ISAAC ASIMOV is regarded as one of
the greatest science fiction writers of our
time, as well as a valued contributor to
the world of science. He holds a Ph.D.
in Chemistry from Columbia University
(1948) and, though he no longer lives in
the Boston area, is an Associate Professor
of Biochemistry at Boston University. He
has received numerous awards for his in-
spiring scientific articles covering a wide
range of subjects.

———————————————

"Devotees of science fiction will
welcome the present anthology."
—*The Booklist*

Before the Golden Age

A Science Fiction Anthology
of the 1930s

BOOK 1

Edited by

ISAAC ASIMOV

A FAWCETT CREST BOOK

Fawcett Publications, Inc., Greenwich, Connecticut

BEFORE THE GOLDEN AGE, Book One

"The Man Who Evolved," by Edmond Hamilton, copyright © 1931 by Gernsback Publications, Inc.; reprinted by permission of the author and the agents for the author, Scott Meredith Literary Agency, Inc.

"The Jameson Satellite," by Neil R. Jones, copyright © 1931 by Radio-Science Publications, Inc.; reprinted by permission of the author.

"Submicroscopic," by Capt. S. P. Meek, copyright © 1931 by Radio-Science Publications, Inc.

"Awlo of Ulm," by Capt. S. P. Meek, copyright © 1931 by Teck Publishing Corporation.

"Tetrahedra of Space," by P. Schuyler Miller, copyright © 1931 by Gernsback Publications, Inc.; reprinted by permission of the author.

"The World of the Red Sun," by Clifford D. Simak, copyright © 1931 by Gernsback Publications, Inc.: reprinted by permission of the author.

"Tumithak of the Corridors," by Charles R. Tanner, copyright © 1931 by Teck Publishing Corporation; reprinted by permission of the author.

"The Moon Era," by Jack Williamson, copyright © 1931 by Gernsback Publications, Inc.; reprinted by permission of the author.

Printed in the United States of America

First printing: April 1975

1   2   3   4   5   6   7   8   9   10

TO SAM MOSKOWITZ, AND MYSELF,
AND ALL THE OTHER MEMBERS OF FIRST FANDOM
(THOSE DINOSAURS OF SCIENCE FICTION),
FOR WHOM SOME OF THE GLITTER WENT
OUT OF THE WORLD IN 1938.

Contents

INTRODUCTION

INTRODUCTION

TO MANY science fiction readers who are now in their middle years, there was a Golden Age of Science Fiction—in capital letters.

That Golden Age began in 1938, when John Campbell became editor of *Astunding Stories* and remolded it, and the whole field, into something closer to his heart's desire. During the Golden Age, he and the magazine he edited so dominated science fiction that to read *Astounding* was to know the field entire.

In that sense, the Golden Age endured till 1950, when other magazines, such as *Galaxy* and *The Magazine of Fantasy and Science Fiction,* entered the field. The editorial personalities of H. L. Gold and Anthony Boucher were as strong in their ways as Campbell's, so the field grew wider and more diverse. In many ways, it improved still further as it spilled out of the magazines and into the books, the paperbacks, and the electronic media.

But then the individual could no longer comprehend the field entire. It grew too large for one to do more than sample, and the Golden Age, when all of science fiction could belong to the reader, was over.

I lived through the Golden Age in the best possible way, for I was among the first of the new writers Campbell discovered, and I am sure there was no other in whom he took so personal and paternal an interest. My book *The Early Asimov* (Doubleday, 1972) is both my memorial to those years and my tribute to John.

But let us forget the capital-letter Golden Age, and let us be more personal. To anyone who has lived a life that has not been utterly disastrous, there is an iridescent aura permeating its second decade. Memories of the first decade, extending back to before the age of ten, are dim, uncertain, and incomplete. Beginning with the third decade, after twenty, life becomes filled with adult responsibility and turns to lead. But that second decade, from ten to twenty, is gold; it is in those years that we remember bliss.

It is the second decade that is the golden age for each individual; it is the memory of life as it was then, that we consider to be life as it ought to be. For any science fiction reader, the gold of the second decade of his life permeates the stories he read at that time, so I frequently hear enthusiasts of thirty speak of "the golden age of the 1950s." If I live out my normal lifetime, I fully expect to hear some rotten kid talk to me of "the golden age of the 1970s." (I will rise from my wheel chair and hit him with my cane.)

Well, then, what about me? My own golden age (small letters) lay in the 1930s. It came in the decade just before the Golden Age (capital letters), and it had a glory for me—and a glory for everyone, for it was in *my* golden age that the personalities that molded the Golden Age, including Campbell himself, were themselves molded.

The science fiction stories I read in the 1930s were in magazines I could not keep. I took each magazine, as it arrived, from my father's newsstand and then, having read it as quickly as I could, I returned it to my father's newsstand so that it might be sold. I cultivated a light hand, which left the magazine in its pristine crispness even though I had read, rabidly, every word on every page. (I *had* to, for if the magazine suffered, my father would have issued a ukase forbidding me to touch any of them, and I don't know about you, but *my* father expected, and got, instant obedience.)

So I never reread those science fiction stories of my personal golden age after that first reading. Oh, a very few of them, yes, when they were reprinted. However, very few stories published before the Golden Age have been reprinted. The Coming of Campbell wiped out all that went before.

The science fiction of the thirties seems, to anyone who has experienced the Campbell Revolution, to be clumsy, primitive, and naïve. The stories are old-fashioned aid unsophisticated.

All right, grant that they are all those things. Nevertheless, there was a rough-hewn vigor about them that sophistication has, to some extent, lost us.

Besides, I remember them. Some of them, although I read them only once at a very early age, I remember over a space of forty years. Through all that has happened and all that I have read and, for that matter, written, I remember them—and love them still.

Those stories were dear to me because they roused my enthusiasm, gave me the joy of life at a time and in a place and under conditions when not terribly many joys existed. They helped shape me and even educate me, and I am filled with gratitude to those stories and to the men who wrote them.

And aside from my personal involvement, the stories form an essential part of the history of science fiction, a part that has been unfairly neglected and is in danger of being forgotten altogether, since virtually no important anthologies have dealt with pre-1938 science fiction.

You would have thought that a person of my incredible ingenuity would have conceived *years ago* the notion of repairing this omission and editing an anthology of the great stories of the 1930s. Oddly enough, that is not so. Never once, in my conscious moments, did so obvious a project occur to me.

Fortunately, I am not always conscious.

On the morning of April 3, 1973, I woke and said to my good lady, "Hey, I remember a dream I had." (I virtually never remember my dreams, so this came under the heading of a stop-the-presses bulletin.)

My good lady is professionally interested in dreams, so she said, "What was it?"

"I dreamed," I said, "I had prepared an anthology of all those good old stories I read when I was a kid and I was getting a chance to read them again. There was 'Tumithak of the Corridors' and 'Awlo of Ulm' and 'The World of the—' "

I think that's about as far as I got. I had been chuckling as I talked about the dream, because it seemed like such a ridiculous thing to do. But was it ridiculous?

Simply talking about it filled me, quite suddenly, with a burning urge to do it. I've had those burning urges before, and I know it means I will have to do it at once regardless of any commitments I may have. But who would publish such a thing?—A ridiculous question. After all, in a quarter century of association, the good people at Doubleday & Company, Inc., had never once said "No" to me.

It was at 7 A.M. that I told my dream, and I had to wait for the opening of the business day to do something about it. At 9:05 A.M. (I gave them five minutes' grace) I was on the phone, talking rapidly and earnestly to Lawrence P. Ashmead and to Michele Tempesta, two splendid editorial representatives of that estimable publishing house. They did not say "No" to me.

I then thought about it some more. As I told you, I did not have those old magazines, and it is most difficult to get copies these days. Difficult, but not impossible.

There was always my old friend Sam Moskowitz, who shared my golden age but bought and kept every magazine that was published, memorized them all, and can quote them all word by word at any time of day or night.

He has put his knowledge and expertise to good use by becoming a historian of science fiction, perhaps the only true specialist in this unusual section of human knowledge in the whole world. He has written two volumes of biographies of great science fiction writers, *Explorers of the Infinite* and *Seekers of Tomorrow*. (One of these biographies dealt with none other than your un-humble servant, Isaac Asimov. Sam, never one to skimp on hyperbole, called that one *Genius in a Candy Store*.)

He also produced *Science Fiction by Gaslight*, a history and anthology of science fiction in the popular magazines of the period from 1891 to 1911, and *Under the Moons of Mars*, a history and anthology of science fiction in the Munsey magazines from 1912 to 1929.

Doubleday published his *The Crystal Man*, dealing with nineteenth-century American science fiction. Sam even wrote an account of the tremendous and earth-shaking feuds among the handful of science fiction fans in the American Northeast, which he very dashingly entitled *The Immortal Storm*.

It was to Sam Moskowitz that I therefore turned. Swearing him to secrecy, I asked him if he had ever himself done an anthology of this sort and if he was in the process of doing so. He answered, no, he hadn't and he wasn't. He would like to if he could find a publisher.

"Well, I can," I said, "and I would make it an autobiographical anthology. Would you object if I moved in on your territory?"

He sighed a little and said that he didn't.

Then I reached the crucial point. "Would you get me the stories, Sam?" I asked.

And goodhearted Sam said, "Oh, sure!" and in three weeks he had them, every one, with word counts and copyright in-

formation and comments on each. (I was only too glad to pay
him for the time and trouble he took.)

So now here I am, all set to do the anthology, and, if you
don't mind, I intend to make it more than a mere anthology. I
am not going to include the stories bareboned.

With your permission (or without, if necessary), I intend
to do as I did in *The Early Asimov* and place the stories within the context of my life. As I told Larry, Michele, and Sam, I
intend the book to be autobiographical.

I am doing this partly because one pronounced facet of my
personality is a kind of cheerful self-appreciation ("a monster
of vanity and arrogance" is what my good friends call me)
but also, believe it or not, as a matter of self-protection and as
almost a kind of public service.

My numerous readers (bless them, one and all) never tire
of writing letters in which they ask eagerly after all the most
intimate statistics of my early life, and it has long since passed
the point where I can possibly satisfy them, one by one, and
still find time to do anything else. *The Early Asimov* has already performed miracles in that respect, since I can send
back post cards saying, "Please read *The Early Asimov* for
the information you request."

And now I will be able to add, "Also read *Before the Gold-
en Age.*"

PART ONE

1920 to 1930

I HAVE always wanted to start a book in the fashion of a nineteenth-century novelist. You know: "I was born in the little town of P——— in the year 19—." Here's my chance:

I was born in the little town of Petrovichi (accent on the second syllable, I believe), in the U.S.S.R. I say the U.S.S.R. and not Russia, because I was born two years after the Russian Revolution.

More than once, I have been asked where Petrovichi is relative to some place that might be considered reasonably familiar. It is thirty-five miles due west of Roslavl and fifty-five miles due south of Smolensk (where a great battle was fought during Napoleon's invasion of 1812, and another during Hitler's invasion of 1941), but that doesn't seem to help any. I had better say, then, that Petrovichi is 240 miles southwest of Moscow and fifteen miles east of the White Russian S.S.R., so I was born on the soil of Holy Russia itself, for what that's worth.

The date of my birth is January 2, 1920. For those of you who are interested in casting horoscopes, forget it! I am not only unaware of the exact hour and minute of my birth but even, actually, of the exact day. January 2 is the official day and that's what I celebrate, but at the time of my birth the Soviet Union was on the Julian calendar, which was thirteen days behind our Gregorian, and my parents in those days didn't even pay much attention to the Julian. They dated things according to the holy days of the Jewish calendar.

Under the Tsars, Russia had never indulged in careful statistical accounting of its less important subjects, and during World War I and the hectic years immediately following, things were more slovenly than ever. So when a birth certificate finally had to be drawn up for me, my parents had to rely on memory, and that worked out to January 2.

And that's good enough. Anyway, it's official.

I remained in the Soviet Union for less than three years and remember nothing of those days except for a few vague impressions, some of which my mother claims she can date back to the time I was two years old.

About the only event of personal note worth mentioning from those years is the fact that sometime in 1921 I fell ill of double pneumonia at a time when antibiotics were non-existent and such medical care as did exist was extremely primitive. My mother tells me (though I never know how much to allow for her innate sense of the dramatic) that seventeen children came down with it in our village at that time and that sixteen died. Apparently, I was the sole survivor.

In 1922, after my sister, Marcia, was born, my father decided to emigrate to the United States. My mother had a half brother living in New York who was willing to guarantee that we would not become a charge on the country; that, plus permission from the Soviet Government, was all we needed.

I am sometimes asked to give the details of how we left the Soviet Union, and I get the distinct feeling that the questioners will be satisfied with nothing less than having my mother jumping from ice floe to ice floe across the Dnieper River with myself in her arms and the entire Red Army hot on our heels.

Sorry! Nothing like that at all! My father applied for an exit visa, or whatever it's called, got it, and off we went by commercial transportation. While we were getting the visa, the family had to go to Moscow, so in the year 1922 I was actually there. My mother says the temperature was forty below and she had to keep me inside her coat lest I freeze solid, but she may be exaggerating.

Needless to say, I am not sorry we left. I dare say that if my family had remained in the Soviet Union, I would have received an education similar to the one I actually did get, that I might well have become a chemist and might even have become a science fiction writer. On the other hand, there is a very good chance that I would then have been killed in the course of the German invasion of the Soviet Union in 1941 to 1945, and while I hope I would have done my bit first, I am glad I didn't have to. I am prejudiced in favor of life.

The four of us—my father Judah, my mother Anna, my sister Marcia, and myself—traveled by way of Danzig, Liverpool, and the good ship *Baltic*, and arrived at Ellis Island in February 1923. It was the last year in which immigration was relatively open and in which Ellis Island was working full steam. In 1924, the quota system was established and the United States began to welcome only sharply limited amounts of the tired, the poor, and the wretched refuse of Europe's teeming shores.

One more year, then, and we wouldn't have made it. Even if we could have come in at some later time, it wouldn't have been the same. Arriving at the age of three, I was, of course, already speaking (Yiddish), but I was still young enough to learn English as a native language and not as an acquired one (which is never the same).

My parents, both of whom spoke Russian fluently, made no effort to teach me Russian, but insisted on my learning English as rapidly and as well as possible. They even set about learning English themselves, with reasonable, but limited, success.

In a way, I am sorry. It would have been good to know the language of Pushkin, Tolstoy, and Dostoevski. On the other hand, I would not have been willing to let anything get in the way of the complete mastery of English. Allow me my prejudice: surely there is no language more majestic than that of Shakespeare, Milton, and the King James Bible, and if I am to have one language that I know as only a native can know it, I consider myself unbelievably fortunate that it is English.

Now my memory starts. I remember, quite distinctly, the first place we lived in after having arrived in the United States. I even remember the address. It was 425 Van Siclen Avenue, in the East New York section of Brooklyn.* I lived

---

* I feel a little silly giving statistics of this sort. I mean, who could possibly care what the exact address is? However, these are among the questions I am sometimes asked: "Exactly where did you live when you first came to the United States?" I hope that no one is thinking of making a pilgrimage to the site. It was a slum when I lived there and it has gone downhill steadily ever since.

in Brooklyn for nineteen years after my arrival in the United States, and my Brooklyn accent is with me to this day.

The Van Siclen Avenue abode was nothing lavish. There was no electricity; we used gas jets. There was no central heating; we had a cast-iron stove, which my mother started with paper and kindling.

Fortunately, I didn't know that this represented slum living. It was home to me, and I was happy. I was particularly fascinated by the stove, and I was always on hand to watch the fire start and my mother knead dough and make noodles. In 1925, when we moved to more advanced quarters, at 434 Miller Avenue, one block away, I cried bitterly.

In February 1925, shortly after my fifth birthday, I began school: kindergarten. If you want further statistics, the school was P.S. 182.

In the ordinary course of events, I would have entered first grade a year later, shortly after my sixth birthday. My mother, however, could not wait.

You see, I had already taught myself to read by hounding the older boys to write out the alphabet for me (which I had learned from a rope-skipping game) and identify each letter and tell me what it "sounds like." I then practiced on street signs and newspaper headlines, sounding the letters till words made sense. To this day, I remember the sudden surge of triumph when I realized there must be such things as silent letters and that the word I was trying to pronounce, ISland, which meant nothing to me, was really EYEland. That made "Coney Island" luminously clear all of a sudden. On the other hand, I remember being completely defeated by "ought." I could not pronounce it, nor could any of the other boys tell me what it meant when *they* pronounced it.

My parents, of course, couldn't read English and so couldn't help me, and the fact that I learned to read without their help seemed to impress them the more. (My sister was much luckier. When she was five years old, I was seven and a past master at the art. Considerably against her will, I taught her to read quite efficiently, so that when it came time for her to enter school, they put her into the second grade directly.)

In September 1925, I remember, my mother took me to school. My mother's half brother came along, too, as interpreter. (He was my "Uncle Joe.") At the time, I did not know what they were doing, but in later years it dawned on me that they must have been altering my birth date. My mother, backed by Uncle Joe, assured the school authorities that I was born on September 7, 1919. (Considering the uncertainty of my birth date, it was less of a lie than it looked, but it was a little of a lie, because, allowing for all uncertainties, I could not possibly have been born earlier than October at the outside.)

With a September 7, 1919 birthday, that made me six years old the day before the fall term started in 1925, and I was allowed to enter the first grade.

The reason I know that this is what must have happened is that when I was in the third grade, the teacher (for some reason) had the children recite their birth dates. In all innocence, I said January 2, 1920, and she frowned and told me it was September 7, 1919.

Well! I have always been quite certain of knowing what I *know*, and I became very emphatic about having been born on January 2, 1920. So energetic did I become in the matter, in fact, that the school records were changed accordingly. If that had not been done, my official birthday would have been September 7, 1919, to this day.

Oddly enough, that turned out to have an important influence on my life. During World War II, I was working at the U. S. Navy Yard in Philadelphia as a chemist and was periodically deferred from the draft because of the war-related importance of my labors. After V-E day, May 8, 1945, the upper age for those liable to the draft was lowered to twenty-six, and those who were still under that age and had thus far escaped being drafted were scrutinized with special care.

On September 7, 1945, I received my notice of induction, and, two months later, was taken into the warm bosom of the Army of the United States as a private. It was no great tragedy, as it turned out, since by that time the war was over, and I remained in the Army only nine months. However, had I kept my little third-grade yap shut, my birthday would have stayed September 7, 1919, and that notice of induction would have arrived on my twenty-sixth birthday and I would have been ineligible for the draft.

My stay in grade school was hectic. On two different occasions, my despairing teachers got rid of me by shoving me ahead a semester. This had its elements of trauma, for on each occasion I lost the friends I had made in the old class and was forced to associate with the strangers of the new one.

Besides that, there was always that panic-laden moment when I realized the class had learned things I didn't yet know and that it would take me days of frightened activity to catch up and move ahead again. On the first occasion on which I was "skipped," I found myself in a class that was solving problems in multiplication, something I had never heard of.

I went home crying. My mother, unable to tell what it was that I did not know, called in a neighboring girl, aged twelve. (I found out in later years that she had been aged twelve; at the time, I thought she was a grownup.) The girl began drilling me in $2 \times 1 = 2$, $2 \times 2 = 4$, $2 \times 3 = 6$, and so on.

After a while it began to seem very familiar. I asked her to wait a moment and got my five-cent copybook. On the back were reference tables telling me that there were 12 inches to a foot, 16 ounces to a pound, and so on. There was also a large square array of mysterious numbers.

"What is this?" I asked.

"That," she said, "is the multiplication table."

"In that case," I said, "I know how to multiply," and I sent her home. Having nothing better to do, I had memorized the numbers long before, and from what she told me, I saw how the multiplication table worked.

The other time when I was pushed ahead, I found the class was studying geography, something of which I was utterly innocent. I remember the teacher had asked me where Yucatan was, and I drew a complete blank and the class laughed. (The less advanced a student was, the louder he laughed at someone else's ignorance.)

Quite humiliated, I asked the teacher after class if we had a book on the subject, and she pointed out the largest of the new books I had been given and said it was the geography book. That night, I went over every map in the book, and you can bet I was never caught again.

It turned out quite early, you see, that I was a child prodigy. My parents apparently knew it, but never told me so, because they didn't believe in giving children swelled heads. I wish they had, though, since then I wouldn't have thought it so unreasonable that every time I came back with less than 100 in any test I took, it would be interpreted as an unsatisfactory performance deserving of punishment. (And my mother, who knew nothing about modern child psychology, always punished by means of a physical assault.)

But then I didn't really need the information from them,

since I gathered it by myself when I made the astonishing discovery that other people didn't understand something till it was explained and then didn't remember it after it was explained.

I don't know how it is with other prodigies, for I have never gone into the subject. Perhaps many of them have had a sense of unhappiness, of isolation, of drudgery, and may have wanted to be like other people.

Not so in my case, however. I enjoyed every minute of my prodigiousness, because, nasty little devil that I was, I enjoyed knowing more than the other kids and being far quicker on the uptake.

Of course, it had its difficulties. By the time I entered the fourth grade, I was a year and a half younger than anyone else in the class, and small for my age at that. And since I was still the smartest kid in the class and very self-appreciative about it, there were many of my schoolmates who lusted for my life. I found, however, that if I picked out the biggest and dumbest kid in the class and did his homework for him, he constituted himself my protector.

Another point that may have helped save my life was that I was never a teacher's pet. Never! I was a loudmouthed extrovert then, as I am now, and I could never resist the chance of upsetting the class with a funny remark. I was forever being disciplined, and when that was insufficient I was sent to the principal's office. (Believe it or not, I was evicted from class as a disruptive influence even as late as my college days.) So, of course, the other kids decided that anyone as badly behaved as I couldn't be all bad, and they resisted the impulse to eradicate me.

During our first years in the United States, my father worked in a knitting factory for a while, and then tried his hand at being a door-to-door salesman. Finally, in 1926, in a search for some sort of security, he put what money he had been able to accumulate into a candy store that existed on Sutter Avenue (good Heavens, I've forgotten the street number), right around the corner from our apartment.

A candy store is a good thing in some ways. You work for yourself and the work is steady. The profits are small but they're there, and we went through the entire period of the Great Depression without missing a meal and without ever having to spend one moment's anxiety that my father might lose his job and that we might all be on the bread lines. To those of you who know nothing of the Great Depression first-hand, let me assure you as earnestly as I can that we were very lucky.

On the other hand, a candy store is a rotten thing in some ways. Back before World War II, candy stores stayed open from 6 A.M. to 1 A.M. seven days a week, with no holidays. It meant that from the age of six I never had any but an occasional, fugitive hour of leisure with either parent. Furthermore, a candy store can be operated only by an entire family, which meant that I had to pitch in. Each year, I did a larger share of the chores.

The work wasn't hard, but it kept me behind the counter for much of my spare time, dishing out candy and cigarettes, making change, delivering papers, running a block and a half to call someone to the telephone, and so on. It kept me from the gay social life of my peers, eliminating punchball and ring-a-levio and many other things of the sort.

Not entirely, of course. In those days (and maybe in ours, too, for all I know) there were "seasons." One day, everyone was playing complicated games with marbles. The next day, all the marbles had disappeared and everyone was out with tops, or checkers (with which to play a marvelous game called "skelly"). I could play all the games with moderate ability, but I was considerably hampered by the fact that I was under strict instructions not to play "for keeps," because my father disapproved of gambling and it was difficult to get other kids to play me "for fun." ("There's no fun in playing for fun," they would say.)

Life was not all work, of course. There was a movie immediately across the street from the candy store. Every Saturday afternoon, my mother gave me a dime and supervised my crossing of the street. For that dime I saw two (silent) movies, a comedy, a cartoon, and, best of all, "an episode," which is what we called the movie serials of those days.

Then, too, I read a good deal. We had no books in the house (they were one of the very many luxuries we could not afford), but my father wangled a library card for me before I was seven. My very first taste of independence was that of going to the library *alone* by bus in order to pick out books.

I could go to the library only at certain times, however, and I could take out only two books at a time when I did go, and I generally finished them both before it was time to go to the library again, no matter how slowly I tried to make myself read. As a result, I constantly felt myself gravitating toward the magazine rack in my father's candy store. It was filled with apparently fascinating reading material.

Along a string stretched across the window, there were draped a dozen paper-backed novels featuring Frank Merriwell and Nick Carter, which I yearned for. There were other paper-backed objects with pictures on the cover, which I learned were called magazines, and some were particularly fascinating; there were pictures of people shooting other people with guns, and that looked great. There were even magazines with names like *Paris Nights*, whose purpose I didn't quite understand but with color illustrations that roused the most intense curiosity in me.

But, standing in the way of all this was my father. He simply would not let me read any of the magazines he sold, for he considered every one of them cheap and sensational trash that would only blunt and ruin my razor-sharp mind. I disagreed, of course, but my father was a remarkably stubborn man and he still had the European notion that Papa was boss.

My fate, however, all unknown to me, was approaching.

In the spring of 1926, the first magazine ever to be devoted to science fiction exclusively was placed on the newsstands for sale. It was entitled *Amazing Stories*, the first issue was dated April, and the publisher was Hugo Gernsback.

To fill the magazine, Gernsback was at first compelled to make heavy use of reprints of the works of European writers. It wasn't till the August 1928 issue that a new world really opened. In that issue there appeared the first installment of a three-part serial entitled *The Skylark of Space*, by Edward E. Smith and Lee Hawkins Garby.

As literature, it was a total flop (may the shade of good old Doc Smith forgive me!), but it had something more than good writing, much more. It had adventure of an unprecedented kind. There was the first introduction of interstellar travel. There were mind-boggling distances and encounters; a kind of never-slowing action centered about indestructible heroes.

The readers whom *Amazing Stories* had been attracting went wild. It became the first great "classic" of American magazine science fiction, and it was the forerunner of native

American science fiction, which ever since has dominated world literature in that field.

But, alas, *The Skylark of Space* came and went and I knew nothing of it. I don't even recall seeing *Amazing Stories* on my father's newsstand during the years 1926 to 1928. I must have, but no trace of it is left in my memory.

Yet 1928, the year of *The Skylark of Space*, was notable for me in a number of ways.

For one thing, I briefly made the acquaintance of a remarkable youngster, who influenced me far more strongly than I could possibly have realized at the time.

He was roughly my age, rather smaller than I was, and rather darker in complexion. Somehow I discovered he had the ability to tell stories that held me enthralled, and he discovered simultaneously that I was an audience most willing to be enthralled.

For some months, we sought each other out so that we could play the roles of storyteller and audience. He would rattle on eagerly while we walked to the library and back, or when we just sat on someone's front steps.

The importance of it was just this: for the first time, I realized stories could be "made up." Until then, I had naturally assumed that stories existed only in books and had probably been there unchanged, from the beginning of time, without human creators.

Of the tales my friend told me, I have only the dimmest of recollections. I seem to remember that they involved the adventures of a group of men who were forever facing and overcoming dangerous villains. The leader of the group, an expert in the use of all conceivable weapons, was named Dodo "Weapons" Windrows, and his lieutenant was one Jack Winslow.

Whether my friend actually made up the stories or retold me material he had read, with adaptations, I don't know. At the time, I had no doubt whatever that he was inventing it as he went along. And looking back on it now, his enthusiasm seems to me to have been that of creation and not of adaptation.

Both of us were careful never to let anyone overhear us in our enjoyment of the process. My friend once explained that the other kids would "laugh at us." I suppose he felt his stories weren't first class and that while I seemed to appreciate them, others might not. Like any true artist, he did not care to expose himself needlessly to the possibility of adverse criticism.

As for myself, my chief fear was that my father would become aware of this. Instinctively, I was certain that my friend's tales would come under the heading of "cheap literature" and that I would be forcibly rescued from their baneful influence. This I most earnestly did not want to happen, and, in so far as I recognized that my friend's stories were akin in spirit to the tales to be found in sensational magazines, my hunger for those magazines sharpened.

Ah, well, it didn't last long. The storytelling spree could not have gone on for more than a few months when my friend's family moved away from the neighborhood and, of course, took my friend with them. He never returned; he never visited; he never wrote. I never knew where they had moved, and shortly my family moved, too. Contact was broken forever.

It seems to me now that my storytelling friend could not possibly have gotten the pleasure he clearly got out of telling stories that he (to all appearances) made up as he went along, without having tried to be a writer as he grew older. I know something about that particular compulsion, and I am certain he would have tried. And if he tried, it would seem to me that he must have succeeded.

And yet I remember his name and I am certain that there is no writer by that name. Can he have used a pseudonym? Is he dead? I don't know; I wish I did.

On a less personal note, and for the sake of statistics, 1928 was also the year of our citizenship. My parents had completed their five-year residency requirement, and in September received their papers. As minor children, my sister and I were mentioned on my father's citizenship papers and automatically became American citizens in consequence. (After I married and left home, I got citizenship papers of my own, dated 1943, so that I need not be forced to send my father to his safe-deposit box every time I needed proof of citizenship. To any future biographer who may find documentation of the 1943 citizenship, however, this is to inform him that I have been a citizen since 1928.)

The year ended with another change of residence. My father, having increased his savings, thanks to the candy store, felt it was time to sell it and buy another. Partly, I suppose, he felt he would welcome a change, and partly there was always the hope that another candy store would be more profitable.

In December 1928, therefore, we moved to 651 Essex Street, on the corner of New Lots Avenue. There the second candy store was located. I had to transfer from P.S. 182 to P.S. 202, something that involved another traumatic readjustment of friendships.

Then came the crucial summer of 1929, in which everything seemed to conspire to change the direction of my life. (It was the last summer of the Roaring Twenties, the last merry spark before the stock-market crash and the beginning of the Great Depression, but no one knew that, of course.)

For one thing, it was a time of crisis for *Amazing Stories*. Though it had been doing well, there were business machinations of a kind that go beyond the capacity for understanding of my essentially simple mind (Sam Moskowitz knows the story in detail), and Gernsback was forced out of ownership of the magazine.

The last issue of what we can call the "Gernsback *Amazing*" was the June 1929 issue, I believe. (I may be wrong by one or two months here.) It had gone thirty-nine issues. The magazine was taken over by Teck Publications, so with the July 1929 issue we can speak of the "Teck *Amazing*."

Gernsback, a man of considerable resource, had no intention of leaving the magazine field or, for that matter, of abandoning science fiction. Without missing a step, he founded another science fiction magazine, which was thereafter to compete with *Amazing Stories* and was to double the supply of reading matter for the science fiction public. Gernsback's new magazine was called *Science Wonder Stories,* and its first issue was dated June 1929.

Gernsback went further indeed and started a companion magazine called *Air Wonder Stories,* which began with the July 1929 issue. The supply of science fiction was thus tripled, and the existence of these new magazines was to prove of crucial importance to me.

The June in which those two new magazines were both on the stands for the first time, I was completing my stay in the fifth grade. The teacher of the course had offered to take a selected group in the class on a post-term trip to the Statue of Liberty. I did not qualify, since my marks in "Deportment" did not meet the minimum standards. I looked so stricken, however, that the teacher (presumably recalling that I was the brightest student in the class) asked the class permission to include me. The nice kids gave it and I went.

The trip was on July 2, 1929. I remember because I was nine and a half years old that day. It was exciting in itself, but the most remarkable thing about it was that for the first time in my life I had gone a considerable distance without my parents. The fact that the teacher was along didn't count. She did not have parental authority. It gave me an extraordinary feeling of having reached manhood.

The third event of the period was the fact that my mother had entered a third pregnancy (this one, I have reason to believe, unplanned) and, in July, was nearing term. It meant she couldn't help much in the store, and my poor father with only a nine-year-old assistant was terribly harried.

Now observe the concatenation of events.

Not long after my trip to the Statue of Liberty, I noted the new magazine *Science Wonder Stories* on the newsstand. It was the August 1929 issue, the third of its existence. I noticed it, first, because it had a cover by Frank R. Paul, the artist Gernsback always used, a man who painted in primary colors exclusively, I think, and who specialized in complex, futuristic machines.

But I also noticed it because it was a new magazine and my eye hadn't grown dulled to it. Finally, I noticed it because of the word "Science" in the title. That made all the difference. I knew about science; I had already read books about science. I was perfectly aware that science was considered a mentally nourishing and spiritually wholesome study. What's more, I knew that my father thought so from our occasional talks about my schoolwork.

Well, then, the loss of my storytelling friend had left a gnawing vacancy within me; my trip to the Statue of Liberty filled me with a desire to assert my independence and argue with my father; and the word "science" gave me the necessary leverage.

I picked up the magazine and, not without considerable qualms, approached my formidable parent. (It is hard for me to believe that at the time he was only thirty-two years old. I took it for granted he was infinitely old—at least as old as Moses.)

I spoke rapidly, pointed out the word "science," pointed to paintings of futuristic machines inside as an indication of how advanced it was, and (I believe) made it plain that if he said

"No" I had every intention of throwing a fit. And that's where the final item in the concatenation of events came in: my father, driven to distraction by the new baby that was on its way, was in no mood to concern himself with trivia. He granted me permission.

I then scanned the newsstand for any other magazine of the same type, planning to maintain with all the strength at my disposal the legal position that permission for one such magazine implied permission for all the others, even when the word "science" was not in the title.

Promptly I found the August 1929 issue of *Amazing Stories* and, of course, the August 1929 issue of *Air Wonder Stories*. I girded myself for the battle. It never came. My mother went to the hospital and my father conceded everything. On July 25, my brother, Stanley, was born.

I wish I could remember the stories in the very first science fiction magazines I ever read, but I can't. The nearest I can come to it is the fact that I remember the cover story in the August 1929 *Amazing Stories* to be "Barton's Island" by Harl Vincent, but I don't remember the plot.

One of the factors that surely must have helped induce my father to let me read the science fiction magazines was their respectable appearance.

At that time, there were two types of magazines on the stands. There were the smaller magazines, 7 by 10 inches in size, which were printed on cheap paper made of wood pulp, unglazed and with ragged edges. These "pulps" featured action stories in different categories, one magazine being devoted to Westerns, another to mysteries, still another to jungle stories, another to sports stories, yet another to air-war stories, and so on.

My father read some of the pulps himself (to improve his English, he said), but nothing could have induced him to let *me* read them. We quarreled over *The Shadow* and *Doc Savage* for years, and eventually, in my mid-teens, I began to read them defiantly without his permission. He would look at me sorrowfully whenever he caught me reading one of them, too; but though those looks stabbed me to the soul, I kept on reading them.

There were, however, also large-size magazines, 8½ by 11 inches or larger, published on glazed paper of good quality with smooth edges. These were the "slicks." I doubt that very many of them were any higher in literary quality than the pulps, but they looked better.

Well, *Amazing Stories, Science Wonder Stories,* and *Air Wonder Stories,* though printed on pulp paper and sometimes featuring authors who wrote regularly for the pulp magazines, were large-size and had smooth edges. They were kept with the slicks on the newsstands, not with the pulps (oh, what a kiss of death that would have been), and they therefore were to be found in respectable company.

What's more, where the pulp magazines usually charged ten cents an issue, the three science fiction magazines charged a lordly twenty-five cents, and, as always, high charge was equated with high quality.

In 1927, Gernsback had been faced with an overflow of stories and had put out a special issue of *Amazing Stories,* which he then still owned, made it thicker than an ordinary one, and called it *Amazing Stories Annual.* It was a success, and from then on he put out such issues at quarter-year intervals. This *Amazing Stories Quarterly* continued under the Teck regime, too, and Gernsback, when he started his new magazines, also began *Science Wonder Quarterly.*

The quarterlies were magnificent. Whereas the ordinary issues of the science fiction magazines contained 96 pages and about 100,000 words of fiction, the quarterlies contained 144 pages and about 150,000 words. The ordinary issues ran novels as serials (usually in three parts), but the quarterlies could run novels entire. Of course, the quarterlies cost fifty cents, an enormous price for those days, and my father didn't always receive them from the distributing companies, so I missed some copies. When I saw them, though, what an enormous feast they were!

(It occurs to me that if my father had not had a newsstand, there would not have been the slightest possibility of my ever reading science fiction magazines at that time except for such issues as I might—a very unlikely supposition—have borrowed. There was no way on Earth that I could have afforded quarters and half dollars for something as unessential as reading matter. . . . Pardon me while I overcome my trembling fit at the thought, and then I will continue.)

Toward the end of 1929, still another science fiction magazine hit the newsstands, with its first issue dated January 1930. It was called *Astounding Stories of Super-Science.* The final phrase was soon dropped and it became *Astounding Stories*. It was published by Clayton Publications and is now referred to as the "Clayton *Astounding*" to differentiate it from later incarnations.

The Clayton *Astounding* was clearly a poor relation. For one thing, it was the size and quality of the pulp magazines and was placed with them on the newsstands. I was taken aback, and almost hesitated to try to read it, thinking that I would surely be stopped. However, my father said nothing. Having retreated, he was not prepared to renew the battle.

Astounding Stories published tales that were heavy on adventure and that seemed, to my boyish mind, to be less sophisticated than those in *Amazing Stories*. In fact, though I read every issue of the Clayton *Astounding,* all thirty-four, there was not one story in any of those issues that has remained with me to this day, and none are included in this anthology.

The very early stories that I still remember almost all appeared in *Amazing Stories,* which called itself "The Aristocrat of Science Fiction." And so it was, in my opinion. During the first four years of my science fiction reading, it was *Amazing Stories* all the way with me.

And it was the novels that were most impressive. The plots were most intricate, the adventures most detailed, and, most of all, there was the cliff-hanger with which each installment ended. You then had to wait the length of an arid month for the next installment. Some readers, I later discovered, saved their issues so that they could read the serials all at once, but I couldn't do that, of course. I had to return each issue to the newsstand.

The earliest serial I remember reading and slavering joyously over was *Cities in the Air,* by Edmond Hamilton, which ran in two parts in *Air Wonder Stories,* in the November and December 1929 issues.* I still remember the dra-

---

* I have a marvelous memory, but it is not so marvelous that I can remember exact issues for all the stories that I quote, or the exact date for the various items of historical interest I refer to in connection with early magazine science fiction. Actually, I am making liberal use of Donald B. Day's *Index to the Science-Fiction Magazines, 1926-1950* (Perri Press, Portland, Ore., 1952), which I bought twenty years ago and which has paid me back a hundredfold in its constant usefulness as a reference book to the early history of magazine science fiction. There have been a number of supplements put out for the period since 1950 by computers at M.I.T., but they lack the taste and flavor of the Day *Index.*

matic Paul cover illustration for that serial, with skyscraper cities shown on huge circular slabs in mid-air.

The next serial I remember is *The Universe Wreckers,* a three-parter in *Amazing Stories,* in the May, June, and July 1930 issues. This one was also by Edmond Hamilton. Considering that, and the fact that Ed is the best-represented in this anthology (three stories) of any of the authors included, I can only deduce that Ed was my favorite author in those very early days.

I have met Ed and his charming wife, Leigh Brackett—also a writer—on many occasions in my grown-up days, and I've never thought to tell him this. I guess I didn't really realize it myself till I began sorting out my memories for this book.

Then, too, there was *The Drums of Tapajos,* by Capt. S. P. Meek, another three-parter in *Amazing Stories,* the November and December 1930 and January 1931 issues. Also *The Black Star Passes,* by John W. Campbell, Jr., published complete in the fall 1930 *Amazing Stories Quarterly*.

These stories, which are full-length novels, can't be included, alas, in this anthology, which is restricted to stories of fewer than forty thousand words.

In my first couple of years as a science fiction reader, I was given an unexpected bonus of time in which to read. When my brother was an infant, I was freed of some of my candy-store chores because I was put in charge of his welfare.

Watching Stanley was much better than standing behind the counter, because virtually no work was required. Aside from giving him his bottle if he cried (or shaking the carriage) and making sure that he didn't fall out or that no eagle swooped down to carry him off, I had only to sit there. I remember the warm summer days of 1930 when I was counting the hours till the Monday after Labor Day, when I could start the adventure of junior high school. I would be sitting next to the carriage, my chair tipped back against the brick wall of the house, and reading a science fiction magazine, dead to all the world beside except for my automatic response to any wail from the carriage.

Sometimes, to avoid being cramped, I would wheel the carriage sixty or seventy times around the block with the science fiction magazine propped against the handlebar.

Of course the nation as a whole was not going through my own idyllic experience that summer. The stock market had crashed in October 1929, and the economic situation had grown steadily worse ever since. The Great Depression was on. My father's customers had less money, so less money was spent in the candy store. Things grew tighter, and the second candy store, after half a year of moderate promise, showed clearly that it was to be no more a highway to riches than the first.

The science fiction magazines suffered along with everyone else. *Amazing Stories* and *Science Wonder Stories,* which never paid their authors very much, paid them more and more slowly. (The grim joke was that they paid a quarter cent a word on lawsuit.) *Astounding Stories,* for all its lower quality, paid higher rates more quickly, and it began to draw the authors its way, which made things harder than ever for the large-size magazines.

Amazing Stories withstood the strain stolidly and continued without apparent alteration. The Gernsback magazines, however, underwent ominous changes.

Air Wonder Stories was simply too specialized. Its stories dealt with futurized air travel in one way or another, and that did not allow for sufficient variety. I presume its circulation suffered, and the May 1930 issue, its eleventh, was also its last. With the next issue, that of June 1930, it was combined with *Science Wonder Stories* and the combined magazine was given the logical name of *Wonder Stories*.

After five issues, however, the combined magazine found that matters were still too tight for it and it attempted to improve its competitive stance by more closely imitating *Astounding Stories*. With the November 1930 issue, *Wonder Stories* went pulp size and left *Amazing Stories* as the only large-size science fiction magazine.

PART TWO

1931

IN 1931, I finished my first year at Junior High School 149. It gave a three-year course: seventh, eighth, and ninth grades. For the better students, it offered, however, a "rapid advance" course in which both seventh and eighth grades were completed in the first year. That was the course I took.

On promotion day in June 1931, therefore, I received my final report card and was told that I would enter ninth grade in September. This was the equivalent of first year high school. I had expected this, of course, and had arranged with my mother that I would not go directly home. I ran to the library instead and came up against the librarian's desk with a bang.

"I want an adult library card, please," I panted, handing her my children's card.

I was still a week short of being eleven and a half, and very skinny, so the librarian said to me, kindly, "You can't have an adult card till you're in high school, little boy."

"I *am* in high school," I snarled, and slammed down my report card. She consulted another official, and I got my card.

This meant I could roam at will among the mysterious stacks containing adult books. The card was stamped "H.S.," however, which still restricted me to two books at a time.

Science fiction helped fill the gaps, and, as it happened, that

35

spring. Three months before my exciting promotion to an adult library card, I had read the first science fiction short story (as opposed to novel) that impressed me so much it stayed in my mind permanently.

I never read it again after that first reading, *never,* until I got a copy of old, fading, and brittle tear sheets of the story from Sam Moskowitz for the preparation of this anthology. And then, when I read it again, after forty-two years, I found I remembered it all in complete detail.

This cannot merely be a quirk of my excellent memory, for there are hundreds of science fiction stories I read both before and after this one that I have completely forgotten, including one or two that I read last month.

No, it's the story, "The Man Who Evolved," by (no surprise!) Edmond Hamilton. It appeared in the April 1931 *Wonder Stories.*

THE MAN WHO EVOLVED

by Edmond Hamilton

THERE were three of us in Pollard's house on that night that I try vainly to forget. Dr. John Pollard himself, Hugh Dutton and I, Arthur Wright—we were the three. Pollard met that night a fate whose horror none could dream; Dutton has since that night inhabited a state institution reserved for the insane, and I alone am left to tell what happened.

It was on Pollard's invitation that Dutton and I went up to his isolated cottage. We three had been friends and roommates at the New York Technical University. Our friendship was perhaps a little unusual, for Pollard was a number of years older than Dutton and myself and was different in temperament, being rather quieter by nature. He had followed an intensive course of biological studies, too, instead of the ordinary engineering courses Dutton and I had taken.

As Dutton and I drove northward along the Hudson on that afternoon, we found ourselves reviewing what we knew of Pollard's career. We had known of his taking his master's and doctor's degrees, and had heard of his work under Braun, the Vienna biologist whose theories had stirred up such turmoil. We had heard casually, too, that afterwards he had come back to plunge himself in private research at the country-house beside the Hudson he had inherited. But since then we had had no word from him and had been somewhat surprised to receive his telegrams inviting us to spend the week-end with him.

It was drawing into early-summer twilight when Dutton and I reached a small riverside village and were directed to Pollard's place, a mile or so beyond. We found it easily enough, a splendid old pegged-frame house that for a hundred-odd years had squatted on a low hill above the river.

Its outbuildings were clustered around the big house like the chicks about some protecting hen.

Pollard himself came out to greet us. "Why, you boys have grown up!" was his first exclamation. "Here I've remembered you as Hughie and Art, the campus trouble-raisers, and you look as though you belong to business clubs and talk everlastingly about sales-resistance!"

"That's the sobering effect of commercial life," Dutton explained, grinning. "It hasn't touched you, you old oyster—you look the same as you did five years ago."

He did, too, his lanky figure and slow smile and curiously thoughtful eyes having changed not a jot. Yet Pollard's bearing seemed to show some rather more than usual excitement and I commented on it.

"If I seem a little excited it's because this is a great day for me," he answered.

"Well, you *are* in luck to get two fine fellows like Dutton and me to trail up to this hermitage of yours," I began, but he shook his head smilingly.

"I don't refer to that, Art, though I'm mighty glad you've come. As for my hermitage, as you call it, don't say a word against it. I've been able to do work here I could never have done amid the distractions of a city laboratory."

His eyes were alight. "If you two knew what—but there, you'll hear it soon enough. Let's get inside—I suppose you're hungry?"

"Hungry—not I," I assured him. "I might devour half a steer or some trifle like that, but I have really no appetite for anything else today."

"Same here," Dutton said. "I just pick at my food lately. Give me a few dozen sandwiches and a bucket of coffee and I consider it a full meal."

"Well, we'll see what we can do to tempt your delicate appetites," said Pollard, as we went inside.

We found this big house comfortable enough, with long, low-ceilinged rooms and broad windows looking riverward. After putting our bags in a bedroom, and while his housekeeper and cook prepared dinner, Pollard escorted us on a tour of inspection of the place. We were most interested in his laboratory.

It was a small wing he had added to the house, of frame construction outside to harmonize with the rest of the building, but inside offering a gleaming vista of white-tiled walls and polished instruments. A big cubelike structure of transparent metal surmounted by a huge metal cylinder resembling a monster vacuum tube, took up the room's center, and he showed us in an adjoining stone-floored room the dynamos and motors of his private power-plant.

Night had fallen by the time we finished dinner, the meal having been prolonged by our reminiscences. The housekeeper and cook had gone, Pollard explaining that the servants did not sleep in the place. We sat smoking for a while in his living room, Dutton looking appreciatively around at our comfortable surroundings.

"Your hermitage doesn't seem half-bad, Pollard," he commented. "I wouldn't mind this easy life for a while myself."

"Easy life?" repeated Pollard. "That's all you know about it, Hugh. The fact is that I've never worked so hard in my life as I've done up here in the last two years."

"What in the world have you been working at?" I asked. "Something so unholy you've had to keep it hidden here?"

A Mad Scheme

Pollard chuckled. "That's what they think down in the village. They know I'm a biologist and have a laboratory here, so it's a foregone conclusion with them that I'm doing vivisection of a specially dreadful nature. That's why the servants won't stay here at night."

"As a matter of fact," he added, "if they knew down in the village what I've really been working on they'd be ten times as fearful as they are now."

"Are you trying to play the mysterious great scientist for our benefit?" Dutton demanded. "If you are you're wasting time—I know you, stranger, so take off that mask."

"That's right," I told him. "If you're trying to get our curiosity worked up you'll find we can scram you as neatly as we could five years ago."

"Which scramming generally ended in black eyes for both of you," he retorted. "But I've no intention of working up your curiosity—as a matter of fact I asked you up here to see what I've been doing and help me finish it."

"Help you?" echoed Dutton. "What can we help you do—dissect worms? Some week-end, I can see right now!"

"There's more to this than dissecting worms," Pollard said. He leaned back and smoked for a little time in silence before he spoke again.

"Do you two have any knowledge at all of evolution?" he asked.

"I know that it's a fighting word in some states," I answered, "and that when you say it you've got to smile, damn you."

He smiled, himself. "I suppose you're aware of the fact, however, that all life on this earth began as simple uni-cellular protoplasm, and by successive evolutionary mutations or changes developed into its present forms and is still slowly developing?"

"We know that much—just because we're not biologists you needn't think we're totally ignorant of biology," Dutton said.

"Shut up, Dutton," I warned. "What's evolution got to do with your work up here, Pollard?"

"It *is* my work up here," Pollard answered.

He bent forward. "I'll try to make this clear to you from the start. You know, or say you know, the main steps of evolutionary development. Life began on this earth as simple protoplasm, and by successive evolutionary mutations or protoplasmic organisms. From these developed in turn sea-creatures, land-lizards, mammals, by successive mutations. This infinitely slow evolutionary process has reached its highest point so far in the mammal man, and is still going on with the same slowness.

"This much is certain biological knowledge, but two great questions concerning this process of evolution have remained hitherto unanswered. First, what is the cause of evolutionary change, the cause of these slow, steady mutations into higher forms? Second, what is the future course of man's evolution going to be, what will the forms into which in the future man will evolve, and where will his evolution stop? Those two questions biology has so far been unable to answer."

Pollard was silent a moment and then said quietly, "I have found the answer to one of those questions, and am going to find the answer to the other tonight."

We stared at him. "Are you trying to spoof us?" I asked finally.

"I'm absolutely serious, Arthur. I have actually solved the first of those problems, have found the cause of evolution."

"What is it, then?" burst out of Dutton.

"What it has been thought by some biologists for years to be," Pollard answered. "The cosmic rays."

"The cosmic rays?" I echoed. "The vibrations from space that Millikan discovered?"

"Yes, the cosmic rays, the shortest wavelength and most highly penetrating of all vibratory forces. It has been known that they beat unceasingly upon the earth from outer space, cast forth by the huge generators of the stars, and it has also been known that they must have some great effect in one way or another upon the life of the earth."

"I have proved that they do have such an effect, and that that effect is what we call evolution! For it is the cosmic rays, beating upon every living organism on earth, that cause the profound changes in the structure of those organisms which we call mutations. Those changes are slow indeed, but it is due to them that through the ages life has been raised from the first protoplasm to man, and is still being raised higher."

"Good Lord, you can't be serious on this, Pollard!" Dutton protested.

"I am so serious that I am going to stake my life on my discovery tonight," Pollard answered, quietly.

We were startled. "What do you mean?"

"I mean that I have found in the cosmic rays the cause of evolution, the answer to the first question, and that tonight by means of them I am going to answer the second question and find out what the future evolutionary development of man will be!"

"But how could you possibly——"

Pollard interrupted. "Easily enough. I have been able in the last months to do something no physicist has been able to do, to concentrate the cosmic rays and yet remove from them their harmful properties. You saw the cylinder over the metal cube in my laboratory? That cylinder literally gathers in for an immense distance the cosmic rays that strike this part of earth, and reflects them down inside the cube.

"Now suppose those concentrated cosmic rays, millions of times stronger than the ordinary cosmic rays that strike one spot on earth, fall upon a man standing inside the cube. What will be the result? It is the cosmic rays that cause evolutionary change, and you heard me say that they are still changing all life on earth, still changing man, but so slowly as to be unnoticeable. But what about the man under those terrifically intensified rays? He will be changed millions of times faster than ordinarily, will go forward in hours or minutes through the evolutionary mutations that all mankind will go forward through in eons to come!"

"And you propose to try that experiment?" I cried.

"I propose to try it on myself," said Pollard gravely, "and to find out for myself the evolutionary changes that await humankind."

"Why, it's insane!" Dutton exclaimed.

Pollard smiled. "The old cry," he commented. "Never an attempt has been made yet to tamper with nature's laws, but that cry has been raised."

"But Dutton's right!" I cried. "Pollard, you've worked here alone too long—you've let your mind become warped——"

"You are trying to tell me that I have become a little mad," he said. "No, I am sane—perhaps wonderfully sane, in trying this."

His expression changed, his eyes brooding. "Can't you two see what this may mean to humanity? As we are to the apes, so must the men of the future be to us. If we could use this method of mine to take all mankind forward through millions of years of evolutionary development at one stride, wouldn't it be sane to do so?"

My mind was whirling. "Good heavens, the whole thing is so crazy," I protested. "To accelerate the evolution of the human race? It seems somehow a thing forbidden."

"It's a thing glorious if it can be done," he returned, "and I know that it can be done. But first one must go ahead, must travel on through stage after stage of man's future development to find out to which stage it would be most desirable for all mankind to be transferred. I know there is such an age."

"And you asked us up here to take part in that?"

"Just that. I mean to enter the cube and let the concentrated rays whirl me forward along the paths of evolution, but I must have someone to turn the rays on and off at the right moments."

"It's all incredible!" Dutton exclaimed. "Pollard, if this is a joke it's gone far enough for me."

For answer Pollard rose. "We will go to the laboratory now," he said simply. "I am eager to get started."

I cannot remember following Pollard and Dutton to the laboratory, my thoughts were spinning so at the time. It was not until we stood before the great cube from which the huge metal cylinder towered that I was aware of the reality of it all.

Pollard had gone into the dynamo-room and as Dutton and I stared wordlessly at the great cube and cylinder, at the retorts and flasks of acids and strange equipment about us, we heard the hum of motor-generators. Pollard came back to the switchboard supported in a steel frame beside the cube, and as he closed a switch there came a crackling and the cylinder glowed with white light.

Pollard pointed to it and the big quartz-like disc in the cubical chamber's ceiling, from which the white force-shafts shot downward.

"The cylinder is now gathering cosmic rays from an immense area of space," he said, "and those concentrated rays are falling through that disk into the cube's interior. To cut off the rays it is necessary only to open this switch." He reached to open the switch, the light died.

The Man Who Evolved

Quickly, while we stared, he removed his clothing, donning in place of it a loose white running suit.

"I will want to observe the changes of my own body as much as possible," he explained. "Now, I will stand inside the cube and you will turn on the rays and let them play upon me for fifteen minutes. Roughly, that should represent a period of some fifty million years of future evolutionary change. At the end of fifteen minutes you will turn the rays off and we will be able to observe what changes they have caused. We will then resume the process, going forward by fifteen-minute or rather fifty million year periods."

"But where will it stop—where will we quit the process?" Dutton asked.

Pollard shrugged. "We'll stop where evolution stops, that is, where the rays no longer affect me. You know, biologists have often wondered what the last change or final development of man will be, the last mutation. Well, we are going to see tonight what it will be."

He stepped toward the cube and then paused, went to a desk and brought from it a sealed envelope he handed to me.

"This is just in case something happens to me of a fatal nature," he said. "It contains an attestation signed by myself that you two are in no way responsible for what I am undertaking."

"Pollard, give up this unholy business!" I cried, clutching his arm. "It's not too late, and this whole thing seems ghastly to me!"

"I'm afraid it is too late," he smiled. "If I backed out now I'd be ashamed to look in a mirror hereafter. And no explorer was ever more eager than I am to start down the path of man's future evolution!"

He stepped up into the cube, standing directly beneath the disk in its ceiling. He motioned imperatively, and like an automaton I closed the door and then threw the switch.

The cylinder broke again into glowing white light, and as the shafts of glowing white force shot down from the disk in the cube's ceiling upon Pollard, we glimpsed his whole body writhing as though beneath a terrifically concentrated electrical force. The shaft of glowing emanations almost hid him from our view. I knew that the cosmic rays in themselves were invisible but guessed that the light of the cylinder and shaft was in some way a transformation of part of the rays into visible light.

Dutton and I stared with beating hearts into the cubical chamber, having but fleeting glimpses of Pollard's form. My watch was in one hand, the other hand on the switch. The fifteen minutes that followed seemed to me to pass with the slowness of fifteen eternities. Neither of us spoke and the only sounds were the hum of the generators and the crackling of the cylinder that from the far spaces was gathering and concentrating the rays of evolution.

At last the watch's hand marked the quarter-hour and I snapped off the switch, the light of the cylinder and inside the cube dying. Exclamations burst from us both.

Pollard stood inside the cube, staggering as though still dazed by the impact of the experience, but he was not the Pollard who had entered the chamber! He was transfigured, godlike! His body had literally expanded into a great figure of such physical power and beauty as we had not imagined could exist! He was many inches taller and broader, his skin a clear pink, every limb and muscle molded as though by some master sculptor.

The greatest change, though, was in his face. Pollard's homely, good-humored features were gone, replaced by a face whose perfectly-cut features held the stamp of immense intellectual power that shone almost overpoweringly from the clear dark eyes. It was not Pollard who stood before us, I told myself, but a being as far above us as the most advanced man of today is above the troglodyte!

He was stepping out of the cube and his voice reached our ears, clear and bell-like, triumphant.

"You see? It worked as I knew it would work! I'm fifty million years ahead of the rest of humanity in evolutionary development!"

"Pollard!" My lips moved with difficulty. "Pollard this is terrible—this change—"

His radiant eyes flashed. "Terrible? It's wonderful! Do you two realize what I now am, can you realize it? This body of mine is the kind of body all men will have in fifty million years, and the brain inside it is a brain fifty million years ahead of yours in development!"

He swept his hand about. "Why, all this laboratory and former work of mine seems infinitely petty, childish, to me! The problems that I worked on for years I could solve now in minutes. I could do more for mankind now than all the men now living could do together!"

"Then you're going to stop at this stage?" Dutton cried eagerly. "You're not going further with this?"

"Of course I am! If fifty million years development makes this much change in man, what will a hundred million years, two hundred million make? I'm going to find out."

I grasped his hand. "Pollard, listen to me! Your experiment has succeeded, has fulfilled your wildest dreams. Stop it now! Think what you can accomplish, man! I know your ambition has always been to be one of humanity's great benefactors—by stopping here you can be the greatest! You can be a living proof to mankind of what your process can make it, and with that proof before it all humanity will be eager to become the same as you!"

He freed himself from my grasp. "No, Arthur—I have gone part of the way into humanity's future and I'm going on."

He stepped back into the chamber, while Dutton and I stared helplessly. It seemed half a dream, the laboratory, the cubical chamber, the godlike figure inside that was and still was not Pollard.

"Turn on the rays, and let them play for fifteen minutes

more," he was directing. "It will project me ahead another fifty million years."

His eyes and voice were imperative, and I glanced at my watch, and snicked over the switch. Again the cylinder broke into light, again the shaft of force shot down into the cube to hide Pollard's splendid figure.

Dutton and I waited with feverish intensity in the next minutes. Pollard was standing still beneath the broad shaft of force, and so was hidden in it from our eyes. What would its lifting disclose? Would he have changed still more, into some giant form, or would he be the same, having already reached humanity's highest possible development?

When I shut off the mechanism at the end of the appointed period, Dutton and I received a shock. For again Pollard had changed!

He was no longer the radiant, physically perfect figure of the first metamorphosis. His body instead seemed to have grown thin and shrivelled, the outlines of bones visible through its flesh. His body, indeed, seemed to have lost half its bulk and many inches of stature and breadth, but these were compensated for by the change in his head.

For the head supported by this weak body was an immense, bulging balloon that measured fully eighteen inches from brow to back! It was almost entirely hairless, its great mass balanced precariously upon his slender shoulders and neck. And his face too was changed greatly, the eyes larger and the mouth smaller, the ears seeming smaller also. The great bulging forehead dominated the face.

Could this be Pollard? His voice sounded thin and weak to our ears.

"You are surprised to see me this time? Well, you see a man a hundred million years ahead of you in development. And I must confess that you appear to me as two brutish, hairy cave-men would appear to you."

"But Pollard, this is awful!" Dutton cried. "This change is more terrible than the first . . . . if you had only stopped at the first . . ."

The eyes of the shrivelled, huge-headed figure in the cube fired with anger. "Stop at that first stage? I'm glad now that I didn't! The man I was fifteen minutes ago . . . fifty million years ago in development . . . seems now to me to have been half-animal! What was his big animal-like body beside my immense brain?"

"You say that because in this change you're getting away from all human emotions and sentiments!" I burst. "Pollard, do you realize what you're doing? You're changing out of human semblance!"

"I realize it perfectly," he snapped, "and I see nothing to be deplored in the fact. It means that in a hundred million years man will be developing in brain-capacity and will care nothing for the development of body. To you two crude beings, of what is to me the past, this seems terrible; but to me it is desirable and natural. Turn on the rays again!"

"Don't do it, Art!" cried Dutton. "This madness had gone far enough!"

Pollard's great eyes surveyed us with cold menace. "You will turn on the rays," his thin voice ordered deliberately. "If you do not, it will be but the work of a moment for me to annihilate both of you and go on with this alone."

"You'd kill us?" I said dumbfoundedly. "We two, two of your best friends?"

His narrow mouth seemed to sneer. "Friends? I am millions of years past such irrational emotions as friendship. The only emotion you awaken in me is a contempt for your crudity. Turn on the rays!"

The Brain Monster

His eyes blazed as he snapped the last order, and as though propelled by a force outside myself, I closed the switch. The shaft of glowing force again hid him from our view.

Of our thoughts during the following quarter-hour I can say nothing, for both Dutton and I were so rigid with awe and horror as to make our minds chaotic. I shall never forget, though, that first moment after the time had passed and I had again switched off the mechanism.

The change had continued, and Pollard—I could not call him that in my own mind—stood in the cube-chamber as a shape the sight of which stunned our minds.

He had become simply a great head! A huge hairless head fully a yard in diameter, supported on tiny legs, the arms having dwindled to mere hands that projected just below the head! The eyes were enormous, saucer-like, but the ears were mere pin-holes at either side of the head, the nose and mouth being similar holes below the eyes!

He was stepping out of the chamber on his ridiculously little limbs, and as Dutton and I reeled back in unreasoning horror, his voice came to us as an almost inaudible piping. And it held pride!

"You tried to keep me from going on, and you see what I have become? To such as you, no doubt, I seem terrible, yet you two and all like you seem as low to me as the worms that crawl!"

"Good God, Pollard, you've made yourself a monster!" The words burst from me without thought.

His enormous eyes turned on me. "You call me Pollard, yet I am no more the Pollard you knew, and who entered that chamber first, than you are the ape of millions of years ago from whom you sprang! And all mankind is like you two! Well, they will all learn the powers of one who is a hundred and fifty million years in advance of them!"

"What do you mean?" Dutton exclaimed.

"I mean that with the colossal brain I have I will master without a struggle this man-swarming planet, and make it a huge laboratory in which to pursue the experiments that please me."

"But Pollard—remember why you started this!" I cried. "To go ahead and chart the path of future evolution for humanity—to benefit humanity and not to rule it!"

The great head's enormous eyes did not change. "I remember that the creature Pollard that I was until tonight had such foolish ambitions, yes. It would stir mirth now, if I could feel such an emotion. To benefit humanity? Do you men dream of benefitting the animals you rule over? I would no sooner think of working for the benefit of you humans!

"Do you two yet realize that I am so far ahead of you in brain power now as you are ahead of the beasts that perish? Look at this . . ."

He had climbed onto a chair beside one of the laboratory tables, was reaching among the retorts and apparatus there. Swiftly he poured several compounds into a lead mortar, added others, poured upon the mixed contents another mixture made as swiftly.

There was a puff of intense green smoke from the mortar instantly, and then the great head—I can only call him that—turned the mortar upside down. A lump of shining mottled metal fell out and we gasped as we recognized the yellow sheen of pure gold, made in a moment, apparently, by a mixture of common compounds!

"You see?" the grotesque figure was asking. "What is the transformation of elements to a mind like mine? You two cannot even realize the scope of my intelligence!

"I can destroy all life on this earth from this room, if I desire. I can construct a telescope that will allow me to look on the planets of the farthest galaxies! I can send my mind forth to make contact with other minds without the slightest material connection. And you think it terrible that I should rule your race! I will not rule them, I will *own* them and this planet as you might own a farm and animals!"

"You couldn't!" I cried. "Pollard, if there is anything of Pollard left in you, give up that thought! We'll kill you ourselves before we'll let you start a monstrous rule of men!"

"We will—by God, we will!" Dutton cried, his face twitching.

We had started desperately forward toward the great head but stopped suddenly in our tracks as his great eyes met ours. I found myself walking backward to where I had stood, walking back and Dutton with me, like two automatons.

"So you two would try to kill me?" queried the head that had been Pollard. "Why, I could direct you without a word to kill yourselves and you'd do so in an instant! What chance has your puny will and brain against mine? And what chance will all the force of men have against me when a glance from me will make them puppets of my will?"

A desperate inspiration flashed through my brain. "Pollard, wait!" I exclaimed. "You were going on with the process, with the rays! If you stop here you'll not know what changes lie beyond your present form!"

He seemed to consider. "That is true," he admitted, "and though it seems impossible to me that by going on I can attain to greater intelligence than I now have, I want to find out for certain."

"Then you'll go under the rays for another fifteen minutes?" I asked quickly.

"I will," he answered, "but lest you harbor any foolish ideas, you may know that even inside the chamber I will be able to read your thoughts and can kill both of you before you can make a move to harm me."

He stepped up into the chamber again, and as I reached for the switch, Dutton trembling beside me, we glimpsed for a moment the huge head before the down-smiting white force hid it from our sight.

The minutes of this period seemed dragging even more slowly than before. It seemed hours before I reached at last to snap off the rays. We gazed into the chamber, shaking.

At first glance the great head inside seemed unchanged, but then we saw that it had changed, and greatly. Instead of being a skin-covered head with at least rudimentary arms and legs, it was now a great gray head like shape of even greater size, supported by two gray muscular tentacles. The surface of this gray head-thing was wrinkled and folded and its only features were two eyes as small as our own.

"Oh, my God!" quaked Dutton. "He's changing from a head into a brain—he's losing all human appearance!"

Into our minds came a thought from the gray head-thing before us, a thought as clear as though spoken. "You have guessed it, for even my former head-body is disappearing, all atrophying except the brain. I am become a walking, seeing brain. As I am so all of your race will be in two hundred million years, gradually losing more and more of their atrophied bodies and developing more and more their great brains."

His eyes seemed to read us. "You need not fear now the things I threatened in my last stage of development. My mind, grown infinitely greater, would no more now want to rule you men and your little planet than you would want to rule an anthill and its inhabitants! My mind, gone fifty million years further ahead in development, can soar out now to vistas of power and knowledge unimagined by me in that last stage, and unimaginable to you."

"Great God, Pollard!" I cried. "What have you become?"

"Pollard?" Dutton was laughing hysterically. "You call that thing Pollard? Why, we had dinner with Pollard three hours ago—he was a human being and not a thing like this!"

"I have become what all men will become in time," the thing's thought answered me, "I have gone this far along the road of man's future evolution, and am going on to the end of that road, am going to attain the development that the last mutation possible will give me!"

"Turn on the rays," his thought continued. "I think that I must be approaching now the last possible mutation."

I snapped over the switch again and the white shaft of the concentrated rays veiled from us the great gray shape. I felt my own mind giving beneath the strain of horror of the last hour, and Dutton was still half-hysterical.

The humming and crackling of the great apparatus seemed thunderous to my ears as the minutes passed. With every nerve keyed to highest tension, I threw open the switch at last. The rays ceased, and the figure in the chamber was again revealed.

Dutton began to laugh shrilly, and then abruptly was sobbing. I do not know whether I was doing the same, though I have a dim memory of mouthing incoherent things as my eyes took in the shape in the chamber.

It was a great brain! A gray limp mass four feet across, it lay in the chamber, its surface ridged and wrinkled by innumerable fine convolutions. It had no features or limbs of any kind in its gray mass. It was simply a huge brain whose only visible sign of life was its slow, twitching movement.

From it thoughts beat strongly into our own horror-weighted brains.

"You see me now, a great brain only, just as all men will be far in the future. Yes, you might have known, I might have known, when I was like you, that this would be the course of human evolution, that the brain that alone gives man dominance would develop and the body that hampers that brain would atrophy until he would have developed into pure brain as I now am!

"I have no features, no senses that I could describe to you, yet I can realize the universe infinitely better than you can with your elementary senses. I am aware of planes of existence you cannot imagine. I can feed myself with pure energy without the need of a cumbersome body, to transform it, and I can move and act, despite my lack of limbs, by means and with a speed and power utterly beyond your comprehension.

"If you still have fear of the threats I made two stages back against your world and race, banish them! I am pure intelligence now and as such, though I can no more feel the emotions of love or friendship, neither can I feel those of ambition or pride. The only emotion, if such it is, that remains to me still is intellectual curiosity, and this desire for truth that has burned in man since his apehood will thus be the last of all desires to leave him!"

The Last Mutation

"A brain—a great brain!" Dutton was saying dazedly. "Here in Pollard's laboratory—but where's Pollard? He was here, too . . ."

"Then all men will some day be as you are now?" I cried.

"Yes," came the answering thought, "in two hundred and fifty million years man as you know him and as you are will be no more, and after passing all the stages through which I have passed through tonight, the human race will have developed into great brains inhabiting not only your solar system, no doubt, but the systems of other stars!"

"And that's the end of man's evolutionary road? That is the highest point that he will reach?"

"No, I think he will change from this great brain into still a higher form," the brain answered—the brain that three hours before had been Pollard!—"am I going to find out now what that higher form will be. For I think this will be the last mutation of all and that with it I will reach the end of man's evolutionary path, the last and highest form into which he can develop!

"You will turn on the rays now," the brain's order continued, "and in fifteen minutes we will know what that last and highest form is."

My hand was on the switch but Dutton had staggered to me, was clutching my arm. "Don't, Arthur!" he was exclaiming thickly. "We've seen horrors enough—let's not see the last —get out of here . . ."

"I can't!" I cried. "Oh God, I want to stop but I can't now—I want to see the end myself—I've got to see . . ."

"Turn on the rays!" came the brain's thought-order again.

"The end of the road—the last mutation," I panted. "We've got to see—to see—" I drove the switch home.

The rays flashed down again to hide the great gray brain in the cube. Dutton's eyes were staring fixedly, he was clinging to me.

The minutes passed! Each tick of the watch in my hand was the mighty note of a great tolling bell in my ears.

An inability to move seemed gripping me. The hand of my watch was approaching the minute for which I waited, yet I could not raise my hand toward the switch!

Then as the hand reached the appointed minute I broke from my immobility and in a sheer frenzy of sudden strength pulled open the switch, rushed forward with Dutton to the cube's very edge!

The great gray brain that had been inside it was gone. There lay on the cube's floor instead of it a quite shapeless mass of clear, jelly-like matter. It was quite motionless save for a slight quivering. My shaking hand went forth to touch it, and then it was that I screamed, such a scream as all the tortures of hell's cruelest fiends could not have wrung from a human throat.

The mass inside the cube was a mass of simple *protoplasm!* This then was the end of man's evolution-road, the highest form to which time would bring him, the last mutation of all! The road of man's evolution was a circular one, returning to its beginning!

From the earth's bosom had risen the first crude organisms. Then sea-creature and land-creature and mammal and ape to man; and from man it would rise in the future through all the forms we had seen that night. There would be super-men, bodiless heads, pure brains; only to be changed by the last mutation of all into the protoplasm from which first it had sprung!

I do not know now exactly what followed. I know that I rushed upon that quivering, quiescent mass, calling Pollard's name madly and shouting things I am glad I cannot remember. I know that Dutton was shouting, too, with insane laughter, and that as he struck with lunatic howls and fury about the laboratory the crash of breaking glass and the hiss of escaping gases was in my ears. And then from those mingling acids bright flames were leaping and spreading, sudden fires that alone, I think now, saved my own sanity.

For I can remember dragging the insanely laughing Dutton from the room, from the house, into the cool darkness of the night. I remember the chill of dew-wet grass against my hands and face as the flames from Pollard's house soared higher. And I remember that as I saw Dutton's crazy laughter by that crimson light, I knew that he would laugh thus until he died.

So ends my narrative of the end that came to Pollard and Pollard's house. It is, as I said in beginning, a narrative that I only can tell now, for Dutton has never spoken a sane word since. In the institution where he now is, they think his condition the result of shock from the fire, just as Pollard was believed to have perished in that fire. I have never until now told the truth.

But I am telling it now, hoping that it will in some way lessen the horror it has left with me. For there could be no horror greater than that we saw in Pollard's house that night. I have brooded upon it. With my mind's eye I have followed that tremendous cycle of change, that purposeless, eon-long climb of life up from simple protoplasm through myriads of forms and lives of ceaseless pain and struggle, only to end in simple protoplasm again.

Will that cycle of evolutionary change be repeated over and over again upon this and other worlds, ceaselessly, purposelessly, until there is no more universe for it to go on in? Is this colossal cycle of life's changes as inevitable and necessary as the cycle that in space makes of the nebulae myriad suns, and of the suns dark-stars, and of the dark-stars colliding with one another nebula again?

Or is this evolutionary cycle we saw a cycle in appearance only, is there some change that we cannot understand, above and beyond it? I do not know which of these possibilities is truth, but I do know that the first of them haunts me. It would haunt the world if the world believed my story. Perhaps I should be thankful as I write to know that I will not be believed.

As I reread "The Man Who Evolved," I tried to remember when I had first learned about cosmic rays and evolution. I failed. It is as though I always knew about both phenomena, even though I was clearly not born with the knowledge.

I honestly believe that I learned about both from science fiction stories to begin with. I might even have come across them first in this story.

There are some pieces of knowledge that I remember clearly having learned from science fiction stories.

For instance, in Hamilton's *The Universe Wreckers,* much of the action took place on the planet Neptune, which was treated in the story as the most distant of the planets. (Pluto had not yet been discovered, and when I heard news of the discovery, in 1931, my first thought was that it messed up

Hamilton's novel.) It was in that novel that, for the first time, I learned Neptune had a satellite named Triton. I remember that piece of learning quite clearly.

It was from *The Drums of Tapajos* that I first learned there was a Mato Grosso area in the Amazon basin. It was from *The Black Star Passes* and other stories by John W. Campbell, Jr., that I first heard of relativity.

The pleasure of reading about such things in the dramatic and fascinating form of science fiction gave me a push toward science that was irresistible. It was science fiction that made me want to be a scientist strongly enough to eventually make me one.

This is not to say that science fiction stories can be completely trusted as a source of specific knowledge. In the case of "The Man Who Evolved," Hamilton was on solid ground when he maintained cosmic rays to be a motive force behind evolution. They are, but only in so far as they help create random mutations. It is natural selection that supplies the direction of evolutionary change, and this works, very painfully and slowly, upon large populations, not upon individuals.

The notion that a concentration of cosmic rays would cause an individual human being to evolve, personally, in the direction inevitably to be taken by the entire species is, of course, quite wrong. Concentrated radiation would merely kill.

However, the misguidings of science fiction can be unlearned. Sometimes the unlearning process is not easy, but it is a low price to pay for the gift of fascination over science.

It was the mark of the early and rather unsophisticated science fiction stories of the 1930s, by the way, that they often opened with one scientist lecturing others on subjects those others could not fail to know in real life (but of which the readers had to be informed).

I remember that the very first story I ever wrote for publication (but which was never published), "Cosmic Corkscrew," began that way, with the scientist-hero lecturing a friend on cosmic rays and neutrinos. No doubt, that opening helped Campbell decide on an immediate rejection (see *The Early Asimov*).

In the very month in which I completed the eighth grade, I read another story that stayed with me: "The Jameson Satellite," by Neil R. Jones, in the July 1931 *Amazing Stories*.

THE JAMESON SATELLITE

by Neil R. Jones

PROLOGUE

The Rocket Satellite

IN THE depths of space, some twenty thousand miles from the earth, the body of Professor Jameson within its rocket container cruised upon an endless journey, circling the gigantic sphere. The rocket was a satellite of the huge, revolving world around which it held to its orbit. In the year 1958, Professor Jameson had sought for a plan whereby he might preserve his body indefinitely after his death. He had worked long and hard upon the subject.

Since the time of the Pharaohs, the human race had looked for a means by which the dead might be preserved against the ravages of time. Great had been the art of the Egyptians in the embalming of their deceased, a practice which was later lost to humanity of the ensuing mechanical age, never to be rediscovered. But even the embalming of the Egyptians—so Professor Jameson had argued—would be futile in the face of millions of years, the dissolution of the corpses being just as eventual as immediate cremation following death.

The professor had looked for a means by which the body could be preserved perfectly forever. But eventually he had come to the conclusion that nothing on earth is unchangeable beyond a certain limit of time. Just as long as he sought an earthly means of preservation, he was doomed to disappointment. All earthly elements are composed of atoms which are forever breaking down and building up, but never destroying themselves. A match may be burned, but the atoms are still unchanged, having resolved themselves into smoke, carbon dioxide, ashes, and certain basic elements. It was clear to the professor that he could never accomplish his purpose if he were to employ one system of atomic structure, such as embalming fluid or other concoction, to preserve another system of atomic structure, such as the human body, when all atomic structure is subject to universal change, no matter how slow.

He had then soliloquized upon the possibility of preserving the human body in its state of death until the end of all earthly time—to that day when the earth would return to the sun from which it had sprung. Quite suddenly one day he had conceived the answer to the puzzling problem which obsessed his mind, leaving him awed with its wild, uncanny potentialities.

He would have his body shot into space enclosed in a rocket to become a satellite of the earth as long as the earth continued to exist. He reasoned logically. Any material substance, whether of organic or inorganic origin, cast into the depths of space would exist indefinitely. He had visualized his dead body enclosed in a rocket flying off into the illimitable maw of space. He would remain in perfect preservation, while on earth millions of generations of mankind would live and die, their bodies to molder into the dust of the forgotten past. He would exist in this unchanged manner until that day when mankind, beneath a cooling sun, should fade out forever in the chill, thin atmosphere of a dying world. And still his body would remain intact and as perfect in its rocket container as on that day of the far-gone past when it had left the earth to be hurled out on its career. What a magnificent idea!

At first he had been assailed with doubts. Suppose his funeral rocket landed upon some other planet or, drawn by the pull of the great sun, were thrown into the flaming folds of the incandescent sphere? Then the rocket might continue on out of the solar system, plunging through the endless seas of space for millions of years, to finally enter the solar system of some far-off star, as meteors often enter ours. Suppose his rocket crashed upon a planet, or the star itself, or became a captive satellite of some celestial body?

It had been at this juncture that the idea of his rocket becoming the satellite of the earth had presented itself, and he had immediately incorporated it into his scheme. The professor had figured out the amount of radium necessary to carry the rocket far enough away from the earth so that it would not turn around and crash, and still be not so far away but what the earth's gravitational attraction would keep it from leaving the vicinity of the earth and the solar system. Like the moon, it would forever revolve around the earth.

He had chosen an orbit sixty-five thousand miles from the earth for his rocket to follow. The only fears he had entertained concerned the huge meteors which careened through space at tremendous rates of speed. He had overcome this obstacle, however, and had eliminated the possibilities of a collision with these stellar juggernauts. In the rocket were installed radium repulsion rays which swerved all approaching meteors from the path of the rocket as they entered the vicinity of the space wanderer.

The aged professor had prepared for every contingency, and had set down to rest from his labors, reveling in the stupendous, unparalleled results he would obtain. Never would his body undergo decay; and never would his bones bleach to return to the dust of the earth from which all men originally came and to which they must return. His body would remain millions of years in a perfectly preserved state, untouched by the hoary palm of such time as only geologists and astronomers can conceive.

His efforts would surpass even the wildest dreams of H. Rider Haggard, who depicted the wondrous, embalming practices of the ancient nation of Kor in his immortal novel, "She," wherein Holly, under the escort of the incomparable Ayesha, looked upon the magnificent, lifelike masterpieces of embalming by the long-gone peoples of Kor.

With the able assistance of a nephew, who carried out his instructions and wishes following his death, Professor Jameson was sent upon his pilgrimage into space within the rocket he himself had built. The nephew and heir kept the secret forever locked in his heart.

Generation after generation had passed upon its way. Gradually humanity had come to die out, finally disappearing from the earth altogether. Mankind was later replaced by various other forms of life which dominated the globe for their allotted spaces of time before they too became extinct. The years piled up on one another, running into millions, and still the Jameson Satellite kept its lonely vigil around the earth, gradually closing the distance between satellite and planet, yielding reluctantly to the latter's powerful attraction.

Forty million years later, its orbit ranged some twenty

thousand miles from the earth while the dead world edged ever nearer the cooling sun whose dull, red ball covered a large expanse of the sky. Surrounding the flaming sphere, many of the stars could be perceived through the earth's thin, rarefied atmosphere. As the earth cut in slowly and gradually toward the solar luminary, so was the moon revolving ever nearer the earth, appearing like a great gem glowing in the twilight sky.

The rocket containing the remains of Professor Jameson continued its endless travel around the great ball of the earth whose rotation had now ceased entirely—one side forever facing the dying sun. There it pursued its lonely way, a cosmic coffin, accompanied by its funeral cortege of scintillating stars amid the deep silence of the eternal space which enshrouded it. Solitary it remained, except for the occasional passing of a meteor flitting by at a remarkable speed on its aimless journey through the vacuum between the far-flung worlds.

Would the satellite follow its orbit to the world's end, or would its supply of radium soon exhaust itself after so many eons of time, converting the rocket into the prey of the first large meteor which chanced that way? Would it some day return to the earth as its nearer approach portended, and increase its acceleration in a long arc to crash upon the surface of the dead planet? And when the rocket terminated its career, would the body of Professor Jameson be found perfectly preserved or merely a crumbled mound of dust?

CHAPTER I

40,000,000 Years After

Entering within the boundaries of the solar system, a long, dark, pointed craft sped across the realms of space towards the tiny point of light which marked the dull red ball of the dying sun which would some day lie cold and dark forever. Like a huge meteor it flashed into the solar system from another chain of planets far out in the illimitable Universe of stars and worlds, heading towards the great red sun at an inconceivable speed.

Within the interior of the space traveler, queer creatures of metal labored at the controls of the space flyer which juggernauted on its way towards the far-off solar luminary. Rapidly it crossed the orbits of Neptune and Uranus and headed sunward. The bodies of these queer creatures were square blocks of a metal closely resembling steel, while for appendages, the metal cube was upheld by four jointed legs capable of movement. A set of six tentacles, all metal, like the rest of the body, curved outward from the upper half of the cubic body. Surmounting it was a queer-shaped head rising to a peak in the center and equipped with a circle of eyes all the way around the head. The creatures, with their mechanical eyes equipped with metal shutters, could see in all directions. A single eye pointed directly upward, being situated in the space of the peaked head, resting in a slight depression of the cranium.

These were the Zoromes of the planet Zor which rotated on its way around a star millions of light years distant from our solar system. The Zoromes, several hundred thousand years before, had reached a stage in science, where they searched for immortality and eternal relief from bodily ills and various deficiencies of flesh and blood anatomy. They had sought freedom from death, and had found it, but at the same time they had destroyed the propensities for birth. And for several hundred thousand years there had been no births and few deaths in the history of the Zoromes.

This strange race of people had built their own mechanical bodies, and by operation upon one another had removed their brains to the metal heads from which they directed the functions and movements of their inorganic anatomies. There had been no deaths due to worn-out bodies. When one part of the mechanical men wore out, it was replaced by a new part, and so the Zoromes continued living their immortal lives which saw few casualties. It was true that, since the innovation of the machines, there had been a few accidents which had seen the destruction of the metal heads with their brains. These were irreparable. Such cases had been few, however, and the population of Zor had decreased but little. The machine men of Zor had no use for atmosphere, and had it not been for the terrible coldness of space, could have just as well existed in the ether void as upon some planet. Their metal bodies, especially their metal-encased brains, did require a certain amount of heat even though they were able to exist comfortably in temperatures which would instantly have frozen to death a flesh-and-blood creature.

The most popular pastime among the machine men of Zor was the exploration of the Universe. This afforded them a never ending source of interest in the discovery of the variegated inhabitants and conditions of the various planets on which they came to rest. Hundreds of space ships were sent out in all directions, many of them being upon their expeditions for hundreds of years before they returned once more to the home planet of far-off Zor.

This particular space craft of the Zoromes had entered the solar system whose planets were gradually circling in closer to the dull red ball of the declining sun. Several of the machine men of the space craft's crew, which numbered some fifty individuals, were examining the various planets of this particular planetary system carefully through telescopes possessing immense power.

These machine men had no names and were indexed according to letters and numbers. They conversed by means of thought impulses, and were neither capable of making a sound vocally nor of hearing one uttered.

"Where shall we go?" queried one of the men at the controls questioning another who stood by his side examining a chart on the wall.

"They all appear to be dead worlds, 4R-3579," replied the one addressed, "but the second planet from the sun appears to have an atmosphere which might sustain a few living creatures, and the third planet may also prove interesting for it has a satellite. We shall examine the inner planets first of all, and explore the outer ones later if we decide it is worth the time."

"Too much trouble for nothing," ventured 9G-721. "This system of planets offers us little but what we have seen many times before in our travels. The sun is so cooled that it cannot sustain the more common life on its planets, the type of life forms we usually find in our travels. We should have visited a planetary system with a brighter sun."

"You speak of common life," remarked 25X-987. "What of the uncommon life? Have we not found life existent on cold, dead planets with no sunlight and atmosphere at all?"

"Yes, we have," admitted 9G-721, "but such occasions are exceedingly rare."

"The possibility exists, however, even in this case," reminded 4R-3579, "and what if we do spend a bit of unprofitable time in this one planetary system—haven't we all an endless lifetime before us? Eternity is ours."

"We shall visit the second planet first of all," directed 25X-987, who was in charge of this particular expedition of the Zoromes, "and on the way there we shall cruise along near the third planet to see what we can of the surface. We may be able to tell whether or not it holds anything of interest to us. If it does, after visiting the second planet, we shall then return to the third. The first world is not worth bothering with."

The space ship from Zor raced on in a direction which would take it several thousand miles above the earth and then on to the planet which we know as Venus. As the space ship rapidly neared the earth, it slackened its speed, so that the Zoromes might examine it closely with their glasses as the ship passed the third planet.

Suddenly, one of the machine men ran excitedly into the room where 25X-987 stood watching the topography of the world beneath him.

"We have found something!" he exclaimed.

"What?"

"Another space ship!"

"Where?"

"But a short distance ahead of us on our course. Come into the foreport of the ship and you can pick it up with the glass."

"Which is the way it's going?" asked 25X-987.

"It is behaving queerly," replied the machine man of Zor. "It appears to be in the act of encircling the planet."

"Do you suppose that there really is life on that dead world —intelligent beings like ourselves, and that this is one of their space craft?"

"Perhaps it is another exploration craft like our own from some other world," was the suggestion.

"But not of ours," said 25X-987.

Together, the two Zoromes now hastened into the observation room of the space ship where more of the machine men were excitedly examining the mysterious space craft, their thought impulses flying thick and fast like bodiless bullets.

"It is very small!"

"Its speed is slow!"

"The craft can hold but few men," observed one.

"We do not yet know of what size the creatures are," reminded another. "Perhaps there are thousands of them in that space craft out there. They may be of such a small size that it will be necessary to look twice before finding one of them. Such beings are not unknown."

"We shall soon overtake it and see."

"I wonder if they have seen us?"

"Where do you suppose it came from?"

"From the world beneath us," was the suggestion.

"Perhaps."

CHAPTER II

The Mysterious Space Craft

The machine men made way for their leader, 25X-987, who regarded the space craft ahead of them critically.

"Have you tried communicating with it yet?" he asked.

"There is no reply to any of our signals," came the answer.

"Come alongside of it then," ordered their commander. "It is small enough to be brought inside our carrying compartment, and we can see with our penetration rays just what manner of creatures it holds. They are intelligent, that is certain, for their space ship does imply as much."

The space flyer of the Zoromes slowed up as it approached the mysterious wanderer of the cosmic void which hovered in the vicinity of the dying world.

"What a queer shape it has," remarked 25X-987. "It is even smaller than I had previously calculated."

A rare occurrence had taken place among the machine men of Zor. They were overcome by a great curiosity which they could not allow to remain unsatiated. Accustomed as they were to witnessing strange sights and still stranger creatures, meeting up with weird adventures in various corners of the Universe, they had now become hardened to the usual run of experiences which they were in the habit of encountering. It took a great deal to arouse their unperturbed attitudes. Something new, however, about this queer space craft had gripped their imaginations, and perhaps a subconscious influence asserted to their minds that here they have come across an adventure radically unusual.

"Come alongside it," repeated 25X-987 to the operator as

he returned to the control room and gazed through the side of the space ship in the direction of the smaller cosmic wanderer.

"I'm trying to," replied the machine man, "but it seems to jump away a bit every time I get within a certain distance of it. Our ship seems to jump backward a bit too."

"Are they trying to elude us?"

"I don't know. They should pick up more speed if that is their object."

"Perhaps they are now progressing at their maximum speed and cannot increase their acceleration any more."

"Look!" exclaimed the operator. "Did you just see that? The thing has jumped away from us again!"

"Our ship moved also," said 25X-987. "I saw a flash of light shoot from the side of the other craft as it jumped."

Another machine man now entered and spoke to the commander of the Zorome expedition.

"They are using radium repellent rays to keep us from approaching," he informed.

"Counteract it," instructed 25X-987.

The man left, and now the machine man at the controls of the craft tried again to close with the mysterious wanderer of the space between planets. The effort was successful, and this time there was no glow of repulsion rays from the side of the long metal cylinder.

They now entered the compartment where various objects were transferred from out of the depths of space to the interplanetary craft. Then patiently they waited for the rest of the machine men to open the side of their space ship and bring in the queer, elongated cylinder.

"Put it under the penetration ray!" ordered 25X-987. "Then we shall see what it contains!"

The entire group of Zoromes were assembled about the long cylinder, whose low nickel-plated sides shone brilliantly. With interest they regarded the fifteen-foot object which tapered a bit towards its base. The nose was pointed like a bullet. Eight cylindrical protuberances were affixed to the base while the four sides were equipped with fins such as are seen on aerial bombs to guide them in a direct, unswerving line through the atmosphere. At the base of the strange craft there projected a lever, while in one side was a door which apparently opened outward. One of the machine men reached forward to open it but was halted by the admonition of the commander.

"Do not open it up yet!" he warned. "We are not aware of what it contains!"

Guided by the hand of one of the machine men, a series of lights shone down upon the cylinder. It became enveloped in a haze of light which rendered the metal sides of the mysterious space craft dim and indistinct while the interior of the cylinder was as clearly revealed as if there had been no covering. The machine men, expecting to see at least several, perhaps many, strange creatures moving about within the metal cylinder, stared aghast at the sight they beheld. There was but one creature, and he was lying perfectly still, either in a state of suspended animation or else of death. He was about twice the height of the mechanical men of Zor. For a long time they gazed at him in a silence of thought, and then their leader instructed them.

"Take him out of the container."

The penetration rays were turned off, and two of the machine men stepped eagerly forward and opened the door. One of them peered within at the recumbent body of the weird-looking individual with the four appendages. The creature lay up against a luxuriously upholstered interior, a strap affixed to his chin while four more straps held both the upper and lower appendages securely to the insides of the cylinder. The machine man released these, and with the help of his comrade removed the body of the creature from the cosmic coffin in which they had found it.

"He is dead!" pronounced one of the machine men after a long and careful examination of the corpse. "He has been like this for a long time."

"There are strange thought impressions left upon his mind," remarked another.

One of the machine men, whose metal body was a different shade than that of his companions, stepped forward, his cubic body bent over that of the strange, cold creature who was garbed in fantastic accoutrements. He examined the dead organism a moment, and then he turned to his companions.

"Would you like to hear his story?" he asked.

"Yes!" came the concerted reply.

"You shall, then," was the ultimatum. "Bring him into my laboratory. I shall remove his brain and stimulate the cells into activity once more. We shall give him life again, transplanting his brain into the head of one of our machines."

With these words he directed two of the Zoromes to carry the corpse into the laboratory.

As the space ship cruised about in the vicinity of this third planet which 25X-987 had decided to visit on finding the metal cylinder with its queer inhabitant, 8B-52, the experimenter, worked unceasingly in his laboratory to revive the long-dead brain cells to action once more. Finally, after consummating his desires and having his efforts crowned with success, he placed the brain within the head of a machine. The brain was brought to consciousness. The creature's body was discarded after the all-important brain had been removed.

CHAPTER III

Recalled to Life

As Professor Jameson came to, he became aware of a strange feeling. He was sick. The doctors had not expected him to live; they had frankly told him so—but he had cared little in view of the long, happy years stretched out behind him. Perhaps he was not to die yet. He wondered how long he had slept. How strange he felt—as if he had no body. Why couldn't he open his eyes? He tried very hard. A mist swam before him. His eyes had been open all the time but he had not seen before. That was queer, he ruminated. All was silent about his bedside. Had all the doctors and nurses left him to sleep—or to die?

Devil take that mist which now swam before him, obscuring everything in line of vision. He would call his nephew. Vainly he attempted to shout the word "Douglas," but to no avail. Where was his mouth? It seemed as if he had none. Was it all delirium? The strange silence—perhaps he had lost his sense of hearing along with his ability to speak—and he could see nothing distinctly. The mist had transferred itself into a confused jumble of indistinct objects, some of which moved about before him.

He was now conscious of some impulse in his mind which kept questioning him as to how he felt. He was conscious of other strange ideas which seemed to be impressed upon his brain, but this one thought concerning his indisposition clamored insistently over the lesser ideas. It even seemed just as if someone was addressing him, and impulsively he attempted to utter a sound and tell them how queer he felt. It seemed as if speech had been taken from him. He could not talk, no matter how hard he tried. It was no use. Strange to say, however, the impulse within his mind appeared to be satisfied with the effort, and it now put another question to him. Where was he from? What a strange question—when he was at home. He told them as much. Had he always lived there? Why, yes, of course.

The aged professor was now becoming more astute as to his condition. At first it was only a mild, passive wonderment at his helplessness and the strange thoughts which raced through his mind. Now he attempted to arouse himself from the lethargy.

Quite suddenly his sight cleared, and what a surprise! He could see all the way around him without moving his head! And he could look at the ceiling of his room! His room? Was it his room! No—It just couldn't be. Where was he? What were those queer machines before him? They moved on four legs. Six tentacles curled outward from their cubical bodies. One of the machines stood close before him. A tentacle shot out from the object and rubbed his head. How strange it felt upon his brow. Instinctively he obeyed the impulse to shove the contraption of metal from him with his hands.

His arms did not rise, instead six tentacles projected upward to force back the machine. Professor Jameson gasped mentally in surprise as he gazed at the result of his urge to push the strange, unearthly looking machine-caricature from him. With trepidation he looked down at his own body to see where the tentacles had come from, and his surprise turned to sheer fright and amazement. His body was like the moving machine which stood before him! Where was he? What ever had happened to him so suddenly? Only a few moments ago he had been in his bed, with the doctors and his nephew bending over him, expecting him to die. The last words he had remembered hearing was the cryptic announcement of one of the doctors.

"He is going now."

But he hadn't died after all, apparently. A horrible thought struck him! Was this the life after death? Or was it an illusion of the mind? He became aware that the machine in front of him was attempting to communicate something to him. How could it, thought the professor, when he had no mouth. The desire to communicate an idea to him became more insistent. The suggestion of the machine man's question was in his mind. Telepathy, thought he.

The creature was asking about the place whence he had come. He didn't know; his mind was in such a turmoil of thoughts and conflicting ideas. He allowed himself to be led to a window where the machine with waving tentacle pointed towards an object outside. It was a queer sensation to be walking on the four metal legs. He looked from the window and he saw that which caused him to nearly drop over, so astounded was he.

The professor found himself gazing out from the boundless depths of space across the cosmic void to where a huge planet lay quiet. Now he was sure it was an illusion which made his mind and sight behave so queerly. He was troubled by a very strange dream. Carefully he examined the topography of the gigantic globe which rested off in the distance. At the same time he could see back of him the concourse of mechanical creatures crowding up behind him, and he was aware of a telepathic conversation which was being carried on behind him—or just before him. Which was it now? Eyes extended all the way around his head, while there existed no difference on any of the four sides of his cubed body. His mechanical legs were capable of moving in any of four given directions with perfect ease, he discovered.

The planet was not the earth—of that he was sure. None of the familiar continents lay before his eyes. And then he saw the great dull red ball of the dying sun. That was not the sun of his earth. It had been a great deal more brilliant.

"Did you come from that planet?" came the thought impulse from the mechanism by his side.

"No," he returned.

He then allowed the machine men—for he assumed that they were machine men, and he reasoned that, somehow or other they had by some marvelous transformation made him over just as they were—to lead him through the craft of which he now took notice for the first time. It was an interplanetary flyer, or space ship, he firmly believed.

25X-987 now took him to the compartment which they had removed him to from the strange container they had found wandering in the vicinity of the nearby world. There they showed him the long cylinder.

"It's my rocket satellite!" exclaimed Professor Jameson to

himself, though in reality every one of the machine men received his thoughts plainly. "What is it doing here?"

"We found your dead body within it," answered 25X-987. "Your brain was removed to the machine after having been stimulated into activity once more. Your carcass was thrown away."

Professor Jameson just stood dumbfounded by the words of the machine man.

"So I did die!" exclaimed the professor. "And my body was placed within the rocket to remain in everlasting preservation until the end of all earthly time! Success! I have now attained unrivaled success!"

He then turned to the machine man.

"How long have I been that way?" he asked excitedly.

"How should we know?" replied the Zorome. "We picked up your rocket only a short time ago, which, according to your computation, would be less than a day. This is our first visit to your planetary system and we chanced upon your rocket. So it is a satellite? We didn't watch it long enough to discover whether or not it was a satellite. At first we thought it to be another traveling space craft, but when it refused to answer our signals we investigated."

"And so that was the earth at which I looked," mused the professor. "No wonder I didn't recognize it. The topography has changed so much. How different the sun appears—it must have been over a million years ago when I died!"

"Many millions," corrected 25X-987. "Suns of such size as this one do not cool in so short a time as you suggest."

Professor Jameson, in spite of all his amazing computations before his death, was staggered by the reality.

"Who are you?" he suddenly asked.

"We are the Zoromes from Zor, a planet of a sun far across the Universe."

25X-987 then went on to tell Professor Jameson something about how the Zoromes had attained their high stage of development and had instantly put a stop to all birth, evolution and death of their people, by becoming machine men.

CHAPTER IV

The Dying World

"And now tell us of yourself," said 25X-987, "and about your world."

Professor Jameson, noted in college as a lecturer of no mean ability and perfectly capable of relating intelligently to them the story of the earth's history, evolution and march of events following the birth of civilization up until the time when he died, began his story. The mental speech hampered him for a time, but he soon became accustomed to it so as to use it easily, and he found it preferable to vocal speech after a while. The Zoromes listened interestedly to the long account until Professor Jameson had finished.

"My nephew," concluded the professor, "evidently obeyed my instructions and placed my body in the rocket I had built, shooting it out into space where I became the satellite of the earth for these many millions of years."

"Do you really want to know how long you were dead before we found you?" asked 25X-987. "It would be interesting to find out."

"Yes, I should like very much to know," replied the professor.

"Our greatest mathematician, 459C-79, will tell it to you." The mathematician stepped forward. Upon one side of his cube were many buttons arranged in long columns and squares.

"What is your unit of measuring?" he asked.

"A mile."

"How many times more is a mile than is the length of your rocket satellite?"

"My rocket is fifteen feet long. A mile is five thousand two hundred and eighty feet."

The mathematician depressed a few buttons.

"How far, or how many miles from the sun was your planet at that time?"

"Ninety-three million miles," was the reply.

"And your world's satellite—which you call moon, from your planet—earth?"

"Two hundred and forty thousand miles."

71

"And your rocket?"

"I figured it to go about sixty-five thousand miles from the earth."

"It was only twenty thousand miles from the earth when we picked it up," said the mathematician, depressing a few more buttons. "The moon and sun are also much nearer your planet now."

Professor Jameson gave way to a mental ejaculation of amazement.

"Do you know how long you have cruised around the planet in your own satellite?" said the mathematician. "Since you began that journey, the planet which you call the earth has revolved around the sun over forty million times."

"Forty—million—years!" exclaimed Professor Jameson haltingly. "Humanity must then have all perished from the earth long ago! I'm the last man on earth!"

"It is a dead world now," interjected 25X-987.

"Of course," elucidated the mathematician, "those last few million years are much shorter than the ones in which you lived. The earth's orbit is of less diameter and its speed of revolution is greatly increased, due to its proximity to the cooling sun. I should say that your year was some four times as long as the time in which it now takes your old planet to circumnavigate the sun.

"How many days were there in your year?"

"Three hundred and sixty-five."

"The planet has now ceased rotating entirely."

"Seems queer that your rocket satellite should avoid the meteors so long," observed 459C-79, the mathematician.

"Automatic radium repulsion rays," explained the professor.

"The very rays which kept us from approaching your rocket," stated 25X-987, "until we neutralized them."

"You died and were shot out into space long before any life occurred on Zor," soliloquized one of the machine men. "Our people had not yet even been born when yours had probably disappeared entirely from the face of the earth."

"Hearken to 72N-4783," said 25X-987, "he is our philosopher, and he just loves to dwell on the past life of Zor when we were flesh and blood creatures with the threat of death hanging always over our heads. At that time, like the life you knew, we were born, we lived and died, all within a very short time, comparatively."

"Of course, time has come to mean nothing to us, especially when we are out in space," observed 72N-4783. "We never keep track of it on our expeditions, though back in Zor such accounts are accurately kept. By the way, do you know how long we stood here while you recounted to us the history of your planet? Our machine bodies never get tired, you know."

"Well," ruminated Professor Jameson, giving a generous allowance of time. "I should say about a half a day, although it seemed scarcely as long as that."

"We listened to you for four days," replied 72N-4783.

Professor Jameson was really aghast.

"Really, I hadn't meant to be such a bore," he apologized.

"That is nothing," replied the other. "Your story was interesting, and if it had been twice as long, it would not have mattered, nor would it have seemed any longer. Time is merely relative, and in space actual time does not exist at all, any more than your forty million years' cessation of life seemed more than a few moments to you. We saw that it was so when your first thought impressions reached us following your revival."

"Let us continue on to your planet earth," then said 25X-987. "Perhaps we shall find more startling disclosures there."

As the space ship of the Zoromes approached the sphere from which Professor Jameson had been hurled in his rocket forty million years before, the professor was wondering how the earth would appear, and what radical changes he would find. Already he knew that the geographical conditions of the various continents were changed. He had seen as much from the space ship.

A short time later the earth was reached. The space travelers from Zor, as well as Professor Jameson, emerged from the cosmic flyer to walk upon the surface of the planet. The earth had ceased rotating, leaving one-half its surface always toward the sun. This side of the earth was heated to a considerable degree, while its antipodes, turned always away from the solar luminary, was a cold, frigid, desolate waste. The space travelers from Zor did not dare to advance very far into either hemisphere, but landed on the narrow, thousand-mile strip of territory separating the earth's frozen half from its sun-baked antipodes.

As Professor Jameson emerged from the space ship with 25X-987, he stared in awe at the great transformation four hundred thousand centuries had wrought. The earth's surface, its sky and the sun were all so changed and unearthly appearing. Off to the east the blood red ball of the slowly cooling sun rested upon the horizon, lighting up the eternal day. The earth's rotation had ceased entirely, and it hung motionless in the sky as it revolved around its solar parent, its orbit slowly but surely cutting in toward the great body of the sun. The two inner planets, Mercury and Venus, were now very close to the blood red orb whose scintillating, dazzling brilliance had been lost in its cooling process. Soon, the two nearer planets would succumb to the great pull of the solar luminary and return to the flaming folds, from which they had been hurled out as gaseous bodies in the dim, age-old past, when their careers had just begun.

The atmosphere was nearly gone, so rarefied had it become, and through it Professor Jameson could view with amazing clarity without discomfort to his eyes the bloated body of the dying sun. It appeared many times the size he had seen it at the time of his death, on account of its relative nearness. The earth had advanced a great deal closer to the great star around which it swung.

The sky towards the west was pitch black except for the iridescent twinkle of the fiery stars which studded that section of the heavens. As he watched, a faint glow suffused the western sky, gradually growing brighter, the full moon majestically lifted itself above the horizon, casting its pale, ethereal radiance upon the dying world beneath. It was increased to many times the size Professor Jameson had ever seen it during his natural lifetime. The earth's greater attraction was drawing upon the moon just as the sun was pulling the earth ever nearer itself.

This cheerless landscape confronting the professor represented the state of existence to which the earth had come. It was a magnificent spread of loneliness which bore no witness to the fact that it had seen the teeming of life in better ages long ago. The weird, yet beautiful scene, spread in a melancholy panorama before his eyes, drove his thoughts into gloomy abstraction with its dismal, depressing influence. Its funereal, oppressive aspect smote him suddenly with the chill of a terrible loneliness.

25X-987 aroused Professor Jameson from his lethargic reverie. "Let us walk around and see what we can find. I can understand how you feel in regard to the past. It is quite a shock —but it must happen to all worlds sooner or later—even to Zor. When that time comes, the Zoromes will find a new planet on which to live. If you travel with us, you will become accustomed to the sight of seeing dead, lifeless worlds as well as new and beautiful ones pulsating with life and energy. Of course, this world being your own, holds a peculiar sentimental value to you, but it is really one planet among billions."

Professor Jameson was silent.

"I wonder whether or not there are any ruins here to be found?" queried 25X-987.

"I don't believe so," replied the professor. "I remember hearing an eminent scientist of my day state that, given fifty thousand years, every structure and other creation of man would be obliterated entirely from off the earth's surface."

"And he was right," endorsed the machine man of Zor. "Time is a great effacer."

For a long time the machine men wandered over the dreary surface of the earth, and then 25X-987 suggested a change of territory to explore. In the space ship, they moved around the earth to the other side, still keeping to the belt of shadowland which completely encircled the globe like some gigantic ring. Where they now landed arose a series of cones with hollow peaks.

"Volcanoes!" exclaimed the professor.

"Extinct ones," added the machine man.

Leaving the space ship, the fifty or more machine men, including also Professor Jameson, were soon exploring the curiously shaped peaks. The professor, in his wanderings had strayed away from the rest, and now advanced into one of the cup-like depressions of the peak, out of sight of his companions, the Zoromes.

CHAPTER V

Eternity or Death

He was well in the center of the cavity when the soft ground beneath him gave way suddenly and he catapulted below into the darkness. Through the Stygian gloom he fell in what seemed to be an endless drop. He finally crashed upon something hard. The thin crust of the volcano's mouth had broken through, precipitating him into the deep, hollow interior.

It must have been a long ways to fall—or so it had seemed. Why was he not knocked senseless or killed? Then he felt himself over with three tentacles. His metal legs were four broken, twisted masses of metal, while the lower half of his cubic body was jammed out of shape and split. He could not move, and half of his six tentacles were paralyzed.

How would he ever get out of there? he wondered. The machine men of Zor might never find him. What would happen to him, then? He would remain in this deathless, monotonous state forever in the black hole of the volcano's interior unable to move. What a horrible thought! He could not starve to death; eating was unknown among the Zoromes, the machines requiring no food. He could not even commit suicide. The only way for him to die would be to smash the strong metal head, and in his present immovable condition, this was impossible.

It suddenly occurred to him to radiate thoughts for help. Would the Zoromes receive his messages? He wondered how far the telepathic messages would carry. He concentrated the powers of his mind upon the call for help, and repeatedly stated his position and plight. He then left his mind clear to receive the thought answers of the Zoromes. He received none. Again he tried. Still he received no welcoming answer. Professor Jameson became dejected.

It was hopeless. The telepathic messages had not reached the machine men of Zor. They were too far away, just as one person may be out of earshot of another's voice. He was doomed to a terrible fate of existence! It were better that his rocket had never been found. He wished that the Zoromes had destroyed him instead of bringing him back to life—back to this!

His thoughts were suddenly broken in upon.

"We're coming!"

"Don't give up hope!"

If the professor's machine body had been equipped with a heart, it would have sung for joy at these welcome thought impressions. A short time later there appeared in the ragged break of the volcano's mouth, where he had fallen through, the metal head of one of the machine men.

"We shall have you out of there soon," he said.

The professor never knew how they managed it for he lost consciousness under some strange ray of light they projected down upon him in his prison. When he came to consciousness once more, it was to find himself inside the space ship.

"If you had fallen and had smashed your head, it would have been all over with you," were the first thought impulses which greeted him. "As it is, however, we can fix you up first rate."

"Why didn't you answer the first time I called to you?" asked the professor. "Didn't you hear me?"

"We heard you, and we answered, but you didn't hear us. You see, your brain is different than ours, and though you can send thought waves as far as we can you cannot receive them from such a great distance."

"I'm wrecked," said the professor, gazing at his twisted limbs, paralyzed tentacles and jammed body.

"We shall repair you," came the reply. "It is your good fortune that your head was not crushed."

"What are you going to do with me?" queried the professor. "Will you remove my brains to another machine?"

"No, it isn't necessary. We shall merely remove your head and place it upon another machine body."

The Zoromes immediately set to work upon the task, and soon had Professor Jameson's metal head removed from the machine which he had wrecked in his fall down the crater. All during the painless operation, the professor kept up a series of thought exchanges in conversation with the Zoromes, and it seemed but a short time before his head surmounted a new machine and he was ready for further exploration. In the course of his operation, the space ship had moved to a new position, and now as they emerged 25X-987 kept company with Professor Jameson.

"I must keep an eye on you," he said. "You will be getting into more trouble before you get accustomed to the metal bodies."

But Professor Jameson was doing a great deal of thinking. Doubtlessly, these strange machine men who had picked up his rocket in the depths of space and had brought him back to life, were expecting him to travel with them and become adopted into the ranks of the Zoromes. Did he want to go with them? He couldn't decide. He had forgotten that the machine men could read his innermost thoughts.

"You wish to remain here alone upon the earth?" asked 25X-987. "It is your privilege if you really want it so."

"I don't know," replied Professor Jameson truthfully.

He gazed at the dust around his feet. It had probably been the composition of men, and had changed from time to time into various other atomic structures—of other queer forms of life which had succeeded mankind. It was the law of the atom which never died. And now he had within his power perpetual existence. He could be immortal if he wished! It would be an immortality of never-ending adventures in the vast, endless Universe among the galaxy of stars and planets.

A great loneliness seized him. Would he be happy among these machine men of another far-off world—among these Zoromes? They were kindly and solicitous of his welfare. What better fate could he expect? Still, a longing for his own kind arose in him—the call of humanity. It was irresistible. What could he do? Was it not in vain? Humanity had long since disappeared from the earth—millions of years ago. He wondered what lay beyond the pales of death—the real death, where the body decomposed and wasted away to return to the dust of the earth and assume new atomic structures.

He had begun to wonder whether or not he had been dead all these forty millions of years—suppose he had been merely in a state of suspended animation. He had remembered a scientist of his day, who had claimed that the body does not die at the point of official death. According to the claims of this man, the cells of the body did not die at the moment at which respiration, heart beats and the blood circulation ceased, but it existed in the semblance of life for several days afterward, especially in the cells of the bones, which died last of all.

Perhaps when he had been sent out into space in his rocket right after his death, the action of the cosmic void was to halt his slow death of the cells in his body, and hold him in suspended animation during the ensuing millions of years. Suppose he should really die—destroying his own brain? What lay beyond real death? Would it be a better plane of existence than the Zoromes could offer him? Would he rediscover humanity, or had they long since arisen to higher planes of existence or reincarnation? Did time exist beyond the mysterious portals of death? If not, then it was possible for him to join the souls of the human race. Had he really been dead all this time? If so, he knew what to expect in case he really destroyed his own brain. Oblivion!

Again the intense feeling of loneliness surged over him and held him within its melancholy grasp. Desperately, he decided to find the nearest cliff and jump from it—head-first! Humanity called; no man lived to companion him. His four metal limbs carried him swiftly to the summit of a nearby precipice. Why not gamble on the hereafter? 25X-987, understanding his trend of thought, did not attempt to restrain him. Instead, the machine man of Zor waited patiently.

As Professor Jameson stood there meditating upon the jump which would hurl him now into a new plane of existence—or into oblivion, the thought transference of 25X-987 reached him. It was laden with the wisdom born of many planets and thousands of centuries' experience.

"Why jump?" asked the machine man. "The dying world holds your imagination within a morbid clutch. It is all a matter of mental condition. Free your mind of this fascinating influence and come with us to visit other worlds, many of them are both beautiful and new. You will then feel a great difference.

"Will you come?"

The professor considered for a moment as he resisted the impulse to dive off the declivity to the enticing rocks far below. An inspiration seized him. Backing away from the edge of the cliff, he joined 25X-987 once more.

"I shall come," he stated.

He would become an immortal after all and join the Zoromes in their never-ending adventures from world to world. They hastened to the space ship to escape the depressing, dreary influence of the dying world, which had nearly driven Professor Jameson to take the fatal leap to oblivion.

"The Jameson Satellite" is a notable example of the faults of pre-Campbell science fiction. The scientific background is not blended with the story but is presented in indigestible blocks that halt the action. The science, moreover, is inaccurate even by the standards of its own time.

In 1931, for instance, radium still had glamour as the richest practical source of radioactivity, so it is natural to have it used vaguely as propulsive power for a satellite (launched in 1958, by the way, almost on the nose). There was no indication, however, in 1931 (or since) that radium possesses "repulsion rays."

Then, too, Jones, at this early stage in his career (he had been publishing for only a year and a half, and this was his fourth science fiction story) was clearly in imperfect command of the English language. He used the words "soliloquized upon" when he should rather have used "considered," "inspiration" rather than the more accurate "impulse," and so on. On the whole, "The Jameson Satellite" is probably the least skillfully written story in this anthology.

None of the flaws in language and construction were obvious to my eleven-and-a-half-year self, however. What I responded to was the tantalizing glimpse of possible immortality and the vision of the world's sad death, to say nothing of the contracting spirals of the planetary orbits forty million years hence (not long enough, by the way; forty billion would have been better if that were the way the Solar System were to end, which it isn't).

More important still were Jones's Zoromes, who were robots really. Their organic brains were just a detail. Jones treated them as mechanical men, making them objective without being unfeeling, benevolent without being busybodies. They made no effort to use force to keep Professor Jameson from committing suicide if he really wanted to, but they did use dignified persuasion.

One of the marks of reader enthusiasm for a story is the demand for more, and an author often wrote a sequel to a popular story. The readers (not just myself) were so taken by "The Jameson Satellite" that Jones wrote about a dozen "Professor Jameson stories" over the next seven years, carrying his Zoromes to a new and startling world in each. Although the Zoromes remained without individual personality, I could easily recite the number-letter combinations of those who appeared most often.

It is from the Zoromes, beginning with their first appearance in "The Jameson Satellite," that I got my own feeling for benevolent robots who could serve man with decency, as these had served Professor Jameson. It was the Zoromes, then, who were the spiritual ancestors of my own "positronic robots," all of them, from Robbie to R. Daneel.

Something else that was very prevalent in the science fiction of the 1930s was the adventure story fitted out with just enough scientific trappings to enable it to pass muster. And in the science fiction magazines of the early part of the decade, no one was better at it than Captain S. P. Meek.

He published some thirty stories in the magazines between 1930 and 1932—his heyday—and of them all, the best was *The Drums of Tapajos*, a lost-civilization-in-the-Amazon story I have already mentioned twice.

Equally typical, and short enough to include here, are his "Submicroscopic" and its sequel, "Awlo of Ulm," which ran in successive issues of *Amazing Stories* (August and September 1931), and which won my heart with their boy-and-girl romance. It was at a level that just suited my time in life.

SUBMICROSCOPIC

by Capt. S. P. Meek

AFTER many weary months of toil my task has been completed. As the sun sank to rest today, I soldered up the last connection on my Electronic Vibration Adjuster and in the fading twilight I tested it. It functions perfectly and as soon as the sun rises tomorrow I will leave this plane, I hope forever. I had originally intended to disappear without trace, as I did once before, but as I sit here waiting for the dawn, such a course seems hardly fair. This plane has treated me pretty well on the whole and I really ought to leave behind me some record of my discoveries and of my adventures, possibly the strangest adventures through which a man of this plane has ever passed. Besides, it will help to pass the time which must elapse before I can start on my journey.

My name is Courtney Edwards. I was born thirty-four years ago in the city of Honolulu, the only child of the richest sugar planter in the Islands. When I arrived at high school age I was sent to the mainland to be educated and here I have stayed. The death of my parents left me wealthy and rather disinclined to return to the home of my youth.

I did my bit in the Air Corps during the war and when it was over I shed my olive drab and went back to the University of Minneconsin to finish my education. My interest in science started when I attended a lecture on the composition of matter. It was a popular lecture intended for non-science students, and so it wasn't over my head. Dr. Harvey, one of our most popular professors, was the speaker and to this day I can visualize him standing there and can even recall some of his words.

"To give you some idea of the size of an atom," he said, "I will take for an example a cubic millimeter of hydrogen gas at a temperature of 0 degrees Centigrade and at sea-level pressure. It contains roughly ninety quadrillions of atoms, an almost inconceivable number. Consider this enormous number of particles packed into a cube with an edge less than one-twentieth of an inch long; yet so small are the individual atoms compared with the space between them that the solar system is crowded in comparison.

"In order to get at the ultimate composition of matter, however, we are forced to consider even smaller units. An atom is not a solid particle of matter, but instead consists of smaller particles called protons and electrons. The protons are particles of positive electricity which exist at the center or the nucleus of the atoms and the electrons are particles of negative electricity some of which revolve about the central portion and in most elements some are in the nucleus. Each of these particles is as small compared to the space between them as is the case with the atoms in the molecule."

I left the lecture hall with my head in a whirl. My imagination had been captured by the idea of counting and measuring such infinitesimal particles and I went to Dr. Harvey's office the next day and sought an interview.

"I wish to ask some questions relative to your talk last night, Doctor," I said when I faced him.

His kindly grey eyes twinkled and he invited me to be seated.

"As I understood you, Doctor," I began, "the space between the atoms and between the electrons and protons in each atom is so vast compared to their bulk that if you were to jam the protons and electrons of a cubic mile of gas together until they touched, you couldn't see the result with a microscope."

"Your idea is crudely expressed, but in the main accurate," he answered.

"Then what in the name of common sense holds them apart?" I demanded.

"Each of the atoms," he replied, "is in a state of violent motion, rushing through space with a high velocity and continually colliding with other atoms and rebounding until it strikes another atom and rebounds again. The electrons are also in a state of violent motion, revolving around the protons and this combination of centrifugal force and electrical attraction holds the atom in a state of dynamic equilibrium."

"One more question, Doctor, and I'll quit. Are these things

you have told me cold sober fact susceptible of proof, or are they merely the results of an overactive imagination?"

He smiled and then leaned over his desk and answered gravely.

"Some of them are solid facts which I can prove to you in the laboratory," he said. "For instance, you, yourself, with proper training could count the number of atoms in a given volume. Other things I have said are merely theories or shrewd guesses which best explain the facts which we know. There is in physical chemistry a tremendous field of work open for men who have the ability and the patience to investigate. No one knows what the future may bring forth."

The Doctor's evident enthusiasm communicated itself to me.

"I'll be one of the ones to do this work if you'll have me as a student!" I exclaimed.

"I'll be very glad to have you, Edwards," he replied. "I believe you have the ability and the will. Time alone will tell whether you have the patience."

I resigned from my course the next day and enrolled as a special student under Dr. Harvey. After a period of intensive study of methods, I was ready to plunge into the unknown. The work of Bohr and Langmuir especially attracted me, and I bent my energies to investigating the supposed motion of the electrons about the nuclear protons. This line of investigation led me to the suspicion that the motion was not circular and steady, but was periodic and simple harmonic except as the harmonic periods were interfered with by the frequent collisions.

I devised an experiment which proved this to my satisfaction and took my results to Dr. Harvey for checking. He took my data home with him that night intending to read it in bed as was his usual custom, but from that bed he never rose. Death robbed me of my preceptor and Dr. Julius became the head of the Chemistry Department. I took my results to him only to meet with scorn and laughter. Dr. Julius was an able analyst, but he lacked vision and could never see the woods for the trees. The result of my interview with him was that I promptly left Minneconsin, and resolved to carry on my work at another school.

The problem on which I wished to work was the reduction of the period of vibration of the atoms and of their constituent parts. If my theory of their motion were correct, it should be possible to damp their vibrations and thus collapse matter together and make it occupy a smaller volume in space. I soon found that men like Dr. Harvey were scarce. Not a man at the head of a university department could I find who had the vision to see the possibilities of my work and in a rage I determined to conduct my experiments alone and hidden from the world until I had proved the truth of my theories.

I was still flying for amusement and one day while flying from Salt Lake City to San Francisco, I passed over a verdant fertile valley hidden in the almost inaccessible crags of the Timpahute range in southern Nevada. I abandoned my trip temporarily and landed at Beatty to make inquiries. Not a person could I find who had ever heard of my hidden valley. Even the old desert rats professed ignorance of its location and laughed at me when I told them that I had seen flowing water and deciduous trees in the barren stretches of the Timpahutes.

I had taken the bearings of my valley and I flew on to San Francisco and made my arrangements. I flew back to Beatty and picked up a pack outfit and landed at the foot of the crags sheltering the valley and started on foot to seek an entrance. It took me a month of careful searching to find it, but find it I did. With a little blasting, the way could be made practicable for pack burros. The stuff I had ordered at San Francisco had been delivered to Beatty and I hired packers to take it out to the Timpahutes for me. I established a dump about a mile from my valley entrance and had the stuff unloaded there. When the packers had left I took my own burros and packed it in to the valley. I didn't care to have anyone find out where I was locating and so far as I know no one ever did.

When I had everything packed in, I started to work.

A few days enabled me to rig an undershot waterwheel in the stream and get enough power to turn an electric generator and thereafter I had the strength of twenty men at my call. I built a small wooden building for a laboratory with a room in it for my cooking and sleeping.

I was fortunate enough not to meet with a single major setback in my work, and in about fourteen months I had my first piece of apparatus completed. I don't intend to tell how I did it, for I do not believe that the world is ready for it yet, but I will give some idea of how it looked and how it was operated. The adjuster has a circular base of silvery metal (it is a palladium alloy) from which rise six supports which hold up the top. The top, which is made of the same alloy as the base, is parabolic in shape and concave downward. In the parabola is set an induction coil with a sparkgap surmounting it, so set that the gap is at the focus of the reflector, which is what the top really is. The coil and gap are connected with other coils and condensers which are actuated by large storage batteries set around the edge of the base. To each of the six uprights is fastened a small parabolic reflector with a small coil and gap at the focus. These small reflectors are so arranged that they bathe the top with the generated ray while the large gap in the top bathes the rest of the apparatus.

When the gaps and coils are actuated by the current, they throw out a ray of such a wavelength that it has the same period as the electronic and atomic vibrations but is half a wavelength out of phase. The ray is effective only when it can flow freely, and the base and top serve not only as conductors, but also as insulators, for they absorb and transform the vibrations falling on them so that nothing outside of the apparatus itself and anything lying between the base and the top is affected.

When I had it completed, I naturally tested it. The whole thing was controlled by a master switch and I reached in with a small steel rod and closed the switch. Immediately the whole apparatus began to shrink. I gave a loud cheer and patted myself on the back. I got down on my knees and watched it as it rapidly diminished in size until I suddenly realized that it would soon get too small to see unless I opened my switch. I tried to reach the switch with my rod but I had waited too long. The rod would not go through the interval between the side columns. I had the mortification of seeing a year's work grow smaller and smaller until it finally vanished.

The loss of my adjuster was a blow, but at least I had proved my theory and as soon as I had rested for a few days I started in to build a duplicate. The way had already been blazed and it took me less than a year to complete my second piece of apparatus. When I tested this one I stopped the shrinking process when the adjuster was about half its original size and reversed the polarity of my coils. To my delight the adjuster began to expand until it had resumed its original proportions. Then I shut it off and began to experiment to find out its limitations.

When I had determined to my satisfaction that inanimate

objects placed on the base would be expanded or contracted, I tried it on living organisms. A jack rabbit was my first subject and I found that I could increase this rabbit to the size of a Shetland pony or reduce it to the size of a mouse without visible ill effects. When I had completed this experiment, I tried the adjuster on myself.

My first experiment was to increase my size. I stepped on the base plate and turned on the current, but I could feel no effects. I looked at the landscape and found to my amazement that something had gone wrong. I was remaining the same size but the house and the surrounding country had come under the influence of my device and was shrinking rapidly. In alarm I shut off my current and got out. The house had shrunk to one-half its normal size and I could not get in the door, even on hands and knees. An idea struck me and I reached in and hauled out a pair of scales and weighed myself. *I weighed a trifle over twelve hundred pounds.* I suddenly realized that I had succeeded beyond my wildest dreams and I reentered the adjuster and shrunk myself down to four inches tall, again with no ill effects and merely the impression that the house and landscape were growing. I returned myself to my normal size and while I was weak from excitement, otherwise I felt perfectly normal.

My first thought was to return and confound the men who had scoffed at me but the more I considered the matter, the more I realized the importance of my invention and the need of caution in introducing it. I felt that I needed a rest anyway, so I remained in my valley to perfect my plans before announcing my discovery.

Time soon lagged on my hands. I have always been fond of big game hunting and I had an excellent rifle and plenty of ammunition, but game does not abound in the Timpahutes. There were quite a few ants in the valley and it struck me that, were I to reduce myself and my rifle to the proper dimensions, I would have some good sport. The novelty of the idea fascinated me as much as the thought of the hunting and I promptly belted on a pistol and a full belt of ammunition and entered the adjuster.

I closed the switch and the house and landscape began to grow to Brobdingnagian proportions, but I kept my power on until the grains of sand began to look like huge boulders and then I tried to open the switch. *It was stuck.* Thoroughly alarmed, I tried to wrench it open and as a result broke the handle—the device kept on functioning and I grew smaller and smaller. The grains of sand grew to be huge mountains and presently I felt myself falling. I realized that my adjuster had been balanced on a grain of sand and that it had slipped and was falling into the chasm between two grains. Soon it became wedged in a gloomy chasm, but it was still functioning and presently I was falling again.

A glance at the dial of my relative size indicator showed me that the needle had almost reached the point which I had indicated as infinity. Desperately I battered at the switch with my rifle butt, but it was solidly made. At last I broke it loose and the whine of my coil became audible and ran down the scale until it was silent. I had stopped shrinking but I was already far smaller than any microscope could detect and an examination of the switch soon convinced me that it was completely wrecked and that it would take me hours to repair it.

When I had finished my examination, I looked around for the first time. I could hardly believe my eyes. My adjuster was standing in a beautiful sunlit glade, which was carpeted with grass and dotted with varicolored flowers. Now I will have to explain one thing. As I said, I felt no change when my size was increased and reduced; it only seemed that the familiar landscape was undergoing a change. As a result, I could never realize while I was in Ulm, that everything was really submicroscopic, but persisted in referring everything to my normal six feet of height. In actual fact, the glade in which the adjuster stood was only a minute fraction of an inch across, but to me it looked like about half a mile and it took me ten minutes to walk it. Even now I have no idea of how small I actually was, so I will not try to describe the absolute size of everything, but will speak of things as they appeared to me; in other words, their *relative* size to me.

I looked over that landscape and rubbed my eyes, trying to convince myself that I was dreaming, but the scene didn't change and I realized that I had stumbled on something heretofore unsuspected—namely that our world is a very complex affair and supports many kinds of life unknown to us. Everything within the range of my vision looked normal, grass, trees and even mosquitos were buzzing around and one lit on my wrist and bit me. Imagine, if you can, what the actual measurements of that mosquito must have been!

Convinced that I was not dreaming, I stepped out of the

adjuster to the grass. Before I repaired that switch I meant to have a look around and see what this miniature world was like. I had gone only a few steps from the adjuster when a lordly buck rose from the grass and bounded away. Instinctively I threw up my rifle and fired and the buck went down kicking. Assured that my weapons were functioning properly, I set off at a brisk pace across the glade. I took careful bearings with my pocket compass and expected to have no trouble in finding my way back. During the ten minutes it took me to cross the glade, I had several more chances to shoot at deer, but I passed them up. I didn't wish to waste ammunition or to call attention to myself until I knew what was ahead of me.

It was hot and sultry in the glade and I glanced up at the sun, expecting it to appear enormous, but it appeared no larger than usual, a matter which I could not explain at the time and cannot even yet. Before I reached the woods which fringed the glade I noticed that the horizon was walled in on all sides with enormous mountains, higher than any I had ever seen and it gave me a shock to realize that these mighty and imposing masses of rock were in reality only grains of sand, or perhaps even smaller; they might be particles of the impalpable dust which lies between the sand grains.

It took me perhaps ten minutes to reach the edge of the jungle, for such it proved to be. Most of the trees were of species unknown to me, although I recognized several trees of peculiarly tropical habit, among them the baobab or one of its relatives and the *lignum vitae*. The scene reminded me more of the Brazilian jungles than anything else. The ground underfoot was deep with rotting vegetation and the creepers made the going hard. I plunged into the tangle and in ten minutes I was as thoroughly lost as I have ever been in my life. The gloom under the trees prevented me from using the sun as a guide and I had not read my compass when I entered the tangle.

I set a compass course and floundered forward as best I could but half an hour of steady going convinced me that I had taken the wrong direction. The jungle was too dense to back trail, so I laid a new course by compass and plunged ahead. I kept on for perhaps ten minutes on my new course when I heard a sound that brought me up standing, hardly able to believe my ears. From ahead of me came a shout, a shout given in a human voice. I strained my ears and soon I heard it again from the same direction and somewhat closer.

Some one was coming toward me and I looked for a hiding place. A tangle of baobab roots concealed me pretty well and I crouched, my rifle ready, waiting for what might appear.

In a few moments I heard a sound of running footsteps and I peered out from my cover. Imagine my surprise when a girl, a white girl, came into view, running at top speed. Not fifty yards behind her came a group of men, or beasts, for I couldn't tell at first glance which they were. They were as black as pitch, with thick heavy lips, flat noses and almost no foreheads. They were or rather seemed to be about seven feet tall on the average, with enormously powerful chests and arms that hung below their knees. At times they dropped forward so that their knuckles rested on the ground and came ahead on all fours at a more rapid rate than their relatively short bandy legs could carry them when they were in an upright position. They were covered on the head, chest and arms with coarse black hair, although their legs, abdomens and backs were almost free from it. Their mouths were wide with the lower jaw protruding somewhat with yellow fangs showing between their lips, giving them a horribly bestial expression. They had two eyes, but they were not placed as is usual with animals of the monkey or human species. One eye was set in the middle of the forehead and the other in the back of the head. They were naked except for a G string and a belt from which hung a short heavy sword, and in their hands they carried spears about ten feet long. The average weight of a full grown male in our world would have been about four hundred pounds. Of course I didn't see all of this at first glance, but later I saw enough of the Mena, as they were called, to get pretty familiar with their appearance.

A glance was enough to show me that the girl was tired and that these brutes were gaining on her. She was human and the sight of these savages made my next action purely instinctive. With a shout I stepped from my hiding place and threw my rifle to my shoulder. The girl saw me and altered her direction to come toward me. The blacks saw me, too, and they turned in my direction, brandishing their spears.

I am a pretty good shot and they were close and an easy target. I had four shells in my rifle and four of the blacks went down as fast as I could work my bolt. The rest paused for a moment and gave me time to ram a fresh clip of cartridges into my rifle. As I reloaded, I picked out one of them

who seemed to be a leader and I dropped him on the next
shot. This made them pause again but another black devil
sprang forward to take the lead and I presented him with a bit
of lead in the face. He went down like a thunderbolt and as
none of the rest seemed to aspire to leadership, I distributed
the other three bullets where I thought they would do the
most good. As I lowered my rifle to reload, another one of the
blacks jumped forward and charged me, and the rest followed. I had no time to load, so I jerked out my Colt .45 and
when he was about twenty-five yards away I let him have a
pill in the chest and then started a little miscellaneous slaughter. By the time the Colt was empty, there were fourteen of
the blacks down and the rest were retreating at full speed. I
first reloaded my rifle and slipped a clip into my pistol and
then looked for the girl.

I didn't see her for a moment and then I spied a lock of
golden hair in the tangle at my feet. She had burrowed into
the vegetation and had got pretty well covered in the few moments I was shooting. I reached down and touched her, but as
soon as she found that her hiding place was discovered, she
bounded up and took to her heels like a scared rabbit. I called
to her and she threw a glance back over her shoulder and
when she saw that I was alone she checked her speed and
stood her ground. She hesitated for a moment and then came
back and dropped to her knees at my feet. I lifted her up and
patted her on the shoulder.

" 'There, little girl, don't cry,' " I quoted inanely, partly because I didn't know what else to say and partly because I was
completely bowled over by her appearance. She was absolutely the most beautiful girl I have ever seen in my life—tall and
lithe, all curves and grace, with eyes as blue as the sea around
Oahu and hair where sunbeams had been imprisoned and
where they struggled continuously for liberty, throwing their
glints out through the meshes of their prison. Bound around
her head was a golden filet with a huge square cut stone of
beautiful sparkle and radiance set in it. Around her waist and
confining her garments of flowing green gauze was another
golden band with a gold-encrusted, gem-set pouch depending
from it. On the buckle of her girdle was another of the square
cut gems such as adorned her head band.

I have always been pretty much at ease in the presence of
girls, principally because I never cared much for them, but to

this dirty little savage, as beautiful as dawn, I didn't know what to say. I could just gulp and stammer.

"Er, do you think these rapscallions will come back for more?" I blurted out at last.

She cast a sideways glance at me that made my head whirl, and my heart do all sorts of funny flip-flops, and then she spoke. Her speech was beautifully liquid and hauntingly familiar. I couldn't understand her, but I was sure that I had heard that language before. Presently I caught a word and like a flash I knew. She was speaking some dialect of Hawaiian. Desperately I strove to recall the speech of Leilani, my old nurse, but the only phrase I could remember was *"E nac iki ne puu wai."* It didn't seem quite appropriate to say "Be true to me, fair one" to a girl I had just met, but it was for the moment the only phrase I could remember so I blurted it out.

She understood it all right and she flew into a royal rage. She shot out a stream of fluent speech so fast that I couldn't understand a word of it. I thought rapidly and then brought fourth another gem of speech, *"Hawaiian pau."* I had to repeat it twice before she understood and then she didn't get the word Hawaiian, but she understood *pau,* finished, all right and she presently realized that my first speech was the only bit of her language which I knew. When she understood my predicament, she forgot her anger and laughed. I was glad to see her cheerful again, but I was still worried about whether those blacks would return.

For lack of language I was forced to fall back on pantomime in order to make myself understood. She readily understood me and looked worried for a moment until her eye fell on my rifle. She touched it questioningly and then spurned the body of the nearest black with her foot and laughed.

Evidently she thought that my weapon made me invincible, but I knew better. I had only two more clips of pistol cartridges and eighty-five rounds for my rifle, not enough to repel a real attack. I tapped my rifle, shook my head sadly and said *"pau."*

The worried look again came into her face and she started talking very slowly and distinctly, repeating the word *"Ulm"* several times. Gradually my Hawaiian was coming back and while her speech was not the language I had learned in my youth, for she made use of the consonants "s" and "t," both of which are unknown in Hawaiian, presently I made out her meaning. She was asking me to go with her to Ulm. I had no idea of where Ulm was but I had given up hopes of finding my adjuster and besides, since I had met this girl, I wasn't so very anxious to find it at once. It seemed to me that it might be a good idea to go to Ulm for a while, and then make a fresh start for the glade with a competent guide, I therefore gave her to understand that her program suited me. She nodded brightly and stepped in front of me and set off toward the northeast.

For perhaps three hours we made our way through the jungle, keeping a pretty straight line as I could tell by my compass. I found later that the people of Ulm have an uncanny sense of direction and can find their way from place to place in their miniature world without the aid of any other guide. The girl kept up a steady talk in her language and as I recalled more of my early Hawaiian, I found that I could understand the sense of most of what she said if she talked very slowly and I was even able to answer her after a fashion.

"What is your name?" I asked her.

"Awlo Sibi Tam," she replied, raising her head proudly as she did so.

"My name is Courtney," I told her.

She tried to repeat it, but she had a little trouble with the "r" sound which was evidently strange to her. She repeated it several times as we went along and at last managed to get a very fair rendition. Anyhow, I thought that I had never heard it pronounced so beautifully before.

Suddenly Awlo paused in her talk and listened intently. She turned a terror-stricken face toward me and said, "They are coming."

"Who?" I asked.

"The Mena," she replied.

I listened but I could hear nothing.

"Are there many of them?" I asked.

"Many," she replied, "hundred, I believe. They are following our trail. Can't you hear them?"

I laid my ear close to the ground and could detect a faint murmur but I would never have recognized what it was.

"What shall we do?" I asked. "This," I held up my rifle, "will kill about a hundred but no more."

"Run," she said, "run as fast as we can. It will be of little use, because the Mena can catch us. You are slow and I am tired, but if we are lucky, we may win to the plains of Ulm and there we are safe."

Her advice sounded good and I started after her as swiftly as I could. I am a fair average runner, but I could not keep up with Awlo, who fled over the ground like an antelope. I was handicapped by the weight of my rifle but I hung to it like grim death. It was not long before I could plainly hear the shouts of the pursuing Mena.

"Have we far to go?" I gasped.

"No," she replied over her shoulder. "Hurry!"

I panted along in her wake. The jungle thinned before us and we debouched onto a huge open plain. Awlo stopped and uttered a cry of dismay.

"What is it?" I demanded.

She did not answer but pointed ahead. Our way was barred by a wide, gently flowing river. Over it had been thrown a bridge but a glance showed me that the center span had been removed and a gap twenty feet wide yawned in the middle of the structure.

"Can you swim?" I asked.

She looked at me interrogatively. Evidently the word was a new one.

"Swim, run through the water," I explained.

An expression of absolute terror passed over her face.

"It is *tabu*," she replied. "It is death to enter."

"It is death to stay on this side," I told her.

"It is better to die at the hands of the Mena than at the hands of the Gods," she answered.

She meant it too. She would rather face certain death at the hands of those hideous savages than to enter the stream. There was only one thing to do and that was to look for a place where I could sell my life dearly. With this in mind, I started along the river bank looking for a depression which would shelter us from the spears of the Mena. We made our way through a clump of trees in front of us and it was my turn to cry out, only the cry was one of joy and not of apprehension. There, between the trees and the river bank, stood a familiar looking object—an Electronic Vibration Adjuster.

"We are saved, Awlo," I cried joyously as I raced for the machine. A glance showed me that it was my first model which I had sent, as I thought, to infinite smallness nearly a year before. I was puzzled for a moment at the fact that it had not shrunk to nothing, but I had no time for philosophical reasoning. The shouts of the Mena were already perilously close.

"Run off a few yards, Awlo," I commanded, "and don't be frightened. I can save you easily."

She obeyed me and I entered the adjuster. A momentary fear came over me that the batteries might be exhausted but I seized the switch and threw it on in the direction of increasing size. The landscape began to diminish its size, although as before, I could feel nothing. I kept my eye on the river until it had shrunk to a point where I knew that I could easily leap it and then I opened my switch and stepped out.

For a moment I could not see Awlo, but I detected her lying face downward on the ground. I bent over her and then I saw something else. The Mena, hundreds of them, had emerged from the jungle and were coming along our trail. I hesitated no longer. As gently as I could, I picked up Awlo and leaped over the river with her. I waited to see whether the Mena were going to make any attempt to follow, but they had evidently caught a glimpse of my gargantuan proportions and they were in full retreat. I found out later that the river was as much taboo to them as it was to Awlo and they would under no circumstances have crossed the stream except by means of a bridge or in boats.

I raised Awlo to the level of my eyes to talk to her but she had fainted. I leaped back to the other side of the river, reentered my adjuster and closed the reducing switch. Since I had the machine under control, I determined not to stop it until I found what had made it cease functioning when it did. My size rapidly grew smaller until I was correctly scaled to my surroundings and then the machine abruptly ceased working. I could not make it reduce either itself or me any further. The only explanation which has ever occurred to me is that the land of Ulm must be at the limit of smallness, that is, the period of vibration of the atoms and their component parts must be at the lower limit of motion and any further reduction would result in contact and consequent nothingness.

My intention had been to swim the river while Awlo was unconscious but it occurred to me that the adjuster might be useful on the other side of the river so I again increased my size until I could step over it. Knowing that the machine would only get so small, I reached in with a piece of wood and closed the reducing switch and watched it grow to toy size. With it in my hand, I again leaped the river and used my pocket knife blade to close the increasing switch. When it had grown to the right size, I stopped it, reentered it and soon had both the adjuster and myself down to the minimum to which it would go.

Awlo was still unconscious and I bent over her and chafed her hands. She soon recovered and sat up. Her gaze wandered and it fell on the adjuster, she shuddered and turned to me with fear in her eyes.

"What happened, Courtney Siba?" she asked with a quaver in her voice. "I thought that you had changed into a *kahuma*, a wizard of the old days. Was I dreaming?"

I thought rapidly. Evidently a *kahuma* was something to be revered but also something not quite human. The advantage and disadvantages of being one flashed before me but a glance at Awlo's scared face decided me.

"I am no *kahuma*, Awlo," I replied. "What I did, I did with the aid of that. It made me appear to the Mena to be larger than I am and they ran. While they were gone, I carried you and the machine over the river. We are perfectly safe now and unless the Mena find some way of crossing, they won't bother us again."

Awlo seemed satisfied with my explanation. I suggested that she rest for a while to recover from her scare but she laughed at the idea.

"Ulm is near at hand," she told me, "and we must hurry on. I would not that my father be unduly worried by my absence."

"That reminds me of something I have been meaning to ask you, Awlo," I said as we resumed our onward way. "How did you happen to be in the jungle with the Mena after you when I found you."

"I was visiting my uncle, Hama, at his city of Ame," she replied. "My visit was at an end and I started homeward yesterday. It has been three years since the Mena have ventured to attack us and the guard was small, only about three hundred soldiers. We were about half way between the two cities and were going peaceably through the jungle when, without warning, the Mena attacked. The soldiers fought desperately but the Mena were too many and too powerful for them and they were all killed. I and two of my maidens were captured. The Mena took us to one of their cities in the jungle and prepared for a feast."

"For a feast?" I inquired.

"We are food for the Mena," she replied simply.

I shuddered at the thought and gritted my teeth as I thought of those flying monsters who were at my mercy a few minutes before. Had I known what brutes they were, I could have taken glorious vengeance on them.

"Last night," went on Awlo, "they took first one and then the other of my maidens out from the cave where we were confined, and killed them and dragged them away to the pot. My turn was next and two of them seized me and dragged me out. They released me and one of them raised a spear to end my life. I dropped to the ground and the spear passed over my head and then I fled. I tried to run toward Ulm, but they suspected the course I would pursue and a party went to head me off while others followed my trail. As long as it was dark I was able to baffle them and go faster than they could trail me, but with the coming of light they found my trail and soon I heard them after me. I ran as fast as I could, but they gained rapidly and I thought that I was lost when I heard your shout. Awlo Sibu Tam will never forget how you saved her and neither will Ulm. My father, Kalu, will honor you highly, Courtney Siba."

"If these Mena are such brutes, why don't your soldiers wage war on them until there are none left?" I asked.

"They have waged war for ages," she replied, "but the Mena are too many and we cannot hunt them all down. In ages past, there were no Mena and then Ulm and Ame fought together. Sometimes one would be victorious and sometimes the other, but always they ceased warring before either was destroyed. Then came the Mena through the passes from the wilderness to the north. They came in thousands and they attacked Ame. The men of Ulm forgot their hatred of their old rival and our armies marched to the assistance of the threatened city. For a time our armies drove the invaders back but more and more came from the north and carried the battle to the gates of Ame itself. There our armies stopped them for they could not climb the walls nor could they break in.

"When they saw that they could not win the city, they attacked Ulm. Our army hurried back to defend the city and the men of Ame came with them, leaving only enough to man the walls. Again the Mena fought their way to the city walls and again they were stopped. When they found they could not take either city, they drew back into the jungle and established cities of huts. Such is the condition today. The Mena fight among themselves and when they are weakened in numbers, the armies of Ulm and Ame march out to attack them. They have always defeated them and tried to hunt them down and sometimes for a generation the Mena are not seen, but eventually they return stronger than ever and attack one of the cities. It has been many years now since war was waged on them and it may be that they are planning to attack again."

"Do Ulm and Ame ever fight now?" I asked.

"No, there is peace between them. Brothers of one blood sit on the two thrones and the old enmity is forgotten. But see, there lies Ulm!"

We had topped a little rise and had come to the cultivated fields. Before us lay row after row of cultivated plots, most of them planted with *keili* bushes, the nut of which is the staple food of the poorer classes of Ulm. Two miles or so across the plain rose a massive walled city. Dotted about on the plain were small stone structures, which reminded me of the old blockhouses which used to be erected on our own plains to guard against Indian raids. That, in fact, was the exact function of these structures.

As we approached the nearest of them a figure appeared on the wall and scrutinized us closely. He called out a musical greeting and Awlo raised her face.

"Awlo Sibi Tam commands your presence," she cried imperiously.

The sentry rubbed his eyes and looked and then came down from that wall in a hurry. The massive gates swung open and an officer appeared and prostrated himself and kissed the ground before Awlo.

"Rise!" she commanded.

He rose and half drew his sword from its sheath and presented the hilt to Awlo. She touched it and he returned it to its scabbard with a sharp motion and stood upright.

"I would go to Ulm," she said. "Send couriers to warn my father of my approach and bid my guard come hither to escort me."

He bowed deeply and Awlo took me by the hand and led me into the building. It was a typical guardroom such as are found in all nations and at all times. We seated ourselves and I heard the sound of hoof-beats rapidly dying away in the direction of the city.

"Who are you, Awlo?" I asked. "Are you a Chief's daughter or what?"

"I am Sibi Tam," she replied.

"I don't know that rank," I answered. "How important is it?"

She looked at me in surprise and then laughed.

"You will find out in time, Courtney Siba," she said with a laugh.

I tried to press the question but she refused to answer and turned the talk to other matters. Half an hour passed and then I was aware of a confused murmur approaching from the city. Awlo rose.

"It is doubtless our escort," she said. "Let us greet them."

I followed her out into the courtyard and up on the thick wall which surrounded the building. Coming down the road was the most gorgeous cavalcade I had ever seen. First came a band of cavalry mounted on superb horses and carrying long lances. They wore golden helmets with nodding crimson horsehair plumes rising from them, a cuirass of gold and golden shin guards. Their thighs were bare. Besides the armor they wore a short crimson garment like a skirt, which fell half way to the knee, and a flowing crimson cape trimmed with brown fur. Heavy swords on the left side of their belts and a dagger on the right, together with their twelve-foot lances made up their offensive weapons.

Following the cavalry came a number of gorgeously decorated chariots, occupied by men gorgeously dressed in every imaginable hue. Another troop of cavalry, similar to the first except that their plumes and clothing were blue, brought up the rear.

As the leading troop came opposite the gate, Awlo stepped to the edge of the wall. Her appearance was greeted by a roar of applause and salutation and the red cavalry reined in their horses and pointed their lances toward her, butt foremost. She answered the salute with a wave of her hand and the troop charged forward at a word of command past the tower and then whirled to form a line facing her. The chariots came up and an elderly man dismounted from the first one and passed in through the gate. He came up the steps to the wall and dropped on one knee before Awlo, half drawing his sword and thrusting the hilt toward her as he did so.

She touched the sword and he returned it and rose to his feet.

"Greeting, Moka," she said. "Come with me for I desire a word with you."

Submissively he followed her a short distance along the wall and I could see that she was speaking rapidly. I could tell from the direction of Moka's glances that I was the topic of conversation, and his actions when Awlo had finished amply proved it. Moka came forward and drew his sword and cast it at my feet. I drew my pistol and placed it beside his weapon. Moka laid his left hand against my breast and I did the same.

"My brother and my lord," he said as he rose.

Awlo interrupted before I could say anything.

"I would go to Ulm," she said.

Moka bowed deeply and we each picked up our weapons. I followed Awlo toward the chariots. The largest and most ornate was empty and into it she sprang lightly, motioning to me to go with Moka in his chariot. I entered it and the whole cortege turned about and proceeded toward the city.

We drove in through a huge gate which was opened before us and down a wide thoroughfare which led directly into the center of the city. This avenue ended in a park in the center of which stood the largest and most beautiful building in the city. We left our chariots and made our way on foot across the park and entered the palace between rows of guards who, as Awlo passed, presented their spears, butt foremost.

At the end of the hall, Awlo paused.

"Courtney Siba," she said, "you are doubtless weary as I am. Go then with Moka, who will supply you with clothing fitting to your rank and with proper refreshment. My father will meet you when you have rested and reward you as you merit."

I had learned a little about the customs of Ulm and I dropped on one knee and presented her my pistol, butt first. She smilingly touched it and I rose and followed Moka. He led me up a flight of steps and into an apartment fit for a Prince of the Blood. Here he summoned servants and surrendered me to their tender mercies.

I did not realize how tired I was until a hot bath revealed the true extent of my fatigue. One of my servants approached and by motions indicated that I was to lie down on a couch. I did so and he massaged me thoroughly with a sweet-smelling oil, which banished my fatigue marvelously. When he had finished, other servants approached with garments which they evidently desired me to put on. I strove to talk to them but they merely shook their heads. Small wonder, for I later found that they were dumb.

The clothing which they brought me consisted of such a skirt, as I had seen on the soldiers, except that it was pure white. In addition they brought me a white cloak which hung well below the waist and which was fastened at the throat with a diamond the size of a walnut. On my feet they placed leather sandals which were thickly encrusted with gold and diamonds and around my calves they wound leather straps also heavily gemmed. About my head they bound a golden filet with a square cut diamond set in the center and around my waist they fastened a belt with a diamond buckle with a long straight sword hanging from the left and a heavily jeweled dagger from the right. As a final touch they set on my head a golden helmet somewhat like those I have seen on ancient Grecian coins, with a white horsehair plume. When they had finished they stood me in front of a mirror to see if I was suited.

I was, in every respect except one. I dug into my old clothes and got my Colt and hung the holster on my belt instead of the silly dagger. It may not have been as handsome, but if I was going to need weapons where I was going, I knew which would be of the most value to me. When I signified that I was suited, my servants withdrew with many bows and left me alone.

I hardly knew what to expect next but I threw myself on the couch to rest a little. For close to an hour I waited before the door swung open to admit Moka.

"My lord," he said with a bow, "Kalu Sabama awaits your presence."

"I am ready," I replied as I rose.

As we passed through the doorway, a detachment of guard met us. As we appeared, they grounded their spears with a ringing clash and closed around us. We passed down a corridor and down a flight of stairs to the main entrance hall and across it to a great closed double door, where we were halted by another detachment of guards and challenged. Moka answered the challenge and the great doors swung open and there was a peal of trumpets. When they had ceased a sonorous voice called out some words which I did not understand, although I was pretty sure that I caught the words "Awlo" and "Courtney." It was evidently an introduction, for, when the voice ceased, Moka motioned me to go forward. I stepped out with my head held high. The guards went with me for a few paces and then opened out and formed a line, leaving me to advance alone down the hall.

It was an immense and spacious hall and while the center was open, the sides were crowded with gaily dressed people. Guards were on all sides and at the far end was a dais or platform raised seven steps above the floor. On the topmost level were four thrones. Before the throne, on the various levels, were a number of men and women, dressed in every color imaginable except the green which was worn by the occupants of the thrones. On the step next to the top level stood a lone figure, who also wore green.

Down the hall I marched until I stood at the foot of the dais. I heard a murmur run down the hall as I passed, but whether of approval or disapproval I could not tell, so I went straight ahead until I came to the foot of the dais and then I bowed deeply. I looked up and looked the occupants of the thrones straight in the eye.

The two center seats were occupied by an elderly couple of great grace and dignity of manner, the throne on the right was vacant and in the one on the left sat Awlo. I had known by the respect accorded her that she must be a rather important personage, but it startled me to realize that she was one of the biggest of them all. She threw me a momentary smile and then looked at me gravely and impersonally as the other two were doing.

The man who occupied one of the center thrones rose and spoke to me.

"Courtney Siba," he said gravely in a sonorous and ringing voice, "my daughter has told before me, where all could hear, the mighty deeds which you have wrought against the Mena. And you who have saved her, in whom the hopes of the dynasty of Kalu are bound up, merit and will receive the gratitude of a nation. The gratitude of a father for the life of his only child I freely give you.

"There is no reward within my power to grant that is great enough for your merits, but if you will name your wishes, they shall be yours if Ulm can supply them. Your rank of Siba I hereby confirm in Ulm and Ame and give orders that your rank is above all others in the empire save only the royal blood. Is there any reward you desire?"

"I thank you, oh King," I replied, "and I will bear your gracious words in mind. Already you have honored me above my poor deserts but the time may come when I will remind you of your words."

"My words are engraven on my memory, Courtney Siba," said the King with a gracious smile, "and time will not erase them. Your rank entitles you to a place on the second level of my throne, below only my beloved nephew, Lamu Siba."

He motioned toward the man who stood on the next to the topmost level and who I noticed was attired in green as was Kalu. I glanced at him and found that he was watching me with a face like a thundercloud. I returned the scowl with interest and took stock of him. He was about two inches shorter than I was and ruggedly built and showed evidence of a great deal of strength. His black hair, which like the hair of all the men of Ulm, was worn long enough to reach his shoulders, matched the swarthy complexion. The thing that set me against him was a crafty expression in his close-set eyes, which were grey instead of the honest black or brown which should have gone with his complexion.

At a gesture from the King (or Sabama as his title really was), I mounted the dais and took my stand on the step below Lamu and directly in front of Awlo. When I had taken my place, the Sabama turned to the court and began again in his sonorous voice what was evidently a regularly recited formula.

"The house of Kalu," he said, "is as a withered tree with but one green branch. Should this branch be cut, the tree would die without trace of life remaining. Already the branch has been almost cut. It is the hope of all Ulm that this branch will make that new life may be given to the tree, yet the immemorial laws of Ulm decree that the Sibi Tam shall be free to choose her own husband when and how she will, nor may even the Sabama force her choice. Awlo, my daughter, the green branch of the tree of the house of Kalu, are you yet ready to declare your choice?"

Awlo rose and stepped forward.

"I am," she declared in ringing tone.

The reply made a sensation. The audience had been listening politely to the words of the Sabama but they evidently expected Awlo to say that she had not yet made up her mind and her reply electrified them. A hastily suppressed murmur ran through the hall and the Sabama started. I noticed that Lamu bit his lip and closed his hand on his dagger hilt.

"Whom, my daughter, have you chosen to be your prince?" asked Kalu.

Awlo stepped down two steps and stood beside me.

"When the branch was about to be cut, one arose who stayed the hand of the Mena and who saved the tree from being a desolate dying trunk today. Who but that one should be chosen to the highest honor in Ulm and as her future ruler. My father, for my husband, I choose Courtney Siba."

As she ended, she took my right hand and raised it high above my head. There was a moment of silence and then cheer after cheer rent the hall. Evidently Awlo's choice was popular. The Sabama stepped forward and held up his hand for silence. The uproar instantly hushed and he started to speak. He was interrupted in a dramatic manner.

Sword in hand, Lamu faced him.

"Grant you permission to the Sibi Tam to make such a choice?" he demanded.

"The Sibi Tam chooses whom she pleases," said Kalu sharply. "Sheath your weapon. You are in the presence of the Sabama."

"My weapon remains drawn until the honor of Ame is revenged," cried Lamu hoarsely. "Have you lost your senses, my uncle, that you give your only child, the pride and hope of Ulm, to a nameless adventurer who comes from no one knows where? Who knows that he is not a *kahuma* who will destroy the land? Awlo says that he slew the Mena by witchcraft."

"Awlo has chosen," said Kalu quietly but with an ominous ring in his voice. "By what right do you assume to question her choice?"

"For years I have sought her, seeking to consolidate the rule of Ulm and Ame," replied Lamu, "and until this stranger came into Ulm, I had reason to think that my suit was favored. Are you seeking, my uncle, to raise a barrier of blood between Ulm and Ame that the Mena may destroy both?"

"What mean you?" thundered Kalu.

"I demand that the stranger be tested before the Court of Lords to prove that he is not a *kahuma*."

"And Lamu presides over the Court of Lords," broke in

Awlo with biting sarcasm. "Do you expect me to let my chosen go before your creatures for judgment?"

The shot struck home and Lamu bit his lips.

"Do you approve Awlo's choice?" he demanded of the Sabama.

"I do," was the reply.

"Then I call upon the ancient laws of Ulm for redress. It is the right of every Siba of royal blood to challenge and fight to the death with the choice of the Sibi Tam. You, Courtney, who claim the rank of Siba, I challenge you to fight to the death."

"Courtney Siba," said Kalu gravely, "do you accept this challenge? Either you must give up your rank or fight for it."

I hesitated but Awlo touched me on the arm. I looked at her and she glanced meaningly at my pistol. An idea came to me.

"I will gladly fight him," I cried, "but not to his death. If he overcomes me, he may do as he wishes, but I fight with my own weapons and if I overcome him, I spare his life."

"Then draw your weapon, Courtney Siba and defend yourself," cried Lamu as he rushed forward.

He aimed a vicious thrust at me before I had time to draw my own weapon and I avoided it only by leaping nimbly back. He came on again and I side-stepped and whipped out my Colt. As he rushed me the third time, I raised my weapon and fired. As I have said, I am a good shot and the range was close, so I didn't shoot to kill. Instead I fired at his sword hand and was lucky enough to hit the hilt of his weapon. The heavy forty-five bullet tore his sword from his grasp and sent it flying through the air. I instantly sheathed my pistol and waited for his next move. It came quickly enough.

He rubbed his right hand for a moment; it must have stung damnably, and then he whipped out his dagger and came at me with it in his left hand. I was a little taller than he was and had the reach on him so I met him half way. He made a sweep at me with his knife which I avoided and then I took his measure and landed my right full on the point of his chin and he went down like a poled ox. A tremendous murmur went around the room and then came a volley of cheers. I judged that Lamu was not popular. When the noise subsided, the Sabama spoke.

"Does any one else wish to challenge the choice of the Sibi Tam?" he asked sardonically.

There was no reply and he nodded to Awlo. She stepped forward and took my right hand in hers and turning it over, she kissed me on the palm and then set my hand on top of her head. When she had finished the ceremony, she looked expectantly at me. I wasn't exactly sure what to do so I took her hand and kissed it and then placed it on top of my head as she had done. In a moment her arms were around me and the assembly room rang with cheers.

Presently Awlo drew back and the Sabama stepped down from his throne. Some officers came forward and removed my white cloak and replaced it with a green one and the Sabama himself bound about my brow a golden filet with a square cut stone in it, similar to the ones which he and Awlo wore, and took me by the hand and led me up the dais and seated me on the vacant throne. There came another blare of trumpets and then the Sabama formally addressed me as "Courtney Siba Tam." Thus it was that I, Courtney Edwards, a citizen of the United States of America, in the year of our Lord one thousand, nine hundred and twenty-two became a Prince of the House of Kalu, the Crown Prince of the Empire of Ulm and the husband of the reigning monarch's only child.

I quickly became settled in my position of Siba Tam. My first official task was to pronounce judgment on Lamu. When I learned the circumstances, I hardly blamed him for his outburst. He was the only son of the ruler of Ame and he had been Awlo's suitor for years. By virtue of his rank he was Commander-in-Chief of the combined armies of Ulm and Ame and when he saw me, a stranger, come in and oust him from his proud position and take his sweetheart as my wife into the bargain, he lost his head. The Sabama wished to reduce him to the grade of commoner and confine him, but Awlo and I interceded and he was eventually pardoned and I appointed him as my second in command of the army. Whatever his faults, he was a good soldier and quite popular with the military. He acted rather formally to me for a couple of years, but he got over it and became one of my closest friends.

One of my first acts was to send a detail of troops out to bring my adjuster into Ulm. There I drained the batteries and went over it thoroughly and stored it in the palace vault. I was perfectly happy and had no idea at all of ever leaving Ulm, but I was guarding against accidents. At any time some prospector might find my valley and wash out a pan of dirt and

dump the rubbish on Ulm. If that happened, I meant to take
Awlo and increase our size and break up through it.

For five years everything was quiet and peaceful in Ulm
and Awlo and I were the happiest pair in the whole empire.
She was the idol of the city and my rescue of her had given
me a good start. I soon grew quite popular and when Lamu
grew to be my friend, the army joined the populace in their
affection for me.

In the fall of 1927 we first began to get rumors of a great
gathering of the Mena. At first both Lamu and I were disposed to scout the idea, but the rumors came with more defi-
niteness and at last we had to face the fact that the Mena were
gathering for an attack in real force. We made what preparations we could for the siege and waited for them to attack.
One of the peculiar things which had struck me about Ulm
was that the art of projecting weapons was unknown to them.
Even the crudest bow and arrow had not been developed. I
thought that I saw my way clear to thrash the Mena hand-
somely and I made up a bow and arrow and showed it to
Kalu, proposing that our army be so equipped. He smiled
enigmatically and advised me to lay it before the council.

I did so and to my surprise Lamu and the council would
not listen to the suggestion. When they explained their rea-
sons, I saw that they were sound ones. The Mena, while they
have no inventive ability, are adept at copying the ideas of
others and the council were afraid that, while we might smash
the first attack by fire superiority, on the next attack we would
find the Mena armed with bows, and in such a case we would
suffer heavily, even if we finally beat off the attack. The principle of the bow and arrow were well known to them, but they
had never used it for this reason.

About a year ago the Mena attacked. There were millions
of them, it seemed to me, and they were utterly reckless and
willing to put up with huge losses to gain a small point. Man
for man they were our superiors, so we did not meet them
outside the walls, but contented ourselves with defending the
city. They brought ladders and tried to climb the walls and
they brought rams and tried to batter down the gates and we
stood on the walls and dropped rocks on them and poured hot
oil on them and when they got a ladder hoisted we hurled it
back and killed with sword and spear those who had gained a
footing on the walls. I had read of such defenses in history,

and I was able to introduce a few new wrinkles which gave the Mena some rather unpleasant surprises. After three months of fighting, the situation hadn't changed a bit. I learned that a siege of ten or even twenty years was nothing unusual. We had enough *keili* nuts stored in the city to last for fifty years and we had an abundant supply of water. We weren't strong enough to take the offensive, so all we could do was to defend ourselves and wait until the Mena got tired and quit or got to fighting among themselves; the latter always happened when the siege drew out to too great a length.

The continual fighting kept me away from Awlo a great deal and I was naturally anxious to end it as soon as possible. As I passed the arsenal one day, I saw my adjuster standing there and a great idea struck me. I was confident that if I could use propelled projectiles, I could break the back of the Mena attack in no time. The council wouldn't let me use bows and arrows for fear our enemies would copy them and use them against us, but I defied any artisan of the Mena, or any artisan of Ulm for that matter, to copy a modern rifle and its ammunition. Why couldn't I use the adjuster to increase my size to the plane where such things were to be had, load it with guns and ammunition and shrink the whole business to usable size. I hastened to lay my idea before Kalu and the council.

I doubt whether any of the council had ever believed the story I told of my origin, although they had never said so. It is never safe to dispute the word of those in high authority. When I soberly offered to increase my size and get them guns and ammunition, they shook their heads and began to wonder. I took them up on the wall and showed them what a rifle would do to the Mena and any opposition to my going vanished. Highly elated, I refilled my batteries with the electrolyte I had drawn years before and got ready for the trip. I soon found that I had reckoned without Awlo. My Princess flatly refused to be separated from me.

For a while I was baffled but Awlo herself suggested a solution of the problem she had raised.

"Why can't I go with you, Courtney?" she asked. "If we come back safely, the trip will be an interesting one and if we do not return, at least we will be together."

The idea had merit and I presented it to Kalu. He didn't like Awlo to leave him, but he gave consent at last on my solemn promise to come back with her. I knew that some of the work up here would be rather heavy and I asked for a volunteer to accompany me. To my surprise, Lamu asked to go. I was glad of his company but I didn't want both the head of the army and the second in command to leave at once. He insisted and pointed out that the danger of the trip should be shared by the two highest ranking men in the army and I gave way and consented.

The adjuster was carried to the palace roof and I made a few adjustments to increase the speed of its action so that it wouldn't crush the whole city beneath its weight before the base expanded enough to get a wider support. At last everything was ready and the three of us crowded in and with final farewells to all I closed the switch.

I had set the machine to work faster than I realized and before I could open the switch we were twelve feet tall. I threw it back into slow speed and reduced our size until the indicator showed that I was my normal six feet and we stepped out into a new world to Awlo and Lamu and almost a new one to me.

We went into my shack and looked it over. Nothing had been disturbed and no one had been there, so there was no reason why Awlo couldn't stay there safely while Lamu and I trekked into Beatty and I got in touch with my bankers and arranged to buy the munitions that I wanted. We talked it over and Awlo wanted to come. There was no real reason why she couldn't come and indeed make a trip to New York with me if she wished, so I agreed to her coming. Lamu suggested that it might be a good idea for me to teach him how to operate the adjuster so that, in case we found it advisable to send the stuff down in several loads, he could take it down and return and thus avoid separating Awlo and me. The thought was a good one so I set the machine on slow speed and soon taught him the simple manipulation. He caught on readily and manipulated it several times to quite a small size and then professed himself satisfied with his ability. I wish that I could have seen what was in the black villain's heart!

The next morning I was in the cabin making up packs for us to carry on our hike to Beatty when I was alarmed by Awlo outside. I dropped everything and rushed out at top speed. For a moment I didn't see either her or Lamu and then I heard a low faint wail in her voice. I looked in the direction from which it came and saw the adjuster. It was less than one-tenth the size it should have been and I realized that it was shrinking. I sprinted toward it hoping to reach the switch and reverse the action, but I was too late. On my hands and knees I dropped and stared into it. Lamu had my Princess captive and his hand was on the switch. He stopped the action for a minute but the thing was already so small that I could not get my finger between the side bars had I tried and I was afraid of wrecking it. Stooping closer, I heard their tiny voices.

"Courtney Siba Tam," cried Lamu with triumph in his voice, "he laughs best who laughs last as I have heard you say. You robbed me of my kingdom once but when we return and tell them how you planned to desert Ulm in her hour of need and to steal away her Princess, I shall win back all I have lost. For years I have planned to thwart you in your ambition and for that reason I throttled my impulses and seemed your friend. Say farewell to Awlo for this is your last glimpse of her."

"Awlo," I cried in a whisper, "can't you free yourself?"

"No, Courtney," came back her tiny voice, "he is too strong for me and I dare not struggle. Come after me, Courtney! Rescue me from this dog who is worse than the Mena from whom you saved me once. I will watch for you, Courtney!" Thus I heard her voice for the last time and responded.

"I'll be after you as soon as I can, my darling," I cried. "As for you, Lamu Siba, the game is not played out yet. When I return, your heart's blood will pay for this!"

"Ah, yes, Courtney Siba Tam," came his mocking voice, "*when* you return."

He turned again to the switch and the adjuster carrying with it all that is dear in life to me disappeared.

I don't remember much about the next few days. Somehow, I made my way to Beatty and established my identity. I made the wires hum to San Francisco, ordering the materials I needed to construct a duplicate of my adjuster. Nor did I forget my people. I ordered the guns and ammunition which I wanted shipped in with the rest of my stuff. It seemed to take forever to get to my valley, but at last it came and I have worked almost day and night since. This afternoon I finished my apparatus and moved it over to the spot where the other had stood and in the morning I will leave this plane and try to take my guns and ammunition to Ulm.

I hope to land in Ulm but I am not at all sure that I will do so. I marked the place where my former machine stood but I may have easily missed placing my new model over the old one. If I have missed setting the center point where it should be by even a fraction of an inch I may come down in Ulm miles from the city. I may even come down into a strange world far from my empire and with no knowledge of which way to go. I have done my best and time alone will tell how well I have done. One thing I know. No matter what Lamu may have done or said, Awlo is still waiting for me and she is still true to me. I have my rifle and plenty of ammunition and even though the whole Mena race block my path, some way I will fight my way through them and once more hold my Princess in my arms.

AWLO OF ULM

by Capt. S. P. Meek

WHEN I allowed my manuscript, "Submicroscopic," to be published, I had no intention of telling to the world the balance of my adventures. Frankly, I did not expect to be believed. The events of which I told were so fantastic, so contrary to the ordinary experiences and preconceived notions of men of this plane of existence, that I expected the story to be passed off as an idle tale, told only to amuse. The editor of AMAZING STORIES was kind enough to forward to me a number of comments received. When I read them over I found, to my astonishment, that there were a small number of discerning thinkers who realized that my story was one of actual facts. Most of them expressed regret that the end of the story was, so they thought, a sealed book to them. It is to this select group, who I feel are my friends, that this story is addressed. The interest they have shown in my welfare and in that of my beloved princess is so heartfelt that I feel that I can do no less than publish for their benefit the extraordinary events which followed that seemingly endless night in my hidden Nevada valley before I started in pursuit of Awlo and her abductor.

Impatiently I watched the sun rise over the Timpahutes. The sunrise is a little later in Ulm than in this plane because of the height of the mountain (grains of sand!) which surround the empire. I judged it best to wait for broad daylight before I plunged into what might easily be the unknown. I had set my electronic vibration adjuster as nearly as possible over the spot where Lamu and my princess had disappeared but I know that a distance which could not be detected under the microscope in this plane might be miles in Ulm and I had little hope of landing in the beleaguered city.

At last I felt that the time had come. I entered my newly

completed adjuster, closed the switch and was on my way. Rapidly the scenery grew to Brobdingnagian proportions and then disappeared as it grew too large for my eyes to see or my mind to comprehend. I watched the indicator dial as the needle crept toward infinity. Presently its motion ceased and the high whine of my generators became audible. The note ran down the scale of audibility and subsided into silence. I looked out from my adjuster and my heart sank. The landscape resembled not in the least the scenery around Ulm. There was no doubt that I had missed my goal by many miles.

My first inclination was to increase my size and move the adjuster but a sober second thought made me realize the futility of such an action. I had set the machine as nearly as I could over the spot where Ulm lay and any change I made would be just as likely to be away from the city as toward it. The only thing to do was to set out on my travels in the hope that I would meet some one, even were it one of the hostile Mena, who could give me some idea of the direction in which to travel. I slung a couple of extra bandoliers of ammunition over my shoulders, picked up my rifle and stepped out of the adjuster. A second thought made me pause. I retraced my steps and opened an arm locker. From it I took two small-caliber .32, automatic pistols, which I placed in shoulder holsters under my shirt. The little guns held six rounds each and while they were small, they carried hollow point bullets which would have a deadly effect at short range. With my armament thus reenforced, I was ready to start my travels.

The country in which I found myself was wild beyond description. In place of the dense semi-tropical vegetation which I had been accustomed to associate with my submicroscopic empire, there was nothing but rock, bare rugged rock. Huge masses of stone, hundreds and even thousands of feet high, lay piled one on another as though a race of giants had tossed them about in sport, recking little of where they fell. There was none of the solidity and symmetry which marks the mountains of the larger plane. Many of the stones seemed to be precariously balanced and even where they were wedged together, the effect was one of insecurity. I shuddered and caught myself afraid to stir lest even my tiny weight would start one of the masses of rock into motion and engulf me and all my possessions in cataclysmic ruin. I walked in a gingerly fashion over to one of the unstable appearing masses of rock and rested my hand against it. It was solid to the touch and I pressed, gently at first, and then with all my strength, trying in vain to budge the mass which must have weighed thousands of tons, if my own negligible weight be taken as being its normal one hundred and eighty pounds. Satisfied that it was beyond my strength to move it, I felt safer, and began to consider in which direction I should start my travels.

I racked my brain for a clue. Somewhere in memory's vaults there was an elusive something that this jumbled phantasmagoria of rock reminded me of. Suddenly I remembered it.

In the days when I had been hailed as the Crown Prince of Ulm, the husband of its ruler's only child, I had been much interested in the ancient legends which told the history of the empire. Ulm had no written language and no records to which I could refer other than the traditions and legends which had been handed down from father to son. These legends were preserved in metrical form. The learning and reciting of them on occasion was the principal duty of the class of persons known as *tamaaini*,* generally elderly men who were not of the noble class, but who, because of their profession, had an *entrée* to the court and many of the privileges of nobility. Some of them had marvelous memories and could repeat without faltering thousands after thousands of lines of the old legends. It was from them that I learned that the Mena had originally come down from the north through the barren passes in the mighty mountains which border Ulm on all sides. I had never been able to gather much information as to derivation of the people of Ulm themselves. It seemed that so far as the *tamaaini* knew, they had always lived in their present location. There were, however, here and there in the legends dim and little understood references to other places and it was one of these passages that I strove to recall. Suddenly, like a flash, the long forgotten tale came to my mind.

It told of the flight of the natural son of a ruler of Ulm who had tried to wrest the throne from his legitimate half-brother, after his father's death, and it described his own defeat and death. The victor pursued him with a handful of guards and caught him in a place where "giants played as children, tossing mountains hand to hand." There they encountered a race of *kahumas* or wizards who flew through the air like birds and who shot fire from their many hands. They could "kill from afar with fire" and they allowed no one who entered their

* Compare the Hawaiian word, *"kamaaini,"* an old inhabitant.

land to return. Evidently, at least one of the party returned to Ulm with the record of the attempted usurper's death, which the legend goes on to detail at great length. The passage had always interested me, for it seemed to hint at a higher civilization than was possessed by the brave and chivalrous warriors of Ulm.

I looked about me and I did not blame the fancy of the ancient bard who had laid the condition of the landscape to the gambols of giants or to the evil machinations of wizards. Certainly his description was an apt one. The forbidden land lay, according to the legend, "toward the setting sun." *If* the tale were true and *if* I were looking on the scene of that ancient tragedy, Ulm should lie to the east and not more than a few days' journey away. It was a pretty slender clue but it was the only one I had. Without it I had no idea of which direction to take, so I decided to trust to the accuracy and authenticity of a legend of unknown antiquity and make my way eastward.

My first step was to fix the landscape in my mind and to take bearings with my marching compass on the most prominent points of the scenery. If I found my way back to Ulm my entire labor and travail would be lost unless I were able to return to the adjuster and its precious load of weapons. Three huge peaks dominated the scene to the north and they stood so that the farther one lay exactly in the middle of the interval between the two nearer ones. The bearing of the farther peak was a quarter point west of magnetic north. Exactly south east was another peak with a peculiar cleft near its summit. A short study enabled me to fix the location of the adjuster so firmly in my mind that I was certain that I could find the place again. With a final look around, I shouldered my rifle, set my face to the east and set out.

Despite the ruggedness of the country I was able, by the aid of my marching compass, to keep going in the general direction of east pretty well although I had to make several lengthy detours around masses of rock. For several hours I pushed on and found the country gradually getting a little less rugged. There were no signs of animal life but once in a while I came across a tuft of vegetation resembling the bunch grass so common in some parts of the West.

As the sun got higher it grew intolerably hot and I began to regret that I had loaded myself so heavily with food and especially ammunition and had brought only two quarts of water.

It was too late to retrace my steps, so I husbanded my water as carefully as possible and kept going. Before noon the heat got so bad that I began to look for a place where I could find a little shelter.

Ahead of me I spied what looked like a cave in the rock and I pressed forward to investigate it. It was not a true cave but it was a fair imitation of one made by two huge masses of rock leaning against one another. I had no idea how far into the rock the cavity extended but it was cool in the shade and I discarded my pack with a sigh of relief. I also unslung the heavy bandoliers of ammunition which I carried and leaned my rifle against the wall of the cavern. According to my pedometer, I had covered about ten miles. I secured a pencil and notebook from my pack and stepped to the mouth of the cavern to sight the directions of the peaks by which I had marked my landing.

I located them without any trouble and was engaged in trying to locate myself by a process of triangulation on a crude map which I had made of my morning's journey when an unfamiliar sound brought me up with a start. I listened intently and the sound faded for a moment only to increase in volume. I puzzled my brains as to what was causing it. It was a dull humming sound and the only thing it reminded me of was the whirling of an airplane propeller, a patent impossibility in Ulm.

The sound came nearer and I started back to the cave and took up my rifle when the cause of the noise came in sight. My flyer's ears had not misled me. Flying along at a moderate speed about a thousand feet above my level was an airplane. It was not the conventional pattern with which I was familiar although it bore certain resemblance to the planes I had flown. The main difference was in the size and shape of the wings. Instead of the usual rectangular wing spread on each side of the fuselage, this machine had a single heart-shaped wing mounted above the fuselage with the point of the heart to the rear. Above the wing was a crisscross network of wires which reminded me of an aerial.

The passenger car was long and cigar-shaped although it did not extend backward much beyond the point of the heart. The sides were pierced with windows which were glazed with glass or some other transparent material through which I fancied I could see figures moving, although the distance was too great for me to be sure.

The machine had three propellers, one mounted directly in front of the car and about on a level with the wing while the other two, which were smaller, were set lower and about midway from the center line of the craft to the extremities of the wing. Now only the small wing spread and other unconventional features of the design attracted my attention but also the complete absence of all motor noise although the three propellers were whirling rapidly.

Stupidly I watched the craft until it was almost overhead and then I had sense enough to start something. Even though the occupants of the ship were not handicapped by the roar of motors, I had no hope of making them hear at that elevation so I hastily took off my hat and waved it frantically. The airship moved serenely on without anyone seeing, or at any rate, heeding my signals of distress. Desperately I ransacked my brains for a means of attracting their attention and inspiration visited me. An old friend of mine had been experimenting with some illuminating bullets and he had given me a handful of cartridges loaded with them. I suddenly remembered that my pistol was loaded with them for I had intended to try them out but had forgotten to do so. Here was an excellent chance to test their value. I pulled my pistol from its holster and fired up into the air.

From the muzzle of the gun a bell of fire rose into the air. Up past the airship it went and still up. It must have traveled fully eight hundred yards before the flame died. I fired again and then turned my attention to the airplane. My signal had evidently been seen, for the ship was swinging around on a wide arc. Again I waved my coat. There was no question that my signal was seen for the ship glided on a long slant toward the ground. I looked at the small open space before me and knew that it would be impossible to land an ordinary plane in it without a crash, but I had not yet learned the possibilities of that stubby ship with its diminutive wing spread. The plane curved down and came to a stop not over a hundred feet from where it first touched ground. The center propeller ceased turning but the two side propellers kept up a steady hum until after the ship had come to a complete stop.

A door opened in the side of the ship and four figures climbed out and came toward me. I hastened to meet them but I stopped short in my stride before I had gone far. They had the general conformation of men but they suddenly gave me an uncanny feeling as though I were looking at huge spiders. I could not understand the feeling for a moment until I concentrated my attention on the one who was leading the advance. From his shoulders projected not one pair of arms but three. The rest of him appeared to be normal as well as I could tell through the bulky shapeless garment which he wore and the helmet which concealed his features.

The four figures spread out as they advanced and I did not interpret the action as a friendly one. I thought momentarily of retreating to the cave where I had left my rifle but I had no idea of how fast these newcomers could travel and they were as close to the cavern mouth as I was. I backed against a nearby boulder and drew my pistol. They might mean no harm but I preferred to be ready for all eventualities.

The four drew near until they were within twenty feet of me. I raised my pistol but hesitated about commencing hostilities until I was sure that they were not friendly. At my action they all stopped and stared and one of them raised an arm and pointed it at me. At this close distance I could see their features through the glass windows which formed the front of their helmets and I realized that they were like no men I had seen before. Their faces were a bright saffron yellow and their eyes were set obliquely in their heads. I raised my left hand in the universal gesture of peace and spoke.

"Pehea oc, malahini?" I said.

The leader looked doubtfully at me for a moment before he replied. He spoke in a strange guttural voice and while his language was not that of Ulm, I was able to understand it.

"Whence came you and what seek you here?" he demanded.

"I come from Ulm," I replied. "I came from the capital which is beleaguered by the race of the Mena and I am seeking to bring assistance to Kalu Sibama, my sovereign lord. I am lost and am trying to find my way thither. Can you direct me?"

"Ulm?" he said slowly and then burst into a harsh laugh. "You lie," he went on. "Ulm is more than a memory. Kalu Sibama has rested, well I hope, in the stomachs of the Mena for many moons."

"Is Ulm fallen?" I gasped, hardly able to believe my ears.

"Ulm is fallen," he said, evidently amused at my horror. "As fleas desert a dying dog, so her leaders deserted her. The Mena stormed the walls and but a remnant fought their way out. That remnant are slaves of my lord, Kapioma Sibama of the Empire of Kau. He will be pleased when I bring him two slaves in place of the one I was sent to seek."

His words answered my question as to his intentions. I thought grimly that he had not captured his slave yet as I carefully covered his chest with my pistol. The illuminating bullet struck him fair in the center of his chest and exploded in a flash of red light. He staggered back under the shock of impact but did not fall. I raised my pistol for a second shot but I never fired it. A flash of blinding green light came from one of his arms and my pistol clattered to the ground. My right arm hung numb and paralyzed from the shoulder. A second flash came and my left arm was in the same condition. I turned to run but I was too late. A dozen hands gripped me and held me helpless.

At a word from their leader, the three subordinates jerked me rudely along the ground toward the strange craft and pulled me inside. I gave a rapid glance around as I entered the craft for I desired to see what type of motors they had which operated so silently. There were none in sight. In the front of the long cabin were a set of dual flying controls of the type with which I was familiar. In the forward end were three tiny motors of an unfamiliar type but there were no batteries, no generators and above all no prime movers, unless such a term could be applied to a large panel board set with switches and dials which was between the two sets of controls. One man stood at this board. There were no other occupants of the ship evident at first glance.

My captors dragged me to the rear end of the cabin and forced me to a sitting position. Two more green flashes filled the interior of the cabin momentarily and my legs from the knee down were as useless as my arms were. The three retreated to the upper end of the cabin and divested themselves of their flying suits. They were men of middle height with rather slight physique but with high foreheads and an air of great intelligence. The leader turned his slanting eyes toward me. There was power in them and intelligence but there was also the very quintessence of cruelty in them. So obsessed was I with his face, that for a moment I failed to notice that four of his six arms had disappeared.

An explanation flashed through my mind and I looked at the rest of the crew. Each of them had only the normal two arms which I had expected. On the wall was a rack and hung there were five flying suits, from the shoulders of each of which projected three sets of arms. As I examined them more closely, I saw that only two arms on each suit ended in gloves. The other arms ended in hollow tubes from which the paralyzing rays had evidently come. The sight of these garments did as much as the coldly merciless faces to impress on my mind the fact that I was dealing, not with the brave chivalrous savages of Ulm, but with a race who had developed their mental powers highly and who were well acquainted with scientific laws.

The leader gave an order and two of the crew stepped to the flying controls. The man at the switchboard manipulated some dials. The ship started upward with a rocketing motion, climbing at what was, to my judgment an entirely unsafe angle. However, the ship made it without any difficulty and leveled off at an elevation of about a thousand feet and continued on her way east. I took a rapid glance at the compass set on the roof and mentally resolved to keep track of our course.

Two of the crew stepped forward and tossed to one side a piece of cloth which had covered some long object lying on the floor. They picked it up and I suppressed an exclamation with difficulty. The object was a man and it needed only a glance to tell me that he was of a different race from the crew of the ship. Long curling yellow locks fell from his head in place of the short black hair of the Kauans and his skin was as white as mine instead of the disgusting saffron yellow which marked our captors.

His arms and legs hung limp and useless as they picked him up and bore him aft. They dumped him unceremoniously on the floor beside me and returned to the forward part of the cabin. I looked at my fellow captive with interest, an interest which he quite evidently felt as well.

"Where from?" he asked me in an undertone. His voice had none of the guttural quality which marked the speech of the crew. It was as soft and liquid as the speech of any man of Ulm.

"Ulm," I replied, also in an undertone.

"But Ulm fell months ago," he said wonderingly. "Surely you did not survive the sack of the city. If you did, how have you survived since then?"

"I was not at the fall of the city," I replied. "I was away seeking aid for Ulm when it fell. I have just returned."

He looked at me curiously.

"What was your rank?" he demanded.

"I was Siba Tam," I replied proudly.

An expression of joy crossed his face.

"My hilt to your hand, Siba Tam," he said, "had I a sword to offer. I have long hoped for a sight of the son of my ruler."

"I was not the son of Kalu," I answered, "I was the husband of his only child."

"Still my hilt to your hand," he replied. "I have not seen my native land since I was a child but no more loyal subject of her Sibama lives. Do you wish to continue on to Kau?"

"I hardly wish to go anywhere as a slave," I said briefly.

"Then we can escape," he replied. "I had planned to try to win my freedom before we reached the city, although I had little hope of success. Two of us should be more than a match for five men of Kau."

"But my legs and arms are paralyzed," I objected.

"That is of no moment. Can you keep them quiet and simulate paralysis if I remove the effects of the ray?"

"I think so."

"Then be careful and do not move them while I work."

He rolled over and fell against me. The Kauans glanced around at him for a moment but paid no further attention. In a moment I felt a sharp pain in my back and then another in my shoulder.

"Now remain perfectly quiet," said my new friend. A dull whir sounded behind me for a moment and an excruciating pain racked my limbs. I bit my lip to keep from crying out. The pain passed and to my joy I found that both feeling and motion had been restored.

"What are your orders?" asked my fellow captive softly.

"I have no plans made. You know what to do much better than I do. Issue your orders and I will obey."

"Then when I give the word, leap to your feet and rush them," he said. "Get between them and their fighting suits and keep them away from them. If they get to their weapons, we are dead or worse. Without them they have nothing but their strength to rely on."

"Wait a moment," I said cautiously, "I think I have a weapon here. I have one that will kill ordinary men but it failed against these men. However, they had their fighting suits on when I tried it. Tell me, are they vulnerable to a sword thrust?"

"Without their fighting suits, yes; with them, no."

"Fine. Lie still and let me try my hand on them. Can you fly the ship after we capture it?"

"Certainly."

"All right, I'll see what I can do. If my weapon fails, we can still rush them with bare hands."

I braced myself for an effort. The distance was short and I felt sure that the little thirty-two automatic pistols which I had providentially armed myself with would be accurate enough for my purpose. Both rested in holsters—one under each arm.

With a sudden swift movement, I sprang to my feet, a pistol in each hand. I raised the right one and fired at the leader. I watched breathlessly for a moment. He swayed back and forth and then fell headlong. The gun was effective.

The other members of the crew stared stupidly at their fallen leader. Again the little gun spoke and the odds were reduced to three to two. The remaining members of the crew made a rush for their fighting suits but they never reached them. Three times the little automatic spat forth a message of death and each time my aim was good. My companion had risen to his feet and he now raced for the controls. He got them just in time, for the pilotless ship was careening badly. In a moment he had it flying once more on a level keel.

I made the rounds of the prostrate crew. At short range the mushroom bullets with which my gun was loaded had done their work. Only one of our enemies lived and it was evident that his wound was fatal. Assured of their helplessness to harm us, I moved up to the control board.

"Which way, Siba Tam?"

I reflected before answering. There was no use in returning to fallen Ulm. The ship would be an excellent aid to me in pursuing my search for my lost princess and I had gained a loyal follower. The first step was to arm him.

"Go back to the place where I was captured and then straight west for a few miles. In the meantime, teach me how to fly this ship. What is your motive power? I see no signs of any source of energy."

"Our power is drawn from the central power house in Kaulani."

"Radio transmission of power!" I gasped.

"I do not understand your words," he said (I had unconsciously spoken in English) "The power to turn our propellers and to actuate the fighting suits is generated in Kaulani and is sent out in the form of waves which are received by wires on the top of the ship."

"I noticed them," I replied, "but did not suspect their use. I thought they were used to receive and probably transmit messages."

"Could messages be sent or received through them?"

"Certainly. Isn't that done?"

"No, Siba Tam."

"In that case we have one bit of knowledge that the Kauans don't have," I said cheerfully. "I will show you how it is done later. Now show me how to control the ship."

He motioned me to take the dual set of controls and started his explanations. It was ridiculously simple for one already well versed in flying and in five minutes I was maneuvering the ship like a veteran. The secret of the small wing spread and the short take-off and landing distance lay in the setting and position of the side propellers. They were so inclined that their blast struck the wings and gave a lifting effect to aid the take-off. Reversing them made them act as a brake and brought the craft to a standstill in a few feet. The central propeller did practically all the work of moving the ship forward.

In a short time we were over the place where I had been captured and we landed and secured my rifle and pack. We took off again and in ten minutes landed safely by the side of my adjuster.

"Now I will repay you for teaching me to fly our ship," I said with a smile, "by teaching you to manipulate a machine which I doubt if even the leader of that crew of brigands who captured us could understand. However, before I do so, tell me about yourself. Who are you and how did you get here? I have lived for years in Ulm and do not know your face and my face was not familiar to you."

"I was taken from Ulm as a child and reared in Kau."

"How did that happen?"

"My name is Olua; Olua Alii by right, for I was born the son of Muana Alii, one of the Council of Lords. When I was a child, I accompanied my father on a trip to Ame. On the way home, the Mena attacked us. My father was killed but I was saved alive and taken as a present to their chief. I was destined for his larder but he never saw me. On the way to his resting place, an airship like this one swooped down on us.

The Mena fled in all directions. Men of Kau in fighting suits came from the ship and one of them, a great Alii, picked me up. His only son had died a few days before and for that reason he spared me, although the men of Kau are entirely without mercy in their dealings with those of other races. He took me to Kau and raised and educated me as his own child. There are a few of the scientific secrets of Kau that I do not know."

"How did you come to be a prisoner?"

"Through loyalty to the land of my birth. Although raised in Kau, I never forgot that I was by birth an Alii of Ulm, one of the Council of Lords. I read all I could of Ulm and the more I learned of their bravery and chivalry, the more glad I became that I was one of them and not a treacherous Kauan. My loyalty was always to Kalu Sibama of Ulm and not Kapioma Sibama of Kau, although I did not speak openly of it.

"When Ulm fell to the Mena, a handful of the warriors of Ulm won their way through to the mountains between Kau and Ulm, where they were captured and brought as slaves to Kaulani. My heart leapt when I saw them come in. They were such men as I had always dreamed of, men who fought their enemies with steel and not with weapons of stealth and treachery. The dream of my life was to rescue them and flee with them to Ame, which had not fallen to the Mena. I laid my plans carefully. I was going to capture one of the largest warships, and fly with them.

"The day before I was to act, I was betrayed. A faithful slave warned me that the Sibama's guards were on their way to arrest me. I did not delay, but raced for the roof of the power house, where I know that the Sibama's private flyers, the fastest craft in Kau, were kept. I selected a fast one-man flyer and fled in the night to the west. My flight was foredoomed to be a failure.

"The power sent out by the power in Kaulani is sent in five wavelengths. One of them is used for all machines of peace, for lighting the house, preparing the food and similar uses. A second actuates the fighting suits and other weapons of war. The other three are assigned to the ships; one to commercial ships, one to war vessels and one to the Sibama's private flyers. All they had to do was to shut down the wavelength on which I was flying and my ship crashed to the ground, a wreck.

"By their meters at Kaulani they can tell where every ship

is and warships were dispatched after me. They could not locate me. Before leaving, I had rigged the flyer with a device I had perfected, which made the meters give false readings and I was many miles from the place where they sought me, I hid the wreckage of my ship under rocks and eked out a precarious living in the hope that some day I would be able to capture a small flyer and make my way to Ame alone. I knew that they would use the paralyzing ray on me when I was found and I labored to make a pocket device which would remove the effects of the ray. After seven months of toil, I perfected it. The search for me had never ended, for the Kauans knew that I could not be beyond the limits of their empire. Many times I had seen the patrol vessels pass over me and each time I had hidden myself. This morning one passed and I deliberately showed myself. Everything went as I had planned. They paralyzed my arms and legs but my pocket neutralizer destroyed the effects. I simulated paralysis and was carried on the ship a prisoner. I bided my time and was about to attack, when they saw your signal and stopped to capture you. You know the rest."

"One question, Olua Alii; you said that the survivors of Ulm were taken to Kaulani. Were there any women among them?"

"There were not, Siba Tam. They were all warriors."

Evidently Awlo and Lamu had not made their way to Ulm. Well, that was about what I had expected.

"Perhaps you had better teach me to use one of these fighting suits," I suggested.

"Certainly, Siba Tam, whatever you desire. As you can see, each suit has six arms. Two of these are control arms, the other four are weapons. Each of the weapons is different. The green ray is a paralyzing ray with whose effects you are familiar. It can be used as a crippling weapon or as a killing weapon. If the heart is paralyzed, death ensues instantly.

"In the second arm is an orange ray which neutralizes the effect of the green ray. It is used as a defensive weapon against an enemy equipped with the green paralyzing ray. It will also restore the functioning of any part of the body which has been paralyzed. The third arm contains a red or heat ray. I will show you the effect of it."

He donned a suit and directed the middle arm on the left side toward a boulder. A ray of intolerable brightness shot from the arm. The granite boulder glowed bright for a moment and a stream of molten rock ran down its face. Olua shut off the ray.

"The fourth ray is a blue one which has the effect of neutralizing the red ray of an opponent," he went on. "You see, each suit is equipped with two offensive and two defensive weapons. These are all that the common soldiers carry. The Alii have suits with more arms and more deadly weapons, both offensive and defensive. It is said that Kapioma Sibama has made a suit with forty arms but it is so heavy that he cannot walk with it on. It operates, not on the usual wavelength, but on the private wavelength on which his flyers operate.

"That, however, is not the most effective suit in Kaulani. The most deadly suit is one which I manufactured in secret and which is hidden there. I had no opportunity to bring it with me or all the forces of Kau could not have harmed me. I will tell you, Siba Tam, where it is concealed. The knowledge may never benefit you but it will do you no harm. In the power house is a laboratory where fighting suits are made and tested. One entire end of the laboratory is taken up by a screen against which all rays are helpless. Unknown to everyone, I have tampered with that screen. If you ever wish to get the suit, go to the laboratory and turn the ordinary red ray, the heat ray of the common suits, against the upper corner of the screen, fourteen inches from the top and eleven inches from the left end. Leave the ray on full force for eight seconds and then apply the orange ray for twelve seconds. A portion of the screen will open and the suit is behind it. It operates on the same wave as Kapioma's."

"Thank you, Olua," I said, after I had practised with one of the suits until I could manipulate it rapidly, "you have told me what I wished to know very frankly and fully. I will reward your confidence by being equally frank with you. Although I am Siba Tam of Ulm, I was not born in that empire. I was born in a much larger world. Do you understand the composition of matter?"

I soon found that the education of an Ali of Kau left little to be desired from a scientific standpoint. Olua was perfectly familiar with the division of matter into molecules and atoms and of the atoms into protons and electrons. One of his statements surprised me a great deal until I had time to reflect on it. He said that the atoms were static instead of in motion and that the same was true of the electrons. I started to correct him, when a sudden thought made me pause. A moment of reflection told me that he was right. In his plane, both atoms and electrons were static.

When I had first started my electronic vibration adjuster, which reduced the amplitude of vibration of the electrons, my switch had jammed and I had broken it in trying to open it. Despite this fact, the adjuster had reduced me to the size of the men of Ulm and had then ceased operation. On each subsequent trip, the same phenomenon had occurred. The reason, on reflection, was obvious. I had reduced the amplitude of vibration to zero and in this minute plane, the electrons did not vibrate.

Once I had that idea in my head, it was a simple matter to explain to Olua the theory of the vibrating atoms of the larger planes. He did not question my theory of simple harmonic vibration of the electrons, which theory had brought so much ridicule on me at one time. He realized at once how the size of a body could be increased under such circumstances but when I told him of the world from which I had first come to Ulm, his eyes opened. He had no more idea of the existence of such a world than we of the larger plane had of the existence of Ulm before my first trip there. His first thought was to flee to the larger plane from the pursuing Kaunas.

"There we will be safe," he said. "They will be after us in a few hours with ships of greater speed equipped with fighting suits against which we have no defence."

"You may go if you wish Olua," I said, "but I have returned to Ulm for a purpose and that purpose has not been accomplished. I will stay and continue my search."

"Where the Siba of Ulm stays, there stays Olua Alii of Ulm," he said quietly. "What are your plans?"

"The only place where I can obtain the information I seek is at Kaulani, where the survivors of Ulm are," I replied. "Let me tell you why I am here and what I seek."

In a few words I told him of Lamu's treachery and of my search for my lost princess.

"You will not find her in Kaulani," he said thoughtfully, "for there were no women brought here. However, some of the prisoners can tell you whether they returned to Ulm before it fell. Since that is your desire, we will wait here until the Kauans come and capture us."

"No, we won't," I replied. "If they come here, they will capture not only us but also my adjuster and the weapons I brought from the larger plane. How long will it be before they are after us?"

"At least four hours."

"Good. In that length of time, I can teach you how to manipulate a rifle and a pistol as well as the adjuster. There is one other thing you want to learn to use. Here is a wireless transmission set. It will enable you to send messages through the air, which a similar instrument will receive, and also to receive messages sent to you. If I can, I will construct one in Kaulani so that we can get into communication. You are not going back to Kaulani with me."

"I will stay with my lord."

"You will obey my orders. If you go there, it will not aid me at all and will result in your death. If you hide out here, it is possible that you may aid me. In the event that I am killed, it is my order that you take up the search for Awlo of Ulm and never abandon it while you live until you have rescued her from Lamu or have looked on her dead body. Do you understand?"

"I do, sire. It will be as you order."

"Good. Now I want to teach you all I can before we have to pull out of here."

Olua was an apt pupil and in two hours he was able to manipulate a rifle and a pistol as well as I could and even to shoot fairly well at short ranges. The weapons would be useless against men equipped with fighting suits, the simplest of which threw about the wearer a repulsive screen which no bullet could penetrate, but I felt that no knowledge was useless, since my ability with a pistol had saved us once. The radio set was elementary to him, his only wonder being that no Kauan had ever thought of so simple a device.

When he was fully instructed we entered the adjuster and increased our size slowly until we were perhaps a hundred yards tall, compared to Ulm standards. We stepped out and I used a rifle to start the adjuster and let it reduce its size to Ulmite standards. When this was done, I could pick it and its entire load up and carry it without difficulty. Olua picked up the Kauan ship and together we set out across the hills for the point where I was captured. I resolved to make that cavern our base of operations.

We found it with no trouble and reduced ourselves to our former dimensions. It was quite a task for us to move the adjuster and its load into the cavern but we did so. When the task was completed, I bade a temporary farewell to Olua and entered the Kauan ship. I drove it about thirty miles due east and then landed. I set the controls of the ship for a maximum climb and pulled the power lever to full speed forward. The ship sprang up into the air and I leaped out just in time. Upward it went for several miles before it fell out of control. When it did, it gave a sickening lurch or two and then dove at full speed toward the ground. I sat down and waited for the next Kauan ship to appear.

I did not have long to wait. In less than an hour a speck appeared in the blue to the east. The new ship was a larger one than the first and it seemed to me to be traveling at a higher speed. I was fearful lest the occupants would see the remains of the ship which had crashed but the Gods of Fate were kind to me and it escaped their notice. It probably dove into some deep dark ravine, for none of the scouts which went out from Kau in search of it ever located it. Hunting for so small an object as a five-man cruiser in the wastes of the Kau mountains was a great deal like the proverbial search for a needle in a haystack.

When the ship came in sight, I walked slowly out into the open and stood quietly awaiting its approach. I thought, and as it turned out I thought rightly, that the figure of a man would hardly escape the attention of an airship sent out to seek for one. The ship swung down on a long slant and came to a standstill less than fifty feet from where I stood. A door opened in the side of the cabin and a half a dozen figures wearing eight-armed fighting suits emerged. I advanced toward them confidently.

"Greetings, men of Kau," I said when I had approached to within twenty feet of them. They paused and their leader stepped a pace in front.

"Greetings, man of Ulm," he replied in his guttural voice. "What seek you in the mountains of Kau?"

"I seek audience with Kapioma Sibama of Kau," I said. "The way to Kaulani is long and weary and I ask your aid in traveling there."

"What manner of man are you?" he demanded. "Your color and speech mark you as a man of Ulm, yet what man of Ulm knows of Kau and Kaulani?"

"I know many things," I said haughtily, "things which I have come to Kau to impart to your Sibama."

"What is your name and rank?"

"I am Courtney Siba Tam, Crown Prince of Ulm."

A peculiar expression flickered for a moment over his face and he bowed low to me.

"Neimeha of Kau is honored to be of service to such a one," he said smoothly. "My poor ship is at your Highness' disposal to carry him to the court of Kapioma Sibama. There you may meet some of your compatriots."

"I believe that a few of my subjects did escape into the Kau mountains when Ulm fell," I said carelessly, "and I would like to see them again. I will mention your courtesy to Kapioma Sibama."

He bowed again at my words and motioned to me to precede him into the flyer. I did so, expecting every moment to feel a paralyzing ray strike me, but evidently my bluff had worked. Neimeha followed me in and he and his followers divested themselves of their fighting suits.

"It is fortunate for me that you took this path," I said cheerfully. "I had little hope of meeting a ship so soon."

"We seek one who has fled from Kau," he replied. "As long as the light holds we will continue our search. Such were my orders."

"It is unfortunate that you men of Kau do not understand some of the laws of nature with which I am familiar," I said. "If you were, it would be a simple matter to communicate with your sovereign and ask for a modification of your orders. The waves which come from your power house could easily carry a message to you."

"How would such a thing be possible?" demanded Neimeha in amazement.

I smiled enigmatically.

"It is but one of the things which I can teach you," I replied. "I could instruct one of your learning in a short time, but I do not choose to do so. Perhaps your Sibama will desire to confine this new knowledge to his Alii. How long will it take us to fly to Kaulani?"

He turned to a map hanging on the wall and I walked over and studied it. It was the first map of the submicroscopic country I had ever seen, for Ulm had not progressed to the stage of map making and probably never would have. The Ulmites were possessed of an uncanny sense of direction which enabled them to find their way readily about their domain without other aid.

I had been captured in what was apparently a "no man's land" between the empires of Ulm and Kau. Ulm lay, as nearly as I could scale distances by the eye, about ninety miles *due west* of where we were. The old legend had lied after all. Kaulani was roughly two hundred miles to the east, a hundred and fifty of which were over barren mountains.

"We can fly to Kaulani in an hour and a half," said Neimeha. "In view of your presence, I am going to alter my instructions on my own initiative and take you directly to the city."

"I thank you," I said. "I am fairly familiar with this type of ship. With your permission, I will take the dual set of controls and guide the ship a part of the way."

He nodded and for the rest of the trip I devoted my attention to improving my technique. There was really nothing to it and long before we reached Kaulani, I was as confident of my ability to fly any ship in the country as I was of my ability to fly a Bach or a Douglas.

It was nearly dark when we landed in Kaulani. The plan of the city resembled the plan of Ulm, but the architecture was of a much lighter and more graceful type. Not that Ulm had not been a beautiful city but its beauty was the beauty of grandeur and massiveness with utter simplicity marking its architectural lines. Kaulani, as well as I could tell in the gathering dusk, was made up of buildings of a much more graceful style. I could not place the type of architecture, although in the daylight it had a strong note of the best Grecian style in it.

We landed in the huge grounds surrounding the royal palace. Neimeha and two of his guards escorted me into the palace to a floor below the level of the ground.

"I am placing you in the slave's quarters," he explained, "not that your status as a guest has changed, but that it is necessary that you be kept under surveillance, until it is learned whether Kapioma Sibama will receive you. The slave's quarters are the only place where this can be done. Besides, I thought that you might like to see some of your old subjects," he added with a touch of malice in his voice.

The room into which I stepped was the central recreation room of a large suite of rooms. It was well lighted and ventilated and was fitted with a number of comfortable looking chairs and divans. At the far end of the room a half dozen men clothed in coarse white garments were grouped together talking. They turned as I entered and surveyed me from head

to foot. As I approached them, one stepped in front of the
rest and looked at me keenly. I suddenly became aware that I
was dressed in corduroy breeches and a flannel shirt and not
in the gorgeous robes of the Crown Prince of Ulm with the
diadem indicative of my royal rank blazing on my brow.
These garments were not suitable for rough work and I had
left them at my adjuster in the care of Olua. With as much of
an air of dignity as I could command, I stepped forward to
face the group. Suddenly I recognized the man who had
stepped forward.

"Moka!" I shouted with joy. It was indeed Moka Alii, Lord
Chamberlain of Kalu's court.

The old nobleman stared at me in unbelief for a moment
and then a red flush stole over his haughty face. Pointedly he
turned his back on me.

"Moka!" I cried again, "Don't you remember me? I am
Courtney Siba Tam, your prince; Courtney Sibama, if Olua
spoke the truth when he said that Kalu Sibama was no more."

Moka turned and faced me coldly, entirely ignoring my
outstretched hand.

"I recognize you, Courtney," he said in a biting tone, carefully avoiding giving me any title, "to my regret, but my lips
will never touch the hand of a traitor, though I be boiled in
oil for my refusal!"

"Moka!" I cried in real anguish, for the coldness of the first
friend I had made in Ulm cut me to the heart. "It is not true.
I am no traitor to Ulm. I was delayed in my task and was on
my way to Ulm with aid when I learned that it had fallen. I
surrendered to the Kauans and hastened here to bring what
aid and comfort I could to those of my subjects who still
lived. Never have I deserted Ulm and never has the thought
of her welfare been absent from my thoughts."

"Traitor! Doubly dyed traitor!" said Moka slowly and bit-
ingly, "and now, it seems, liar to boot! Well, I know the plan
with which you left Ulm. You planned to aid her enemies and
to depose Kalu Sibama, your lord, and reign in his stead.
Thankful I am that Kalu, who foolishly loved you, died before he knew of your treachery."

"I am no traitor, Moka," I cried, "and who says I am, lies
in his throat! Hold up, old friend," I exclaimed as he sprang
at me, "I am not hitting at you but at the one who told you
this pack of lies. Where did you learn what you thought were
my plans?"

"Your smooth tongue, which deluded Kalu Sibama, will not avail you, Courtney," he said cöldly. "Cover your face in confusion and learn that your treachery was told by Lamu Siba, whom you tried to corrupt and failed."

"Lamu!" I gasped—"Did Lamu return to Ulm?"

"He is here and he has told of the plans which you broached to him to destroy Kalu and of how he fled from you when he learned of your baseness. Your treachery is proven indeed, Courtney."

"So he got back to Ulm safely," I said. Somehow I had always had an idea that he must have missed the city as I did and thought that he and Awlo were wandering somewhere in the submicroscopic world. The news that he had reached Ulm and had managed to turn my friends against me was a bitter blow for it could mean only one thing, that Awlo was dead. Had she been alive, he could never have told that tale and been believed. With a sinking heart I put my next question.

"What of Awlo?" I asked.

I reeled back as Moka struck me a blow on the mouth.

"Dog!" he cried. "The name of a Sibama of Ulm must not be uttered by the lips of a perjured traitor! To complete your confusion, I will tell you that the Sibama of Ulm is in Kaulani."

"Said she that I was a traitor?" I demanded bitterly. Moka paused.

"No," he admitted slowly, "she did not, but it is unnecessary. Lamu Siba has told enough. We men of Ulm need no word from her to damn you further."

My heart leaped with joy at the thought that Awlo was alive and in the same city with me, and while her silence was inexplicable, I knew that she must have some good reason for it. Awlo knew that I was no traitor to Ulm and I would have staked my life on her love and loyalty.

"Listen, old friend," I said to Moka, "it was never your way to condemn a man unheard in his own defense on the testimony of his enemies. You have known me as your lord and as your friend for years; have you ever known me to speak an untruth?"

"No," he admitted.

"Then listen, old friend, while I tell you the truth. Lamu Siba is the traitor, not I."

Rapidly, but in great detail, I told him all that had happened since the fatal day when I left Ulm in my adjuster with

Awlo and Lamu to bring back the guns and ammunition with which I hoped to rout, if not destroy the besieging Mena. I told how Lamu had learned to operate the adjuster, how he had stolen my princess and had fled with her, leaving me desolate. I told of my struggle to get material and of the months of feverish work while I had constructed a duplicate of my machine and gone in pursuit. Last, I told of how I had landed with my guns and ammunition and had met Olua and how I had surrendered to the Kauans in order to be brought to Kaulani.

Moka's face grew graver as my story progressed. My sincerity almost convinced him, but for months he had thought me a traitor. The struggle was evident in his face. He wanted to believe and yet he could not. When I had ended my tale and again held out my hand to him, he hesitated, but another of the auditors, a young officer named Hiko, who had at one time been my personal aide, had no doubts.

"My sword to your hand, Courtney Sibama!" he cried, as he dropped on one knee and pressed my hand against his forehead and then to his lips. "My life is yours to command!"

His enthusiasm carried the day and in a moment, not only Moka, but the rest of the group were on their knees professing their loyalty to me.

"Forgive me for doubting you, Courtney Sibama," cried Moka with tears in his voice, "but the words of a Siba carry weight."

"Where is my Sibimi?" I demanded.

"Alas, my lord," said Moka, "she is a prisoner in the palace of Kapioma Sibama, Lord of Kau. I have seen her twice but none of us has ever spoken to her."

"Did you not speak to her in Ulm?" I asked.

"No, my lord. She or Lamu never returned to Ulm. Four months after you left us, Ulm fell to a night assault of the Mena. Had you been there, it would never have happened, but discipline was relaxed after you left and they kept watch poorly. Besides, the Mena had never before attacked at night.

"The city was given over to slaughter, but a remnant of the royal guard gathered about the palace of the Sibama and we held them at bay for eight days. At the end of that time they fired the palace and we fought our way out hardly. Both Kalu and the Sibimi were killed and most of the guards, but a few of us held together and fought our way toward the waste places where we hoped the kahumas, who were said to rule, would either defend us or kill us with honor.

"The Mena ringed us about and mile by mile our numbers lessened. There were but a hundred and twenty left and many of them sore wounded when the pressure of the Mena suddenly ceased and we saw them flying like leaves before a gale. We heard a strange noise overhead and looked up and saw a multitude of strange birds flying over us. Some of these birds lit near us and disgorged men with many arms who took us prisoners and dragged us into the interior of the birds. We thought they were kahumas. When they were in the birds they divested themselves of all their arms but two and we prepared for death. They did not kill us but saved us alive and brought us here to Kaulani.

"We had been here about a month when we learned that an Alii of Kau had planned to rescue us. We rejoiced but his plot failed and he had to flee for his life. Two months later Lamu Siba was brought to us as a slave. He told us a tale of treachery on your part and of how he and Awlo Sibimi had fled from you but had been captured in the waste places of Kau. Him we foolishly believed, the more because Awlo Sibimi was a prisoner in the palace of Kapioma and none of us could speak with her.

"Aside from the fact that we are slaves and not free men, we have no complaint. The kahumas have treated us well and mercifully, although we are forced to labor, and dire is the punishment of one who shirks. We hope that our condition will be improved, for Kapioma means to make Awlo his Sibimi as soon as the present one is killed."

"Is killed?" I echoed.

"Yes. The kahumas have a barbarous custom in Kau. A Sibimi is chosen and in one year, unless she is with child, she is slain and a new one is chosen. The present Sibimi dies in a month. Thinking you dead, Kapioma meant to make Awlo Sibimi of Kau. Hark! Here come the others from work. Hide behind us for a moment, Courtney Sibama, until I tell them of your presence."

I knew the love of the men of Ulm for dramatic scenes and I stepped behind the ranks of my followers. The door opened and in trooped a hundred men, all attired alike, in the coarse white garb which is the Kauan mark of a slave. Moka stepped forward and held up his hand for silence.

"We harbor in our midst a traitor!" he cried dramatically.

"One who is a traitor to his Sibama, a worse traitor to his Sibimi and a traitor to Ulm. What is the punishment for such a one?"

"Death!" came a cry from the men of Ulm. Lamu stepped forward and confronted Moka.

"Death is his punishment and it shall be meted out when he is known," he said. "Name this traitor."

This was the answer that Moka had hoped for. He drew himself up to his full height and pointed his finger dramatically at the prince.

"Thou art the man!" he thundered. "On your knees and beg for mercy from Courtney, Sibama of Ulm!"

Taking my cue from his words I stepped forward into full view. Lamu started and turned pale as he saw me, but an ominous growl rose from the rest.

"What means this, Moka?" demanded one of them. I recognized the man as Hama Alii, a noble of Ulm and one of the Council of Lords. He was, if my memory did not play me false, a distant cousin of Lamu's. "Courtney is a traitor, as we all well know. To him shall the sentence of death be meted out."

A murmur of assent came from the ranks of the Ulmites behind him and my handful of followers closed up behind me.

"Slay him!" cried Lamu pointing at me. The crowd surged forward.

"Hold!" I cried and they paused for a moment. "Every man is entitled to a hearing. Let me tell my tale and then let the Council of Lords judge my tale. One of royal blood may be tried only by that tribunal."

My point was well taken and it appealed to the justice of the men and a cry of assent went up. Briefly, and as eloquently as I could, I retold my story. It made an impresssion but there was no loyal aide to turn the tables in my favor this time and at the end of my speech there was silence for a moment.

"It is a lie!" cried Lamu suddenly. "Kill the traitor and make an end of it."

There was a murmur, half of assent and half of dissent and I played the same card again.

"How many of the Council of Lords of Ulm are here?" I asked.

"Hama Alii and I," replied Moka.

"A matter touching the royal family of Ulm can be decided only by the Council of Lords," I insisted. "Neither Lamu Siba nor I can be tried by any lesser tribunal. Let Hama and Moka decide."

There was a roar of assent to my proposition and the two nobles retired into a corner to talk the matter over. For half an hour they argued the matter back and forth. Knowing Hama's relation to Lamu, I had rather expected a deadlock and that was what eventually happened. The two came forward and Moka, as the elder, announced their decision.

"When the Council of Lords is evenly divided, the decision rests with the Sibama," he said, "but here the Sibama is an interested party and it would not be fair to let him decide the matter, for traitor or not, Courtney is Sibama of Ulm until the Council of Lords declare the throne vacant. Both Courtney Sibama and Lamu Siba have spoken and the voice of each sounds as that of a true man in our ears. It is our decision that Courtney Sibama and Lamu Siba be each given the honors of their rank and both held blameless, until the matter can be laid before the Sibimi for decision. In the meantime, the disputants shall swear friendship to one another for the time being, and we will all live in harmony as becomes brothers in misfortune."

Lamu and I looked speculatively at one another. After all, there was nothing that we could do except agree with the decision, which was manifestly a just one. I knew that once Awlo spoke, the question would be settled and he doubtless hoped that she would get no chance to speak or else he had another idea in the back of his head. At any rate, he spoke first.

"The Prince of Ame defers to the Council," he said. "As Moka Ali has spoken, so shall it be."

"So shall it be," I echoed.

As Lamu and I approached one another for the ceremony of swearing temporary friendship, there came an interruption. The door opened and there stood Neimeha with a detachment of guards.

"Courtney Sibama," he said, "Kapioma Sibama requires your presence in his throne room."

With a shrug of my shoulders I followed him out of the slaves' quarters and to the ground flooor of the palace. The building was a beautiful one, much more ornate than Kalu's palace in Ulm, but what it gained in beauty, to my mind at least, it lost in grandeur. At the door of the throne room we were challenged, but a word from Neimeha opened a way for us.

The scene was very similar to one of the dozens of Kalu's audiences I had taken part in. On all sides blazed the colors of the nobles and ladies, their flashing gems set off by the sombre black worn by the guards. The throne room was long and impressive, with a dais at the head bearing four thrones, the central two of which were occupied. Kapioma Sibama of Kau was a tall, slender man of about my age. He had a splendid breadth of forehead but his slanting eyes, like those of all the Kauans, were mercilessly cold and cruel. The first thing, however, that attracted my attention was the sadness of the face of the Sibimi who sat beside him. She was a slim young girl and despite her yellow skin, was beautiful, but the sadness of the ages was in her tragic eyes. Suddenly I remembered what Moka had told me of the customs of Kau and I realized that she saw death before her in a few short weeks. I squared my shoulders and advanced to the foot of the dais. Slave or prisoner, condemned to death, I might come from that interview, but as Sibama of Ulm I would go to it. I looked Kapioma squarely in the eye and he returned my gaze with an expressionless face.

"Courtney of Ulm," he said in a guttural voice, "Neimeha tells me that the wonders we have heard of you are true and that your subjects in Ulm looked on you as a powerful kahuma because you knew more of nature and her laws than they dreamed of. You are no barbarian of Ulm, fit only to be a slave, but a man of intelligence and learning. He tells me that you are able to navigate a flyer."

I bowed without speaking.

"I am duly sensible of the misfortunes which have thrown you from your high position, where you might with propriety have sat by my side, and it is not my desire to add to the burdens or sorrows of a man of royal rank. Since you are able to take your part in this community as an equal with my nobles, it is in my mind to create you an Alii of Kau and attach you to my court."

Again I bowed deeply in silence.

"Neimeha tells me further that you know ways of sending messages through the air from the power house to a ship miles away."

"I do, sire, it is a relatively simple matter."

"I am glad to hear it, for I believe that the art will be of much use. To the rank of Alii of Kau I will raise you, but in return I will ask of you one small favor."

"I will be glad to put my knowledge at your service," I replied.

He frowned slightly at my answer.

"It is not that; that I took for granted. The favor I ask of you is of a different nature. You were married in Ulm to Awlo, daughter of Kalu Sibama. Since his death she is now Sibimi of Ulm. In a month or so," here he paused and shot a glance at the Sibimi, who quailed under it as though under a lash, "there will be no Sibimi in Kau and it is my intention to elevate the daughter of Kalu to that exalted rank in lieu of the throne she has lost. The favor I ask of you is that you divorce her."

"Divorce Awlo? Never!" I cried.

"You had better consider well before you decide so," he said with a frown. "As the wife of an Alii, I could not marry her without first getting rid of you. Were I to order your execution, I would be no better off, for the widow of an executed criminal could not be elevated to the rank of Sibimi. However, under the laws of Kau, a slave may not legally have a wife. Unless you consent, I will degrade you to the position of a slave, which will effectually dissolve the tie which binds her and leave her free to mount the throne by my side. It is immaterial to me, but it means much to you. You may have a day in which to decide. Either you become an Alii of Kau and divorce her, or you become a slave of Kau and I will marry her in either event."

"It doesn't take a day or a minute to decide that, Kapioma Sibama," I replied, "I will never divorce her."

He shrugged his shoulders.

"At any rate, I tried to be kind to you," he replied. "Neimeha, this man is a slave of Kau. Clothe him as such and take him to the slaves' quarters. He will work in the laboratory of the power house and show us a method of sending messages to our ships, which he boasts is so simple. If he refuses, or fails, flay him alive."

The guards seized me and half dragged and half led me from the throne room. Once outside the room, my clothing was stripped from me and the white garb of a slave thrown over my shoulders. Thus dressed, I was led back to the slaves' quarters which I had left a short time before. Moka and my other friends hastened to greet me and to express their indignation at the tale I had to tell. They applauded my action vociferously, although Lamu suggested that it might have been a good plan for me to have fallen in with Kapioma's plan and won the rank of Alii, which might have enabled me to aid all of them to escape. A withering glance from Moka stopped his mouth. After a short talk we dispersed to our beds in the dormitories attached to the central room.

I lay awake for some time making my plans. So far everything had fallen out better than I had dared to hope. Awlo was alive and well and in no immediate peril. I had a hundred loyal friends at my back and best of all, I was assigned to work in the laboratory to construct a wireless set, the very thing I needed to communicate with Olua with. I dropped to sleep with a feeling that fortune was favoring me.

When the slaves were turned out for work the next morning, a guard was waiting for me. He took me to the power plant, which was located in the grounds of the royal palace. I was taken to the laboratory and told shortly to show how I proposed to send messages over power waves. I protested that I was unfamiliar with their methods of power transmission and that I would have to familiarize myself with their methods and equipment before I could be expected to show them anything new. After a consultation, my stand was decided to be a reasonable one and that I was handed over to one of the laboratory men with orders that I be taught all that could be taught about power transmission.

My guide and instructor was a young man, about my own age. Despite his slant eyes and yellow skin, he proved to me quite likeable fellow as well as an erudite scientist. He was a son of one of the higher Alii of Kau. During the period I worked with him, we became in a measure friends and he confided to me one day that one of his great-grandmothers had been a slave brought from Ame, the second city of the empire of Ulm. This probably accounted for the fact that he showed less interest in science and more in human beings than most of his compatriots. Altogether, I found him the most human and likeable person I met among the Kauans. Only the fact that he was passionately loyal to Kapioma prevented me from approaching Waimua, which was his name, on the subject of joining forces with us. His tragic death later was a source of lasting sorrow to me.

I had little trouble following Waimua's explanations. The power for the entire empire of Kau was generated in one building in Kaulani and was sent out broadcast for general use. There were five distinct and separate installations, each sending out one of the five wave-lengths earlier described to me by Olua. I was appalled at first by the enormous waste of energy involved in general broadcasting until I found out that only a low-power pilot wave was so sent out. The generators were so built that when a demand was received by the pilot wave, a directional wave of the proper power was automatically sent out to fill the demand. Meters registered the direction and distance from the power house of the consumption and, as a result, the location of any ship flying over the empire could be plotted to within a dozen miles on a map hung near the flying broadcasters. The smallest installation of the five was naturally the one on which the Sibana's private flyers and his fighting suits were operated.

The day passed before we were half through with the power installation but I took the time to give Waimua a rough outline of the methods of radio telegraphy. He understood the principle at once and promised to assemble everything we needed for our experiments and start the best instrument makers in the empire making tubes according to my specifications. As soon as the needed equipment could be got together, we would be in a position to start our experiments. I readily located the screen in the laboratory, behind which Olua had hid his fighting suit, but naturally I made no attempt to get possession of it and did not mention its existence to Waimua.

While I was going over the power plant, a germ of an idea came to me, which seemed to make our escape not altogether impossible. While I had no intention to strike before I had established communication with Olua and given him orders as to the part he was to play in it, nevertheless, I broached the idea to Moka in strict confidence. He promptly promised to see that our men gathered as promptly as possible certain information which I needed. He proposed to speak at first only to the most discreet and trustworthy of our men and avoid giving out information until the time came for action. As we were not interrupted that night, the remnant of the Council of Lords decided that the moment was propitious and Lamu and I swore a temporary oath of friendship.

The next day I finished my course of instruction and on the third day the instrument makers presented for my approval a dozen radio tubes which they had manufactured. Considering the fact that they had never seen a small tube for the sending of messages, they had done a very creditable job and I had little doubt of the success of my efforts. Waimua and I at once started assembling a transmitter and two receivers. One of the receivers was constructed to work only on one definite wavelength, but the other was made adjustable, so that I could not only receive from my own transmitter but also from Olua, if I finally established communication with him. A week passed before I was ready to make a test.

The receivers worked all right while they were in the room with the transmitter and on the pretext of testing them at a longer distance, I sent Waimua fifty miles away in a military flyer. As soon as he was out of the way, I set my transmitter to the wave-length of the receiver on the adjuster and called frantically. It seemed hours before an answer came. Olua had diligently studied the international code since I had left him and he had no difficulty in receiving my messages and answering them. I quickly acquainted him with the state of affairs in Kau and told him of our plans. He was able to make some excellent suggestions, based on his knowledge of Kaulani, suggestions which I gladly fitted into my plans. On the offchance that they might be useful, I directed him to make a trip to the larger plane in the adjuster and bring back certain supplies. I had left quite a sum in gold in my hidden Nevada valley and I told him where to find it. He promised faithful performance of his duties and I turned to the wave-length on which the receiver, which Waimua was carrying, was set.

I sent out a garbled message, varying my power from time to time so that the signals would come in strong and then fade out. I was fairly sure that Waimua would be able to get only a few words of the message, yet he would feel much encouraged. By means of a proposed modification, I intended to prolong the work for a few more days until we were ready to strike for freedom. My plan worked perfectly and Waimua came back wildly enthusiastic about the partial success we had achieved on our first attempt. We tore down both the receivers and the transmitters and proposed rebuilding them with slight modifications, which I assured him would make them entirely successful.

That night Moka reported that Hiko had brought in the last bit of information we had needed and there was no need to delay longer. Everyone, even Lamu, had by this time been informed of the plan and of the part assigned to him in carrying it out.

Briefly, our plan was this. At a given time, we were to divide into two bands. One band, under my personal leadership, was to attack the power house and shut off all power. As soon as this was done, the remainder, under the command of Moka, was to enter the palace and secure Awlo. The rest of us would sally out and meet them and we would all take refuge in the power house. We expected to capture several of the Kauan scientists in the power plant and we would force them to modify a hundred-man military flyer, which was always kept in a hangar on the roof of the power house, to fly on the Sibama's private wave-length. We would disable all generating units except the small one which sent out this power. All but a picked detail were then to leave on this modified ship and the devoted band who remained would try to hold the power plant until we were well away from Kau.

The plan was a risky one but it was the best we could think of and I resolutely refused to allow any discussion of what would happen after those staying behind had been overpowered and our ship brought to the ground. I had another plan, which I did not divulge, even to Moka. I meant to head for my adjuster and arm my band. Kau had no firearms so far as any of us had seen and before a hundred well-armed and resolute men, the entire army of Kau would be helpless, once their fighting suits were put out of business by the shutting off of power which actuated them. What we would do after our escape would depend on Awlo's wishes. We might wipe out the Mena and refound the empire of Ulm (Ame had not yet fallen to the Mena so far as we knew), or we might found a new empire in some remote part of our tiny world some place where neither the Mena nor the Kauans would find us.

The weakest part of our plan was the fact that we were forced to strike in broad daylight, for we were locked in at night. This could not be helped, however, and we set high noon for our attempt. We trusted to the surprise and to the fact that many of the palace attendants would be at lunch. When we left our quarters in the morning, I could not help wondering how many of my brave subjects would be alive that night.

About ten o'clock, as Waimua and I were working away at the radio transmitter, two guards appeared in the laboratory and ordered me to follow them. They refused to answer any questions, merely stating that I was wanted at once in the throne room. With a few words of instruction to Waimua, I took my place between them and walked out. As we emerged from the power house, I saw that something had gone wrong with our plans. Between rows of guards wearing fighting suits, the Ulmites were being herded to the slave's quarters. I was taken to the door of the throne room, where I found Lamu, Moka, and Hama all waiting under guard. The door opened and I was ordered to enter the presence of the Sibama. Shaking off the hands of my guards, I walked with my head up, to the foot of the dais and stared defiantly at Kapioma. He stared back at me with an expressionless face.

"I have been informed, Courtney," he said in his guttural voice, "that there is a plot on foot among the slaves from Ulm to capture the power plant and then to escape in a military flyer, with you at the controls. What have you to say?"

"Nothing, sire," I replied briefly.

"All of the details of the plot are in my hands," he went on, "and any denial would be useless. As the ringleader, your fate is naturally death. What form it will take, I have not decided, nor has my Council of Lords yet debated the fate of your followers."

"Of course, I realized long ago that you had decided on my death, Kapioma Sibama," I said coldly, "since only thus can you free Awlo from her bonds to me. The laws of Kau may say what they please about a slave but we were wed by the laws of Ulm when I was free and a Prince. My enslaving does not dissolve the tie which may be set aside only by the Sibama of Ulm with the consent of his Council of Lords. I would like to know how you learned of our plan."

"One of your members, whom you basely planned to leave behind through jealousy, overheard the plan and found out the details and told them," he replied.

"None were to be left," I exclaimed in surprise.

"Did you not plan to leave Lamu here?"

"We did not. He was the leader of the band who were to seize and protect the power installation by means of which we hoped to escape."

"Then Lamu lied," said Kapioma slowly. "This is not the first lie in which he has been detected. Courtney, it seems that even a Prince of Ulm may be a traitor. Bring in the slave, Lamu!"

The trembling Lamu was dragged by guards to the foot of the dais. He prostrated himself at the foot of the throne and looked abjectly upward. His subserviency disgusted me and I kicked him sharply.

"Get up and take you medicine like a man!" I said.

Kapioma smiled coldly as Lamu struggled to his feet with a black look at me.

"Lamu," he said, "you have lied once too often. The penalty for lying to the Sibama of Kau is death and that fate you have merited. The reward for treachery to your ruler in all countries is death and you have betrayed him who is your lawful Sibama, slave though he may be in Kau. Twice do you merit death and so slowly shall you die that it will seem to you that twice have you passed through the agonies of dissolution. You were planning to escape despite what you told me."

"I was not," cried Lamu. "I first learned of the plot last night through overhearing Moka and Courtney talk. I told my guards at the first opportunity."

"Bring in Moka and Hama," directed Kapioma.

The two Alii were brought in and it pleased me to see that each of them bowed with just the right amount of deference due to a throned monarch and not a speck more.

"Was the slave, Lamu, included in the plot to escape and did he know of it before last night?" demanded the Sibama.

The two nobles glanced at me for orders.

"Speak the truth!" I said.

"He was included in the plot to escape and he was told of it four nights ago, Kapioma Sibama," said Hama. Moka nodded assent.

"By the voices of your countrymen are you condemned, Lamu," said Kapioma. "His death shall be a thing to bring the sweat of terror to the brows of condemned criminals for a generation. Courtney, the laws of Kau are not inexorable. You have been the victim of one you trusted and your suffering to learn that one of your Princes is a traitor is already a heavy punishment. It may be that you may not have to die. If you will divorce Awlo as I have requested, I will submit the question to my Council of Lords with a recommendation for clemency. No, do not answer me now; I know what your answer will be before you have had time to think the matter over. Reflect on this matter. If you die, with you will die every one of your followers who were concerned in the plot. As criminals shall die by torture. For you, I decree a soldier's death."

"Not through any regard for me, Kapioma Sibama, but because you cannot elevate the widow of one who has died as a criminal to the rank of Sibimi," I replied hotly.

"Exactly, Courtney. Your refusal to accede to my terms will accomplish nothing. You may have two days in which to make your decision. In the meanwhile, it is my pleasure that any reasonable wish of yours be granted. Have you a desire?"

"Yes," I replied with my blood boiling, "let me be the one to execute your decree of death on that rat who has been the source of all my trouble."

Kapioma smiled slightly, while Lamu shuddered.

"Gladly," said the Sibama. "It will be an amusing spectacle. I will even let you choose the manner of his death."

"I wish to kill him in a fair fight."

Kapioma studied the two of us for a moment.

"So be it," he said. "Should he kill you, the question of Awlo would be settled pleasantly. If he is the victor, his life will be spared and he shall serve as a slave in Kau for the rest of his days. If you kill him, both you and your subjects will be free. You will be taken to the Kau mountains and liberated with two weeks' supply of food and water and with arms. If any of you return to Kau, you will be put to death with torture. If you win through the mountains, the Mena will kill you? What say you?"

"And Awlo?" I asked.

"In any event, Awlo remains here and becomes my Sibimi," he said sharply.

"Then I will—" I paused in thought. I had been about to declare my preference for death in Kau rather than for a separation from Awlo, but a plan occurred to me. My death in Kau would rob Awlo of her only protector and the Kau mountains were where my precious firearms were stored.

"I accept your terms, Kapioma Sibama," I said.

"Bring fighting suits!" commanded the Sibama.

A guard hastened up with two fighting suits, each equipped with eight arms.

"A scientist such as you are, Courtney, needs no instruction to use such a simple appliance," said Kapioma in a cold voice. "Since Lamu has not your knowledge, I will personally instruct him so that the fight may be more even."

I saw at once that it was his plan that Lamu should kill me and I thought regretfully of the thirty-armed suit which Olua had told me was concealed in the laboratory. However, there was no use in crying for the moon and I devoted my attention to studying the six controls with which my suit was equipped. I soon had them located.

Kapioma put in some time instructing Lamu. When he was satisfied that my adversary understood his weapons, he gave orders for us to don the suits. We did so and the guards brought in a huge dome of some transparent crystalline material which they sat down over us. I have no idea what it was made of. It looked like glass, but since it was thirty feet in diameter and ten feet high and four men carried it with ease, it must have been made of some exceedingly light material. I could hear Kapioma's voice as plainly as though the dome were not over us.

"Let no one interfere," said the Sibama. "I will count to five. When I have given the final number you may fight, but not before. Are you ready? One! Two!"

A blinding green flash came from one of the arms of Lamu's suit. My left arm fell useless, paralyzed by the deadly ray. Lamu threw back his head and raised an arm to shield his eyes from the brilliance. The ray passed from me with no further damage. I waited for the further counting of Kapioma. I was sure that he had instructed Lamu to start the battle before the final count, but I was equally sure that I would be punished if I did the same.

"Three!" came his voice after a pause. "Four!"

Lamu had recovered from the shock and with a crafty expression he was slowly bringing his green ray, which had been blazing harmlessly against the crystalline dome covering us, to bear on me. Nearer and nearer it came and still Kapioma did not give the final word. The ray touched my paralyzed arm and traveled down toward my leg.

"Five!" came Kapioma's voice at last.

My orange ray blazed forth and Lamu's green ray disappeared. I wasted a moment by turning my orange ray against my paralyzed arm and restoring it to usefulness. With it again normal, I could use two of my weapons at once.

I turned the orange ray again on Lamu and then turned on in rapid succession my red and my green. This was a fighting trick which Olua had taught me. There was a blinding flash from Lamu's suit and his green ray disappeared. One of his most powerful weapons was out of commission.

A scared look came on his face and his red ray blazed out. I was resolved to act only on the defensive until his weapons were destroyed and I turned off my orange, green and red rays and let my blue one blaze forth. Vainly Lamu strove to pierce the shield of blue light with which I covered myself. He reached toward his suit again and a white ray began to play beside the red. Olua had told me of this terrible ray, which extracted the water from any substance on which it struck and I hurriedly turned on my yellow ray to combat it. Round and round one another we circled, his rays trying vainly to find a hole in my armor of light. I strove to remember other tricks which Olua had told me of and one came to my mind. I suddenly turned off both my rays. Lamu swung the two blazing arms of his fighting suit toward my heart. I waited until the two rays overlapped one another and then turned on my green and yellow. With only one ray to guard against, it was a simple matter to keep him at bay.

I could remember no method of putting his white ray out of operation and to avoid prolonging the battle indefinitely, I turned on my green ray suddenly and directed it against his legs. Before he could switch to his orange ray to combat it, the paralyzing ray had got in its deadly effect and he fell in a heap. I hastened forward and stood over him. Olua had told me that almost any ray was deadly against the force which generated it. I seized the arm from which the white ray was blazing and slowly twisted it around. Lamu strove to fight, but a touch of my paralyzing ray made his arms as useless as were his legs. Slowly I twisted his arm until the white ray bore back against the arm from which it came. In another moment the ray ceased to glow and Lamu was shorn of his weapons.

A touch of either of my three offensive rays would have finished him, but I was not minded to kill him in that way. I bent over him and stripped his wrecked fighting suit from him. I tossed it to one side and stepped back. My orange ray glowed for an instant and Lamu rose as well and strong as he had been at the start of the battle.

"This fight is between you and me, Lamu Siba," I said slowly and menacingly. "Prepare to die at my hands."

Quickly I ripped my fighting suit from me. Lamu watched me like a cat. Once my arms were engaged in getting out of the suit he straightened up and rushed. I stepped back and to one side and gave him an opening. His right foot flew out and caught me a violent blow in the groin. With a cry of anguish I doubled up in pain and Lamu threw himself on me, a dagger gleaming in his hand.

I had sense enough left to twist to one side and Lamu's dagger merely scored my back. The pain of his foul blow was terrible and I was unarmed, but as he closed again I wriggled out of my suit and launched myself at his throat. His dagger flashed before my eyes but I disregarded it and closed with him. I grasped him by the throat and hurled myself to the ground, dragging him with me. I felt a burning pain in my shoulder and another in my side before my knee found his chest and I could wrench the dagger from his grasp and hurl it away. My hands closed again on his throat and I began to squeeze. His face grew purple and he looked at me appealingly. I released the pressure for a moment and put my head down.

"Mercy, Courtney Sibama," came in a coarse whisper from his lips.

"When did you show mercy?" I demanded. "Where is Awlo? Where is Kalu Sibama? Where is ravaged Ulm? Your life is trebly forfeit for your treachery and there is no mercy in my heart."

Slowly I tightened my grip on his throat. His breath came in gasps and then in a rattling wheeze. His head sank back, his eyes starting from their sockets and staring horribly. I can see those eyes yet. Still kneeling on his chest, I released my grip on his throat and seized his head and twisted it slowly around. Further and further it went until the vertebrae gave with a snap and his head fell limp. So died Lamu Siba, Prince of Ame of the Empire of Ulm at the hands of his ruler, whom he had betrayed.

I staggered to my feet and faced Kapioma.

"Your decree has been executed, oh Sibama," I cried between gasps. "When may I and my subjects depart?"

"As soon as you are recovered from your wounds and can travel, Courtney," he said gravely. "I am disappointed at the showing that dog made, but the word of the Sibama once pledged, may not be recalled. You are only changing the quick and honorable death of a soldier for a lingering death of thirst and starvation in the mountains. You have made your choice. Remember, however, that my offer of your life is still open. Divorce Awlo and I give it to you freely."

I straightened up to hurl a defiance into his teeth, but I could do no more. I had lost more blood than I realized and I swayed a moment and then everything went black. I seemed to be falling through an endless distance and then I could remember nothing more.

It was four days before I recovered consciousness, but when I did, I was ready to travel. The physicians of Kau had treated me with healing rays which had healed my wounds and restored my strength. I really felt little the worse for the terrible battle I had been through. Moka wished me to rest for a few more days, but I did not dare. The date of the death of the Sibimi of Kau was only fourteen days away and unless we could return to Kau before that time, I shuddered to think of the fate of Awlo. Accordingly, I sent word to Kapioma that I held him to his promise and desired to depart at once.

Somewhere in his heart there must have been a speck of chivalry which had not been bred out, for he came to the power house in person to see our departure.

"Farewell, Courtney Sibama," he said, "for once I have released you from slavery, your royal rank returns. I am sorry that you would not accede to the very lenient terms I offered you, for I believe you would be a useful member of my court. However, I have pledged my word and you may depart. I am merely changing the form of your death. You cannot return to Kau. If you stay in the mountains, you starve, and if you go to Ulm the Mena will kill you. In any event, you will be removed from my path in a few weeks."

I humbled myself to ask one favor before I left.

"Since I am going to death, Kapioma Sibama," I said, "I ask of your mercy one thing. I wish to see Awlo before I go."

His brow darkened.

"That is impossible," he said coldly. "Awlo does not know of your presence here and thinks you are dead. You soon will be and I have no wish to refresh her memory and reawaken her sorrows. It would turn her against me."

I did not trust myself to speak further but entered the waiting transport. My men followed me and in a few moments we rose rapidly into the air and headed away to the west.

"Where shall we land you, Courtney Sibama?" asked Nei-meha, who was in command.

"Land us at the spot where you found me," I replied.

He shrugged his shoulders and spoke to the pilot. Two

hours after leaving Kaulani, the transport dropped to a landing and we debarked. The ship hovered over us for a few minutes and then turned back toward the capital of Kau. Moka approached me as the Kauan ship disappeared.

"What are your plans, Courtney Sibama?" he asked.

"We will return to Kau and rescue our Sibimi. Thereafter we will do as circumstances direct."

"We are but a hundred and two," said Moka doubtfully, "and the army of Kau numbers thousands. Can we hope to win through to victory?"

"A hundred men properly armed can do wonders, Moka," I replied. "Have you forgotten the weapons which I went from Ulm to bring? They are hidden in these mountains. We will go to where they are and then make our plans. With them we will find an Alii of Ulm who has lived in Kau for years and knows their weapons. Do you think that the Kauan ship will return to watch our movements?"

"Since we are forbidden to return, I think it will."

"I hope so. If they do, I have an idea that may enable us to reach Kaulani without a fight. The first thing to do is to get proper arms."

My marching compass was one of the things which the Kauans had returned to me before they left us. My automatic pistols they had kept, although they were not familiar with their use. I laid off a course with the compass and, laden down with food and water, we started our journey toward the adjuster.

Moka had been right when he said that the Kauans would keep track of us. Late that afternoon, while our cavalcade was struggling wearily over the bare rocks, the transport which had brought us to the mountains sailed over us at a low elevation. The sight of our progress evidently satisfied them, for after a careful survey of our column, they returned toward Kaulani. Night fell before we had covered more than half the distance which I calculated separated us from the adjuster, but I was confident that we were going in the right direction.

The night was bitterly cold and as we had nothing resembling blankets, all we could do was to huddle together and pass the night as best we could. The men of Ulm were unaccustomed to cold weather and they suffered horribly but none of them complained. The next morning we took up our march.

By noon I was confident that we had come far enough, yet

none of the landscape was familiar. I halted the column and sent parties of scouts off in various directions. They were all ordered to reassemble at the central point before sundown.

It was a hard task to find one's way about the rugged country, even with a compass. I nearly got lost and the sun was setting when my party returned to camp. Two of the parties were still unaccounted for. We had no material with which to make fires and all we could do was to send up occasional shouts to guide the stragglers. One party came in about eight o'clock but morning dawned without trace of the other one. I was surprised at this, for I knew of the wonderful sense of direction and location which is the gift of all Ulmites. I made some tests and soon found that this sense was not operative in the mountains. Why, I can't explain. It just wasn't.

I held a consultation with Hama and Moka the next morning. I was sure that we were close to the adjuster and the ammunition and yet we had combed the country the day before and found nothing. I had a feeling that we were too far south and favored moving the camp, but the problem of the lost party remained to be solved. We finally decided to leave ten men under Hama at our first camp and move the rest some five miles north, keeping in touch by means of messengers. At the new camp I would send out fresh search parties. This programme we carried out, but another two days of combing the hills failed to locate the adjuster and I began to fear that the Kauans had found it and moved it. The fourth and fifth days passed in similar fashion and even my staunchest supporter, Moka, began to look dubious.

The morning of the sixth day we were about to start fresh parties out on their interminable search when a faint shout was heard from the south and we saw one of Hama's party approaching at top speed. As he came nearer, it was evident that he was laboring under great excitement.

"We have found the place, Sibama!" he gasped as he came within hearing. "Hiko's party found it the first day but the messenger they sent fell and broke a leg. It was not until today that he crawled into our camp, nearly dead from pain and thirst. He says that Hiko and two men stayed there, but he does not know where it is."

The fact that the adjuster had been found near our camp was a heartening thing and we swiftly broke camp and retraced our steps to join Hama's party. We found that Hama had sent off all his men in the direction in which Hiko had left the camp and all we could do was to wait until they found the place. We had not waited more than three hours when a man arrived and told us that he had located it. He said that they had found the cave and the boxes in it, but that there were no signs of Olua or the adjuster. I started at once with a party with food and water for Hiko's men, leaving most of the men in camp until all of Hama's men returned. They were to move camp and join me the next morning.

The report of the scout was correct. In the cave were the arm chests and the boxes of ammunition, but there was no trace of either Olua or the adjuster. I racked my brains as to what could have happened. The only explanation which seemed logical was that when he had returned to the larger plane at my orders, his adjuster got moved. In such a case he might easily have come down miles away and was earnestly seeking us. The loss of the adjuster was a blow, but we still had our arms and ammunition and everything was not lost.

It was a short task to break open the rifle chests and the ammunition boxes and I felt better when I saw my tiny force armed with modern rifles and pistols, even though none of them had the slightest idea of their use and I had grave doubts of their value against the fighting suits of the Kauans. The fact that they did not know how to use the weapons did not worry me especially, for I knew that I had eight days before the Sibimi of Kau was doomed to die and I had a plan which, if successful, would enable us to travel over the two hundred miles which separated us from Kaulani in a short time. The Kauan transport had flown over us each afternoon, evidently checking our movements and my plan was a no less daring one than attempting its capture. I blessed the fact that I had not completed my radiotelegraphic apparatus before I left the city.

My first task was to teach my men the use of the pistols and rifles. I had loaded a hundred rifles and thirty thousand rounds of ammunition on the adjuster together with a hundred pistols and ten thousand rounds of pistol ammunition. I felt that I could safely expend one hundred rounds of rifle ammunition per man and half that amount of pistol ammunition on target practise. We improvised a range and posted guards to warn us of the approach of Kauan ships. The Ulmites took to the guns as ducks take to water. In five days I felt my fire discipline was adequate and I anxiously awaited the arrival of the ship I had planned to capture.

To my horror, the ship did not appear on that day, nor the next day, nor yet on the next. Our food and water were about exhausted, for we had been allowed only a fourteen-day supply. Apparently the Kauans knew that we could not return to their country and had decided that we were afraid to face the Mena and thought it useless to keep further track of us. As the sun went down on the fourteenth day after we had left Kaulani, I was in black despair. That was the day set for the execution of the Sibimi of Kau and the thought of my princess at the mercy of Kapioma nearly drove me insane.

We could not possibly cover the two hundred miles separating us from Kaulani in less than five days of forced marching, even were we adequately supplied with food and water and unopposed. I had based all my plans on the capture of a Kauan ship. The morning of the fifteenth day found us with no water and almost no food and despair settled over the camp. We felt the urge to be moving but there was no place where we could go and nothing that we could do. We went through some rifle drill in the morning in a perfunctory manner and with the feeling that it was merely a waste of time.

In an endeavor to keep my men from brooding, I took them out on the improvised range again in the afternoon, but there was no enthusiasm. We were all suffering badly from thirst. I was about to order them back to camp when a shout from one of the lookouts whom we had posted as a routine matter, brought us to our feet. The lookout was shouting and pointing to the east. In the sudden silence which fell, I could feel rather than hear, the distant hum of propellors. Our plans had been made long ago and my men rapidly took the ambush formation I had laid out, while others, as the Kauans appeared, started a dropping fire at the distant targets.

I had counted on the curiosity of the Kauans to bring them to the ground to see what we were doing, nor was I disappointed. The ship hovered over our range for fifteen agonizing minutes before it swooped to a landing, a hundred yards from our firing point. A detachment of Kauans, wearing six-armed fighting suits, debarked and approached the firing line. I was hidden behind a rock perhaps fifty yards from the ship. The angle at which the ship landed was such that I could not see the control board through the open door, a vital necessity, if we were to capture the ship. I waited until the Kauans had passed me and blew my whistle.

A burst of fire came from the line and the Kauans staggered back under the impact of the heavy bullets at short range. The fighting suits held and none of them were injured. Green and red rays shot out from the arms of the fighting suits. Half a dozen of my men dropped helpless and the Kauans advanced slowly in a line. This was the moment for which I had been waiting. Holding my fire at ready, I raced across the ground behind the fighters. The angle at which I ran brought the control panel into view through the open door. I dropped prone and cuddled my rifle to my cheek. I had been nervous, but when the moment came to fire, I was as steady as a rock. I picked out the switch which controlled the current which fed the fighting suits. The switch sat for a moment on top of my front sight as I slowly squeezed my trigger. With a crash the rifle went off. In an instant the rays died out in mid-air, and with a cheer my men leaped to their feet. A volley rang out and the ground was sprinkled with dead and dying Kauans. I had effectually disabled every fighting suit in the ship.

The pilot of the ship was not napping. My men raced toward the ship, but when the nearest was still fifty yards away, the central propeller began to whir and the ship moved forward. Hiko was the nearest and he almost reached it when a blinding white flash came from its side and he dropped in his tracks. The ship moved forward with rapidly gathering momentum.

My men raced after it, but I knew the use of a rifle better than they did. I rammed a fresh shell into my piece and took careful aim. As my shot rang out, the central propeller slowed down for a moment and I hastily reloaded my gun. My second shot went wild, but the third scored a bull's eye and the propeller slowed visibly and ran out of true. A fourth shot, the last in my magazine, stopped it entirely and the ship, with only the two wing propellers turning, sank toward the ground.

"After it!" I shouted, and my men toiled valiantly toward the dropping ship. I did not dare to risk a shot at a wing propeller lest the ship crash so badly that we would be unable to repair it. The ship touched the ground and came to a standstill. My men rushed forward with a shout of triumph. They had almost reached it when another blinding crash came from the side and two of the Ulmites crumpled in their tracks.

It was apparent that the Kauans possessed other means of offense than their fighting suits, but they seemed to be effective only at short range. I called my men back and a volley from our rifles riddled the transport. A second and third volley were poured into the cabin for safety's sake before we cautiously approached. No flash greeted us and we opened the doors to find the interior of the cabin a shambles.

The soldiers removed the dead bodies while I inspected the ship. Aside from my first shot, not a one had struck the control panel, but the central propeller was wrecked. A cursory inspection showed me that the switch which controlled the fighting suits was hopelessly wrecked, but as my men did not know how to use those terrible weapons, it was a matter of small moment. I knew that every Kauan ship carried a set of spare propellers and I soon located them and set some of my men at work removing the damaged one. The Ulmites were about as clumsy with tools as it is possible to imagine and in the end I had to do most of the work myself. The result was that the sun had nearly set before I tested the new propeller with the control panel and found that it had been properly installed. Our party embarked and I took my place at the controls. A hundred-man transport was not built for one man to fly and I had my troubles. How I cursed the luck which had made Olua miss the place when he returned to Kau in the adjuster. I would have given a great deal to have him at my side. However, what must be done can be done and I got the ship into the air and headed for Kaulani.

For half an hour we made our way east without incident. A shout from the forward lookout apprised us of danger and Moka hastened to his side. He glanced through the telescope and informed me that three Kauan warships were approaching at high speed. I dared not leave the controls for an instant, so I hastily gave him directions for the fight which I felt was approaching and I drove forward.

The leading Kauan ship approached to within fifty yards and a string of illuminated signals broke out above her wings. I had no idea what they meant. The ship passed by, swung around in a circle and flew parallel to us about a hundred yards away with the strange signals flying. I gave the word to Moka.

A burst of rifle fire came from our ports and I had the satisfaction of seeing the Kauan ship reel wildly for a moment and then plunge headlong toward the ground. The other ships had not been fired on and they approached rapidly, one on either side. As the first one swept past us there was a blinding flash of purple light from her side. I was conscious of a feeling as though I had been struck a heavy blow, but they had miscalculated the range. While our ship reeled in the air, she righted herself and went on. The fire of our riflemen was deadly and the second ship plunged to the ground after the first.

The third ship had learned caution. It swung past us at a much greater range. When it was opposite us, a tiny spot of intense light shone for an instant and every switch on our power panel flew open. Our ship reeled and started to fall, but I dropped the flying controls and rushed to the panel. With both hands I closed the switches and then grasped the controls again and tried to right the ship. I had barely succeeded when the spot of light shone again and I had to repeat the task.

"Fire at them, Moka!" I cried. "Never mind the range!"

At my words, the burst of fire came from our ship but again the light glowed, this time before I had the ship under control. We turned nose down and fell rapidly. Apparently satisfied that they had put us out of commission, the Kauan ship turned her tail to us and sped away in the gathering darkness. I closed the switches and with all three propellers whirling at top speed, I strove desperately to right the ship. Nearer and nearer we came to the ground, but I wrenched at the controls with all my strength. Just before we struck I felt the craft respond to my efforts and slowly start to gain altitude. A dropping fire had been kept up at the flying Kauan and just as we started to climb, a shout of joy from Moka, who was at the telescope, told us that it was in trouble. At our best speed we drove it and soon it was again visible, flying slowly and in evident distress. A few well-directed shots ended the fight. We left it in ruins and resumed our course for Kaulani. Again I thanked my lucky stars that Kau did not have wireless communication.

Darkness came on rapidly, but I held my course by compass and in less than an hour the lights of Kaulani loomed before us. With all my lights blazing I headed boldly for the power house and landed on the roof. A detachment of the guard came to meet us and we opened the door and emerged. Ten of my men had donned the useless fighting suits of the dead Kauans and they led the way with me in their midst and the rest of the Ulmites trooped along after as though they were prisoners.

"What means this, Homena?" demanded the officer who had approached us.

These were the last words he spoke, for Moka had him by the throat before he could utter another. Before the menace of the lifted arms of the fighting suits, the unarmed Kauan guards surrendered and were taken into the flyer and bound and gagged. The ten men equipped with fighting suits, with me again an apparent prisoner in their midst, trooped down the stairs to the laboratory. We paused outside and I heard the buzz of a wireless transmitter. Waimua was apparently at work.

I motioned my men aside and softly opened the door. Waimua was alone in the laboratory and he looked up with a smile when I entered.

"Ah, Courtney," he said, "you are just in time. I have been hearing some signals on my receiver—"

He broke off as I covered him with my pistol.

"I want to save your life, Waimua," I said, "for you were kind to me, but to do so you must surrender to me. I am in control of the power house and my men are outside. If you make a sound, I will kill you where you stand."

"What do you mean?" he asked in amazement.

"Exactly what I say. We have returned from the Kau mountains to rescue our Sibimi and we will brook no interference. Raise your hands in token of surrender or I'll shoot."

Slowly he raised his hands as I ordered. I turned to call my men, and he sprang. Not at me, but toward a button which was on his laboratory table. I liked Waimua, but it was his life or mine and with mine, Awlo's. My pistol spat out a message of death and the luckless scientist fell in a heap. At the sound of my weapon, my men burst in. We barred the door and waited breathlessly. Not a sound came from outside. Apparently the Kauans were enough accustomed to strange sounds from the laboratory to remain unalarmed at my shot.

Satisfied that we would not be interrupted, I took an ordinary six-armed fighting suit from the wall and donned it. I measured a distance of fourteen inches from the top of the huge testing screen, which covered one entire end of the laboratory and eleven inches from the left edge. I marked the place and stepped back. I pointed my red ray at the intersection of the two lines I had drawn and left it on full force for eight seconds. I shut it off and supplied the orange ray for twelve seconds. As I shut the orange ray off, a section of the screen opened slowly forward and there, in a recess cut behind the screen, lay the fighting suit of which Olua had told me. I drew it out and examined it.

The suit weighed less than twenty pounds, despite its thirty arms. I took off the six-armed suit which I was wearing and donned the new garment. It fit me like a glove and was not much more uncomfortable than an ordinary suit of clothes.

Olua had explained the suit to me and I found detailed instructions with it. I stepped back and spent several minutes in practising the use of the various controls against the protective screen. I did not have time to try all of them and no time to learn which control actuated which weapons, but I did locate the master control, which threw on all of the protective rays at once. Satisfied that I had learned enough, I led the way out of the laboratory.

For some unknown reason, we passed through the building and into the grounds without a challenge, although the sight of a detachment of eleven men in fighting suits in the Sibama's palace ground was enough to attract attention. We stole quietly toward the royal palace until we were under the south wing, where we knew Awlo to be confined. Moka pointed out her window to me and I gave my rifle to him and grasped a creeper which clothed the wall. It was a hard climb and I was tempted several times to return to the ground and take off the cumbersome fighting suit which I wore, but better judgment prevailed and I struggled on. At last I climbed to a point where I could look into her room. It was apparently empty and I inserted the point of my dagger and pried the window open and stepped into the room.

I found myself in a luxuriously furnished apartment, but a hasty search through the rooms proved them to be as empty as the grave. My heart fell, for I feared that Awlo had already been dragged to Kapioma's chambers. I tried the doors leading from the rooms and one of them opened at my touch. I found myself in a deserted corridor and I stole softly along it. I had almost reached an intersecting way when a slight noise behind me made me swing around. A hidden panel in the wall I had just passed was slowly opening and I stepped beside it.

A Kauan Alii made his appearance and turned toward me. As he saw me, he opened his mouth to shout, but my green ray blazed forth for an instant and he stopped petrified. He had done me no harm and with my orange ray I removed the paralysis from his brain. His tongue I left helpless and before I left him I treated both his legs with a dose from my paralyzing ray. I left him helpless and went on.

I found myself in a secret passage, dimly lighted, and I stole along it for a few yards and found it ended in a stairway. I debated for a moment as to what course to pursue and then stole back to the panel. It was closed and I could not find the spring or lever which operated it. It would have been an easy matter to have burnt my way through with my heat ray, but I did not care to start a possible fire in the palace. I thought of restoring to speech the Alii who lay helpless before me, but knowing the Kauans as I did, I felt certain that his first action would be to give the alarm. Despite their cruelty and treachery, they were intensely loyal to their Sibama.

There was only one alternative. With a prayer in my heart, I returned to the stairway and proceeded down it. I went down a long flight and paused on a landing place where I could hear a murmur of voices. I touched the wall before me and found that it was no wall but a hanging. Cautiously I cut a slit with my dagger and peered through.

I was looking into the throne room from a point behind and slightly to one side of the two central thrones. The room was empty save for a small group which stood before the throne. I didn't stop to count them, for my eyes were focused on one of them and my heart gave a bound which threatened to burst my ribs. The central figure was my adored princess, Awlo of Ulm. I could hear a voice speaking from the throne which was concealed from my gaze and I recognized it as Kapioma's.

"The Sibimi's throne of Kau is empty," he said in a voice which sounded as though he were repeating an argument for the hundredth time, "and I offer you the honor of filling it. I could take you without this formality, but such is not my wish. You blood is royal and your children would be worthy of the throne of Kau, which they would occupy some day. Will you bid me lay aside the panoply of war and don the robes of peace that I may wed you honorably?"

Awlo threw back her proud head.

"Never!" she cried. "My lord, Courtney Sibama, lives and will rescue me. I could not be your Sibimi if I wished and would not if I could."

"I tell you that Courtney is dead," protested Kapioma.

"Not until I see his corpse will I believe that and when I do, my life will end as well," she said haughtily. "Beware what you do, Kapioma Sibama, the arm of my lord is long and he knows how to avenge any indignity to which I am subjected."

"Enough of this!" cried Kapioma angrily. "I am offering you no indignity but honorable marriage and the rank of Sibimi of the greatest empire in the world. If you will not wed me willingly, you will by force. Wedlock is essential that your children may be lawfully called to the throne of Kau. Where is the Mayor of the Palace?"

A gorgeously dressed functionary stepped forward.

"You shall wed us, Wiki," said Kapioma, "and as I have on her by conquest, I will be wed in the panoply of war."

He stepped down from the dais into the range of my vision. Had it not been for his voice, I would not have known him, for he wore a fighting suit from which fully forty arms protruded. The weight must have been great for he moved slowly and as if with an effort. As he approached, the Mayor of the Palace stepped forward toward Awlo, but recoiled as though she had been a deadly snake. In her hand gleamed a jeweled dagger.

"One step nearer and I will sheath this weapon in my heart!" she cried.

The Mayor stopped but Awlo could not fight alone the weapons of Kau. A green flash came momentarily from Kapioma's suit and the dagger dropped from her paralyzed arm. She turned to run but another flash, this time of a paler green, filled the room for an instant and she stopped in her tracks. Kapioma's guttural laugh rang out as he advanced to where she stood motionless. He took her hand in his and kissed it and then placed it for a moment on top of his head. He held out his hand and the Mayor of the Palace took it respectfully and raised it toward Awlo's lips. A sharp report rang out and the Mayor staggered and fell headlong. Unfamiliar as I was with Olua's fighting suit, I preferred to use the weapon I knew. I have mentioned before that I am a good shot, especially at short range.

A sweep of my dagger opened a way for me through the tapestry and I stepped out into view. The time for ordinary weapons had passed and I dropped both pistol and dagger and placed my hands on the control buttons of my fighting suit. I swung the deadly offensive arms toward Kapioma and prepared to launch my deadly assortment of rays at him. The guards, armed with spears, were approaching from all sides.

"One step nearer and your Sibama dies!" I shouted.

The Sibama stared at me for a moment and a look of wonder came into his eyes.

"Courtney Sibama!" he cried.

I bowed my head in acknowledgement but I did not take my eyes off him. It was well that I did not. Slowly his hands sought the control buttons of his massive fighting suit.

"Stop that!" I warned sharply. "If you try to use a weapon you are a dead man."

He dropped his hand and stared fixedly at me. The situation was a stalemate. Kapioma did not dare to move and I could not pick the helpless Awlo up and leave with her. I thought of trying a blast of one of my rays at Kapioma but I was not sure just which ones his fighting suit would stop instantly. Besides, if I opened hostilities, Awlo might be killed in the blasts of rays which would fill the throne room. For a full minute we stared at one another and then Kapioma spoke.

"Courtney Sibama," he said slowly, "one of us will never leave this room alive. You are wearing a fighting suit of a type I do not recognize. I wear the most powerful suit in Kau. Which of the two will win in a conflict, neither of us knows. If we fight in the open, no one can prophesy what the result to all in this room will be."

He paused and I nodded assent to his word but did not relax my vigilance.

"We both desire the same thing—the life and person of Awlo of Ulm," he went on, "and one of us will win it. Let her be won in fair fight and to the victor she shall belong."

"What do you mean?" I asked.

"Let a fighting dome be brought and placed over us. When the signal is given, we will prove which of our fighting suits is the most powerful. To the survivor shall belong the princess."

"If I win, have I the promise that Awlo and I can leave Kau with our subjects without hindrance?" I demanded.

"You may, without hindrance from me. Further than that I cannot promise. The word of a dead Sibama does not bind his successor. However, if you win, you should be able to fight your way out of the kingdom with fighting suits."

I hesitated for a minute. If I fought him and lost, my princess was doomed. If I won, all I could hope for was the chance to battle my way out with her in my arms. If, on the other hand, I refused his terms, she might easily be sacrificed during the battle in the open, which would ensue. I quickly made up my mind.

"Bring your fighting dome," I cried.

Guards hastened out to get it. Still keeping my hands on the control buttons of my suit, I walked down the steps of the dais and took my place facing Kapioma. The dome was brought in and placed over us.

"Take your hands from your controls, Courtney Sibama," said Kapioma, "in order that we may start equally."

I dropped my hands to my side. The Sibama turned to the ring of spectators.

"Noma," he said to an Alii who stood there, "take a spear from a guard and drop it. When that spear strikes the ground, the battle will commence."

The Alii took a spear and poised it. He stood in such a position that each of us could see him equally well. He poised the spear above his head for an instant and then let it fall.

The fractions of a second that passed before that spear reached the floor seemed like days and weeks. It seemed to move with infinitesimal slowness. I stole a glance around and the scene burned itself on my brain. Kapioma stood a few feet from me with a confident smile on his yellow face, his slant black eyes gleaming fiercely. All about us stood the Alii and guards of Kau, their yellow faces alight with excitement. Like a white flower stood out the form of my beloved princess, rigid in the grasp of the rays which Kapioma had poured out on her. I looked back and saw that the spear had almost reached the floor. Another glance at Kapioma showed that he had not moved but stood with muscles tense, waiting for the signal. At least, he was a fair fighter.

The spear struck the floor and my hands flew to the control buttons of my suit. I tugged the master button of the defensive buttons in the nick of time for the red and green rays flashed out from half a dozen of the arms of Kapioma's suits. They were absorbed harmlessly in the refulgence with which I was bathed. He stepped back a moment and shifted his hands.

His first attack with his simpler weapons had failed and he was prepared to use weapons which were individual to his suit.

I remembered what Olua had told me and shut off my general protective ray. I hastily tugged at my fifth, sixteenth and seventeenth buttons. A dazzling kaleidoscope of colors surrounded me and I heard a report from Kapioma's suit. His simple paralyzing and heat rays had been rendered useless.

His hand found the buttons he wished and a fresh menace threatened me. From him came a cloud of purple gas which rolled rapidly toward me. I knew the weapon to use against that and I tugged at my eleventh button. The cloud of gas was drawn rapidly into one of the arms of my suit. I pressed my twelfth button and a cloud of yellow vapor rolled toward him. As his hands sought his defensive weapons, I tugged my ninth button and the gas dissolved into a blinding flash which rushed toward him. It struck him full on the chest and drove him back with the violence of the shock. I followed up my advantage with my violet ray, but he had recovered from the momentary effects, of the surprise he had received and shot out a furry spiral of red flame, which twisted in and out before him and rendered the purple ray helpless.

From another arm came alternate flashes of red and white. I pulled on a defensive weapon but it had no effect. Through my protective screens the deadly ray was eating its way. I felt as though my veins were filled with liquid fire. Frantically I tugged at button after button. Cloud of deadly gases and vivid rays of various sorts leaped from the arms of my suit but Kapioma met each attack with a weapon of his own and rendered my efforts futile. And still that deadly red and white ate into my screen. It was a matter of seconds only before the end would come.

In desperation I used my final weapon. Olua had cautioned me not to use, except as a last resort. With a sob I tugged at my thirtieth button. As I did so, a blinding flash came from one of the arms of my suit. It struck Kapioma and coiled itself around him. Fighting against the strange power at every step, he was dragged relentlessly toward me. The red and white still glowed and my body seemed parched and dried up but I could not think of that. In another moment he would be within reach.

Despite his struggles, he was drawn closer until I could

reach him with my hands. I understood why Olua had warned me against this weapon for my strength was rapidly oozing away. It took a tremendous toll of the user. Kapioma reached for other buttons but he was unable to use them. This thirtieth weapon of Olua's was nothing less than an electrical harnessing of the will of the user and while Kapioma was in its grasp, his will was a slave to mine. As I realized the nature of the strange force I was wielding, I concentrated on what I wished him to do. Slowly and reluctantly his hand sought his controls. He tugged at one and the deadly red and white which was eating into my very brain died out. I was temporarily safe.

I threw all the force of my will into the struggle and the force I exerted was magnified a thousand times by the instrument which Olua's genius had evolved. Kapioma tugged button after button, until not a ray gleamed from his suit and not a single deadly gas even oozed from it. With almost my last effort I pulled my second button and bathed him for an instant in the common green paralyzing ray carried by even the simplest fighting suits. He wavered a moment and then dropped in a heap. I shut off the terrible weapon with which I had conquered and swayed in weakness for a moment.

I thought I was going to fall, but I didn't. My eyes caught a glimpse of Awlo and it acted like a dash of cold water in my face. I braced myself up and faced the spectators.

"Remove the fighting dome!" I cried, "and make way for Courtney, Sibama of Ulm!"

The dome was hastily lifted from me. As I approached Awlo, there was a disturbance at the door. I looked up and a more welcome sight never met my eyes. In the doorway stood Moka with a half dozen Ulmites with rifles in their hands ranged behind him. Four figures in six-armed fighting suits stood beside him.

"Way!" I cried imperiously, "Way for the men of Ulm! Way ere I blast a path through your living bodies!"

There was a general scurry at my words and the space between Moka and me opened. Down the path came my loyal Ulmites. At my orders two of them handed their rifles to comrades and tenderly picked up the form of my beloved princess. Down through the ranks of the scowling Kauans we passed until the door of the palace opened before us. Guards stepped forward to bar our way, long black tubes in their hands. I hesitated only a moment. The poor fellows wore no fighting suits and it was almost murder but I did not dare to hesitate. I tugged my fourteenth button and a flash of violet flame leaped in front of me. The guards went down like ten-pins, their black tubes exploding with brilliant flashes of light. As we emerged from the doorway, a distant crackle of rifle fire told us that Hama's party had left the roof and were fighting their way down through the power house. In a compact group we raced across the lawn toward the building.

We had covered about half the distance before we were opposed. I heard a shout behind us and turned and looked Emerging from the trees at one side were a group of figures in fighting suits. We were a little closer to the power house than they were, but we were handicapped by our rifles and we had to carry Awlo. It looked as though we would arrive at the door at about the same moment. My decision was made in an instant. Warning Moka to hold straight for the door, I turnd at an angle and raced to meet them.

As I approached the newcomers stopped and rays began to flash from the arms of their fighting suits. None of the suits carried more than ten arms, so I pulled on my general protective rays and charged them. They strove to run but they were too late. Again my fourteenth button came into play and they toppled in heaps. I glanced over my shoulder and saw that Moka's party had gained the doorway.

I bounced through the door and Hama slammed it shut behind me. I was positive that there were protective rays of some sort that could be brought into action but I did not dare to look for them. Hama told me that the power house was clear of Kauans except for one room in which a few were barricaded. I knew that they would soon emerge wearing fighting suits and that more men from the palace would be using more potent weapons against us in a few minutes. With Hama and Moka at my back, I ran for the central control room. I reached it just in time.

My hand was on the switch controlling the fighting suit power when a door opened and a dozen figures wearing many-armed suits entered. I let them approach a few feet and pulled the switch just as their hands were seeking the control buttons. When I pulled that switch every fighting suit and every weapon of war in the empire of Kau became useless. It took me only a few seconds to pull the other four controlling switches and everything which depended on power in the empire was useless. The science of our enemies was at an end and the battle, if battle there was, would be fought out hand to hand in the same manner as the old battles with the Mena. The only power left in the land was a tiny auxiliary generator which fed the lights in the power house itself. As we saw in the morning, my action in pulling the switches came none too soon. Two huge Kauan warships had crashed in ruins not a hundred yards from the building. Had I been a little slower, they would have landed on the roof and we would have been caught between two fires.

I left Awlo in the laboratory and hastened out to look after our defense. Although crippled by the loss of power, the Kauans were not altogether helpless. They were present in tremendous numbers and they still had a quantity of the black tubes which I had noticed in the hands of the guards at the palace gates. These tubes were not dependent on power for their discharge, although once fired, they could not be reloaded while the generators were shut down. They carried a large charge of static electricity and at short range they were very deadly.

Armed with the tubes and with spears, the Kauans made a determined assault on our fortress. The attack was doomed to failure from the first. The flash tubes were not dangerous at ranges of over fifty yards and we mowed down the attackers with our deadly rifle fire. The attack waned after a few minutes and I returned to the laboratory.

Awlo lay on a table, cold and rigid. There was a complete absence of respiration and I could not detect the slightest flicker of a pulse. I would have unhesitatingly pronounced her dead, had I not seen what had happened to her. I knew that Kapioma would never have fought for the possession of a dead body and I was confident that there was some method of reviving her, could I only find it. I ordered Moka to turn on the switch which controlled the fighting suit I had worn. He did so and I bathed her in a refulgence of the orange antiparalysis ray. It had not the slightest effect. For an hour I experimented with various rays and combinations of them without result. I did not dare to use most of the weapons in Olua's fighting suit for I was not aware of all of their properties and I might easily do more harm than good.

As I studied her prostrate figure, I was alarmed by a crash at the main door of the house. I started down to investigate, but a messenger from Hama met me before I got there.

"A Kauan!" the man gasped, "a Kauan in a fighting suit has broken in the door and has killed a dozen of our men!"

The explanation rushed to my mind. When I had connected up the generator which had actuated my fighting suit, I had also supplied power to Kapioma's, which worked on the same wave-length. I hurried to the control room and pulled off the switch. A crackle of fire from below told me that my men were engaged. I rushed down the steps to take charge, but I was no longer needed. When the fighting suit was rendered helpless, our rifles came into their own and they made short work of the Kauans, who had followed their leader in through the wrecked door.

In an hour the door was repaired and we were again in a position to bid defiance to the armies of Kau, but I learned with regret that the fleeing Kauans had carried off the body of their leader and so, of course, his fighting suit. If we had it, two of us could have walked unopposed throughout Kaulani. As it was, I did not dare to again turn on any of the generators which would arm our enemies. Since I had no idea of what to do for Awlo, even had I had plenty of power, it did not seem to matter much.

In point of fact, our situation had many elements devoid of cheer in it. To be sure we were comparatively safe in the power house, but we had no way of getting out. We had a hundred-man flyer at our service, but if we turned on power to run it, we mobilized every warship in Kau. We plenty of powerful fighting suits, but there were more powerful ones in the hands of some of the Alii of Kau and arming our suits meant arming theirs. As far as I could figure out, in capturing the power house, I had put myself in the classic position of the man who had caught the bear by the tail; I needed a lot of help to hang on and a darned sight more help to let go.

I went back to the laboratory and studied the rigid figure of Awlo, but no new suggestion came to me and I lay down for a few minutes of rest, hoping that time would solve the problem. In any event, I felt sure that we could hold the power house indefinitely. In thinking this, however, I had underestimated the power and resourcefulness of the Alii of Kau, as the morning showed.

All night we heard the sounds of men working and saw faint lights flickering back and forth across the lawn. We tried them with a shot occasionally but we had no ammunition to waste and I ordered the men to hold their fire. When day broke, we saw on the lawn between the palace and the power-house, an enormous machine made of metal. As we watched, it moved slowly forward toward the power house. I had forgotten that the Alii and even the soldiers and commoners of Kau were familiar with electricity in all of its forms. The obvious thing had occurred to them. Since their regular source of power had been shut off, they had collected or constructed batteries and were driving this tank, for that is what it looked like, toward us with direct current. From the moving mass of metal, heavy cables trailed back toward the palace.

I took a rifle and fired at that cable, directing my best shots to do the same. Despite the fire we poured in, the machine continued to advance until it was only a few yards from the building. From its side a bolt of what looked like lightning came and the power house door was again splintered and driven from its hinges. The machine moved forward for a few feet and stopped. No fresh bolts came from it and it was apparently helpless. At last a lucky shot had severed their connection with the source of power. We were temporarily saved.

As no fresh attack seemed imminent, I left Moka in charge of the defense and returned to the laboratory. It had occurred to me that direct current might have some effect on Awlo.

As I entered the laboratory, a familiar sound struck my ear. I paused and looked around but I could not locate the source. It was an intermittent buzzing and cracking and as I listened, it began to form itself into letters and words in my mind. "—.—. ———— ... .—. — —. . —.——," I heard and then "—.—. ———— ... .—. — —. . — .— ... . .—— ——.—." "COURTNEY, COURTNEY SIBAMA." There was only one person in the world who would be calling me by wireless and calling me by that title. I jumped for the radio set which had stood unheeded on the laboratory table since Waimua's death. As I clamped the headphones on my ear, the message came through plainly and distinctly. It was a matter of seconds only until I had the transmitter hooked up and ready to send. Luckily both sender and receiver drew their power from the auxiliary generator which normally supplied only the lights in the power house. I pounded my key rapidly.

"Olua," I called. "Olua, can you hear me?"

"Yes, Courtney Sibama," came the reply.

"Where are you?" I tapped out.

"At the cave, where we parted. The arms are gone. Did you return for them or did the Kauans get them?"

"I have the arms here."

"Where is here?"

"At the power house in Kaulani. I'll tell you the situation."

"All right, but send a little slower."

As briefly as possible I told him the events which had happened and the situation in which we were. I told him of the deadlock and that we were afraid to turn on any power. Last I told him of the attack launched by battery driven appliances that morning.

"How long can you hold out?" he asked.

As the message came in, a crash from below, followed by a burst of rifle fire, told me that a fresh attack had been launched. I told Olua of this fact.

"Battery apparatus won't do much harm," he answered. "If you can hold out for a few hours, I'll be with you and help you."

"How can you get here?" I asked, "There is no power being broadcast."

"I'll get there," he replied. "Look for me in three hours or less."

"Wait," I demanded. "I want one bit of information."

In a few words I described the condition of Awlo.

"Was it a light green ray with yellow flecks?" he asked.

"Yes."

"Use button twenty-eight on my suit for two seconds. Goodbye. I'll be with you soon."

Without regard to the risk I was running, I dashed to the control room and threw on the switch which actuated Olua's fighting suit. Back in the laboratory, I donned the garment and with trembling hands pulled button twenty-eight. Nothing happened for two seconds and then Awlo sat up. With a shout of joy I released the button and started for her. She gave me a cry of terror and strove to run. I stopped aghast at her reception of me, until I remembered the fighting suit which I wore. She took me for a Kauan.

"Awlo!" I cried as I threw back my helmet. "It is Courtney, your Courtney! Don't you know me?"

She looked at me in wonder and then with a sob of utter thankfulness threw herself into my arms. As I clasped her, there came an interruption. Moka dashed into the room.

"Sibama!" he cried. "Come quickly or we are lost. The Kauans are winning their way in."

So excited was he that he failed to notice Awlo. As I released her, his jaw dropped and he fell on one knee.

"Sibimi!" he cried and the worship in his voice made me realize anew the depth of affection which these tiny men had for their rulers. I gave him no further time.

"Come, Moka," I cried, as I pulled my helmet back into place, "we must go to the rescue."

I led the way down the stairs to the doorway. A number of Kauans equipped with fighting suits from which long leads trailed back to the palace, had crossed the lawn and forced their way through the shattered door. Bullets had no effect on them and my men went down like tenpins before the deadly rays which poured from them. Their feeble fighting suits, however, were no match for the one I wore and in three minutes after I arrived, not a live Kauan remained in the powerhouse. My violet ray disposed of them. As the last one fell, a figure wearing Kapioma's forty-armed suit came from the palace and lumbered slowly across the lawn. Before he was close enough to do any damage I had the power shut off and he fell before a well aimed bullet from Hama's rifle. The danger was again temporarily averted and I turned my attention to my men. The improvised suits did not have enough power to kill, or else it was not a killing ray that was used, for they were merely stunned and a few minutes of care brought them to, as well as ever.

Leaving Moka in command, I hurried back to the laboratory. Awlo threw herself into my arms again as I entered. I embraced her fervently and then turned to the key of my wireless. Not an answering signal could I get. I gave up at last and devoted my attention to Awlo. Her story was soon told.

The adjuster must have been moved slightly without our knowledge when Lamu had stolen it and fled with her, for they landed in Kau, not far from Kaulani. Lamu had attempted to force his attentions on her and had threatened her with death if she did not substantiate his story of my treachery. When I heard this, I gritted my teeth and wished that I had killed Lamu more slowly and painfully.

They attempted to make their way to Ulm but they were
seen and taken prisoners. They were taken to Halekala, one
of the cities of Kau, several hundred miles from the capital.
There they were held as prisoners for several months. Word
of their presence was finally brought to Kaulani and Kapioma
had ordered them sent to him. He had at once made Lamu a
prisoner and confined him with the survivors of Ulm who had
been meanwhile captured and brought to the city. Awlo he
treated at first as an honored guest, but during the last few
months he had tried unavailingly to win her consent to their
union. The final scene of his attempt was the one which I had
interrupted in the throne room.

She had consistently refused to give him any cause for
hope, for she assured me that she never would believe that I
was dead but always expected me to rescue her. Until I entered the throne room she had no idea that I had been in
Kaulani.

An hour later the Kauans attacked in earnest. Wearing
their improvised direct current fighting suits they came in
force and repaired the broken cable which led to their machine. I went down in my fighting suit to rout them, but I did
not dare to turn the power on. One of them was wearing Kapioma's suit and any attempt to render mine active would
have activated his. He kept behind a screen of men and was
effectually protected from our rifles.

Slowly the huge tank-like machine moved forward. We
poured a storm of rifle and pistol bullets into it but they had
no effect. Like the heroes they were, the loyal Ulmites threw
themselves before it and strove to stop it with their bodies,
only to fall before the deadly rays which it poured out. Half
of my men were down and the tank was slowly but inexorably
approaching the open doorway. At intervals blinding flashes
of white light came from it and whatever stood in their path,
be it man, wood or stone, was shattered to fragments. On it
came despite all our efforts. I was about to order the power
turned on and make a last desperate attempt to stop it with
Olua's fighting suit, despite the one I would have opposing
me, when an unfamiliar sound stopped the fighting for a moment. There was a silence and I heard a sound I had never expected to hear again, the drone of an airplane motor. The
Kauans looked up and gave vent to cries of surprise. Half of

them raced back toward the hangars where their war machines were kept.

Louder and louder became the sound and over the palace grounds swooped the familiar form of a tri-motored Fokker. I gave a shout of joy when I saw it and another one of exultation when I realized who the pilot must be. I suspected what Olua was up to and I called my men under shelter.

The Fokker swooped down low over the palace grounds and then up. A second time it swooped, and as it passed, a few hundred feet above our heads, something was thrown from the cockpit. It was a long black object and it fell slowly toward the ground. Square on the Kauan machine it landed. There was a deafening crash and a burst of smoke. Fragments of the machine flew in all directions. The Kauans who remained on their feet fled with cries of alarm.

Again the Fokker swept up and back over the palace. Another black cylinder fell and a huge hole was torn in one corner of Kapioma's stately residence. Apparently satisfied with the damage he had done, the pilot swung down with idling motor. I raced to the roof to meet him. The Fokker came down and made a perfect landing, although it would have rolled off the roof had not several of my men been there to check it. Removing his flying goggles, Olua climbed out and knelt at my feet.

"You came just in time, Olua Alii," I said as I raised him to his feet. "I feared that your adjuster had been moved and that you could not find your way back."

"I had no trouble, Courtney Sibama," he replied. "I exceeded your orders somewhat but I felt certain that you would approve what I did. I got to the larger plane all right and learned to fly your ship with no trouble but it took me a long time to get the explosives you wanted. I could make myself understood only with difficulty and when they understood, they would not give me what I wanted, although I offered them the metal you told me to use. At last I found one who knew you in the place they call Beatty and he got them for me. Then I returned as quickly as I could."

"And just in time," I repeated, "And you are more than welcome. I was about at the end of my resources, but with your knowledge of Kauan fighting methods, the battle will be on a more even footing now."

Olua inquired as to the details of the fight and expressed

himself as surprised at the stubborn resistance we had made. As a member of the Council of Lords, he requested a private interview with Moka and Hama, a favor which I promptly granted. In an hour the three of them entered the laboratory where I was talking to Awlo and requested permission to speak.

"Speak on," I said puzzled at their grave faces.

"It is the law of Ulm," said Moka gravely, "that when dire peril threatens the persons of the Sibama or the Sibimi, the word of the Council of Lords shall rule, if it will promise safety. Is that not so, my lord?"

"It is," I replied.

"Grave danger now threatens you and Awlo Sibimi, my lord. It is the word of the Council of Lords that you take the flying ship in which Olua Alii arrived and take the Sibimi to a place of safety."

"I'll do nothing of the sort," I said shortly.

"You must, Courtney Sibama," said Moka earnestly. "All of us have risked our lives and Olua Alii has returned from a place of safety to one of peril to assure the safety of our rulers. Unless you avail yourself of this chance, the sacrifice of those who have already died for you will be in vain. For countless generations my fathers have served the royal family of Ulm and it is just and fitting that the last member of my family should die that the royal family of Ulm should live on. Besides, the ammunition is running short."

This last was serious news. I inquired and found that we had less than sixty rounds of rifle cartridges per man left and another serious attack would settle matters. Olua gave another argument.

"You do not know the power of Kau," he said. "They have tried to conquer you quickly so far but now I think they will settle down to do it slowly. It is only a matter of time until they will construct a new power house or at least a power unit sufficient to power their fighting suits and when they do, the battle is over. I can make suits for our men but they would be outnumbered by a thousand to one. No, Courtney Sibama, what Moka says is true. You and our Sibimi must fly to safety. For this reason, I brought you your ship."

Thus reenforced, Moka returned to the attack.

"Ame has not yet fallen to the Mena," he said, "and there you and the Sibimi will find refuge and can build up again the empire of Ulm. We here are few and worthless, but the hopes of a mighty people are bound up in you. It may even be that when the Mena are defeated that you can lead a rescue party here for us."

"Wait a minute," I cried. His voice gave me an idea. I had forgotten the possibilities of my electronic vibration adjuster. Could I win my way to that, I could make my Fokker large enough to carry the entire population of Ulm, Ame and Kaulani. As the possibilities of the plan became clear, I gave a shout of joy.

"We will go," I exclaimed. "We will go, but we will return and carry you all to Ame."

In a few words I outlined my plan and Moka, Hama and Olua enthusiastically agreed to it. I don't think that any of the three expected me to succeed but the fact that Awlo and I would be safe was the thing that was uppermost in their loyal minds. In a few minutes we were on the roof and I was examining the Fokker prior to taking off. Satisfied with my inspection, Awlo and I went the rounds of our subjects to say farewell. Our plan had been told to them and man after man, the brave fellows thrust forward their gun butts for me to touch and knelt at Awlo's feet. To each of them we gave a hearty hand clasp and then, with only the three Alii in attendance, we ascended to the roof to take our departure. At the last moment I suggested that Olua accompany me to help me with the adjuster but he objected on the grounds that his knowledge would be needed to ward off the next attack. Moka dropped on one knee with the tears suspiciously near overflowing in his blue eyes.

"Farewell, my lord; farewell, my lady," he said. "It is the best end to die bravely for those we love."

"Die, nothing!" I exclaimed. "I'll be back here in five hours at the outside to take you all to Ame and safety."

"If it be so written," he replied, "but if not, remember ever, my friends, that Ulm was loyal to the last."

Awlo was sobbing openly and the tears were coming into my own eyes, so I brusquely put my princess into the plane and took the controls. Olua spun the propeller and the little craft soared into the air and at her best speed flew to the west toward the Kau mountains.

In two hours we were over the mountains and I was searching for my adjuster. At last I saw it and on a long slope we glided down toward it. We were within a hundred yards of the ground when the sun suddenly darkened and a terrific gust of wind turned the ship completely over. I strove to right it, but we were too close to the ground and in the semi-darkness, we crashed. I staggered to my feet and found that neither of us had been more than badly shaken by the fall.

As we climbed free from the wreck, the wind nearly carried us from the ground while crashes which shook the earth came from all around us. The sun was still partially obscured and I looked up and saw a marvel. Through the air were flying rocks the size of mountains, some of them apparently miles in diameter. They were flying toward the east and I realized that some of them must be falling on or near Kaulani.

"The kahumas! The giants!" cried Awlo.

"Kahumas, nothing!" I replied. "I don't know what it is, but it is no witchcraft."

As I spoke, another blast of wind came and again the sun was darkened. When it cleared, more of the huge masses of rock were flying through the air. One boulder, which must have weighed a million tons, fell not over two miles from us.

"Quick, Awlo!" I gasped. "Come with me!"

I grasped her hand and we raced for the adjuster. The only defence against such masses of rock was to increase our size until they were small in comparison to our bulk. We entered the machine and I turned the speed control to maximum, at the same time setting an automatic stop I had put on my new model, which would halt our increase when I arrived at my normal six feet. My hand reached for the increasing switch when a fresh cloud of rock masses came hurtling through the air, this time falling to the west of us. One of them struck the mountain above us and started a slide. I looked up and saw thousands of tons of rock rushing madly toward us. Awlo gave a cry of despair and fear but before they reached us, my hand closed on the switch and I pulled downward with all my strength.

I stepped from the adjuster and faced with clenched fists a grizzled old prospector, who lay on the ground where he had been thrown by the adjuster, as it had grown almost instantaneously to its original size.

"What do you mean by digging here and killing my friends?" I demanded hotly. "This is private property."

"Taint so on the map," he retorted as he rose. "It's public

domain and I reckon a man can prospect where he pleases. Where in hell did you come from?"

Without bothering to answer him, I hastily pulled the adjuster to one side. Under where it stood was piled dirt that that wretched fool had thrown and the weight of the adjuster had packed it smooth. Ulm, Ame, Kau; all were gone; buried under what was to them miles on miles of rock.

"Where did you come from?" demanded the prospector again as he dusted off his knees. "You weren't here a minute ago!"

"I came from a better land than you'll ever see," I replied grimly. "Hand me your shovel for a moment."

I took his tool and reached in and changed the speed of the adjuster to slow and closed the reducing switch. Sadly I watched it as it shrunk down to nothing and vanished from our sight. When it disappeared, I turned to Awlo, ignoring for the moment the ancient prospector who had watched the proceedings with dropping jaw and eyes as big as saucers.

"Farewell, Awlo, Sibimi of Ulm," I said solemnly. "My dear, you have lost forever your royal title but you have gained another fully as honorable, if it is slightly less exclusive."

"What do you mean, Courtney?" she asked.

"I mean that through the action of God and this ignorant agent of his, the Empre of Ulm has ceased to exist. You have ceased to be Awlo, Sibimi of Ulm, and will henceforth have to content yourself with being Mrs. Courtney Edwards, citizen of the United States of America."

When I reread "Submicroscopic" and "Awlo of Ulm," I was made very uneasy by the touches of racism it contained. The thought crossed my mind that I ought to try to edit them out, but, you know, I can't do that. Once I started tampering with stories, where would I stop?

The trouble is that racial stereotypes, unfavorable to everyone but white men of northwest European extraction, were completely accepted, and indeed, scarcely noted in those days of only forty years ago (except perhaps by members of the groups victimized thereby).

I'm sure the readers of that day were not particularly disturbed by the fact that the brave and chivalrous people of Ulm were blond, white people; and that so was the Earthman hero. (That hero is rich, athletic, and the kind of square-shooter who longs to kill ants for sport, and who does kill an inoffensive deer the instant he sees it, even though he is not hungry at the time and has no intention of eating it.) The one member of the Ulm group who is vallainous is, of course, swarthy in complexion.

The chief villains in "Submicroscopic," however, are the Mena, who are black, brutal, disgusting, and cannibalistic. In "Awlo of Ulm" the villains are the men of Kau, who are intelligent and scientifically advanced, but who are yellow in color and very, very cruel. This picture of the savage Black (given in almost every adventure story dealing with the far corners of the world, from *Robinson Crusoe* on) and the cruel Oriental (remember Fu Manchu and Ming the Merciless) was drummed into young heads until it became second nature.

Indeed, when my storytelling friend of 1928 told his tales of derring-do, the band of heroes he invented included both a Black and an Oriental, each with a full and insulting list of stereotypical characteristics. Neither he nor I knew there was anything wrong in that.

That we have come as far as we have in forty years is hopeful, though I believe it is more through the fact that Hitler's excesses made racism poisonous to any humane individual than through our own virtue. That we have much farther to go even now is incontestable.

The stories also included naïvetés of drama characteristic of the adventure stories of the day. There is the love at first sight, the princess who accepts a strange adventurer as her husband, and who threatens, "One step nearer and I will sheath this weapon in my heart!" (I had to read that line twice to make sure it was there.)

There are also the naïvetés of science that assume that slowing atomic and subatomic movement reduces size (it actually cools an object) or that mass automatically increases and decreases with size, or that the living creatures of the submicroscopic world would be of the same species as ourselves and would speak a kind of Hawaiian (which the hero fortunately understands).

But never mind. The action is rapid and violent; the hero is utterly heroic, the heroine utterly beautiful, the various villains utterly despicable. Everything breathed a kind of knightly chivalry, and at the time I asked no more.

"Submicroscopic" and "Awlo of Ulm" did not directly affect my own writing. I have never been able to throw myself into the kind of tale in which virtue just happens to have stronger muscles, readier fists, and better weapons.

Two things lingered, though. One was the seductive vision of a world in a grain of dust. (something handled with much superior force in "He Who Shrank," which will appear later in the book). The notion is an old one, but it seemed to gain scientific backing in 1910, when the atom was briefly pictured as an ultramicroscopic Solar System.

Science quickly abandoned the picture as impossibly simplistic, but it caught on with science fiction writers. I never used it, because by the time I became a writer I had too good a grounding in the physical sciences to make me comfortable with the notion.

However, in 1965, when I was asked to do a novelization of a motion picture that had already been made, I found myself brought face to face with a similar notion. The picture was *Fantastic Voyage,* and it dealt with the miniaturization of human beings to the size of bacteria and with their adventures in a human blood stream. It was not the type of situation I would have chosen to use of my own accord, but since it was handed me, the dim memory of "submicroscopic" helped persuade me to accept the task.

The other aspect of the stories that particularly impressed me was the duel with the rays in "Awlo of Ulm." The ray gun was a staple of science fiction (and came true, after a fashion, with the laser). That and the disintegrator gun were the two great hand weapons of the future. No one, however, had gone as all out as had Meek in "Awlo of Ulm."

I don't think I ever actually used ray guns myself in my stories, but the "neuronic whip" in my book *Pebble in the Sky* is a definite reminiscence of the weapons of "Awlo of Ulm."

It was not long after "Awlo of Ulm" that I read "Tetrahedra of Space," in the November 1931 issue of *Wonder Stories,* and was nearly as impressed. That was an important issue to me anyway, for after twelve months of experiment with pulp size, *Wonder Stories* went back to the large size with that issue, to my great relief.

TETRAHEDRA OF SPACE

by P. Schuyler Miller

A MOON of mottled silver swam in the star-flecked sky, pouring its flood of pale light over the sea of blue-green vegetation that swelled up and up in a mighty, slow wave to break in the foaming crest of the Andes. The shadow of the plane raced far below, dipping into the troughs, breasting the summits of that vast, unbroken sea of emerald stretching on and on beyond reach of vision.

And the stars—blinking Mira nearly overhead, a great Fomalhaut blazing over the far off mountains, and to the south a host of exotic strangers, burning with a fire that we of the north seldom know—clustered like great glowing fireflies around the invisible Pole. But I paid little heed to moon and stars and silvered jungle, for night had caught me unawares, and it is no simple matter to lay down supplies in a little clearing, marked only by a flickering camp-fire, lost somewhere among the jungles of Brazil.

Or was it Brazil? Here three great states mingled in an upland of forest and mountain and grassy valley—Peru, Bolivia, Brazil. Here ancient races had made their home, raised their massive temples in the little valleys, wrested a fortune from the mountains, given their lives to the jungles—a people more ancient by far than those others beyond the ranges whom the Incas conquered. Here none had come before to study, yet now, somewhere in the gloom beneath me, was a little oval valley hung midway between crag and forest, and there would be the tents and fires of scientists, men of my own world.

I must swoop and circle and loose my load, then soar off into the silver night like some great moth spurning the flame, out into the world of the moon and the jungles, back to the government that had sent me, to plunge once more into the hum-drum routine of government flight, the moon and the silvered jungle forgotten and forever gone.

But there came no glimmer of flame in the darkness, no flicker of white tents in the moonlight. Alone the outflung cross of the plane swam the unbroken sea of green, dark and boding against its wan beauty. It takes little error of judgment to miss a tiny clearing in the dark. So, as the western ranges crept out of their alignment, I swooped and soared, and was roaring back, higher now, over the silent moon-lit forests.

But one gap had I seen in the jungle—a harsh, black scar seared by some great fire from the bowels of the planet, ugly and grim in the soft beauty of the night. Again it slipped beneath, and as the shadow of the plane vanished against its harsh blackness it seemed to me that there came a scurry of furtive motion, an instant's flicker of shadow against its deeper gloom. I half checked the course of the plane, to wheel and search it closer, then of a sudden the air about me blazed with a dull crimson fire that burned into my body with a numbing fury of unleashed energy, the drone of the engines gasped and died, and we were spinning headlong toward the silver sea beneath!

As it had come, the tingling paralysis passed, and I flattened out the mad dive of the crippled plane, cut the ignition, and dived over the side. As in a dream I felt the jerk of the parachute, saw the deserted plane, like a huge, wounded bat of the jungles, swoop and check and swoop again in a long flat dive that broke and pancaked into the upper reaches of the forest. Then the heavy pendulum of my body alone beat out the dull seconds as I swung and twisted beneath the silken hemisphere of the 'chute. And then the leafy boughs, no longer silver but like hungry, clutching talons of black horror, swept up and seized me. I crashed through a tangle of vine and brittle bough into a hot, sweet-scented darkness where little hidden things scurried away into the night and the silence.

The rain-forest is like a mighty roof stretched over the valleys of tropical America. Interlacing branches blot out the sun from a world of damp and rotting dark, where great mottled serpents writhe among tangled branches and greater vines strangle the life out of giants of the forest in the endless battle for light. And there are little, venomous things of the dark ways—savage two-inch ants with fire in their bite, tiny snakelets whose particolored beauty masks grim death—creatures of the upper reaches and of the glorious world above the tree-tops. With the sunrise, a blaze of life and flaming color breaks over the roof of the jungle—flame of orchid and of macaw, and of the great, gaudy butterflies of this upper world. Beneath, there comes but a brightening of the green gloom to a wan half-light in which dim horrors seem to lurk and creep and watch, and giant lianas twist and climb up and ever up to the living light. And lowest of all is death and damp decay— the dull, sodden carpet of mold and rotting vegetation where fat white grubs burrow in blind fear and huge centipedes scurry underfoot.

The sun was an hour gone when I fell, but it was not until its second coming when I managed to writhe and slip through the tangle as if I too were of the jungle, moving toward the spot where my memory placed that blasted clearing, and the light. And with the deepening of the gloom in the upper branches, I came upon it, quite by accident, from above.

It was a little valley, perhaps a mile long and two thirds as wide, lying in an oval of glittering jet against the side of the mountain. Here the Andes were beginning their swift climb up from the jungles to the snows, and beneath me fifty-foot cliffs of sheeer, black rock dropped to the valley floor.

I have spoken of it as blasted, seared into the living heart of the jungle. It was all of that, and more! There was a gentleness in its rocky slopes that spoke of centuries of hungry plant-life, prying and tearing at jagged ledges, crumbling giant boulders, dying, and laying down a soft, rich blanket of humus over the harsh, under-rock, forming a little garden-spot of life and light in the dark heart of the forest.

Then came fire—an awful, scourging blast of fierce heat that even Man's Hell cannot equal! It blasted that little valley, seared its verdant beauty horribly, crumbling blossoms and long grasses into dead white ash, stripping the rich soil of past ages from its sleeping rocks, fusing those rocks into a harsh, glittering slag of seared, burnt black, cold and dead and damned! The sheer cliffs of its sides, once draped with a delicate tracery of flowered tendrils, had cloven away under the terrible heat, split off in huge slabs of the living rock that had toppled into the holocaust beneath and died with the valley.

The few thin shrubs that screened me at their summit showed blackened, blistered leaves and twigs, though here the heat had been least. As no other spot on Earth that little upland valley was awfully, terribly dead, *yet at its center something moved!*

Eagerly, fearfully, I peered through the gathering dusk. Full and golden, the moon was rising over the forest, throwing new shadows across the valley floor, brightening new corners, revealing new motion. And as its smoky orange cleared to white gold and waned to limpid silver, that glorious light seemed to soften the harsh jet of the valley. It wakened a lustrous opalescence in the two great spheres that nestled like mighty twin pearls against the dark rock, to create beings of the rock and of the shadow, gliding wraithlike among the shattered boulders!

Painfully I crept through the dense growth of the brink, nearer to those great spheres and their dreadful cargo. Within me my brain whirled and throbbed, my throat froze against the cry of shocked incredulity that rushed to my lips, cold, clammy sweat oozed from gaping pores! It was beyond all reason—all possibility! And yet—it *was!* Now I could see them clearly, rank on rank of them in orderly file, some hundred of them, strewn in great concentric rings about the softly glowing spheres—harsh as the black rock itself, hard, and glittering, and angular—a man's height and more from summit to base—great, glittering tetrahedra—*tetrahedra of terror!*

They were tetrahedra, and they were alive—living even as you and I! They stirred restlessly in their great circles, uneasy in the dim light. Here and there little groups formed, and sometimes they clicked together in still other monstrous geometric shapes, yet always they moved with an uncanny stillness, darting with utter sureness among the scattered rocks. And now from the nearer of the twin spheres came another of their kind, yet twice their size, the pearly walls opening and closing as by thought-magic for his passing! He swept forward a little, into the full light of the moon, and the rings followed him, centered about him, until the spheres lay beyond the outermost and the giant tetrahedron faced alone the hosts of his lesser fellows!

Then came their speech—of all things the most mind-wracking! I felt it deep within my brain, before I sensed it externally, a dull, heavy rhythm of insistent throbbing, beating at my temples and throwing up a dull red haze before my staring eyes!

And then I knew it was no fancy—that the great things of the blasted valley were indeed speaking, chanting, in low, vibrant monotone that beat physically upon me in long, slow waves of the air! You have heard those deepest notes of a great organ, when the windows tremble, even the walls, the building itself vibrate in resonance, beat and beat and beat to its rhythm until you feel it throbbing against your skull, pulsing in your mind in a vast, relentless sea of thundrous sound!

Such was the speech of the tetrahedra, only deeper still beneath the threshold of sound—so deep that each tiny nerve of the skin sensed its monotonous pressure and shouted it to a reeling brain—so deep that it seemed like a great surf of more-than-sound thundering dismally against desolate, rocky shores!

For it was without inflection—only the dull, dead beat and beat and beat, mounting throb on throb in my pulsing brain, and bringing madness in its wake! I think now that it was a sort of chant, the concerted cry of all the scores of tetrahedra, dinning savagely, angrily at their giant leader in a dismal plaint of discontent and unease! I think they were restless, aware of unfulfilled promises and purposes, anxious to make sure their mission, or to be gone. I think that the seed of tetrahedral mutiny was sown among them, and that as angry convicts will drum at their prison bars and scream in monotone, even so these things of another world, another life-stuff, drummed their grievances at their mighty leader!

For soon I sensed a deeper, stronger voice beating against the din, drowning it out, thundering command and reproof, shouting down the mob until its lesser drumming sank to a mutter and ceased. But the voice of the giant tetrahedron rang on, inflected now as our own voices, rising and falling in angry speech and command, pouring out burning sarcasm, perhaps, cowing them with its great insistence!

Like all great leaders, his followers were as children to him, and the hard, harsh beat of sound swept off into a soothing, cajoling murmur of whispering ripples, tapping ever so lightly against the packed sand of some distant tropic breach, almost sibilant, if such a sound can be so, yet none the less dominant and definite in its message. And it sank to a far, hinting rumble and vanished.

For a long instant they lay quiet, like graven things of the stone itself, then through the circles, like a spreading wave, rose a thrill of slow motion, quickening, livening, until all were astir! The ranks parted, the giant tetrahedron swept swiftly over the valley floor to the two great spheres, his angular hordes flowing in swift, soft motion in his wake! Again, with that speed and silent mystery of thought, the spheres gaped open and the ranks of the tetrahedra were swallowed up within! Alone, the twin pearls of fire-flecked opalescence nestled among the black rocks—great orbs of soft light, glowing with the magic of the full moon.

For a long moment I lay there under the bushes at the cliff's edge, staring out over the valley, stunned by the weird unreality of the thing I had seen. Then, out of the dark behind me, came a hand, gripping my shoulder in a vise of iron! Mad with sudden terror I twisted free, struck blindly at the thing that had seized me, a thing that fastened with the grip of a Hercules upon my flailing arms, pinioned them to my sides—a thing that spoke, its words a hoarse mutter that barely penetrated the gloom!

"For God's sake, man, be still! Do you want *them* to hear?"

It was a man—a human like myself. My frozen tongue stammered reply.

"Who are you? What are those things out there? What Hell of Earth did they spring from?"

"None of Earth, you may rest sure!" came the grim answer. "But we will tell you that later. We must get clear of this place! I am Marston of the Museum expedition—the biologist. I suppose you are the aviator—Valdez saw them burn you down last night. Follow me."

"Yes, I'm Hawkins. The plane is somewhere over there, if it didn't burn, with all your supplies in it. I was held up crossing the mountains. But tell me, first—those things, there—are they *alive?*"

"You've wondered that? I suppose anyone would. The Indians make them gods of a kind—realize they're beyond all experience and tradition. But I'm a biologist. I have had some experience in strange forms of life. They are as much alive as we—perhaps even more than we. After all, if life is energy, why should it not rest where it will? Need we—soft, puny things of carbon and water and a few unstable elements—be the only things to harbor life? But this is no place to moralize —come on!"

He vanished into the dark, and I followed, plunging blindly after the sound of his crashing progress, away from the seared valley and the tetrahedra, to safety of a sort in the sombre depths of the rain-forest.

They crouched beside a tiny fire of bark and twigs, like men of old Cro-Magnon, fifty thousand years ago—two gaunt skeletons hung and swathed with soiled rags, brooding over their pitiful little flame. With the crackle of our approach they sprang at bay—two hunted things of the jungle—then relaxed as we came into the firelight.

I will always remember them as I saw them then—Hornby, the Museum archaeologist, tall, grey-haired, his haggard face seamed with deep wrinkles of sleeplessness and fear and puzzled wonderment. Valdez, his colleague of the government that had sent me, short, dark, his Portuguese blood blended with that of the squat tribes of the interior, teeth gleaming in a snarl like that of some great jungle cat, cornered, crazed, and dangerous! He seemed plumper than the others, and I felt that he could and would care for himself very well if need be.

Now, too, I saw my guide for the first time as something more than a black hulk in blackness. Marston, the biologist, looked like an old-time blacksmith, a massive man of bone and muscle, with keen grey eyes under heavy brows and the beginnings of a mighty beard. A Hercules, I have said—more like an Atlas, upholding the burden of this little wilderness world from the shoulders of one who could not and one who would not share it! Muscles that had had scant padding of reserve flesh now lacked it utterly, jutting like knotted tree-roots from his rugged frame, making him seem a being rudely hewn from some twisted cypress stump by the master hand of a forest god, and given life.

"We're all there are, Hawkins," he rumbled, his unhushed voice bearing much of the quality of the speech of the tetrahedra. "We've got to find that plane soon, if it's still whole. Did you see flames, Valdez?"

"Flames, Senor Marston? No—as I have so often said, I saw merely the falling of the plane, like a great wounded bird seeking the shelter of the jungle, and Senor—Hawkins, is it—with his parachute. I am not certain that I can find it, now that a day and a night have passed, but I will try. With the guides gone, it is not easy to feed even three mouths—eh, Senor Marston?"

"Four is no worse than three, Valdez. I'm glad Hawkins is here. He's new blood, a new brain, and with his help we may lick the damn' things yet!"

Then Hornby's voice—dry and withered as his shrunken body—weary as his tired old eyes.

"You have seen the tetrahedra, Lieutenant Hawkins? You realize that they are living, intelligent beings? You can comprehend the menace of their presence here on our Earth?"

"Yes, Professor," I answered slowly, "I have seen them and heard them. I can see that they're not like anything I know of, on Earth or off, and that there is some sort of purpose behind them. But I saw them only in the half-light, for a few moments at best. They had a great leader, twice the size of any of them, and the rest seemed to be dissatisfied with the way he was running things."

"You hear that, Marston?" cried the Professor, almost savagely. "You hear—they are impatient—they will act, as soon as they have fed again! We dare not wait longer! We must do something, Marston—we must act now—now!"

"Yes, I saw them too," said Marston slowly. "They're on the brink, all right. But I don't know what we can do—four men with three rifles and a couple of machetes against a hundred of them and what they can do. I don't know that we can even puncture one—they look almighty hard to me!"

"Marston," I put in eagerly, "if it's guns you want, there are two machine-guns and plenty of ammunition in the plane —it was a government ship, fresh from the uprising in the North. If we can find that, there'll be guns as well as food. I think I could find it, from the valley, in daylight."

"Valdez—you hear that? Can you help him search? You are the one who saw him fall, and you have been out with the Indians more than once. How about it?"

"Very well, Senor Marston, I will do what I can. But do not hope for too much—remember, there has been a day and a night, and I had only a glimpse. And the guns—what can they do against those devils from the spheres? We are fools to stay here, I tell you—we would do better to flee, now that there is food, and warn the world of what has come upon it!"

"I've heard that stuff preached before. Valdez. Stow it! If it comes to announcing them to the world, those things will do it for themselves faster than we could! It would be our own hides we'd be saving, and that not for long! Besides, you know the reputation these Indians have, once they're roused!

Looks like you're the fool of the lot, Valdez. You'll hunt with Hawkins in the morning!"

Professor Hornby had said little—he merely crouched against a tree, staring blankly at the flames. Now, at Marston's words, he roused again.

"Marston," his voice came petulantly, "have you seen the Indians in the forest, as I have? Have you seen them, felt them staring at your back, fingering their little darts in the dark? Marston, they take those tetrahedra for gods, or devils —things to worship and propitiate with sacrifice! The forest is full of them—I feel it—I can tell! Marston, *what are they doing?*"

CHAPTER II

The Coming of the Tetrahedra

Marston's bluff rumble drowned out that final wail. "Sure, Prof, they're here, all right—all about us, out there in the jungle with the beasts. I can feel them too—watching us from the dark. But they're harmless—just inquisitive, that's all. It's the things yonder that draw them—gods, maybe, or devils, like you said, but something out of old times and old tales, when the Old People had their forts and palaces here under the shadow of the hills. It's a legend come true, for them, and until they find out different, I reckon they link us with the things that have appeared in the place where we used to be—we, with our white magic and our questions of the Old People. They're not apt to hurt us for a while yet, but it won't hurt to slip a mite closer to the valley, where we can watch the things and keep the association fresh for the Indians."

Then Valdez slipped his acid wedge of dissent, smoothly and blandly as ever, yet deadly sharp beneath the flashing smile.

"You remember, of course, Senor Marston, that these poor Indios retain the superstitions of their ancient masters, and that in time of peril it was the way of the Old People to make blood sacrifice to their gods—the blood of their most holy priests! Old customs linger long among savages, Senor! You have a proverb, I think—'Out of sight, out of mind', is it not? There is truth in such old maxims, Senor Marston."

"Meaning we can skip out and let them forget us? We're

not playing that game, as I think I've said before, Valdez. None of us—get that! We're staying, and we're fighting, just as soon as you and Hawkins locate those guns, which is to-morrow. Your memory will improve with a little sleep, I think. And, Prof—I reckon Hawkins here would like to hear about those things yonder. Tell him what there is to tell—you have it clearest of any of us, I guess."

And so, huddled there by the tiny, flickering fire, I listened as the thin, dry voice of the old Professor marched through the awful story of the coming of the tetrahedra. It was graven deep in his mind, and with every telling the tale grew more vivid to him. Even now the sweat oozed from his face as he spoke staring in fascination at the dying flames. The eyes of Marston and Valdez watched us across the embers and those other, unseen eyes in the darkness that hung its velvet shroud beyond the waning flicker of the fire-light, peered furtively out of the night.

They had come to the little valley in the hills, three white men and a half-dozen Indian guides from the more civilized tribes to the north. Here in its oval bowl they had made their camp among flowers and waving grasses, with the dark rampart of the jungle standing about them like the walls of a prison. And from those walls, in the end, came the Indians of the forests—poor, savage creatures hag-ridden by superstition and ignorance, wracked by famine and disease—a feeble remnant of those who had been servants to the Old People in days long gone.

For they treasured weird legends and aborted ceremonies where understanding of other things had passed. Perhaps they had never known the reality of the great deeds with which they had served the Masters—cunningly fitting huge boulders into smooth-cut walls and terraces, hacking long roads into jungle and mountain, eking out a livelihood for the decadent ruling race.

But true it was that they bore memories of things that even the savage mind can ponder, memories of magic and ritual, and the adoration of fierce and powerful gods. As the newer magic of this younger, paler race gripped their childish minds, they told of the things that their fathers before them had learned of grandfathers through the centuries, tales not only of custom and life in those long-gone days, but of cities swallowed up in the rain-forest, cities of massive stone and untarnishing metal—"the metal of the Sun," that sleeps in long, fat serpents in the white rock of the mountains. In Hornby's old eyes gleamed a new, young frenzy of hope and joy, and in the little eyes of Valdez another, older lust-light wakened at the tale of the golden serpents. Marston saw it, but Marston had known that it would come, and he went about his study of the plants of valley and forest as if it had not been there—worked, and watched.

Then, one day—and Professor Hornby's hoarse voice sank almost to a whisper as he told of it—there came the little group of savages who were to lead the way to the buried ruins of a great city of the Old Ones, four little brown men with blow-guns and deadly darts, waiting patiently for the great White Ones to take up their magic and follow. Hornby had stepped to the door of his tent to call their chieftain to conference, and as he went he gazed up at the towering Andes, whence the Old Ones had sprung. There, drifting like wind-tossed bubbles just above the tree-tops, floated the spheres of the tetrahedra!

Gently they sank to rest at the other end of the little valley —lay there in the thick grass like the eggs of some huge moth out of fable. The Indians had fled in terror, but as Hardy and Marston raced down the slope toward the twin globes they sensed that furtive eyes would be peering from the undergrowth, half-fearful, half-wondering, waiting with timeless patience for new magic—new masters.

The three came to the spheres as they lay there in the lush grass—Hornby, Marston, Valdez—and in each heart must have been something of the wonder that I in my turn had felt. For the spheres were unbroken by any opening, were as twin orbs hewn from mother-of-pearl, iridescent, with delicate hues of blue and rose tinting their snowy white, and yet there came a force from them, a tingling of excess energy that thrilled in every nerve and set their minds on edge with unwonted keenness!

It grew in strength, slowly, and it was Marston who first sensed its lurking hostility, who turned his gaze from the enigmatic spheres to see the long grasses about their bases wither and shrivel to soft grey ash under the blasting radiation! It was he who cried the alarm, and in sudden panic they fled a little way up the valley, to stand like startled sheep, then flee anew as the surge of energy poured forth in ever-quickening pulses from the opal spheres.

It swept all life before it into sudden, luxuriant growth that as suddenly dropped into blighted destruction! Beside their tents, nearly in the shadow of the brooding forest, they stood at last and watched the slow torrent sweep the life of their little valley home into the sullen ash of death. And then its invisible van drifted up the slope to their feet, and again its subtle venom thrilled evilly in their veins, and they ran crazily, headlong, into the jungle!

But they could not long shun the brain-troubling enigma that had engulfed their little home. Marston, Hornby, Valdez —they struggled back and stared from the damp dark of the forest at the thing that was happening there in the sunlit oval on the mountainside. Then it was that Marston broke the spell of fear that had been laid upon him—seized rifles, blankets, food from the deserted tents in the ebbing of the invisible waves, and fled again as the second billow of devastation poured from the silent spheres! The grasses and delicate blossoms of the valley had passed under the first blight, but here and there grew hardier blooms and bushes, akin to the life of the forest, and higher forms of life—insects, rodents, birds. Again the wave of death surged, and again, and now they could see a faint flush of crimson burning angrily where it passed, a glow more of the atmosphere than of the blighted, seared life of the valley! Then, for a time, there came a lull—a peace almost of the days and hours when this little spot of light in the green dark was the home of happy, busy men—almost, yet not quite!

For there was a boding in it, an ominous sense of oppression, a tension of the very ether, a stress that spread to mind and brain and sucked hungrily at the dazed consciousness! Now they saw that the spheres were alight with a cold green radiance that glowed vividly even above the glare of the sun upon the bleaching ash! Almost an incandescence they might have called it, yet there was no feeling of heat, only a great, overpowering energy that was being hurled from those unearthly spheres upon the little valley and its walling forests. And they were not wrong, for of a sudden, with an awful violence that shook even the stolid Marston, the storm burst in its full fury over the valley!

It did not touch the forests—indeed, it seemed to shun their cool, damp dark—and so the three could watch its awful progress and live. In an instant's time the tension burst into a seething, chaotic turmoil of blue-green flame, electric fire akin to lightning, yet far surpassing any lightning of Earth in its fury!

In a great beating sea of horrid flame it lashed the oval valley, driving into the soil, into the very rock, waking them into an angry answer of leaping, burning crimson fires. The fires swept the thin black soil from the underlying rock and scored the naked face of the rock itself with an awful furnace of consuming fury. Filling all the bowl of the valley and beating high against its bounding walls, licking away their flowery curtain of lacing vines, rending from them huge flakes of rock that burst like monster bombs as they toppled into the fiery sea below, it rushed in a mighty pillar of roaring fires hundreds of feet into the shuddering air!

And through the curtain where fire of heavens and fire of Earth met in that terrible holocaust, those three saw the curving flames of the twin spheres gape wide, saw huge angular shapes file from the darkness within—shapes never yet associated in the Mind of Man with the meaning of life! Careless of the flame that seethed about them, they glided out over the fusing rock of the valley floor, score on score of them, showing in the fierce glare as mighty, eight-foot tetrahedra of dark, glistening crystal. They were of a purple that seemed to be of the essence of the things themselves, rather than a pigmentation of their surface; and near one apex each had two green-yellow unstaring, unseeing eyes!

Within them one glimpsed a spherical body—purple too— from which ran hundreds of curious filaments to the smooth surfaces. Tetrahedra they were—living tetrahedra of chilling terror that feared neither flame nor lightning and spread destruction on every side!

Sick at heart the three men watched, while the flames died and the winds came and stripped the blanket of dust and ash from the blasted rock. The tetrahedra meanwhile glided about their endless affairs, forming and reforming in geometric pattern. Or they clicked swiftly into many-faceted forms that in turn mounted into monolithic, crystalline monstrosities, then melted with startling suddenness into their original components. These were idle, pointless maneuverings from the human viewpoint, yet fraught with some hidden meaning and purpose as alien to Earth as the things themselves. They suggested the terrible energies that were under their control—energies such as our little science has never hinted at.

"I cannot tell you of the feeling that came to me," the

weary, dried-out voice of the Professor droned despairingly on. "Here was a power absolutely at odds to all the great, painfully evolved civilization of mankind, a power that could and would crush us as a fly, if we came into conflict with the motives of the tetrahedral race! Here were beings endowed by nature with powers beyond our science—alien to our ideas of evolution, well-nigh to our imagination and reason. I felt the latent doom of mankind and of the very life-forms of all Earth, squatting here in our little, blasted valley with an ominous, cruel indifference that struck chill fear into my heart! And I knew that if Man must die, I would die too—die fighting for *my* race and *my* civilization! I think we all felt it, knew it in our hearts, and swore our oath of undying feud upon the violated rock of our valley home!"

His voice trailed off into silence as his deadened eyes saw once more the vision of that awful day. I thought he had done, but again his voice broke the quiet.

"Perhaps we can flee, even now—hide away in some corner where they can have no motive for searching—exist for a few dreadful months or years while our planet sinks under their unearthly tyranny. Perhaps, for a little, we can save our lives, and yet—I wonder if it is not better to die foolishly, futilely, but to die with the knowledge that we have been closer than any man to the unfathomable, to the reality that underlies all life."

From the dark beyond the glowing embers came Marston's quiet rumble:

"We can't do less, Prof, and we won't. We will fight, as men fight, and if our way is greater and better than their way, you know, down in your heart, that we will win as Man has always won—and that science will have another doubtful bone to quarrel over. In the morning we must lay our plans. They are getting restless—they may strike any minute, and we must be ready and waiting. We're going to die, I guess, but we'll die as men should!" That was all.

The events of the past few hours had crowded in upon me with such staggering force and complexity that I found my mind in a whirl. I could get no clear-cut impression—no broad meaning—only a blurred, fantastic cyclorama of unearthly event and taut emotion, piling thought on thought in an orgy of color and sound and feeling that completely swamped me. Even now, with it all past and much of it clarified by time, I feel that same vagueness, that groping for concepts, that I felt then. With the morning all this changed—changed swiftly and utterly as event after event rushed upon us, broke like a tidal wave upon our outraged consciousness, and vanished before the tumultuous onslaught of another, greater clash of mind and matter.

We were up with the dawn, and after a scant breakfast of dried fruits, salvaged from the tents before the destruction of the valley, Valdez and I set out to find the plane. I wanted to return to the valley to get my bearings, but Valdez protested —claimed it was uselessly dangerous, that he could make better time from where we were. We struck into the tangle of dank underwood, Valdez leading, and within seconds of our leaving camp I was utterly lost. My companion seemed sure of his way, slipping through the maze of fine growth like a beast of the jungle, almost as if he were following an invisible trail.

For nearly an hour we plunged ahead, then of a sudden came a gap in the forest roof as the level of the ground fell in a narrow ravine, and I woke to angry realization of what was happening! The sun, on our right when we started, lay behind us! *We were traveling dead away from the valley, the camp, and the plane!*

Angrily I sprang forward, seized Valdez by the shoulder! He spun like a striking snake, fury in his half-closed eyes, fury and crazed fear! In his hand was a gun!

"So—you have awakened at last, Senor Hawkins," he sneered. "You feel that things are not quite as they seemed— is it not so? You fool—did you for one moment think I would cast my lot with those idiots back there? Do I seem mad, that I should offer my life for fools like them? You—you were not invited to our little party, but you came—you are here, and on my hands—and you will do as I say or wish you had! Am I clear?"

"You're too damn' clear!" I shouted. "You're not fit to live, Valdez, and it's high time someone told you so to your sneaking face! So you're going to sneak off and leave your comrades to the tender mercies of those tetrahedra—you want to make sure of your precious hide! Why, damn you, it's you that's a bigger fool than any of us! How can you expect to get clear of this filthy jungle, with the guides gone? Where are you going to find food when your shells run out? What do you think these damn' stinking savages will do to you when

they catch you out here alone, running away from their new
gods? You haven't the least chance in the world—you're
crazy, that's it! You're stark, staring mad—a damned, yellow,
mad dog!"

"You say unfortunate things, Senor Hawkins," he replied
coldly, the ugly sneer still on his thin, red lips. "I think that I
can dispense with your company. It might interest you to
know that Valdez is the name of my father by adoption,
Senor. My people are those whom you have so kindly classi-
fied as 'damned stinking savages'—my home is these very
forests that you seem to find so unpleasant! And, Senor Hawkins, have I not said that I can always find your plane?"

"What do you mean by that?"

"I mean, Senor, that it has always been I who could find the
plane, and I who *did* find it, not very many minutes after it
crashed. You would be disappointed, Senor Hawkins, were
you to see it now. The food, the guns and ammunition of
which you boasted—they can never have existed save in a
mind disordered by jungle fevers. Or can it be that the Indios
—the 'stinking savages' that even now are all about us, there
behind you in the shadows, have stolen them? It would be
most interesting to know the truth of the matter, would it
not?"

I stared up through the matted branches at the blandly
shining sun, red hate clouding my vision! I raised both hands,
fists clenched, as if to crash them down upon the evilly smil-
ing face! But the little snub-nosed gun that bored into my
belly spoke eloquent warning, and of a sudden came clear
thought and cool, calculated words:

"So even in this you must lie, Valdez! It is bred in the
blood, I think! I do not question that you stole the food and
weapons that meant life to your comrades—it is much too
characteristic an act to doubt—but, *Senor* Valdez, no Indian
would so steal another's food. *Was it, perhaps, your mother
who was white?*"

Blind fury glazed his little, bloodshot eyes and drew back
his thin lips in an ugly snarl of rage! I saw murder staring at
me from those eyes, and in the instant when he stood frozen
with his hate I leaped—swung with all my weight on the great
liana that was looped over the branch above me! Even as the
gun spat flame, the tautening vine caught him full at the base
of the skull and toppled him forward into the black mold of
the forest floor, out and out for good!

CHAPTER III

The Tetrahedra's Power

It was his life or mine, but I had not contemplated killing him. The vine was heavy and swung loose on the limb, and it whipped taut with the force of a snapping hawser, catching him squarely at the base of his maddened brain! It was an awful blow, every bit as heavy as the swing of a sledge hammer, and it broke his spine free from his skull as I would snap an apple from its stem! I turned him over, his features purple and contorted, and as I lifted him his head flopped forward like that of a rag dummy! With a shudder I dropped him and turned away.

Yet part of him was white, and all of him was human, and so I scooped a shallow trench in the soft mold and buried him, first searching his body for weapons and food. In his breast pocket was a rough sketch-map, showing the valley, the camp, and a small cross where the plane had fallen. Across its penciled contours ran a fine dotted line, due north from the camp nearly to the place where the plane lay, then bearing off to the west, toward the mountains, and toward a little upland river that ran down from the snows.

There was the gulley where I stood, a dried-out stream-bed leading up into the lower end of the valley, and just beyond a second little cross, to the south of the trail. I knew what it meant—the food and guns from the looted plane! I could see now that the way was cunningly marked by untangled vines and diverted branches—a path of least resistance, more than a trail—and within five minutes I had uncovered Valdez' cache, under the cover of an outcropping ledge of quartz, and loaded one of the packs we had brought along.

How to return to camp with my news was another question entirely. I knew it was hopelessly futile for me to try to follow the back trail, or to run by the rude map for either plane or camp. There remained the valley—straight south along the ravine—and I felt certain that once there I could regain my lost sense of direction or wait until one of the others found me. The valley—and the tetrahedra! Driven by instinct or intuition, I shouldered one of the very light machine-guns and wrapped three belts of ammunition about my waist, under my shirt.

The going was easier along the rim of the little ravine than at its bottom, where extra moisture made the tangle thicker. Indeed, it seemed almost like the trail Valdez had followed— a path of least resistance, carved invisibly into the underbrush by unknown hands. To right and left the thicket held like a tightly woven fabric, but ahead, parallel to the gulley, the branches slipped silently apart under a slight pressure of the hand and closed us quietly behind. It was obvious that either Valdez or the Indians had made this way to the valley, and it was not on Valdez' map.

The trail finally swung away from the stream-bed, toward the east, and suddenly emerged on a sort of peninsula jutting into the valley just above the point where the twin spheres lay. I saw the glare of sunlight through the trees, for there was a sort of clearing overlooking the parade-ground of the tetrahedra. Here were gathered the forest Indians, clustered behind the thin screen of vegetation, gazing in dumb adoration at the things below. So rapt were they that my approach went unnoticed, and I was able to retreat and bear to the west, creeping up to the edge of the valley midway between clearing and ravine.

It was nearly noon, and the fury of the blazing sun made the valley a black cauldron of flickering air-currents. They boiled up from the naked rock in vast, shimmering waves of heat that made the distant jungle and the rocky valley floor seem to engage in a weird witches' caper with the unearthly things that basked at the valley's heart.

Now, in the full light of day, I could see that it was as Professor Hornby had said. The tetrahedra were formed from some hard, crystalline mineral, black almost to invisibility, with a faint wash of rich purple running through it. As they moved, the sun sent up glittering flashes of brilliance from their polished flanks, dancing like little searchlight rays along the shadowed face of the forest. For the tetrahedra were restless, were weaving aimlessly in and out among the boulders in weird arabesques as of some unearthly dance of the crystal folk, were condensing in little groups of half a dozen or less that formed and broke again even as do restless humans, waiting impatiently for some anticipated event.

Apart from the rest, motionless in a sort of circular clearing among the rocks, squatted the giant leader of the tetrahedra. In him the deep violet of the crystal became a rich, plum-like hue, purple flushed with warm red, and the underlying black seemed less harsh. It was warmer and more like the calm velvet of the tropic night. But these are impressions, qualitative terms with which to distinguish him in some way other than by mere size from his fellows. To an observer, the distinction was apparent, but it is not easy to express in every-day terms. It must suffice that he was indefinably different from the others, that he seemed to have character and person-ality, where the rest were but pyramidal crystals, albeit terri-bly alive.

And now the giant leader was dinning out his mighty call in long, slow billows of beating sound that seemed to thrust me back, press me into the dark of the forest, away from the alien monsters of the valley! In response came thirty of the lesser tetrahedra, chosen seemingly at random from the scat-tered ranks, to range themselves at equal intervals about their master, forming a single great circle a dozen yards in diame-ter.

Again the throbbing call shattered against the cliffs about me, and now all the hordes of the tetrahedra broke into flow-ing motion, converging in a torrent of glittering purple crystal upon the natural amphitheater, clustering in threes at the spots that their fellows had marked—all but ten, who glided into place before every third group, forming a giant toothed wheel with hub and rim and spokes of living, sentient crystal —*crystal with a purpose!*

There under that blazing sun they lay, gleaming like giant purple gems against the jetty rock. I thought of the great stone wheel of Stonehenge, and of the other monolithic circles that men have found in England and on the Continent. Strange re-semblance, between the pattern of living monsters of another world and the ancient temples of a prehistoric race! And yet, is it too far-fetched to suggest that the superstitious savages should pattern their greatest temples after the unearthly gods of their worship—gods of purple crystal that came and smote and vanished again into the skies, leaving the memory of their inevitable circling, and the thunder of their language in the great drums of worship? May it not be that they have come before, and found Earth unfitted for their usage, and passed on to other worlds? And if they have so come, and found us wanting, what lies beyond that has prevented them from bear-ing back the tale of their findings, marking Earth as useless for their tetrahedral purposes? Why have they had to come again and again?

I could see that the groups of three that formed the toothed rim of the giant crystal wheel were tipping inward, bringing their peaks together in a narrow focus, and more, that the ten that were the spokes, the binding members of the wheel, were of the same rich hue as their master. The shadows of the myriad tetrahedra squatted short and black about their shining bases, against the shining rock.

As the sun soared higher, pouring its blazing rays straight down upon the sweltering world, I sensed the beginning of a vague roseate glow at the foci of the circling trios, a glow as of energy, light, focussed by the tetrahedra themselves, yet not *of* themselves, but sucked from the flood of light that poured upon them from above. For the light that was reflected from their sides gleamed ever bluer, ever colder, as they drank in the warm red rays and spewed them forth again into the seething globes of leashed energy that were forming just beyond their pointing tips!

The rose-glow had deepened to angry vermillion, seemingly caged within the spheres defined by the tips of the tilted tetrahedra. Thirty glowing coals against the black, ninety great angular forms gleaming ghastly blue in the pillaged sunlight, forms that were slowly closing in upon the center, upon their mighty master, bearing him food, energy of the sun for his feasting!

Now the scarlet flame of the prisoned light was mounting swiftly in an awful pinacle of outrageous color—pure fire torn from the warm rays of the sun—raw energy for the glutting of these tetrahedral demons of another world! It seemed to me that it must needs burst its bounding spheres and fuse all that crystal horde with its unleashed fury of living flame, must win free of the unimaginable forces that held it there between the eager, glittering facets, must burst its unnatural bonds and sweep the valley with a tempest of awful fire that would consign the furnace of the tetrahedra to pitiful insignificance! It did none of these, for the power that had reft it from the golden sunbeams could mould it to the use and will of the tetrahedra, as clay before the potter!

Slowly the great ring contracted, slowly the tetrahedra tipped toward their common center, bearing at their foci the globes of angry flame. Now they stopped, hung for a long moment in preparation. Then in an instant they loosed the cradled energy of the spheres in one mighty blaze of blinding crimson that swept out in a single huge sheet of flame, blanketing all the giant wheel with its glory, then rushing into the blazing vortex of its center. Here, all the freed energy of the flame was flowing into the body of the mighty ruler of the tetrahedra, bathing him in a fury of crimson light that sank into his glowing facets as water into parched sand of the desert, bringing a fresh, new glow of renewed life to his giant frame!

And now, as in recoil, there spouted from his towering peak a fine, thin fountain of pale blue fire, soundless, like the blaze of man-made lightning between two mightily energized electrodes—the blue of electric fire—the seepage of the giant's feast! Like slaves snatching at the crumbs from their master's board, the ten lesser tetrahedra crowded close. As their fierce hunger voiced itself in awful, yearning force, the fountain of blue flame split into ten thin tongues, barely visible against the black rock, that bent down into the pinnacles of the ten and poured through them into the crowding rim of the giant wheel, a rim where again the spheres of crimson fire were mounting to their climactic burst!

Again the crimson orbs shattered and swept over the horde in a titanic canopy of flame, and again the giant master drank in its fiery glory! Now the fountain of seepage had become a mighty geyser of sparkling sapphire light that hurtled a hundred feet into the shimmering atmosphere, and, bent by the fierce hungering of the lesser creatures, curved in a glorious parabola above the crystal wheel, down over them and into them, renewing their substance and their life!

For as I watched, each tetrahedron began to swell, visibly, creeping in horrid slow growth to a magnitude very little less than that of their giant leader. And as they mounted in size, the torrent of blue fire paled and died, leaving them glutted and expectant of the final stage!

It came, with startling suddenness! In an instant each of the hundred clustering monsters budded, burst, shattered into four of half its size that cleaved from each corner of the parent tetrahedron. They left an octohedral shape of transparent crystal, colorless and fragile, whence every evidence of life had been withdrawn into the new-born things—a shell that crumpled and fell in fine, sparkling crystal dust to the valley floor. Only the giant ruler lay unchanged beneath the downward slanting rays of the sun. The hundred had become four hundred! The tetrahedra had spawned!

Four hundred of the monstrous things where a hundred had lain the moment before! Drinking in the light of the noonday sun, sucking up its energy to give them substance, these tetrahedral beings from an alien world held it in their power to smother out the slightest opposition by sheer force of ever-mounting numbers! Against a hundred, or four hundred, the armies and the science of mankind might have waged war with some possibility of success, but when each creature of these invulnerable hosts might become four, with the passing of each noon's sun, surely hope lay dead! Man was doomed!

On the jutting point to my left I sensed new activity. The Indians were chanting, in weird low tones, to the rhythm of a great, deep-throated drum. It was some monotonous hymn or supplication to their ancient gods—gods now personified in the things below. Through the screen of shrubbery between us, I glimpsed their chieftain, taller by a head than the rest, his arms up-raised, leading the exhortation. Their voices rose, broke in an angry clamor as a dozen of their kind burst from the forest dragging the bound form of a white man—*of Marston!*

I must be closer. Here, separated from them by a hundred feet of space and a double screen of matted vines, I dared not fire for fear of slaying friend with foe! Headlong I dived into the tangle, shoving the machine gun ahead of me! Had they not been utterly engrossed in their savage ritual, the Indians must surely have heard my blundering approach, ripping blindly through the undergrowth with caution flung to the winds! By chance or fortune the tangle was less matted than elsewhere, and I burst into the cleared space barely in the nick of time.

For all of his traitorous hypocrisy, Valdez had spoken truly of old customs and old sacrifices! Marston's huge, straining frame was bent back over a rounded slab of polished rock in the center of the clearing, the dwarfed forest-men fairly swarming over him to hold him in place! Arms raised in supplication, their chieftan stood over him, his features distorted by something more than fear of his gods, and frenzy of sacrifice! Hate and terrible rage had seized upon his bronzed visage, making of it a veritable devil-mask! And in his clenched fist he grasped a glittering knife of steel, a knife that half an hour ago I had seen buried in the black soil of the forest floor—*Valdez' knife!*

Again he was raising his chant of dedication and sacrifice, screeched to the thunderous rhythm of the drum in the manner of those Old Ones before the Incas! Again it mounted to its climactic crescendo of frenzied adoration and black hate— rose to a maddened scream, and broke as his arm swept down against that bearded throat! With a merry cackle of savage laughter, my gun woke the echoes, sweeping leaden death across the clearing, mowing its swath of lives in sacrifice more terrible than any savage mind could plan!

Through a bloody haze I saw the brown, broken bodies twisted and flung bodily from their feet by thudding missiles that tore their unresisting flesh from their broken bones and bathed the altar and the gaunt form stretched over it with spouting, smoking blood! Blood lust was in me as I raked their bewildered ranks with the laughing death, then the belt of cartridges was gone, and as I fumbled for a second the few cowering survivors fled screaming into the sheltering jungle!

Sanity came, and horror at the slaughter I had done, and with them an awful fear that in my unreasoning rage I had murdered friend as well as foe! Stumbling over the torn and bleeding windrows of slain humanity, I raced across the bloody clearing to where he lay, the gun forgotten! And as I reached the rude altar where he lay, Marston heaved his blood-soaked frame free of the bodies that covered it, sat up, and growled whimsically:

"Are you quite sure you've killed enough for the day? Or didn't you know it was loaded?"

"Marston, man!" I shouted frantically, "Are you all right? Did I hit you?"

"Oh, not at all. I'm quite all right. You're a rotten shot if I do say it—bring in a blasted flail, and then you can't hit me! Though I'll not say you didn't try hard enough. You did well by the innocent bystanders, and of course the public must come first in the mind of every good citizen."

As a matter of fact, I had nicked a chunk out of his arm—a nice, clean hit—and the blood on him was not all Indian. Still, his sarcastic joshing served its purpose and brought me out of my near-hysteria, where I was doing nobody the slightest good, into a sort of sanity in which I could at least talk without dithering like a crazy fool. Not until we were well clear of the shambles around the altar did he speak of Valdez.

"What happened?" he asked. "Did Valdez bolt?"

"He tried to," I replied glumly. "He had the stuff from the plane cached on the trail out, and—well, I wouldn't listen to reason, he pulled a gun, and we had it out. I broke his neck—killed him."

"I'm not blaming you for it. I saw it coming, and I reckon it was you or he. But it's stirred up merry hell among the Indians. Did you know he was a breed? He claimed to be pure Indian, son of a jungle chieftain and a princess of some remnants of the Old People, but he was a breed, and crossed the wrong way! The least hint that anyone had guessed the truth made a beast of him. I've seen him deliberately bash a man's head to jelly because the fellow, a Portuguese muleteer, claimed relationship—on his mother's side! He was one of their priests, a heritage from his father, and I guess they found his body. Hornby doesn't know, though, and if I were you I'd lay the blame to the Indians—the dead ones. Right?"

"I suppose so. It happened as you guessed. I slugged him in the neck with a heavy liana, too hard. But how did they get you?"

"I told you I was suspicious of Valdez. I tried to follow you, and they jumped me, south of here, near the ravine. It must have been shortly after they found Valdez, for they were all crazy mad. I think the Doc is safe, though. Do you realize that this spawning means that they're ready to go ahead and burn their way right through everything—make this whole planet a safer and better place for tetrahedra? Doc has figured they're from Mercury—overcrowded, probably, by this wholesale system of reproduction in job-lots, and hunting for new stamping-grounds. I don't know what our chances are of bucking them—about a quarter of what they were an hour ago—but they're mighty slim, armed as we are. You've got the other machine-gun?"

"It's at the cache, with most of the food, if the Indians didn't find it when they found Valdez. I have a map here, that he was using."

"Good. Let's have it. You keep an eye on the Professor tomorrow, now that the Indians are out for blood, and I'll get the stuff back to camp. Now I know they're hostile, I'll keep my weather eye open for trouble and I'll guarantee I won't be caught napping again. Come on—let's hunt him up now, while they're still scared."

"Wait, Marston," I replied. "You get the stuff now. I have a hunch we'll need it, and that soon. I can find Professor Hornby well enough, and I don't think the Indians will want any more for some time to come."

"Right you are!" he exclaimed. "So long then." And he swung off along my back-track.

CHAPTER IV

At Bay!

I had no trouble in finding the Professor. In truth, he found me. He was all but boiling over with excitement, for he had seen something we had not.

"Hawkins," he exclaimed, grabbing my shoulder fiercely, "did you see them spawn? It is remarkable—absolutely unequalled! The speed of it all—and, Hawkins, they do not have to grow before cleaving. I saw two that divided and redivided into three-inch tetrahedra—over a thousand of them! Think of it—Hawkins, they can overrun our little planet in a few days, once they start! We're done for!"

"I guess you're right, Professor," I replied. "But tell me—have you seen anything of the Indians?"

"The Indians? Yes—there seems to be something wrong with them now, Hawkins. They seem to have lost their reverence for the tetrahedra. These tribes do not paint much, but those I have seen were decorated for battle, and one old man was cursing the things from the edge of the forest, working himself up into a regular frenzy of invective. They may resist, now, if the tetrahedra try to start anything."

"Marston will be glad to hear that! Right now, I think we had better strike for the high ground across the ravine, where their flame is less likely to reach us. I'll leave you there and then look for Marston and the guns. We're going to need them before long."

"Very well, Hawkins. Your plan sounds good, and I'm glad you found the plane. But where is Valdez? Isn't he with Marston?"

"No. He's dead."

"Dead! You mean—the Indians?"

"Um. They nearly got Marston too, but I had one of the guns. Come on, we'll pick it up, and my pack of food, and find a place where we can see what happens and still be fairly safe. Follow me."

We found an ideal fortress, high on the west side of the ravine, where a little spur ran down from the highlands to the valley of the tetrahedra. Indeed, it had been used as a lookout by the ancient inhabitants of the region, ages ago, when great cities of cut stone lay in the valleys now choked by vegetation. Enough of the ancient walls remained to provide a decent bulwark against attack, and I left Professor Hornby with the gun to hold the fort until I could find Marston.

I had little difficulty in locating him, and between us we transferred the supplies from cache to lookout, while the Professor kept a perfunctory guard over them. As a matter of fact, he was more interested in digging around in the ancient floor of potsherds and tools of the former inhabitants. He explained that the ancient Pleistocene wave of immigration from Asia, via Alaska and North America, had split at Panama to pass down both sides of the Andes. On the west, along the coast, arose the ancient American civilizations, culminating in the Incas. On the east were the forest Indians, poor savage creatures of the thick jungles, such as we had seen. And here, on the boundary between these two regions, he sought a link between the two. Perhaps he had found it. We were never to know.

It was two days before the hostilities began. Meanwhile we had found the wreck of the plane, very nearly intact but quite useless in this dense jungle. We drained the tanks of what gasoline they contained, storing it in great glazed jars of painted earthenware that Professor Hornby had found intact in a niche below our present floor-level. His idea was to fight fire with fire, incidentally clearing a space about the spur on which our little fort was perched, so that we could see what we were about in case of trouble.

Marston and I cleared out the brush as best we could, and cut deep slots in the larger trees on the down-hill side. A back-fire is ticklish work in the forest, but we worked it, piling the quickly drying underbrush at the far side of our little swath, saturating it with gasoline, then digging in to one of the Professor's excavations while the fireworks went off. In a drier climate we would not have lived to tell the tale. As it was, we more or less leveled the thick forest for about two hundred feet on all sides, before the fire petered out, leaving a tangled mess of blackened wreckage that effectively kept us in and others out, as well as clearing the field of view.

Our fire may have served to set off the onslaught of the tetrahedra. Certainly, with the next morning, there was renewed activity in their rocky pocket. They cleared out a sizeable ring of forest before sun-set. The next noon they had another sunfeast, and now the blackened valley was fairly teeming with their angular forms, large and small, for many seemed to have split without growing, as the Professor had seen one do before.

Now, their army of destruction assembled, the tetrahedra began their conquest of Earth! In vast waves of horrid destruction with rays of angry yellow flame darting from apexes their flaming floods of energy swept over the jungle, and now not even its damp dark could resist. Mighty forest-giants toppled headlong, by the cleaving yellow flame, to melt into powdery ash before they touched the ground. Giant lianas writhed like tortured serpents as their juices were vaporized by the awful heat, then dropped away in death to lie in long grey coils along the stripped rock of the forest floor—rock that was fast taking on the glassy glare of the little valley, rock fused by heat such as Earth had never known.

By evening, our spur of rock was a lone peninsula, an oasis in a desert of harsh black, a height which the tetrahedra, for some unknown reason, had not attempted.

Now we could watch their plan of campaign, and our hearts sank in fear for our race, for while half of the tetrahedral army engaged in its holocaust of destruction, the remaining half fed and spawned in the full blaze of the sun. With every day dozens of square miles were added to their hellish domain and thousands of tetrahedra to their unnatural army. For now we could see that more and more of them were taking the second course, were splitting into hosts of tiny, three-inch creatures which, within a few days' time, had swelled to full size and on the following day could spawn anew! It was dreadful, but now we were hopelessly isolated—an island in a sea of black rock, untouched as yet by the blasting fires, but utterly unable to save ourselves or our world.

Aside from the vegetation which they were so methodically blasting, the Mercutian tetrahedra—for such Professor Hornby swore they were and such we later found them to be—had not yet come into real contact with the life of our planet, much less its master, Man. The worship of the Indians had been carried on from afar, and we ourselves were careful not to tempt our visitors from space. Now all that was changed in something of a double-barreled fashion. It began with the Indians. It ended with us.

Now that we were shut off from the jungle, we no longer sensed the unease and stealthy activity of the forest people. Their gods had betrayed them—perhaps they thought them devils now—their sacrifice had been interrupted and their chief men slaughtered unmercifully by the slayers of their half-white brother. Their whole life and legend had gone wrong. The tetrahedra were to blame, and the tetrahedra must pay!

The invaders did not start their daily program of devastation until the sun was high. Of late, the people of the forest had become creatures of the night, and so it was that Marston roused us about midnight to watch the fun, as he put it. As a matter of fact, we all realized that what the Indians did would probably be of vital importance to our own situation.

The spheres were too small to hold all the tetrahedral hosts, now, and they lay crowded in great confocal ovals about them, sleeping, if such things can be said to sleep. The first indication of the attack was a tiny fire of leaves and twigs on the rocks above the ravine, now choked with slabs of rock scaled from its walls by the terrific heat. It was barely visible —merely a smudge in size, kindled for some magical purpose. Then there came a low, wailing chant, rising swiftly in vehemence and bitter hatred—a curse designed to blast the unearthly invaders where they lay. Professor Hornby was fairly gasping at the enormously ancient background of legend and superstition which it revealed, when it suddenly broke in a shrill, senile yammer of sheer madness! The strain was more than the old priest could stand.

As in answer, other, greater fires sprang up all along the walls of the valley, and by their light we could see the Indians closing in from the edge of the forest—thousands of them, drawn to worship over untold leagues of jungle paths, and now racing into battle with all the mad fanaticism of an outraged religion! It was like a tidal wave of screeching humanity, pouring down over the black rock to break over the sleeping tetrahedra! Yet, as the last Indian burst from shelter of the jungle, the attacking force was revealed as pitifully small, compared to the ranks of those whom they attacked. Like a great city of black, tetrahedral tents the Mercutians lay, dim-lit by the failing moon, as if unaware of the savage swarm, led by its gibbering priest, that raced upon them. But they were far from unaware!

It was I who first noticed the faint, rosy glow that hung over the silent ranks—a glow like that which had brought down my plane. I whispered to Marston, and he told me that it had not been there before—that the tetrahedra must be awake, and waiting!

He was right. The red glow was spreading swiftly, out over the valley floor, and there must have been another, invisible emanation that preceded it, for I saw the old priest falter, beat with clawed fists at an unseen wall, then topple with a choking scream and lie still. Now, all round the valley, the first ranks of the savages were meeting this slowly advancing wall of un-seen death—meeting it, and falling before it! In long win-drows they lay, body after body piling up before the momen-tum of the unleashed rush of the red-skinned hordes! Stones, arrows, spears flew through the thickening red mist to clatter harmlessly upon the quiescent tetrahedra! But not as harm-lessly as it seemed, for here and there among them showed a little spurt of pale blue flame as one of the smaller things was crushed by a hurtling stone! They were hard, but their skins of crystal were thin, and a well-flung stone might break them! *They were not invulnerable!*

The Indians sensed this, too, for they had deserted spears and darts in favor of a hail of stones, large and small, that clattered among the tetrahedra in a veritable downpour, deal-ing really telling destruction among those who had not at-tained a fair size.

The savages were yelling in triumph, now, thrilled with suc-cess, and their blind onslaught was checked, but still the in-visible barrier crept on, dealing death all along their evilly grimacing front, and still the rose-red haze followed after, dis-solving the crumpled bodies in fine white ash that in turn van-ished in the deepening red. The yelling circle was thinning fast, yet they had not realized the futility of their attack when suddenly the tetrahedra deserted quiet defense for active com-bat!

The cause was evident. Five Indians on the upslope had shoved over the cliff a huge rounded boulder that bounded like a live thing among the rocks and crashed full into the side

of a great eight-foot tetrahedron, splintering its flinty flank
and freeing the pent-up energy in a blinding torrent of blue
flame that cascaded over the nearby ledges, fusing them into a
white-hot, smoking pool of molten lava that glowed evilly in
the ill-lit gloom! It was the last straw! The mad attack had become a thing of real menace to the tetrahedra, and they
sprang into swift retribution. From their apexes they flashed
out the flaming yellow streaks of destruction.

Now at last the Indians broke and fled before the advancing
hordes, but flight came too late, for the tetrahedra were
aroused and they gave no quarter! Long tongues of yellow
reached out, beating down like awful flails on the fleeing savages and searing them with swift agony, dropping them in
their tracks, driving them down in shapeless horror against
the smoking rock, where the scarlet sea swept over them and
dissolved them in drifting, fusing ash! The doomed Indians
seemed to float in a yellow sea and what the sea touched was
gone in an instant! Before that awful barrage nothing living
could stand!

Of a sudden the tragedy was borne forcibly to our own
quarter, as a handful of Indians sought the refuge of our
rocky spur! Like brown apes they scrambled up its precipitous
side toward our fortress and burrowed through the tangled
debris of our back-fire. They were men like ourselves, men in
awful danger of their lives, and Marston and Hornby sprang
to the parapet, shouting at them in their native tongue. But
the frightened savage knows no friend, and their reply was a
volley of long arrows that toppled the Professor into my arms
and sent Marston cursing for the guns! Lips set grimly, he
sprayed the rocky slope with whining leaden death, mowing
down the frenzied savages as I had done in the place of sacrifice! At sight of us, their madness burst forth anew and they
broke their flight to rush our pinnacle, voices raised in wild
vituperation!

Laying Professor Hornby under the shelter of the wall, I
dragged out the other gun and kicked open a case of ammunition, joining Marston in the defense of the fort. That other
time I had had surprise and superstition to aid me in my
single-handed victory, but now we two were leagued against
outraged fanaticism, and the odds were great. Like locusts
they came on, from every side, eyes red with blood-lust, teeth
bared in hate—beasts of the jungle, ravening for the kill! It

was the debris of our back-fire, piled in a matted belt around the spur, that saved us, for here the mad charge must halt and here our guns took their toll. Nor were we two alone, for now I heard the crack of a rifle and knew that Professor Hornby was covering the ledge of rock that ran back at our rear to join us to the hills.

Even so, I think our defense must have failed but for the tetrahedra. They had not been slow to recognize the changed nature of the Indians' fight, and they turned that realization to their own advantage, curving around the spur to cut off a second retreat, then laying down their fiery yellow barrage upon the rear of the clamoring savage host, licking them up as a bear licks ants. It was a matter of minutes before the last Indian lay in grey ash on the rocky slope of the crag.

For a moment matters were at a deadlock. We paused and took stock—three men with their guns against thousands of tetrahedra, armed with lightnings. Hornby had slumped back against the low wall, his eyes closed, his spare frame racked with coughs that brought back blood to his twisted lips. An arrow had pierced his lungs. Marston dropped the machine-gun, now smoking-hot, and grabbed up a rifle. I followed suit. So for perhaps two minutes the rival forces held silent, waiting.

The Mercutians took the initiative. Their yellow tongues of flame crept slowly up the hillside, scouring it clean—up, up toward our little refuge on the peak. Now they began to glide forward, on every side, beginning the ascent. In answer our rifles rang out, and now there was no doubt as to their vulnerability, for wherever the steel-jacketed lead hit, there the thin crystal splintered and the night was lit by the glare of freed energy, the life-blood of the tetrahedra! We could not save ourselves, but we would do no puny damage!

Now came a dull thunder from the rear, and by the dim light of the red mist I could see the giant leader of the Mercutians, standing at the summit of the cliff above the valley, commanding the attack. In reply, the yellow barrage began to beat upward along the rock, toward us, and with the same signal a faint, blurred scheme leapt into my fuddled brain! I raised my rifle, fired—not at the advancing front but farther back, into the body of the horde, slowly driving my fire back toward the giant commander, picking off monster after angular monster, nearer and nearer to where he squatted!

Then he was flinching, gliding back before the sea of flame

that burst around him as his crystal warriors fell, and in reply I brought down one after another of those toward whom he was retreating, hemming him in with death, threatening—but not striking! I cannot tell why we did not destroy him, for Marston had followed suit, neglecting the threat of the flame, which waned and died as the tetahedra woke to the meaning of our fire. Somehow we felt that it was wiser to spare him, and our intuition was good. For a moment he hesitated, then thundered his drumming command, and the ranks of the tetrahedra drew slowly back, leaving us in peace and safety.

So we remained, virtually prisoners, for eight days. On the third, Professor Hornby died—a blessing, for he suffered greatly. He was the only one who really understood these tetrahedra, and we shall never know how he deduced that they were from Mercury, a fact which Marston later proved. The archaeological data collected by the expedition are lost, too, since both he and Valdez are dead and we could bring out no specimens. The tetrahedra left us alone, barring us from flight with their haze of red energy, which extended up the slope to a level above that of the saddle connecting us with the forested mountain-slopes. Meanwhile they continued their barrage of the jungle, laying it waste on every side, mile after mile, day after day.

Through the binoculars we had watched them slowly advance, and noted their very human surprise as they burned the covering jungle from the great ruined city which the expedition had sought. It was their first real experience with the works of Man, and it caused a great commotion among them. Led by the purple giant, they swarmed over and through its ruined labyrinth, studying its every niche and angle, learning it. Here was their proof that Earth harbored a civilization—that they might expect real opposition. I do not think they ever realized that our puny defense was a fair example of what that civilization could do.

Later in the same day they found the wreck of the plane, and this time consternation indeed reigned. Here was a machine of some sort, evidently the product of that civilization that they feared. Moreover, it was recent where the city was ancient. Could it mean that they were watched—that the unseen creatures of this unknown ruling race were lurking in the dark of the jungle, with their engines of war and destruction—*waiting?* Now, as never before in their descent on

Earth, the tetrahedra were faced by the stark blankness of the utterly unknown, and I think that they began to be afraid.

The little valley was still the center of their activity, and every day we watched their spawning as the sun rode high, saw the piling up of the hordes that would overwhelm our race and planet, and make of it a dead, black thing like that little pocket on the east slope of the Andes. There was always a double ring of the tetrahedra about us now, and their crimson sea of energy beat high about our prison. The giant who led them came often to observe us, to sit and stare with invisible eyes at our fortress and ourselves. Their drumming speech had grown familiar, too, and I felt that it would not be hard to understand, given the key to its meaning.

Marston seemed fascinated with the things and their ways. There was a spring, just above the limit of the red haze, where we got our water, and he would sit there by the hour, as close to the things as he could get, watching and listening. I could see him sway to the rhythm of their thunderous speech, see his lips move in low response, and I wondered if he were going mad.

Ever since Marston had first mentioned Professor Hornby's theory that the things were Mercutians, I had been trying to find some way of verifying it. Now that we were on semi-intimate terms with the tetrahedra, I wondered if I might not get them, somehow, to supply this evidence. I thought of stories I had read of interplanetary communication—of telepathy, of word-association, of sign-language. They had all seemed far-fetched to me, impossible of attainment, but I resolved to try my hand at the last.

There was some rather soft rock in the structure of the watch-tower, and as Valdez had rescued my tool kit from the plane, I had a hammer and chisel. With these, and a faulty memory, I set out to make a rough scale diagram of the inner planets, leaning a bit on the Professor's theory. I cut circular grooves for the orbits of the four minor planets—Mercury, Venus, Earth, Mars—and dug a deep central pit. In this I set a large nugget of gold, found in the ruins of the fortress, for the Sun, and in the grooves a tiny black pebble for Mercury, a large white one for Venus, and a jade bead from the ruins for Earth. Earth had a very small white moon, in its own deep-cut spiral orbit. Mars was a small chunk of rusty iron with two grains of sand for moons. I had a fair-sized scale, and there was no room for more.

Now I was prepared to attempt communication with the tetrahedra, but I wanted more than one diagram to work with. Consequently I attempted a map of Earth, with hollowed oceans and low mountain-ridges. All this took plenty of time and trouble, but Marston was not at all in evidence, and I was not sorry, for my scheme seemed rather pointless, and I did not relish his ridicule.

CHAPTER V

Face to Face

So things stood when the tropical storm broke over us. Its cause is not hard to explain. Remember, when those scathing fires blasted the jungle, all the superabundant moisture of the region was vaporized. Even our little spring, as it ran down into the crimson haze, vanished in plumes of steam as it passed the scarce visible boundary between life and death. To add to this, during all the long summer, the sun had been literally boiling the moisture out of the rain-forests all over the Amazon Basin. The air was nearly saturated with water-vapor, though the rainy season was normally a month off. The electrical disturbances set up by the continual barrage of fire added to the general effect. Things were ripe for a storm, and it came!

A cloud-burst, it would be called in the United States. The heavens opened in the night, and water fell in torrents, streaming from every angle of the rock, standing in pools wherever a hollow offered itself, drenching us and the world through and through. Day came, but there was no sun for the tetrahedra to feed on. Nor were they thinking of feeding, for very definite peril threatened them. *To the tetrahedra, water was death!*

As I have said, their fires had flaked huge slabs of rock from the walls of the ravine leading from the high-walled valley where they slept, choking its narrow throat with shattered stone. And now that the mountain slopes, shorn of soil and vegetation, were pouring water into its bed, the stream that had carved that ravine found its course dammed—rose against it, poured over it, but not until the valley had become a lake, a lake where only the two pearly spheres floated against the rocky wall, the thousands of tetrahedra gone forever—*dissolved!*

Water was death to them—dissolution! Only in the shelter of the spheres was there safety, and they were long since crowded. The hordes of the tetrahedral monsters perished miserably in the night, before they could summon the forces that might have spun them a fiery canopy of arching lightnings that would drive the water back in vapor and keep them safely dry beneath. A hundred had come in the twin spheres. A hundred thousand had been born. A bare hundred remained. Our way of escape was clear!

But escape had been possible before, and we stayed then as now. Flight was delay—nothing more. A miracle might save us, and I think we believed in miracles. So we vainly sought shelter from the deluge in the ruins of the tower, and stared through the falling rain at the two spheres, now clear of the water and perched on the ravine's edge, above the dam.

Our "local shower" lasted for three days. Then came the sun, and the mountains began to drain. Only the new-born lake remained to remind us of the rains, a lake stained deep violet with the slowly dissolving bodies of the crystal tetrahedra. Those in the two spheres waited for a day, then came forth to survey the ruins of their campaign—the giant leader and a scant hundred of his richly purple subordinates. And now, too, came proof of the method in Marston's madness.

The tetrahedra had resumed their guard about the base of our crag, although the crimson barrage did not beat so high nor so vividly. Their master squatted outside the ring, brooding, watching us—perhaps pondering our connection with the tempest that had wrecked his hopes. And now Marston took under his arm the great Indian drum that I had brought away from the place of sacrifice, a drum of ancient ritual, headed with well-tanned human skin, and stalked down the slope to confront the tetrahedra. I stuck by the guns and waited.

I can see them yet, giant leaders of two utterly different races, born on two planets sixty millions of miles apart at their nearest, inherently opposite and inherently enemies, squatting there on the black rock, watching each other! A rumble of speech from the great leader and the rose-hue of the barrage deepened, climbed higher about the crag. A bluff, it was. Marston did not move.

And then he took up the great drum. He had cared for it as for a child during the long rain, sheltering it as best he could, testing the tautness of its grisly membrane, drying it carefully with sun and fire during all the previous day. Now I learned the reason.

Slowly, softly, using the heel of his palm and his fingers in quick succession, he began to drum. This was not the rhythmic throb of native dances, not the choppy voice of signal drums. Faster, ever faster the great drum of sacrifice boomed forth its message, until the beats melted into a low, continuous thunder of bottomless sound, mounting in volume to a steady, rolling roar, rising and swelling in delicate inflection. His wrist must have been wonderfully strong and flexible to so control the sound! On and on in great throbbing billows rolled the drumming, and but for its thunder all the world lay still—Marston and I on the slope of the spur, the tetrahedra about its base, the purple giant beyond, on the shore of the lake. On and on, thundering through my brain in dull, insistent beatings of dead surf on the beaches of a dead world, possessing me, filling me, speaking to me in the voice of the storm—speaking—that was it! *Marston was speaking to the tetrahedra with the voice of his giant drum!*

During those long, empty days on the crag-side he had been listening, learning, drilling into his scientist's brain the meaning of every voiced command that the great master of the Mercutian tetrahedra thundered to his crystal hosts, learning their inflections, storing them in his mind! He had memorized a simple vocabulary—sounds that signified the great commander, the horde, the tetrahedra as a class; simple verbs for coming and going, for altering the barrage; words for human beings, for their planet and our own—a host of nouns and verbs that even yet seem behind the power of any man to glean from the muttering of an alien race, coupled with the actions that fitted the words. But Marston *had* learned, and with the sullen voice of the giant drum he was replying, in rough, broken, ill-chosen words, falteringly expressed, words that the tetrahedron understood!

For the crimson mist faded, vanished. The crystal ranks split, and through the lane between them glided the giant ruler, coming to where Marston sat with his drum. He stopped, spoke in words very like those that Marston had used —simple words, such as our own babies learn, roughly connected.

"What—you?"

And the drum: "We—tetrahedra—Earth." I translated rudely, as they spoke. His words were not so literal as I must make them, to suit our limited tongue—were ideas, rather than words. And yet, they got their message across!

The giant was startled. How could we, misshapen, flabby monstrosities, be rulers of a planet, equal to themselves? He was incredulous:

"You—tetrahedra?"

The drum muttered approval, as for a fulfilled command. The idea had been transferred, but the purple giant did not seem to think much of it.

"You—weak! (Easily vulnerable, like vegetation, was the sense of the term used.) You—dead—easy. (Here he used a term with which he had designated the tetrahedra shattered in the battle with the Indians.) *We*—tetrahedra—our planet—and Earth!"

There wasn't much answer to that one. They could rule both planets with ease. And yet—Marston called to me.

"Hawkins, bring down those stones you've been chipping, and a flask of water. Wait—bring two flasks, and a gun."

So he had seen me at work and guessed my plan. Well, his own beat it hollow, but if he had an idea, I wasn't going to hinder him. I lugged the slabs down and went back for the stoppered canteens of water and the gun. At his directions I set one flask against the rock of the hillside, above him. He took the other. And all the while his drum was murmuring reassurance to the giant and his horde.

"You work the slabs, Hawkins," he said, "while I talk. I'll translate, and you act accordingly." The drum spoke:

"Sun—Sun—Sun." He pointed. "Your Sun—our Sun."

The tetrahedron approved. He came from our own Solar System.

Now he was pointing to my diagram, to the Sun, the Earth and its orbit. "Sun. Sun. Earth. Earth." I rolled the jade bead slowly along its groove, the white moon-pebble following in its spiral course. I rolled the other planets, showed him their colors and relative sizes. Marston was drumming again, as I touched planet after planet, questioning.

"You planet—your planet? Your planet—what? This?"

The giant disapproved. It was not Mars.

"This?" It was anything but Venus! Venus must have been pretty wet for the completest comfort.

Eagerly—"This?" Assent! The Professor was right! They came from Mercury! But Marston wanted to be sure. He found a white speck of quartz in the black stone that was Mercury, and now he turned it to the golden Sun—held it there as Mercury revolved slowly in its orbit. There was emphatic approval. Mercury it was—the planet with one side always to the sun. So far, so good. Marston took my other plaque—the relief map of Earth.

"Earth—Earth."

Yes, the Mercutian recognized it. He had seen it thus from space.

With a crystal of quartz, Marston gouged our particular section of South America, pointed to the ground, to the lake, the forests. "This—this," he said.

More approval. They knew where they were, all right.

Now he reopened a closed subject. He started up the monotone of reassurance, then superimposed on it a few deft words.

"You—tetrahedra—Mercury." They sure were!

"*We*—tetrahedra—*Earth!*" Not so good! He repeated: "*You*—Mercury. *We*—Earth. We—tetrahedra!" There were evident signs of dissent! Marston swelled the reassurance-tone, then added a sharp call to attention, raised his gun, fired twice, threw the weapon down, and redoubled his assurance of well-meaning and safety.

His aim had been good. The flask was pierced at top and bottom, and a thin stream of water was jetting forth, trickling over the glassy rock toward us. It made a little pool at his feet, lipped over, and the double rank of tetrahedra drew back to let it pass. It formed another little pool, close to the base of their giant leader. He wasn't taking bluffs! A flash of blinding energy and the pool was steam and the rock white-hot! Marston learned another word.

"*Water—dead!* We—tetrahedra—Mercury and Earth!"

Not so good! Marston tried another.

"You — tetrahedra — Mercury. *Water* — tetrahedron — Earth!"

An alarming idea that! Water the lord of Earth!

"Water—*no*—dead!" Decided negation in the drum. He pointed. True enough, the steam was condensing and running down the smooth rock in little droplets. Water could not be killed! It always came back!

"*We—tetrahedra—water!*"

Phew! That *was* a statement! He proved it. He dabbled his fingers in the pool at his feet, took some up in his hand and slicked back his hair. I gave a thunderous grunt by way of attracting attention, uncapped the other canteen, and poured a long and very visible stream of water down my throat. Marston took the canteen and did the same, then sent me for more water, a pailful.

"Water—tetrahedron—Earth!" he reiterated. He illustrated his point, dipped water from the pail with much splashing and poured it over my relief of the Earth, filling the hollows of the seas. He emphasized it, with a gloomy note in his drumming. *"Water*—tetrahedron—Earth. Water. *Water!"*

He had another hunch, rolled Venus around its orbit. "What?" asked the drum. He was answered, glumly. He dipped Venus in the water. Venus was pumice and floated.

"Water—tetrahedron—Venus?" Oh, decidedly. The purple giant was sure of that. Marston tried Mercury. Mercury sank. Time after time it sank. Water didn't like Mercury.

"You—tetrahedra—Mercury. Water—*no*—tetrahedron—Mercury." A pause. Then slowly, ominously—*"Water—tetrahedron—you!"*

And he was right. Water had them licked. I had a bright idea, and Marston moved camp to the brink of the lake, striding like a conqueror between the double file of tetrahedra. Arrived beside the water, with the giant fairly close and the army very much in the background, I stripped and dove in—"brought up bottom"—brought up a chunk of half-dissolved purple crystal! Marston rubbed it in, gleefully.

"Water—tetrahedron—*you!"* They had to admit it. Now he tried to coin a word—pointed to the sky and shuffled syllables on the drum. "Up—up. Water—up." The giant caught on and supplied the correct term. Marston coined a real one—a genial, murmured "Thank-you"—on his drum. I tried my hand again, dipped up a bucket of water and doused Marston, then stepped toward the great tetrahedron with another. He retreated. I wallowed in it myself instead—childish, but convincing. By now the idea was definitely set that water was rank poison to the tetrahedra and a second home to us. Now for the real information!

Marston drummed attention and reassurance, and the great leader glided back, carefully avoiding puddles. I could see that he floated about three inches clear of the ground. Perhaps, with the lesser gravitation of Mercury, he flew.

I started demonstrating my little Solar System again, while Marston announced again that Earth was largely water—no fit place for tetrahedra—water that could be killed, but that came down again in rain. He drilled in the idea of rain, until he was sure he had made his point, securing various Mercutian expressions of disgust and dislike. He found a word for "rain"—really coined one, for it did not seem to exist in Mercutian. It was a combination of "water" and "up," so as to be quite clear, with a double-ruffle of emphasis to characterize it. The etymology of the word was quite clear to all concerned. They knew what rain was, now.

I had poked a hole through the soft, thin rock of Mercury's orbit and put clay plugs in Earth's orbit at diametrically opposite points. Now Marston demonstrated. He poured water on Mercury. It vanished.

"Mercury—no—rain. No!" The entire host had crowded in, and there was a general murmur of assent.

Venus, on the other hand, being a deep groove, held plenty of water. "Venus—rain. Water—tetrahedron—Venus."

They got that, too. Weather of Venus is ideal for ducks and frogs—*not* for tetrahedra.

He moved out one planet, and I could feel a tensing. They knew what he was driving at! He was going to describe weather-conditions of Earth. Half Earth's orbit held water to the brim. The other half was rather damp. He slowly moved Earth around her circles, showing that six months were wet and six not so wet. He took to the drum for emphasis.

Water—tetrahedron—Earth. *We*—tetrahedron—water. Water—tetrahedron—*you*." A delicate inference. Then, slowly, emphatically, "Water—Venus. Water—earth." And now his final card.

He set Mercury in its orbit, placed Venus almost opposite, paused. The giant assented. That was where the planets were at present. He skipped Earth and went to Mars, rolled it along its orbit, stopped it. Assent. All true, so far. And now I saw his point, for when he dropped Earth in place, very nearly in line between Mars and Mercury, *it fell in the middle of the dry half of the orbit!*

A hundred tetrahedra slid back a yard or so in recoil. This rain which had drowned out practically all of their army of thousands, was an example of our *dry* season! By inference, our real wet weather must have been sheer Mercutian hell to every tetrahedron of them!

But Marston was too good a diplomat to give them a hands off without suggesting an alternative. He slowly poured water on Mars. Mars apparently, and actually, had a hole in its bottom, for it drained bone dry. Mars, now, was very nice. But Earth was nasty and wet, as bad as Venus or worse. And it was inhabited by a race of super-intelligent fish, to judge from the impression he gave the tetrahedra. He picked up the drum for a last word.

"Earth—*rain*. Mars—*no*—rain. *We*—Earth. You—*no*—Earth. You—Mars?" He dwelt on the question. "Mars? Mars???" He rolled out an endless question-mark, then suddenly quit, took a long, flashing drink of water from the flask, and dove into the lake, clothes and all. I followed him, and together we splashed to the other shore, making our mastery of the water very evident, them climbed out, waiting. If things worked out, all well and good. If they didn't—well, we had the lake between us.

And it did work! For a moment they stood motionless, the mighty sixteen-foot tetrahedron of royal purple and his eight-foot purple retinue, silent, considering. Then came a sudden command, and the hundred flowed in orderly motion to the spheres, entered. Their mighty master was alone. For an instant he hesitated, then swept forward to the very edge of the lake. From this towering peak beat the white lightnings, lashing the purple waters into great billowing clouds of steam that threw up a dense wall of mist between us! Through the hiss of the steam came his thunderous voice, in last comment upon the invastion of his tetrahedral race! Marston translated, softly:

"Water—tetrahedron—Earth. *You*—tetrahedron—water. *We*—*kill*—*water!* You—Earth. We—Mars. Mars!" And a long, rolling assent, an infinitely underlined *"YES!"*

Water and Earth seemed to be synonymous, and we were perfectly at ease in that dangerous element. For all that, they, the tetrahedra of Mercury, could "kill" it, which, by inference, we could not. They weren't going to admit defeat, by Man or water, but this was a big Solar System. We could have our soggy Earth! They were going to Mars!

Up from behind the wall of "killed" water rose two great, glorious pearls, marvelously opalescent in the rays of the setting sun—up and up, smaller and smaller, until they vanished into the deepening blue above the Andes. Ironically, it began to rain.

As you see, "Tetrahedra of Space" belongs in the same tradition as the stories of Meek. The setting is South America, and it is the Indians this time who are superstitious savages and clearly subhuman. When the half-breed, Valdez, is killed, the hero buries him saying, ". . . all of him was human," but also says, ". . . part of him was white."

P. Schuyler Miller has been the book reviewer for *Astounding* now for almost as many years as I have been writing, and I know him to be a liberal and humane person, one of the gentlest and most generous souls I have ever met. It is a measure of how far the unthinking stereotypes can penetrate and of how taken-for-granted they were in this type of adventure fiction, that even Miller could fall victim to them.

What fascinated me in this story and what caused it to live on in my memory was the picture of extraterrestrials who were utterly non-human. This wasn't often done in those days, or, for that matter, in the more primitive forms of science fiction even today. In so many cases, intelligent creatures are assumed to be quite human if they are virtuous, and distortedly human if they are villainous, as in "Submicroscopic."

There was, further, the picture of the tetrahedra spawning and of the final communication of the two intelligences, which was handled rather subtly, I thought then—and thought again recently, when I reread it.

One other thing that occurs to me in connection with the story is the mere word "tetrahedra." Miller doesn't define the word anywhere in the story, but the illustrations by Frank R. Paul (one of them on the cover of the magazine) made it clear to me that they were solids with four, triangular faces.

It was the first time I had ever heard the word, and, of course, I never forgot it. Any form of reading will improve one's vocabulary, but science fiction automatically improves one's scientific vocabulary.

"Tetrahedra of Space," incidentally, contains another common characteristic of early magazine science fiction: elephantiasis of the adjectives. Especially in the first portion of the story, every sentence carries a load of them that breaks it in two. Combine that with inverted word order and unnecessary italics, and you find yourself breathing heavily and losing track of the sense.

To me in my younger days, and to others in theirs, and to some, I fear, in all their days, this thick layer of fatty adjectival froth seems to be a mark of good writing. And, indeed, adjectivitis was most common in the fantasy of the time and in such admired writers as A. Merritt, H. P. Lovecraft, and Clark Ashton Smith (whom, however, I am afraid I never admired, even when I was young and might have been excused the error).

Clark Ashton Smith, in particular, had a second interesting literary aberration. He used long and unfamiliar words as another way of impressing the naïve with the quality of his writing. In the same issue with "Tetrahedra of Space," for instance, there is Smith's "Beyond the Singing Flame," and since Sam Moskowitz had sent me the complete issue in this particular case, I looked at the Smith story for old times' sake.

In the very second paragraph, I found him using "veridical" when he meant "true," and I read no further. Yes, "veridical" does mean "true," but I cannot imagine any occasion (outside a certain specialized use among psychologists) when "true" is not very greatly to be preferred.

In my early days, I tried to imitate these adjectival examples of writing. My style was most ornate in the days before I had published anything. Some of the fat had been steamed out by the time I was publishing, and my writing has grown progressively leaner with the years. I am not sorry.

During 1931, I reached the stage where my pleasure in science fiction had bubbled over and could not be confined. I began to retell the stories I had read. I did this, I remember, in distinct imitation of my storytelling friend of three years earlier. Now it was *I* who had the audience.

Of course, the stories weren't my own, but I made no pretense that they were. I carefully explained that I had read them in science fiction magazines. My classmates couldn't afford to buy the magazines any more than I could and were glad to listen.

As for myself, I discovered, for the first time in my life, that I loved to have an audience and that I could speak before a group, even when some of them were strangers to me, without embarrassment. (It was a useful piece of knowledge, for twenty years later I was to become a professional after-dinner speaker at what turned out to be, eventually, very respectable fees. The childhood experience and training helped, I am sure.)

I well remember sitting at the curb in front of the junior high school with anywhere from two to ten youngsters listening attentively while I repeated what I had read, with such personal embellishments as I could manage.

And the specific story that I most vividly recall telling was "The World of the Red Sun," by Clifford D. Simak, which appeared in the December 1931 issue of *Wonder Stories*.

THE WORLD OF THE RED SUN

by Clifford D. Simak

"READY, Bill?" asked Harl Swanson. Bill Kressman nodded.

"Then kiss 1935 good-bye!" cried the giant Swede, and swung over the lever.

The machine quivered violently, then hung motionless in pitch blackness. In the snap of a finger the bright sunlight was blotted out and a total darkness, a darkness painted with the devil's brush, rushed in upon the two men.

Electric lights glowed above the instrument boards, but their illumination was feeble against the utter blackness which crowded in upon the quartz windows of the machine.

The sudden change astounded Bill. He had been prepared for something, for some sort of change, but nothing like this. He half started out of his seat, then settled back.

Harl observed him and grinned.

"Scared," he jested.

"Hell, no," said Bill.

"You're traveling in time, my lad," said Harl. "You aren't in space any more. You are in a time stream. Space is curved about you. Can't travel in time when you're still in space, for space binds time to a measured pace, only so fast, no faster. Curve space about you, though, and you can travel in time. And when you're out of space there's absolutely no light, therefore, utter darkness. Likewise no gravity, nor any of the universal phenomena."

Bill nodded. They had worked it all out before, many, many times. Double wall construction of a strength to withstand the vacuum into which the flier would be plunged at the move of the lever which would snatch it out of space into the time stream. An insulation to guard against the absolute zero that would rule where there could be no heat. Gravity grids at their feet so that they would still be able to orient themselves when flung into that space where there was not gravity. An elaborate heating system to keep the motors warm, to prevent the freezing of gasoline, oil and water. Powerful atmosphere generators to supply air to the passengers and the motors.

It had represented years of work, ten years of it, and a wealth that mounted into seven figures. Time after time they had blundered, again and again they had failed. The discoveries they had made would have rocked the world, would have revolutionized industry, but they had breathed no word of it. They had thought of only one thing, time travel.

To travel into the future, to delve into the past, to conquer time, to this the two young scientists had dedicated all their labors, and at last success lay beneath their hands.

It was in 1933 they had at last achieved their goal. The intervening months were spent in experiments and the building of the combination flier-time machine.

Miniature fliers were launched, with the miniature time machines set automatically. They had buzzed about the laboratory, to suddenly disappear. Perhaps at this very instant they were whirling madly through unguessed ages.

They managed to construct a small time machine, set to travel a month into the future. In a month's time, almost to the second, it had materialized on the laboratory floor where it had dropped at the end of its flight through time. That settled it! The feasibility of time travel was proved beyond all doubt.

Now Harl Swanson and Bill Kressman were out in the time stream. There had been a gasp of amazement from the crowd, on the street, which had seen the giant tri-motored plane suddenly disappear into thin air.

Harl crouched over the instrument board. His straining ears could distinguish the wheezy mutterings of the three motors as, despite the elaborate precautions taken to safeguard them, the inexorable fingers of absolute zero clutched at their throbbing metal.

This was a dangerous way, but the only safe way. Had they remained on the surface to plunge into the time stream they might have halted to find themselves and their machine buried by shifting earth; they might have found a great building over them, they might have found a canal covering them. Here in the air they were safe from all that might occur beneath them in the passing centuries through which they sped at an almost unbelievable pace. They were being fairly hurled through time.

Furthermore, the great machine would serve as a means of travel in that future day when they would roll out of the time stream back into space again. Perhaps it might serve as a means of escape, for there was no foreknowledge to tell them what they might expect a few thousand years in the future.

The motors wheezed more and more. They were operating on a closed throttle. At full speed they might dash the propellers to bits.

However, they must be warmed up. Otherwise they would simply die. It would be stark tragedy to roll out into space with three dead engines. It would mean a crash which neither of them could hope to survive.

"Give her the gun, Bill," said Harl in a tense voice.

Bill pushed the accelerator slowly. The motors protested, sputtered, and then burst into a roar. Here, in the machine, because of the artifical air, sound could be heard. Out in the time stream there could be no sound.

Harl listened anxiously, hoping fiercely that the propellers would stand.

Bill cut the acceleration and the motors, once more barely turning over, ran more smoothly.

Harl glanced at his wrist watch. Despite the fact they were in time, where actual time could not be measured by clocks, the little watch still ticked off the time-space seconds and minutes.

They had been out eight minutes. Seven minutes more and they must roll out of time into space.

Fifteen minutes was all that the tortured motors could stand of this intense cold and vacuum.

He glanced at the time dial. It read 2816. They had traveled 2816 years into the future. They should be well over 5000 when the fifteen minutes were at an end.

Bill touched his arm.

"You're sure we're still over Denver?"

Harl chuckled.

"If we aren't, we may find ourselves billions of miles out in space. It's a chance we have to take. According to all our experiments we should be in exactly the same position we were when we snapped into the time stream. We are occupying a hole in space. It should remain the same."

Their lungs began to ache. Either the atmosphere generators were failing or the air leakage out into the vacuum was
greater than they had expected. Undeniably the air was becoming thinner. The motors still ran steadily, however. It
must be a leakage from the cabin of the ship.

"How long?" bellowed Bill.

Harl glanced at his watch.

"Twelve minutes," he reported.

The time dial read 4224.

"Three minutes," replied Bill, "I guess we can stand it. The
motors are running all right. It's getting colder, though, and
the air's pretty thin."

"Leakage," said Harl gruffly.

The minutes dragged.

Bill tried to think. Here they hung, hypothetically, over the
city of Denver. Less than a quarter of an hour ago, they were
in the year 1935, now they were passing over years at a
lightning-like speed—a speed of over 350 years in each space-
minute. They must now be in about the year 6450.

He glanced at his hands. They were blue. It was intensely
cold in the cabin. Their heat was leaking—leaking swiftly. It
was hard to breath. The air was rare—too rare for safety.
Suppose they became unconscious. Then they would freeze—
would drive endlessly through time. Frozen corpses, riding
through the aeons. The earth beneath them would dissolve in
space. New worlds might form, new galaxies be born as they
whirled on in the time stream. The time needle would reach
the pin, bend back upon itself and slip past the pin, to slam
against the side of the dial, where it would still struggle to record the flight of the years.

He chafed his hands and glanced at the time dial. It read
5516.

"A quarter of a minute," snapped Harl, his teeth chattering, his right hand on the lever, his wrist watch held in front
of him.

Bill placed his hands on the wheel.

"All right!" shouted Harl.

He jerked the lever.

They hung in the sky.

Harl uttered a cry of astonishment.

It was twilight. Beneath them were the ruins of a vast city.

To the east lapped a sea, stretching to a murky horizon. The sea coast was a desert of heaped sand.

The motors, warming to their task, bellowed a mighty challenge.

"Where are we?" cried Harl.

Bill shook his head.

"It's not Denver," said Harl.

"Doesn't look much like it," agreed Bill, his teeth still chattering.

He circled, warming the motors.

There was no sign of humanity below them.

The motors blasted a throaty defiance to the desert sands and under Bill's hand, the machine came down in a long swoop, headed for a level stretch of sand near one of the largest of the white stone ruins.

It hit the ground, bounced high in a cloud of sand, struck and bounced again, then rolled to a stop.

Bill cut the motors.

"We're here," he said.

Harl stretched his legs wearily.

Bill glanced at the time dial. It read 5626.

"This is the year 7561," he said slowly, thoughtfully.

"Got your gun?" asked Harl.

Bill's hand went to his side, felt the reassuring touch of the .45 in its holster.

"I have it," he said.

"All right, let's get out."

Harl opened the door and they stepped out. The sand glittered under their boots.

Harl turned the key in the door lock and locked the ring to his belt.

"Wouldn't do to lose the keys," he said.

A chill wind was blowing over the desert, moaning among the ruins, carrying with it a freight of fine, hard granules. Even in their heavy clothing, the time explorers shivered.

Harl grasped Bill by the arm, pointing to the east.

There hung a huge dull red ball.

Bill's jaw fell.

"The sun," he said.

"Yes, the sun," said Harl.

They stared at one another in the half-light.

"Then this isn't the year 7561," stammered Bill.

"No, more likely the year 750,000, perhaps even more than that."

"The time dial was wrong then."

"It was wrong. Badly wrong. We were traveling through time a thousand times faster than we thought."

They were silent, studying the landscape about them. They saw only ruins which towered hundreds of feet above the sands. They were ruins of noble proportions, many of them still bearing the hint of a marvelous architecture of which the twentieth century would have been incapable. The stone was pure white, gleaming beautifully in the twilight which the feeble rays of the great brick-red sun could not expel.

"The time dial," said Bill, thoughtfully, "was registering thousands of years instead of years."

Harl nodded cheerlessly.

"Maybe," he said. "For all we know it may have been registering tens of thousands of years."

A creature, somewhat like a dog, dull gray in color, with tail hanging low, was silhouetted for a moment on a sand dune and then disappeared.

"These are the ruins of Denver," said Harl. "That sea we saw must cover the whole of eastern North America. Probably only the Rocky Mountains remain unsubmerged and they are a desert. Yes, we must have covered at least 750,000 years, perhaps seven million."

"What about the human race? Do you think there are any people left?" asked Bill.

"Possibly. Man is a hardy animal. It takes a lot to kill him and he could adapt himself to almost any kind of environment. This change, you must remember, came slowly."

Bill turned about and his cry rang in Harl's ear. Harl whirled.

Running toward them, leaping over the sands, came a motley horde of men. They were dressed in furs and they carried no weapons, but they charged down upon the two as if to attack.

Harl yanked his .45 from its holster. His great hand closed around the weapon and his finger found the trigger. It gave him a sense of power, this burly six-shooter.

The men, their furs flying behind them, were only a hundred yards away. Now they yelled, blood-curdling, vicious whoops which left no doubt that they were enemies.

No weapons. Harl grinned. They'd give 'em hell and plenty of it. There were about fifty in the mob. Big odds, but not too great.

"We might as well let them have it," he said to Bill. The two guns roared. There was disorder in the running ranks, but the mob still forged ahead, leaving two of its members prone on the ground. Again the .45's barked, spurting a stream of fire.

Men staggered, screaming, to collapse. The rest hurdled them, raced on. It seemed nothing could stop them. They were less than fifty feet away.

The guns were empty. Swiftly the two plucked cartridges from their belts and reloaded.

Before they could fire the mob was on top of them. Bill thrust his gun into the face of a running foeman and fired. He had to sidestep quickly to prevent the fellow tumbling on top of him. A knotted fist connected with his head and he slipped to his knees. From that position he drilled two more of the milling enemies before they piled on top of him.

Through the turmoil he heard the roar of Harl's gun.

He felt the grip of many hands, felt bodies pressing close about him. He fought blindly and desperately.

He fought with hands, with feet, with suddenly bared teeth. He felt bodies wilt under his blows, felt blood upon his hands. The sand, kicked up by many feet, got into his nostrils and eyes, half strangling, half blinding him.

Only a few feet away Harl fought, fought in the same manner as his companion. With their weapons knocked from their hands they resorted to the tactics of their ancient forebears.

It seemed minutes that they battled with their attackers, but it could not have been more than seconds before the sheer weight of numbers subdued them, wound thongs tightly about their hands and feet and left them, trussed like two fowls ready for the grid.

"Hurt, Bill?" called Harl.

"No," replied Bill. "Just mussed up a bit."

"Me, too," said Harl.

They lay on their backs and stared up at the sky. Their captors moved away and massed about the plane.

A loud banging came to the ears of the two. Evidently the others were trying to force an entrance into the machine.

"Let them bang," said Harl. "They can't break anything."

"Except a propeller," replied Bill.

After more banging, the men returned and untying the bonds on the feet of the captives, hoisted them up.

For the first time they had an opportunity to study their captors. They were tall men, well proportioned, clean of limb, with the stamp of well-being about them. Aside from their figures, however, they held a distinctly barbarous appearance. Their hair was roughly trimmed, as were their beards. They walked with a slouch and their feet shuffled in the sand with the gait of one who holds a purposeless existence. They were dressed in well-tanned furs, none too clean. They bore no arms and their eyes were the eyes of furtive beings, shifty, restless, as are the eyes of hunted beasts, always on the lookout for danger.

"March," said one of them, a large fellow with a protruding front tooth. The single word was English, with the pronunciation slightly different than it would have been in the twentieth century, but good, pure English.

They marched, flanked on either side by their captors. The march led back over the same route as the future-men had come. They passed the dead, but no attention was paid them, their comrades passing the sprawled figures with merely a glance. Life apparently was cheap in this place.

CHAPTER II

Orders of Golan-Kirt

They passed between monstrous ruins. The men talked among themselves, but, although the tongue was English, it was so intermixed with unfamiliar words and spoken with such an accent that the two could understand very little of it.

They reached what appeared to be a street. It led between rows of ruins and now other humans appeared, among them women and children. All stared at the captives and jabbered excitedly.

"Where are you taking us?" Bill asked a man who walked by his side.

The man ran his fingers through his beard and spat in the sand.

"To the arena," he said slowly that the twentieth century man might understand the words.

"What for?" Bill also spoke slowly and concisely.

"The games," said the man, shortly, as if displeased at being questioned.

"What are the games?" asked Harl.

"You'll find out soon enough. They are held at high sun today," growled the other. The reply brought a burst of brutal laughter from the rest.

"They will find out when they face the minions of Golan-Kirt," chortled a voice.

"The minions of Golan-Kirt!" exclaimed Harl.

"Hold your tongue," snarled the man with the protruding tooth, "or we will tear it from your mouth."

The two time-travelers asked no more questions.

They plodded on. Although the sand beneath their feet was packed, it was heavy going and their legs ached. Fortunately the future-men did not hustle their pace, seeming to be content to take their time.

A good-sized crowd of children had gathered and accompanied the procession, staring at the twentieth century men, shrieking shrill gibberish at them. A few of them, crowding too close or yelling too loudly, gained the displeasure of the guards and were slapped to one side.

For fifteen minutes they toiled up a sandy slope. Now they gained the top and in a depression below them they saw the arena. It was a great building, open to the air, which had apparently escaped the general destruction visited upon the rest of the city. Here and there repairs had been made, evident by the decidedly inferior type of workmanship.

The building was circular in shape, and about a half-mile in diameter. It was built of a pure white stone, like the rest of the ruined city.

The two twentieth century men gasped at its size.

They had little time, however, to gaze upon the building, for their captors urged them on. They walked slowly down the slope and, directed by the future-men, made their way through one of the great arching gateways and into the arena proper.

On all sides rose tier upon tier of seats, designed to hold thousands of spectators. On the opposite side of the arena was a series of steel cages, set under the seats.

The future-men urged them forward.

"They're going to lock us up, evidently," said Bill.

He of the protruding tooth laughed, as if enjoying a huge joke.

"It will not be for long," he said.

As they approached the cages, they saw that a number of them were occupied. Men clung to the bars, peering out at the group crossing the sandy arena. Others sat listlessly, regarding their approach with little or no interest. Many of them, the twentieth century men noticed, bore the marks of prolonged incarceration.

They halted before one of the cells. One of the future-men stepped to the door of the cage and unlocked it with a large key. As the door grated back on rusty hinges, the others seized the two, unbound their hands and roughly hurled them inside the prison. The door clanged to with a hollow, ringing sound and the key grated in the lock.

They struggled up out of the dirt and refuse which covered the floor of the cell and squatted on their heels to watch the future-men make their way across the arena and through the archway by which they had come.

"I guess we're in for it," said Bill.

Harl produced a pack of cigarettes.

"Light up," he said gruffly.

They lit up. Smoke from tobacco grown in 1935 floated out of their cell over the ruins of the city of Denver, upon which shone a dying sun.

They smoked their cigarettes, crushed them in the sand. Harl rose and began a minute examination of their prison. Bill joined him. They went over it inch by inch, but it was impregnable. Except for the iron gate, it was constructed of heavy masonry. An examination of the iron gate gave no hope. Again they squatted on their heels.

Harl glanced at his wrist watch.

"Six hours since we landed," he said, "and from the appearance of the shadows, it's still morning. The sun was well up in the sky, too, when we arrived."

"The days are longer than those back in 1935," explained Bill. "The earth turns slower. The days here may be twenty-four hours or longer."

"Listen," hissed Harl.

To their ears came the sound of voices. They listened intently. Mingled with the voices was the harsh grating of steel. The voices seemed to come from their right. They grew in volume.

"If we only had our guns," moaned Harl.

The clamor of voices was close and seemed to be almost beside them.

"It's the other prisoners," gasped Bill. "They must be feeding them or something."

His surmise was correct.

Before their cell appeared an old man. He was stooped and a long white beard hung over his skinny chest. His long hair curled majestically over his shoulders. In one hand he carried a jug of about a gallon capacity and a huge loaf of bread.

But it was neither the bread nor the jug which caught the attention of Harl and Bill. In his loincloth, beside a massive ring of keys, were thrust their two .45's.

He set down the jug and the loaf and fumbled with the keys. Selecting one he unlocked and slid back a panel near the bottom of the great door. Carefully he set the jug and the loaf inside the cell.

The two men inside exchanged a glance. The same thought had occurred to each. When the old man came near the door, it would be a simple matter to grasp him. With the guns there was a chance of blazing a way to the ship.

The oldster, however, was pulling the weapons from his loincloth.

Their breath held in wonder, the time-travelers saw him lay them beside the jug and the loaf.

"The command of Golan-Kirt," he muttered in explanation. "He has arrived to witness the games. He commanded that the weapons be returned. They will make the games more interesting."

"More interesting," chuckled Harl, rocking slowly on the balls of his feet.

These future-men, who seemed to possess absolutely no weapons, apparently did not appreciate the deadliness of the .45's.

"Golan-Kirt?" questioned Bill, speaking softly.

The old man seemed to see them for the first time.

"Yes," he said. "Know you not of Golan-Kirt? He-Who-Came-Out-of-the-Cosmos?"

"No," said Bill.

"Then truly can I believe what has come to my ears of you?" said the old man.

"What have you heard?"

"That you came out of time," replied the oldster, "in a great machine."

"That is true," said Harl. "We came out of the twentieth century."

The old man slowly shook his head.

"I know naught of the twentieth century."

"How could you?" asked Harl. "It must have ended close to a million years ago."

The other shook his head again.

"Years?" he asked. "What are years?"

Harl drew in his breath sharply.

"A year," he explained, "is a measurement of time."

"Time cannot be measured," replied the old man dogmatically.

"Back in the twentieth century we measured it," said Harl.

"Any man who thinks he can measure time is a fool," the future-man was uncompromising.

Harl held out his hand, palm down, and pointed to his wrist watch.

"That measures time," he asserted.

The old man scarcely glanced at it.

"That," he said, "is a foolish mechanism and has nothing to do with time."

Bill laid a warning hand on his friend's arm.

"A year," he explained slowly, "is our term for one revolution of the earth about the sun."

"So that is what it means," said the old man. "Why didn't you say so at first? The movement of the earth, however, has no association with time. Time is purely relative."

"We came from a time when the world was much different," said Bill. "Can you give us any idea of the number of revolutions the earth has made since then?"

"How can I?" asked the old man, "when we speak in terms that neither understands? I can only tell you that since Golan-Kirt came out of the Cosmos the earth has circled the sun over five million times."

Five million times! Five million years! Five million years since some event had happened, an event which may not have occurred for many other millions of years after the twentieth century. At least five million years in the future; there was no telling how much more!

Their instrument had been wrong. How wrong they could not remotely have guessed until this moment!

The twentieth century. It had a remote sound, an unreal significance. In this age, with the sun a brick red ball and the city of Denver a mass of ruins, the twentieth century was a forgotten second in the great march of time, it was as remote as the age when man emerged from the beast.

"Has the sun always been as it is?" asked Harl.

The old man shook his head.

"Our wise ones tell us that one time the sun was so hot it hurt one's eyes. They also tell us it is cooling, that in the future it will give no light or heat at all."

The oldster shrugged his shoulders.

"Of course, before that happens, all men will be dead."

The old man pulled the little panel shut and locked it. He turned to go.

"Wait," cried Harl.

The old one faced them.

"What do you want?" he asked, mumbling half-angrily in his beard.

"Sit down, friend," said Harl. "We would like to talk further."

The other hesitated, half wheeling to go, then turned back.

"We came from a time when the sun hurt one's eyes. We have seen Denver as a great and proud city. We have seen this land when the grass grew upon it and rain fell and there were broad plains where the sea now lies," said Harl.

The oldster sank to the sand in front of their cage. His eyes were lighted with a wild enthusiasm and his two skinny hands clutched the iron bars.

"You have looked upon the world when it was young," he cried. "You have seen green grass and felt rain. It seldom rains here."

"We have seen all you mention," Harl assured him. "But we would ask why we have been treated as foes. We came as friends, hoping to meet friends, but ready for war."

"Aye, ready for war," said the old man in trembling tones, his eyes on the guns. "Those are noble weapons. They tell me you strewed the sands with the dead ere you were taken."

"But why were we not treated as friends?" insisted Harl.

"There are no friends here," cackled the old man. "Not since Golan-Kirt came. All are at one another's throats."

"Who is this Golan-Kirt?"

"Golan-Kirt came out of the Cosmos to rule over the

world," said the old man, as if intoning a chant. "He is neither
Man nor Beast. There is no good in him. He hates and hates.
He is pure Evil. For after all, there is no friendliness or good-
ness in the universe. We have no proof that the Cosmos is benevolent. Long ago our ancestors believed in love. This was a
fallacy. Evil is greater than good."

"Tell me," asked Bill, moving closer to the bars, "have you
ever seen Golan-Kirt?"

"Aye, I have."

"Tell us of him," urged Bill.

"I cannot," there was stark terror in the old man's eyes. "I
cannot!"

He huddled closer to the cage and his voice dropped to an
uncanny whisper.

"Men out of time, I will tell you something. He is hated,
because he teaches hate. We obey him because we must. He
holds our minds in the hollow of his hand. He rules by suggestion only. He is not immortal. He fears death—he is afraid
—there is a way, if only one with the courage might be
found—."

The old man's face blanched and a look of horror crept
into his eyes. His muscles tensed and his clawlike hands
clutched madly at the bars. He slumped against the gate and
gasped for breath.

Faintly his whisper came, low and halting.

"Golan-Kirt—your weapons—believe nothing—close your
mind to all suggestion—."

He stopped, gasping for breath.

"I have fought—" he continued, haltingly, with an effort. "I
have won—. I have told you—. He has—killed me—he will
not kill you—now that you—know—."

The old man was on the verge of death. Wide-eyed, the two
saw him ward it off, gain a precious second.

"Your weapons—will kill him—he's easy to kill—by one
who does not—believe in him—he is a—"

The whisper pinched out and the old man slid slowly to the
sands in front of the cage.

The two stared at the crumpled form of humanity.

"Killed by suggestion," gasped Harl.

Bill nodded.

"He was a brave man," he said.

Harl regarded the corpse intently. His eyes lighted on the
key ring and kneeling, he reached out and drew the body of

the future-man close. His fingers closed on the ring and ripped it from the loincloth.

"We're going home," he said.

"And on the way out we'll bump off the big shot," added Bill.

He lifted the guns from the floor and clicked fresh cartridges into the chambers. Harl rattled the keys. He tried several before he found the correct one. The lock screeched and the gate swung open protestingly.

With quick steps they passed out of the cell. For a moment they halted in silent tribute before the body of the old man. With helmets doffed the twentieth century men stood beside the shriveled form of a man who was a hero, a man who had flung his hatred in the face of some terrible entity that taught hate to the people of the world. Scanty as was the information which he had given, it set the two on their guard, gave them an inkling of what to expect.

As they turned about they involuntarily started. Filing into the amphitheater, rapidly filling the seats, were crowds of future-men. A subdued roar, the voice of the assembling people, came to their ears.

The populace was assembling for the games.

"This may complicate matters," said Bill.

"I don't think so," replied Harl. "It's Golan-Kirt we must deal with. We would have had to in any case. These men do not count. As I understand it he exercises an absolute control over them. The removal of that control may change the habits and psychology of the future-men."

"The only thing we can do is fight Golan-Kirt and then act accordingly," said Bill.

"The man who captured us spoke of his minions," Harl said thoughtfully.

"He may be able to produce hallucinations," Bill hazarded. "He may be able to make one believe something exists when it really doesn't. In that case, the people would naturally believe them to be creatures which came at his beck and call."

"But the old man knew," objected Harl. "He knew that it was all mere suggestion. If all the people knew this the rule of Golan-Kirt would end abruptly. They would no longer believe in his omnipotence. Without this belief, suggestion, by which he rules, would be impossible."

"The old man," asserted Bill, "gained his knowledge in some mysterious manner and paid for its divulgence with his life. Still the old fellow didn't know all of it. He believed this entity came out of the Cosmos."

Harl shook his head, thoughtfully.

"It may have come out of the Cosmos. Remember, we are at least five million years in the future. I expect to find some great intelligence. It is physical, for the old man claimed to have seen it, and that should make our job easier."

"The old man said he was not immortal," commented Bill. "Therefore, he is vulnerable and our guns may do the work. Another thing—we are not to believe a single thing we feel, hear, or see. He seems to rule wholly by suggestion. He will try to kill us by suggestion, just as he killed the old fellow."

Harl nodded.

"It's a matter of will power," he said. "A matter of brain and bluff. Apparently the will power of these people has degenerated and Golan-Kirt finds it easy to control their minds. They are born, live, and die under his influence. It has almost become hereditary to accept his power. We have the advantage of coming out of an age when men were obliged to use their brains. Perhaps the human mind degenerated because, as science increased the ease of life, there was little need to use it. Some fine minds may still remain, but apparently they are few. We are doubters, schemers, bluffers. Golan-Kirt will find us tougher than these future-men."

CHAPTER III

The Struggle of the Ages

Bill produced cigarettes and the two lighted up. Slowly they walked across the vast arena, guns hanging in their right hands. People were filing into the place and the tiers were filling.

A roar came out of the tiers of seats before them. They recognized it. It was the cry of the gathering crowd, the cry for blood, the expression of a desire to see battle.

Harl grinned.

"Regular football crowd," he commented.

More and more poured into the arena, but it was apparent that the inhabitants of the ruined city could fill only a very small section of the thousands upon thousands of seats.

The two seemed lost in the mighty space. Above them, almost at the zenith, hung the vast red sun. They seemed to move in a twilight-filled desert rimmed in by enormous white cliffs.

"Denver must have been a large city at the time this place was built," commented Bill. "Think of the number of people it would hold. Wonder what it was used for?"

"Probably we'll never know," said Harl.

They had gained the approximate center of the arena.

Harl halted.

"Do you know," he said, "I've been thinking. It seems to me we must have a fairly good chance against Golan-Kirt. For the last fifteen minutes every thought of ours has been in open defiance of him, but he has not attempted our annihilation. Although it is possible he may only be biding his time. I am beginning to believe he can't read our minds as he could the mind of the old man. He killed him the moment he uttered a word of treason."

Bill nodded.

As if in answer to what Harl had said, a great weight seemed to press in upon them. Bill felt a deadly illness creeping over him. His knees sagged and his brain whirled. Spots danced before his eyes and a horrible pain gripped his stomach.

He took a step forward and stumbled. A hand clutched his shoulder and fiercely shook him. The shake momentarily cleared his brain. Through the clearing mist which seemed to hang before his eyes, he saw the face of his friend, a face white and lined.

The lips in the face moved.

"Buck up, old man. There's nothing wrong with you. You're feeling fine."

Something seemed to snap inside his head. This was suggestion—the suggestion of Golan-Kirt. He had to fight it. That was it—fight it.

He planted his feet firmly in the sand, straightened his shoulders with an effort, and smiled.

"Hell, no," he said, "there's nothing wrong with me. I'm feeling fine."

Harl slapped him on the back.

"That's the spirit," he roared. "It almost floored me for a minute. We've got to fight it, boy. We've got to fight it."

Bill laughed harshly. His head was clear now and he could feel the strength flowing back into his body. They had won the first round!

"But where is this Golan-Kirt?" he burst out.

"Invisible," snarled Harl, "but I have a theory that he can't put in his best licks in such a state. We'll force him to show himself and then we'll give him the works."

The frenzied roar of the crowd came to their ears. Those on the bleachers had seen and appreciated the little drama out in the middle of the arena. They were crying for more.

Suddenly a spiteful rattle broke out behind the two.

They started. That sound was familiar. It was the rat-a-tat of a machine gun. With no ceremony they fell flat, pressing their bodies close against the ground, seeking to burrow into the sand.

Little puffs of sand spurted up all about them. Bill felt a searing pain in his arm. One of the bullets had found him. This was the end. There was no obstruction to shield them in this vast level expanse from the gun that chuckled and chattered at their rear. Another searing pain caught him in the leg. Another hit.

Then he laughed—a wild laugh. There was no machine gun, no bullets. It was all suggestion. A trick to make them believe they were being killed—a trick, which, if carried far enough, would kill them.

He struggled to his knees, hauling Harl up beside him. His leg and arm still pained, but he paid them no attention. There was nothing wrong with them, he told himself fiercely, absolutely nothing wrong.

"It's suggestion again," he shouted at Harl. "There isn't any machine gun."

Harl nodded. They regained their feet and turned. There, only a couple of hundred yards away, a khaki-clad figure crouched behind a gun that chattered wickedly, a red flame licking the muzzle.

"That isn't a machine gun," said Bill, speaking slowly.

"Of course, it's not a machine gun," Harl spoke as if by rote.

They walked slowly toward the flaming gun. Although bullets apparently whistled all about them, none struck them. The pain in Bill's arm and leg no longer existed.

Suddenly the gun disappeared, and with it the khaki-clad figure. One moment they were there, the next they were not.

"I thought it would do just that," said Bill.

"The old boy is still going strong, though," replied Harl. "Here is some more of his suggestion."

Harl pointed to one of the arching gateways. Through it marched file upon file of soldiers, clad in khaki, metal helmets on their heads, guns across their shoulders. An officer uttered a sharp command and the troops began to deploy over the field.

A shrill blast of a bugle drew the attention of the two time-travelers from the soldiers and through another gateway they beheld the advance of what appeared to be a cohort of Roman legionnaires. Shields flashed dully in the sun and the rattle of arms could be distinctly heard.

"Do you know what I believe?" asked Harl.

"What is it?"

"Golan-Kirt cannot suggest anything new to us. The machine guns and the soldiers and legionnaires are all things of which we have former knowledge."

"How is it," asked Bill, "that we see these things when we know they do not exist?"

"I do not know," replied Harl, "there are a lot of funny things about this business that I can't understand."

"Anyhow, he is giving the crowd a good show," observed Bill.

The bleachers were in an uproar. To the ears of the two came the shrill screaming of women, the loud roars of the men. The populace was thoroughly enjoying itself.

A lion, large and ferocious, growling fiercely, leaped past the two men. A thunder of hoof-beats announced the arrival of more of the brain creatures.

"It's about time for us to do something," said Harl.

He lifted his .45 high in the air and fired. A hush fell.

"Golan-Kirt, attention!" roared Harl, in a voice that could be heard in every part of the arena. "We challenge you to personal combat. We have no fear of your creatures. They cannot harm us. You are the one we wish to fight."

An awed silence fell over the crowd. It was the first time their god had ever been openly challenged. They waited for the two lone figures out in the arena to be stricken in a heap.

They were not stricken, however.

Again Harl's voice rang out.

"Come out of hiding, you fat-bellied toad!" he thundered. "Come and fight if you have the guts, you dirty, yellow coward!"

The crowd may not have gathered the exact meaning of the words, but the full insult of them was plain. A threatening murmur rolled out from the bleachers, and there was a sudden surging of the crowd. Men leaped over the low wall in front of the seats and raced across the arena.

Then a sonorous voice, deep and strong, rolled out.

"Stop," it said. "I, Golan-Kirt, will deal with these men."

Harl noticed that the soldiers and the lion had disappeared. The arena was empty except for him and his comrade and the score of future-men who had halted in their tracks at the voice which had come out of nothingness.

They waited, tensed. Harl wriggled his feet into a firmer position. He slipped a cartridge in the gun to take the place of the one which had been fired. Bill mopped his brow with the sleeve of his coat.

"It's going to be brains now," Harl told his friend.

Bill grinned.

"Two mediocre intelligences against a great one," he joked.

"Look Bill!" shouted Harl.

Directly in front and slightly above the level of their heads a field of light had formed, a small ball of brightness in the murky atmosphere. Slowly it grew. Vibrations set in.

The two watched, fascinated. The vibrations quickened until the whole field was quivering. As the vibrations increased the light faded and a monstrosity began to take form. Only vaguely could it be seen at first. Then it became clearer and clearer, began to take definite form.

Hanging in the air, suspended without visible means of support, was a gigantic brain, approximately two feet in diameter. A naked brain, with the convolutions exposed. It was a ghastly thing.

The horror of it was heightened by the two tiny, pig-like, lidless, close-set eyes and a curving beak which hung directly below the frontal portion of the brain, resting in what was apparently an atrophied face.

The two were aghast, but with a tremendous effort they kept close hold on their self-control.

"Greetings, Golan-Kirt," drawled Harl, sarcasm putting an edge to the words.

As he spoke, his arm swung up and under the pressure of his finger, the hammer of the gun slowly moved backward. But before the muzzle could be brought in line with the great brain, the arm stopped and Harl stood like a frozen man, held rigid by the frightful power which poured forth from Golan-Kirt.

Bill's arm flashed up and his .45 broke the silence with a sullen roar. However, even as he fired, his arm was flung aside as if by a mighty blow and the speeding bullet missed the huge brain by the mere fraction of an inch.

"Presumptuous fools," roared a voice, which, however, seemed not a voice, for there was no sound, merely the sense of hearing. The two, standing rigidly, as if at attention, realized that it was telepathy: that the brain before them was sending out powerful emanations.

"Presumptuous fools, you would fight me, Golan-Kirt? I, who have a hundred-fold the mental power of your combined brains? I, who hold the knowledge of all time?"

"We would fight you," snarled Harl. "We are going to fight you. We know you for what you are. You are not out of the Cosmos. You are a laboratory specimen. Unknown ages ago you were developed under artificial conditions. You are not immortal. You fear our weapons. A bullet in that dirty brain of yours will finish you."

"Who are you to judge," came the thought-wave, "you, with your tiny, twentieth century brain? You have come unbidden into my time, you have defied me. I shall destroy you. I, who came out of the Cosmos aeons ago to rule over the portion of the Universe I chose as my own, do not fear you or your ridiculous weapons."

"Yet you foiled us when we would have used our weapons on you. If I could reach you I would not need my weapon. I could tear you apart, destroy you with the strength of my two hands."

"Say on," rumbled the thought-waves. "Say what you believe me to be, and when you are done I shall obliterate you. You shall be dust floating in the air, ashes on the sands."

There was an unveiled tone of mockery in the brain emanations.

Harl raised his voice, almost shouting. It was a deliberate act, done in hopes the future-men would hear, that they might realize not too late the true nature of the tyrant Golan-Kirt. They did hear and their mouths gaped as they listened.

"You once were a man," Harl roared, "a great scientist. You studied the brain, specialized in it. At last you discovered a great secret, which gave you the power of developing the brain to an unheard-of degree. Sure of your technique, and realizing the power you might enjoy, you transformed yourself into a brain creature. You are a fraud and an impostor. You have mis-ruled these people for millions of years. You are not out of the Cosmos,—you are a man, or what once was a man. You are an atrocity, an abomination—"

The thought emanations which flowed from out the brain trembled, as if with rage.

"You lie. I am out of the Cosmos. I am immortal. I shall kill you—kill you."

Suddenly Bill laughed, a resounding guffaw. It was an escape from the terrible tension, but as he laughed a ludicrous angle presented itself—the twentieth century travelers millions of years ahead of their time wrangling with a cheat pawning himself off as a god on a people who would not be born until long after he was dead.

He felt the horrible power of Golan-Hirt centering upon him. Perspiration streamed down his face and his body trembled. He felt his strength leaving him.

He stopped laughing. As he did so, he seemed to be struck, as if by a blow. He staggered. Then sudden realization flashed through him. Laughter, that was it. Laughter and ridicule! That would turn the trick.

"Laugh, you fool, laugh," he screamed at Harl.

Uncomprehendingly, Harl obeyed.

The two rocked with laughter. They whooped and roared.

Hardly knowing what he did, almost involuntarily, Bill screeched horrible things at the great brain, reviled it, taunted it, called it almost unspeakable names.

Harl began to understand. It was all a great game that Bill was playing. A supreme egoism such as was lodged in the brain pitted against them could not bear ridicule, would lose its grip before a storm of jeers. For uncounted centuries, through some miraculous power, it had lived and in all that time it had been accorded only the highest honor. Derision was something with which it was unacquainted, a terrible weapon suddenly loosed upon it.

Harl joined with Bill and hurled gibes at Golan-Kirt. It was a high carnival of mockery. They were not conscious of their words. Their brains responded to the emergency and their tongues formed sentences of unguessed taunts.

Between sentences they laughed, howling with satanic glee.

Through all their laughter they felt the power of the brain. They felt its anger mount at their taunting. Their bodies were racked with pain, they wanted to fall on the sands and writhe in agony, but they continued to laugh, to shout taunts.

It seemed an eternity that they fought with Golan-Kirt, all the time shrieking with laughter, while they suffered fine-edged torture from the tops of their heads to the soles of their feet. Still they dare not stop their laughter, dare not cease their hideous derision, poking fun at the huge intelligence which opposed them. That was their one weapon. Without it the engulfing waves of suggestion which poured with relentless fury upon them would have snapped asunder every nerve in their bodies.

They sensed the raging of the great brain. It was literally crazed with anger. They were "getting its goat!" They were ridiculing the very life out of it.

Unconsciously they allowed the pitch of their laughter to lower. From sheer exhaustion they lapsed into silence.

Suddenly they felt the terrible force of the brain renewed, as it drew upon some mysterious reserve strength. It struck them like a blow, doubling them over, clouding their eyes, dulling their minds, racking every nerve and joint.

Hot irons seemed to sear them, hundreds of needles seemed thrust in their flesh, sharp knives seemed to slash their bodies. They reeled blindly, gropingly, mouthing curses, crying out in pain.

Through the red haze of torture came a whisper, a soft, enchanting whisper, a whisper beckoning to them, showing them a way of escape.

"Turn your weapons on yourselves. End all of this torture. Death is painless."

The whisper fluttered through their brains. That was the way out! Why endure this seemingly endless torture? Death was painless. The muzzle against one's head, a pressure on the trigger, oblivion.

Bill placed his gun against his temple. His finger contracted against the trigger. He laughed. This was a joke. A rare joke. Robbing Golan-Kirt by his own hand.

Another voice burst through his laughter. It was Harl.

"You fool! It's Golan-Kirt! It's Golan-Kirt, you fool!"

He saw his friend staggering toward him, saw his face pinched with pain, saw the moving of the livid lips as they shouted the warning.

Bill's hand dropped to his side. Even as he continued that insane laughter, he felt chagrin steal over him. The hideous brain had played its trump card and had failed, but it had almost finished him. Had it not been for Harl he would have been stretched on the sand, a suicide, his head blown to bits.

Then suddenly they felt the power of the brain slipping, felt its strength falter and ebb. They had beaten it!

They sensed the gigantic struggle going on in that great brain, the struggle to regain the grip it had lost.

For years on end it had lived without struggle, without question that it was the ruler of the earth. They sensed the futile anger and the devastating fear which revolved in the convolutions of Golan-Kirt.

But he was beaten, beaten at last by men from out of a forgotten age. He had met defeat at the hands of ridicule, something he had never known, a thing he had not suspected.

His strength ebbed steadily. The twentieth century men felt his dread power lift from them, sensed the despair which surged through him.

They stopped their laughter, their sides sore, their throats hoarse. Then they heard. The arena resounded with laughter. The crowd was laughing. The horrible uproar beat like a tumult upon them. The future-men were roaring, bent over, stamping their feet, throwing back their heads, screaming to the murky skies. They were laughing at Golan-Kirt, screaming insults at him, hooting him. It was the end of his rule.

For generations the future-men had hated him with the very hate he had taught them. They had hated and feared. Now they feared no longer and hate rode unchained.

From a god he had fallen to the estate of a ridiculous fraud. He was a thing of pity, an uncloaked clown, simply a naked, defenseless brain that had bluffed its way through centuries of kingship.

Through bleared eyes the twentieth century men saw the great brain, writhing now under the scorn of its erstwhile subjects, being laughed powerless. No longer did it hold control over these creatures of a dying world. Its close-set eyes glowed fiercely, its beak clicked angrily. It was tired, too tired to regain its rule. It was the end of Golan-Kirt!

The revolvers of the time-travelers came up almost simultaneously. This time the sights lined on the brain. There was no power to ward off the danger.

The guns roared rapidly, spitting hateful fire. At the impact of the bullets the brain turned over in the air, blood spurted from it, great gashes appeared in it. With a thump it struck the ground, quivered and lay still.

The time-travelers, their eyes closing from sheer weariness, their knees suddenly weak, slumped to the sand, the .45's still smoking.

Over the arena floated the full-toned roar of the future-men.

"Hail to the Deliverers! Golan-Kirt is dead! His rule is ended! Hail to the saviors of the race!"

Epilogue

"It is impossible to reverse time. You cannot travel back to your own age. I have no idea of what will occur if you attempt it, but I do know it is impossible. We of this age knew travel into the future was possible, but we lacked the technique to build a machine to try it. Under the rule of Golan-Kirt there was no material progress, only a steady degeneration. We know that it is impossible to reverse time. We, as a people, beg you not to attempt it."

Old Agnar Nohl, his white beard streaming in the wind, his hair flying, spoke seriously. There was a troubled frown on his face.

"We love you," he went on, "you freed us of the tyranny of the brain which ruled over us for uncounted time. We need you. Stay with us, help us rebuild this land, help us construct machines, give us some of the marvelous knowledge which we, as a race, have lost. We can give you much in return, for we have not forgotten all the science we knew before the coming of Golan-Kirt."

Harl shook his head.

"We must at least try to go back," he said.

The two twentieth century men stood beside the plane. Before them was a solid mass of humanity, a silent humanity in the shadow of the silent ruins of the city of Denver, the future-men who had come to bid the time-travelers a regretful farewell.

A chill wind howled over the desert, carrying its freight of sand. The furs of the future-men fluttered in the gale as it played a solemn dirge between the ruined walls of humbled buildings.

"If there was a chance of your success, we would speed you on your way," said old Agnar, "but we are reluctant to let you go to what may be your death. We are selfish enough to wish to hold you for ourselves, but we love you enough to let you go. You taught us hate was wrong, you removed the hate that ruled us. We wish only the best for you.

"It is impossible to go back in time. Why not remain? We need you badly. Our land grows less and less food every year. We must discover how to make synthetic food or we shall starve. This is only one of our problems. There are many others. You cannot go back. Stay and help us!"

Again Harl shook his head.

"No, we must try it. We may fail, but we must try it at least. If we succeed we shall return and bring with us books of knowledge and tools to work with."

Agnar combed his beard with skinny fingers.

"You'll fail," he said.

"But if we don't we will return," said Bill.

"Yes, if you don't," replied the old man.

"We are going now," said Bill. "We thank you for your thoughtfulness. We must at least try. We are sorry to leave you. Please believe that."

"I do believe it," cried the old man and he seized their hands in a farewell clasp.

Harl opened the door of the plane and Bill clambered in.

At the door Harl stood with upraised hand.

"Good-bye," he said. "Some day we will return."

The crowd burst into a roar of farewell. Harl climbed into the plane and closed the door.

The motors bellowed, droning out the shouting of the future-men and the great machine charged down the sand. With a rush it took the air. Three times Bill circled the ruined city in a last mute good-bye to the men who watched silently and sorrowfully below.

Then Harl threw the lever. Again the utter darkness, the feeling of hanging in nothingness.

The motors, barely turning, muttered at the change. A minute passed, two minutes.

"Who says we can't travel back in time!" Harl shouted triumphantly. He pointed to the needle. It was slowly creeping back across the face of the dial.

"Maybe the old man was wrong after—"

Bill never finished the sentence.

"Roll her out," he screamed at Harl, "roll her out. One of our engines is going dead!"

Harl snatched at the lever, jerked frantically at it. The faulty motor choked and coughed, sputtered, then broke into a steady drone.

The two men in the cabin regarded one another with blanched faces. They knew they had escaped a possible crash —and death—by bare seconds.

Again they hung in the air. Again they saw the brick-red sun, the desert, and the sea. Below them loomed the ruins of Denver.

"We couldn't have gone far back in time," said Harl. "It looks the same as ever."

They circled the ruins.

"We had better land out in the desert to fix up the engine," suggested Harl. "Remember we have traveled back in time and Golan-Kirt still rules over the land. We don't want to have to kill him a second time. We might not be able to do it."

The plane was flying low and he nosed it up. Again the faulty engine sputtered and missed.

"She's going dead this time for certain," yelled Bill. "We'll have to chance it, Harl. We have to land and chance getting away again."

Harl nodded grimly.

Before them lay the broad expanse of the arena. It was either that or crash.

As Bill nosed the plane down the missing motor sputtered for the last time, went dead.

They flashed over the white walls of the amphitheater and down into the arena. The plane struck the sand, raced across it, slowed to a stop.

Harl opened the door.

"Our only chance is to fix it up in a hurry and get out of here," he shouted at Bill. "We don't want to meet that damn brain again."

He stopped short.

"Bill," he spoke scarcely above a whisper, "am I seeing things?"

Before him, set on the sands of the arena, only a few yards from the plane, was a statue of heroic size, a statue of himself and Bill.

Even from where he stood he could read the inscription, carved in the white stone base of the statue in characters which closely resembled written English.

Slowly, haltingly, he read it aloud, stumbling over an occasional queer character.

"Two men, Harl Swanson, and Bill Kressman, came out of time to kill Golan-Kirt and to free the race."

Below it he saw other characters.

"They may return."

"Bill," he sobbed, "we haven't traveled back in time. We have traveled further into the future. Look at that stone—eroded, ready to crumble to pieces. That statue has stood there for thousands of years!"

Bill slumped back into his seat, his face ashen, his eyes staring.

"The old man was right," he screamed. "He was right. We'll never see the twentieth century again."

He leaned over toward the time machine.

His face twitched.

"Those instruments," he shrieked, "those damned instruments! They were wrong. They lied, they lied!"

With his bare fists he beat at them, smashing them, unaware that the glass cut deep gashes and his hands were smeared with blood.

Silence weighed down over the plain. There was absolutely no sound.

Bill broke the silence.

"The future-men," he cried, "where are the future-men?"

He answered his own question.

"They are all dead," he screamed, "all dead. They are starved—starved because they couldn't manufacture synthetic food. We are alone! Alone at the end of the world!"

Harl stood in the door of the plane.

Over the rim of the amphitheater the huge red sun hung in a sky devoid of clouds. A slight wind stirred the sand at the base of the crumbling statue.

Cliff Simak is a particularly prominent figure in the science fiction world. "The World of the Red Sun" was his first published story, and it was simply and straightforwardly told. It had a sad ending, too, and I remember that impressed me at the time. I could not help but recognize the force of a dramatic and ironic ending. ("The Man Who Evolved" had possessed one, too.)

Simak was unusual among the early authors in that he survived the Coming of Campbell. Most early authors did not. (It was rather like the coming of talking pictures, which proved the ruin of so many actors who had learned their job in the world of the silents.)

Meek, for instance, hardly wrote anything after 1932, and Miller wrote infrequently. Jones and Hamilton continued to write frequently but hardly ever appeared in Campbell's *Astounding,* which was all that counted through the 1940s.

Simak was quite different. He published four more stories in 1932 and then nothing more until the Campbell era began, in 1938. He then began to write prolifically for the various magazines, including *Astounding,* and was soon numbered among the recognized members of Campbell's "stable"—that is, those authors whom he had discovered or developed (or both).

Indeed, Simak went on to grow even larger in stature as the field expanded in the 1950s and 1960s, when Campbell no longer held the monopoly. Simak was Guest of Honor at the World Science Fiction Convention held in Boston in 1971, and just the other day I received the hardback edition of his most recent novel, *Cemetery World.*

In the gap between 1932 and 1938, I had forgotten Clifford Simak, though not "The World of the Red Sun." I rediscovered him when he wrote "Rule 18," which appeared in the July 1938 issue of *Astounding Science Fiction.* What followed from that and how we grew to be close friends I mentioned in *The Early Asimov.*

It was not till a number of years after I had become friends with Cliff that I discovered, quite by accident, that it was he who had written the story I had once told with such pleasure and success to my junior high school classmates. What a happy discovery that was!

Simak was the first to teach me, by example, of the value of an unadorned style. I explained that in *The Early Asimov*, and I want to mention that here, too.

In the fall of 1931 (inspired, perhaps, by my success in interesting my friends in the science fiction tales I retold), I began to try my hand at making up stories of my own.

I didn't write science fiction, however. I had a most exalted notion of the intense skills and vast scientific knowledge required of authors in the field, and I dared not aspire to such things. Instead, I began to write a tale of ordinary planet-bound adventure called "The Greenville Chums at College."

I worked with a pencil and a five-cent notebook and eventually wrote eight chapters before fading out. I remember trying to tell the story of the Greenville Chums to one of those friends who had listened steadily to my retelling of science fiction. With a certain precocious caution, I had chosen the one who seemed most consistently enthusiastic. After I had told him what I had written that day, he asked eagerly if he could borrow the book when I was done.

I had either neglected to make it clear to him, or he had failed to understand, that I was *writing* the book. He thought it was another already printed story I was retelling. The implied compliment staggered me, and from that day on, I secretly took myself seriously as a writer.

PART THREE

1932

IN THE SPRING of 1932, I completed my stay at Junior High School 149. The class held the graduation ceremonies at a fancy auditorium somewhere in Brooklyn. My father gave me a fountain pen as a graduation present (the traditional gift, of course, but very appropriate in my case—though neither my father nor I realized that at the time).

More important, he and my mother actually managed to shake off the candy-store duties (I don't remember whether they closed the store or hired a temporary store sitter) in order to attend the graduation. They took it *very* seriously.

I remember only two things. First, the glee club sang "Gaudeamus Igitur," which included the line "Glorious youth is with us." I was at once overwhelmed with a sharp and sorrowful pang at the thought that I was graduating and that youth was slipping fast away.

Yet I was only twelve years old at the time, and here it is over forty years later and youth *still* hasn't slipped away. (Well, it hasn't, you rotten kids.)

The second thing I remember was that two awards were given out, one for excellence in biology and the other for excellence in mathematics. Both winners marched forward and onto the stage and were covered with glory in the sight of their proud parents. And I knew that somewhere in the audience my father's face was setting into lines of grim disapproval, since neither winner was I.

Sure enough, when we were all home, my father, in awful, patriarchal tones, demanded to know why it was that I had won neither prize.

"Papa," I said (for I had had time to think out the best way of putting it), "the kid who won the mathematics prize is lousy in biology. The kid who won the biology prize can't add two and two. And as for me, I was second in line for *both* prizes."

That was quite true and it took me neatly off the hook. Not another word was said.

The last months at the junior high school were enlivened for me by "Tumithak of the Corridors," by Charles R. Tanner, which appeared in the January 1932 *Amazing Stories*.

TUMITHAK OF THE CORRIDORS

by Charles R. Tanner

FOREWORD

IT is only within the last few years that archeological science has reached a point where we may begin to appreciate the astonishing advances in science that our ancestors had achieved before the Great Invasion. Excavations in the ruins of London and New York have been especially prolific in yielding knowledge of the life that those ancestors led. That they possessed the secret of flying, and a knowledge of chemistry and electricity far beyond ours is now certain; and there is even some evidence that they surpassed us in medicine and some of the arts. Taking their civilization as a whole, it is quite doubtful if we have even yet surpassed them in general knowledge.

Until the time of the Invasion, their discoveries of the secrets of Nature seem to have been made steadily in regular geometric progression, and we have good cause to believe that it was the people of earth who first solved the secret of interplanetary flight. The many romances that have been written by novelists dealing with this time, testify to the interest which we of today take in the history of what we call the Golden Age.

But the present story deals neither with the days of the Invasion, nor with life as it was in the Golden Age before it. It tells, instead, of the life of that semi-mythical, semi-historical character, Tumithak of Loor, who, legend tells us, was the first man to rebel against the savage shelks. Although innumerable facts are still lacking, recent investigations in the Pits and Corridors have thrown much light on what was obscure in this hero's life. That he really lived and fought is now certain to be true; that he accomplished the miracles accredited to him by legend is just as certain to be untrue.

We can feel sure, for instance, that he never lived for the two hundred and fifty years that are ascribed to him; that his wonderful strength and imperviousness to the rays of the shelks are mythical, as are doubtless the stories of his destruction of the six cities.

But our knowledge of his life increases as our credibility in the legends decreases, and the time has come when we can grasp dimly, but with a more rational viewpoint, the truth about his deeds. So, in this tale, the author makes an attempt to rationalize, to place properly in its historical setting, the early life of a great hero who dared to strike boldly for Mankind, in the days when the Beasts of Venus held all the earth in thrall . . .

CHAPTER I

The Boy and the Book

As far as eye could see the long somber corridor extended. Fifteen feet high and as many wide it ran on and on, its brown, glassy walls presenting an unvarying sameness. At intervals along the center line of the ceiling large glowing lights appeared, flat plates of cool white luminescence that had shone without attention for centuries. At intervals equally frequent, were deep-cut doors, draped with a rough burlap-like cloth, their sills worn down by the passing generations of feet. Nowhere was the monotony of the scene broken unless it were in some places, where the corridor was crossed by another of equal simplicity.

The passage was by no means deserted. Here and there, throughout its length, scattered figures appeared—men, for the most part blue-eyed and red-haired and dressed in rough burlap tunics that were gathered at the waist by wide, pocketed belts with enormous buckles. A few women were also in evidence, differing from the men in the length of their hair and tunics. All moved with a furtive slinking air, for though it was many years since the Terror had been seen, the habits of a hundred generations were not easily thrown off. And so the hall, its frequenters, their clothes and even their habits combined to complete the somber monotone.

From somewhere far below this corridor came the steady beat and throb of some gigantic machine; a beat that continued unceasingly and was so much a part of the life of these people that it was only with difficulty that they could be brought to notice it at all. Yes its beat bore down on them, penetrated their minds, and, with its steady rhythm, affected all that they did.

One part of the hall seemed to be more populous than any other. The lights here glowed brighter, the cloths that covered the doorways were cleaner and newer, and many more people appeared. Sneaking in and out of the doorways they went, for all the world like rabbits engaged in some big business enterprise.

Out of one of the side doorways, a boy and girl appeared. About fourteen years of age, they were exceptionally tall for children, apparently having already reached their full growth, though their immaturity was evident. They, too, like their elders, were blue-eyed and red-haired; a complexion due to the eternal lack of sunshine and lifelong exposure to the rays of the corridor lights. There was a certain boldness and quickness about them that caused many of the folk of the corridor to frown disapprovingly as they passed. One could see that these older ones felt that the younger generation was fast riding to destruction. Certainly, sooner or later, this boldness and loudness would bring down the Terror from the Surface.

But sublimely indifferent to the disapproval that was so in evidence around them, the two youngsters continued upon their way. They turned from the main corridor into one less brilliantly lighted, and after traversing it for nearly a mile, turned into another. The hall in which they now found themselves was narrow and inclined upward at a decided angle. It was entirely deserted and the thick dust and neglected condition of the lights showed that it was long since men had lived here. The many doorways were without the draped curtains that concealed the interior of the inhabited apartments in the larger corridors; but many of the doorways were almost entirely covered with draperies of cobwebs covered with dust. The girl drew closer to the boy as they continued up the passage; but aside from this she showed no sign of fear. After some time the passageway grew steeper, and at last ended in a cul-de-sac. The two seated themselves in the rubble that littered the floor and presently began to talk in a low tone.

"It must have been years since men have come here," said the girl, softly. "Perhaps we will find something of great value which was left here when men deserted this corridor."

"I think Tumithak is too hopeful, when he tells us of possible treasures in these halls," answered the boy. "Surely there have been men in these halls, searching as we are, since they were abandoned."

"Tumithak should be here by now," the girl said, after a while. "Do you think he will come?" Her eyes strove vainly to pierce the gloom down the hallway.

"Why, of course, he will come, Thupra," said her companion. "Has Tumithak ever failed to meet us as he promised?"

"But to come here, alone!" protested Thupra. "I should die of fright, Nikadur, if you weren't here."

"There isn't really any danger here," he said. "The men of Yakra could never enter these halls without passing through the main corridor. And many, many years have passed since Loor has seen a shelk."

"Grandfather Koniak once saw a shelk," reminded Thupra.

"Yes, but not here in Loor. He saw it in Yakra, years ago, when he fought the Yakrans as a young man. Remember, the Loorians were successful in their campaign against the Yakrans and drove them out of their city and into the corridors beyond. And then suddenly there was flame and terror, and a band of shelks appeared. Grandfather Koniak saw but one, and that one almost caught him before he escaped." Nikadur smiled. "It is a wonderful tale, but I think we have only Grandfather Koniak's word for it."

"But really, Nikadur—" the girl was beginning, when she was interrupted by a rustling noise from one of the web-hung doorways. Like a flash, boy and birl both leapt to their feet and sped in panic down the passage without so much as a single glance backward, totally unaware of the youth who had stepped from the doorway and who was now leaning against the wall, watching their flight with a cynical smile on his face.

At a glance, this youth seemed not unlike the others who lived in the corridors. The same red hair and clear translucent skin, the same rough tunic and enormous belt characterized this lad as it did all the others of Loor. But the discerning eye would have noticed in the immense brow, the narrow, hooked nose and the keen eyes, a promise of the greatness that was to some day be his.

The boy watched his fleeing friends for a moment and then gave a low bird-like whistle. Thupra stopped suddenly and turned around, and then, seeing the newcomer, called to Ni-

kadur. The boy stopped his flight, too, and together they returned, rather shamefaced, to the end of the passage.

"You frightened us, Tumithak," said the girl, reproachful-
ly. "What in the world were you doing in that room? Weren't
you afraid to go in there alone?"

"Nothing is in there to hurt me," answered Tumithak, lofti-
ly. "Often and often I have browsed around through these
corridors and apartments and never yet have I seen any living
thing, save the spiders and the bats. I was seeking for forgotten things," he went on, and his eyes grew suddenly brighter.
"And look! I have found a book!" And, reaching into the
bosom of his tunic, he drew forth his prize and exhibited it
proudly to the others.

"This is an *old* book," he said. "See?"

It certainly was an old book. The cover was gone, more
than half the leaves were missing, and the thin metal sheets of
which the leaves were composed were even beginning to oxi-
dize on the edges. Certainly, this book had been lying forgotten for centuries.

Nikadur and Thupra looked at it in awe, the awe that an il-
literate person naturally holds for all the mysteries of the
magic black marks that transmit thoughts. But Tumithak
could read. He was the son of Tumlook, one of the food men,
the men who held the secret of preparing the synthetic food
that these people lived on, and these food men, as well as the
doctors and the light and power men, retained many of the secrets of the wisdom of their ancestors. Foremost among these
secrets was the very necessary art of reading; and as Tumithak was intended to follow in his father's footsteps, Tumlook
had early trained him in this wonderful art.

So, after the two had looked at the book and held it in their
hands, and wondered, they beseeched Tumithak to read it to
them. Often, they had listened in wide-eyed wonder as he read
to them from some of the rare works the food men owned,
and they never wasted a chance to watch the apparently mys-
tifying process of changing the queer marks on the metal
sheets into sounds and sentences.

Tumithak smiled at their importuning, and then, because
secretly he was as anxious as they to know what the long-
forgotten script contained, he motioned them to be seated on
the floor beside him, and opening the book, began to read:

"The manuscript of Davon Starros; written at Pitmouth,

Sol 22nd, in the year of the Invasion, 161, or in the old style —A.D. 3218."

Tumithak paused.

"That *is* an old book," whispered Nikadur in an awed voice, and Tumithak nodded.

"Nearly two thousand years!" he answered, "I wonder what the figures A.D. 3218 stand for?"

He puzzled over the book for a moment and then resumed his reading.

"I am an old man, in these latter days, and to one who can remember the day when men still dared to fight, now and then, for liberty, it is indeed a bitter thing to see how the race has fallen.

"There is growing up among men in these days a hopeless superstition to the effect that man can never conquer, and must never attempt to even battle with the shelks, and it is to combat this superstition that the author here writes the story of the conquest of earth, in the hope that at some future time, a man will arise who will have the courage to face the conquerors of Man and again do battle. In the hope that this man will appear and that he may know the creatures against whom he fights, this story is written.

"The scientists who tell of the days before the Invasion, inform us that man was once little more than a beast. Through thousands of years he gradually worked his way upward to civilization, learning the arts of living, until he conquered all the world for his own.

"He learned the secret of producing food from the very elements themselves, he learned the secret of imitating the life-giving light of the sun, his great airships sped through the atmosphere as easily as his waterships sped through the sea. Wonderful, disintegrating rays dissolved the hill that stood in his way, and as a result, long canals brought water from the ocean to inaccessible deserts, making them blossom like earth's most fertile regions. From pole to pole, man's mighty cities grew, and from pole to pole man was supreme.

"For thousands of years, men quarreled among themselves, and great wars tore the earth, until at last their civilization reached a point where these wars ceased. A great era of peace settled down upon the earth, sea and land alike were conquered by man, and he began to look out to the other worlds that swung about the sun, wondering if these, too, might not be conquered.

"It was many centuries before they learned enough to attempt a journey into the depths of space. A way had to be found to avoid the countless meteors that filled the paths between the planets. A way had to be found to insulate against the deadly cosmic rays. It seemed that no sooner was one difficulty overcome that another arose to take its place. But one after another the difficulties in the way of interplanetary flight disappeared and at last the day came when a mighty vessel, hundreds of feet long, lay ready to leap into space to explore the other worlds."

Tumithak again paused in his reading.

"It must be a wonderful secret," he said. "I seem to be reading words, but I do not know what they mean. Some one is going somewhere, but that's about all I can make of it. Shall I go on?"

"Yes! Yes!" they cried; so he continued:

"It was under the command of a man named Henric Sudiven; and, of all the great company that manned it, only he returned to the world of men to tell of the terrible adventures that they met with on the planet Venus, the world to which they traveled.

"The trip to Venus was a highly successful one, and quite uneventful. Week after week passed, while the evening star, as men called it, grew ever brighter and larger. The ship worked perfectly, and though the journey was a long one to those who were used to crossing an ocean in a single night, the time did not hang heavy on their hands. The day came when they sailed over the low rolling plains and broad valleys of Venus, under the thick mantle of clouds that forever hides the surface of that planet from the sun, and marveled at the great cities and works of civilization that were in evidence everywhere.

"After hovering over a great city for some time, they landed and were welcomed by the strange, intelligent creatures that ruled over Venus; the same creatures that we know today by the name of shelks. The shelks thought them demi-gods and would have worshipped them; but Sudiven and his companions, true products of earth's noblest culture, scorned to dissemble; and when they had learned the language of the shelks, told them quite truthfully just who they were and from whence they came.

"The astonishment of the shelks knew no bounds. They were skilled far more than men in mechanical science; their knowledge of electricity and chemistry was quite as great; but astronomy and its kindred sciences were totally unknown to them. Imprisoned as they were under the eternal canopy of clouds that hides forever the sight of outer space, they had never dreamed of other worlds than the one they knew; and it was only with difficulty that they were at last persuaded that Sudiven's story was true.

"But, once convinced, the attitude of the shelks underwent a decided change. No longer were they deferential and friendly. They suspected that man had come only to conquer them and they determined to beat him at his own game. There was a certain lack of the more humane feelings in the make-up of the shelks, and they were quite unable to conceive of a friendly visit from strangers of another world.

"The Tellurians soon found themselves locked up in a great metal tower many miles from their space flier. In a moment of carelessness, one of Sudiven's companions had let drop the remark that this flier was the only one yet built upon the earth, and the shelks decided to take advantage of this fact, to begin at once the conquest of earth.

"They took possession at once of the Tellurians' vessel, and with that unity of purpose that is so characteristic of the shelks and so lacking in man, began at once the construction of a vast number of similar machines. All over the planet, the great machine-shops hummed and clattered with the noise of the work; and while the earth waited the triumphal return of her explorers, the day of her doom drew nearer and nearer.

"But Sudiven and the other Tellurians, locked up in their tower, had not given up to despair. Time after time, they attempted to escape, and there is no doubt but that the shelks would have slain them to a man, had they not hoped to extract further knowledge from them before they killed them. For once the shelks were in error; they should have slain the Tellurians, every one; for about a week before the date set for the departure of the shelks' great fleet of machines, Sudiven and about a dozen of his companions managed to escape.

"At terrific risk they made their way across the country to the place where their space car lay. An idea can be had of the dangers of the journey when one realizes that on Venus, that is, on the inhabited side, it is always day. There was no concealing night to enable the Tellurians to travel without hope of discovery. But at last they came upon their car, guarded only by a few unarmed shelks. The battle that ensued is one that should go down in man's history, to inspire him in all the ages to come. When it was over the shelks were all dead and only seven men were left to man the space-flier on its journey back to earth.

"For weeks, the great bullet-shaped flier sped across the vast emptiness of space and at last landed upon the earth. Sudiven alone remained alive when it landed; the others had succumbed to some strange disease, a disease that had been given to them by the shelks.

"But Sudiven was alive and remained alive long enough to warn the world. Faced with this sudden terror, the world had little time for any but defensive measures. The construction of vast underground pits and caverns was begun at once, the intention being to construct great underground cities, in which man could hide himself and from which he could emerge to conquer his enemies at his leisure. But before they were well started, the shelks arrived and the war was on!

"Never, in the days when man warred with man, had anyone dreamed of a war like this. The shelks had arrived by the millions; it was estimated that fully two hundred thousand space cars took part in the invasion. For days man's defensive measures kept the shelks from gaining a landing space on the earth; they were forced to fly far above the surface, dropping their deadly gases and explosives where they could. From his subterranean halls, man sent up vast quantities of gases as deadly as those of the shelks, and their disintegrating rays sent hundreds of the space-cars into nothingness, killing off the shelks like flies. And from their fliers, the shelks dropped vast quantities of flaming chemicals into the pits that men had dug, chemicals that burned with terrific violence and exhausted the oxygen of the caverns, causing men to perish by the thousand.

"Ever, as men found themselves defeated by the shelks, they drove deeper and deeper into the earth, their wonderful disintegrations dissolving the rock almost as fast as man could walk through the corridor it dug. Men were forced from the Surface at last, and a million intricate warrens of corridors and passages honeycombed the earth for miles beneath the surface. It was impossible for the shelks to ever thread the mazes of the innumerable labyrinths, and so man reached a position of comparative safety.

"And thus came the deadlock.

"The Surface had become the property of the savage

shelks, while far below them in the pits and corridors, man labored to hold on to the dregs of civilization that were left him. An unequal game it was, for man was sadly handicapped —the supplies of elements that produced the disintegrating rays gradually diminished, and there was no way of renewing them; they were unable to secure wood, or the thousand and one varieties of vegetation on which their industries were based; the men of one set of corridors had no way of communicating with the men of another; and always came hordes of shelks, down into the corridors, hunting men for sport!

"The only thing that enabled them to live at all was the wonderful ability to create synthetic foods out of the very rock itself.

"So it was that man's civilization, fought for and won after centuries of struggle, collapsed in a dozen years; and over it was imposed the Terror. Men, like rabbits, lived a life of fear and trembling in their underground holes, daring less each year, as time went by, and spending all their time and energy in devising means to sink their pits deeper and deeper into the ground. Today it seems that man's subjugation is complete. For over a hundred years, no man has dared to think of revolt against the shelks, any more than a rat would think of revolt against man. Unable to form a unified government, unable even to communicate with his brethren in the neighboring corridors, man has come to accept far too willingly, his place as merely the highest of the lower animals. The spider-like Beasts of Venus are the supreme Masters of our planet, and—"

The manuscript had come to an end. Although the book had originally been much longer, although, indeed, what was left of it was probably little more than an introduction to some work on the life and customs of the shelks, the remainder was missing and the droning sing-song voice of Tumithak ceased as he read the concluding unfinished sentence. For several moments there was silence and then—

"How hard it was to understand," said Thupra. "I only know that men were fighting with shelks, just as though they were Yakrans."

"Who could have conceived such a story?" murmured Nikadur, "Men fighting with shelks: Of all the impossible tales!"

Tumithak did not answer. For quite a while he sat in silence and stared at the book as one who suddenly beheld some dazzling vision.

At last he spoke.

"Nikadur, that is history!" he exclaimed. "That is no strange impossible tale of fancy. Something tells me that those men really lived; that that war was really fought: How else can we explain the life that we live. Have we not wondered often—have not our fathers wondered before us—how our wise ancestors ever gained the wisdom to build the great pits and corridors? We know that our ancestors had great knowledge; how did they come to lose it?

"Oh, I know that no legend of ours even suggests such a thing as men ruling this world," he went on, as he saw the incredulous look in the eyes of his companions. "But there is something—something in that book that tells me it is surely true. Just think, Nikadur! That book was written only a hundred and sixty years after the savage shelks invaded the earth! How much more that writer must have known than we who live two thousand years later. Nikadur, once men fought with shelks!" He arose, his eyes gleaming with the first glow of the fanatical light that, in after years, was to make him a man apart from his fellows, *"Once men fought with shelks:* and with the help of the High One, they shall do so again! Nikadur! Thupra! Some day *I* shall fight a shelk," he flung his arms wide, "some day I shall *slay* a shelk!

"And to that I dedicate my life!"

He stood for a moment with his arms outstretched, and then, as if oblivious of their presence, he dashed down the hallway and in a moment was lost in the gloom. For a moment the two stared after him in amazement, and then, clasping hands, they walked slowly, soberly after him. They knew that something had suddenly inspired their friend, but whether it was genius or madness they could not tell. And they were not to know with certainty for many years.

CHAPTER II

The Three Strange Gifts

Tumlook contemplated his son proudly. The years that had passed since he had discovered the strange manuscript and acquired his strange obsession may have ruined his mind, as some said, but they had certainly been kind to him, physically. Six feet tall, Tumithak stood (an exceptional height for these dwellers in the corridors), and every inch seemed to be of iron muscle. Today, on his twentieth birthday, there was not a man that would not have hailed him as one of the leaders of the city, had it not been for his preposterous mania. For Tumithak was resolved to kill a shelk!

For years—in fact, since he had found the manuscript, at the age of fourteen—he had directed all his studies to this end. He had pored over maps of the corridors, ancient maps that had not been used for centuries—maps that showed the way to the Surface—and he was known to be an authority on all the secret passages in the pit. He had little idea of what the Surface was really like; there was little in the stories of his people to tell him of it. But of one thing he was certain, and that was, that on the Surface he would find the shelks.

He had studied the various weapons that man could still rely on—the sling, the sword, and the bow; and had made himself proficient in the use of all three. Indeed, in every way possible, he had prepared himself for the great work to which he had decided to devote his life. Of course, he had met with the opposition of his father, of the whole tribe, for that matter, but with the singleness of purpose that only a fanatic can attain, he persisted in his idea, resolved that when he was of age he would bid his people adieu, and set out for the Surface. He had given little thought to the details of what he would do when he arrived there. That would all depend on what he found. One thing he was sure of—that he would kill a shelk and bring its body back to show his people that men could still triumph over those who thought they were man's masters.

And today he became of age; today he was twenty and Tumlook could not resist being secretly proud of this astounding son of his, even though he had done everything in his power to turn him from the impossible dream that he had conceived. Now that the day had come when Tumithak was to start on his absurd quest, Tumlook had to admit that in his heart, he had long been one with Tumithak, and that now he was eager to see the boy started on his way. He spoke:

"Tumithak," he said. "For years, I have sought to turn you from the impossible task that you have set yourself. For years, you have opposed me and persisted in believing in the actual possibility of achieving your dream. And now the day has come when you are to actually set out to achieve it. Do not think that it was anything other than a father's love that led me to oppose your ambition, and to try and keep you in Loor.

But now that the day has come when you are free to do as you please, and as you are still determined to make your incredible attempt, you must at least allow your father to help you all he can."

He paused and lifted to the table a box about a foot square. He opened it and drew from it three strange-looking objects.

"Here," he said, impressively, "Are three of the most precious treasures of the food-men; implements devised by our wise ancestors of old. "This one," and he picked up a cylindrical tube about an inch in diameter and a foot long, "is a torch, a wonderful torch that will give you light in the dark corridors, by merely pressing this button. Take care not to waste its power, it is not made of the eternal light that our ancestors set in the ceilings. It is based on a different principle and after a certain time its power is exhausted."

Tumlook picked up the next object gingerly.

"This, too, is something that will surely help you, though it is neither so rare nor so wonderful as the other two. It is a charge of high explosive, such as we use occasionally for closing a corridor, or in mining the elements from which our food is made. There is no telling when it may come in handy, on your way to the Surface.

"And here," he picked up the last article, which looked like a small pipe with a handle set on one end, at right angles. "Here is the most wonderful article of all. It shoots a small pellet of lead, and it shoots it with such force that it will pierce even a sheet of metal! Each time this small trigger on the side is pressed, a pellet is ejected from the mouth of the pipe, with terrific force. It kills, Tumithak, kills even quicker than an arrow, and much surer. Use it carefully for there are but ten pellets, and when they are gone, the instrument is useless."

He laid the three articles on the table before him, and pushed them across to Tumithak. The younger man took them and stowed them carefully in the pockets of his wide belt.

"Father," he said, slowly, "You know it is not anything in my heart that commands me to leave you and go on this quest. There is something, higher than either you or I, that has spoken to me and that I must obey. Since mother's death, you have been both mother and father to me, and so I probably love you more than the average man loves his father. But I have had a Vision! I dream of a time when Man will once again rule on the Surface and not a shelk will exist to oppose him. But that time can never come as long as men believe the shelks to be invincible, and so I am going to prove that they can really be slain—and by men!"

He paused and before he could continue, the door opened and Nikadur and Thupra entered. The former was a man now, the responsibility of a householder having fallen upon him at his father's death, two years before. And the latter had grown into a beautiful woman, a woman that Nikadur was soon to marry. They both greeted Tumithak with deference and when Thupra spoke, it was in an awed voice, as one who addressed a demi-god; and Nikadur, too, had obviously come to look upon Tumithak as something more than mortal. These two, with the possible exception of Tumlook, were the only ones who took Tumithak seriously, and so they were the only ones that he would call his friends.

"Do you leave us today, Tumithak?" asked Thupra.

Tumithak nodded. "Yes," he answered. "This very day. I start for the Surface. Before a month has gone by, I will lie dead in some distant corridor, or you shall look on the head of a shelk!"

Thupra shuddered. Either of these alternatives seemed terrible enough to her. But Nikadur was thinking of the more immediate dangers of the journey.

"You will have no trouble on the road to Nonone," he said, thoughtfully, "But mustn't you pass through the town of Yakra on the way to the Surface?"

"Yes," answered Tumithak. "There is no road to the Surface, except through Yakra. And beyond Yakra are the Dark Corridors, where men have not ventured for hundreds of years."

Nikadur considered. The city of Yakra had for over a century been the enemy of the people of Loor. Situated as it was, more than twenty miles nearer the Surface than Loor, it was inevitable that it should be much more conscious of the Terror. And it was just as inevitable that the people of Yakra should envy the Loorians their comparative safety, and continually make attempts to seize the city for their own. The small town of Nonone, located between the two larger cities, found itself sometimes fighting with the Yakrans, sometimes against them, as suited the convenience of the chiefs of the more powerful cities. Just as present, and indeed for the past twenty years, it was allied to Loor, and so Tumithak expected no trouble on his journey until he attempted to pass through Yakra.

"And the Dark Corridors?" questioned Nikadur.

"Beyond Yakra, there are no lights," replied Tumithak. "Men have avoided these passages for centuries. They are entirely too near the Surface for safety. Yakrans have at times attempted to explore them, but the parties that went out never returned. At least, so the men of Nonone have told me."

Thupra was about to make some remark, but Tumithak turned and busied himself with the pack of foodstuff that he intended to take with him on his journey. He slung it over his back and turned toward the door.

"The time has come for me to begin my journey," he said impressively. "This is the moment that I have awaited for years. Farewell, father! Farewell, Thupra! Nikadur, take good care of my little friend, and—if I do not return, name your first-born after me."

With a dramatic gesture that was characteristic of him, he thrust the door curtain aside and strode out into the corridor. The three followed him, calling and waving as he walked on up the hallway, but without so much as a backward glance, he strode along until he disappeared in the distant gloom.

They stood then, for a while, and then, with a dry sob, Tumlook turned and re-entered the apartment.

"He'll never return," he muttered to Nikadur. "He'll never return, of course."

Nikadur and Thupra answered nothing, only standing in uncomfortable silence. There was nothing consoling that they might say. Tumlook was right and it would have been foolish to attempt words of condolence that would have obviously been false.

The road that led from Loor to Nonone inclined very gradually upward. It was not an entirely strange road to Tumithak, for long ago he had been to that small town with his father, but the memory of the road was faint and now he found much to interest him as he left the lights of the populous portion of the town behind him. Then entrances of other corridors continually appeared, corridors that were constructed to add to the labyrinthine maze, that made it impossible for the creatures from the upper Surface to find their way into the great pits. The way did not lead along the broad main corridor for long. Often Tumithak would take his own way down to what appeared to be quite an insignificant hallway, only to have it suddenly branch into another larger one, farther on.

It must not be supposed that Tumithak had so quickly forgotten his home in his anxiety to be on his quest. Often, as he passed some familiar sight, a lump would come into his throat and he would almost be tempted to give up his journey and return. Twice Tumithak passed foodrooms, rooms where the familiar mystic machines throbbed eternally, building up out of the very rocks their own fuel and the tasteless biscuits of food that these people lived on. It was then that his homesickness was the greatest, for many times he had watched his father operating such machines as these, and the memory made him realize poignantly all that he was leaving behind. But like all the inspired geniuses of humanity, at times such as this, it almost seemed as if something outside of himself took charge of him and forced him on.

Tumithak turned from the last large corridor to a single winding hall not more than a half dozen feet in width. There were no doorways along this hall and it was much steeper than any he had yet climbed. It ran on for several miles and then entered a larger passage through a door that was seemingly but one of a hundred similar ones that lined this new passage. These doors were apparently those of apartments, but the apartments seemed to be unused, for there were no signs of inhabitants in this district. Probably this corridor had been abandoned for some reason many years ago.

There was nothing strange in this to Tumithak, however. He knew quite well that these doorways were only to add extra confusion to the ones who sought to thread the maze of corridors, and he continued on his way, without paying the slightest attention to the many branching hallways, until he came to the room he sought.

It was an ordinary apartment, to all appearances, but when Tumithak found himself inside, he hastened to the rear and began to feel carefully over the walls. In a corner, he found what he was searching for—a ladder of metal bars, leading upwards. Confidently, he began the ascent, mounting steadily upward in the dark; and as minute followed minute, the faint glow of light that shone in from the corridor below grew smaller and smaller.

At last he reached the top of the ladder, and found himself standing at the mouth of the pit, in a room similar to the one he had left below. He strode out of the room into another of the familiar door-lined corridors and turning in the direction that led upward, continued his journey. He was on the level of Nonone now, and if he hurried, he knew that he might reach that town before the time of sleep.

He hastened along, and presently he perceived a party of men in the distance, who gradually approached him. He drew into an apartment from which he peered out cautiously, until he assured himself that they were Nononese. The red color of their tunics, their narrow belts and the peculiar way they had of dressing their hair convinced him that these were friends and so Tumithak showed himself and waited for the party to approach him. When they saw him, the foremost man, who was evidently the leader, hailed him.

"Is not this Tumithak of Loor?" he asked, and as Tumithak replied in the affirmative, he continued, "I am Nennapuss, chief of the people of Nonone. Your father has acquainted us with the facts of your journey and asked us to be looking for you about this time. We trust that you will spend the next sleep with us; and if there is anything that we can do to add to your comfort or safety on your journey, you have but to command us."

Tumithak almost smiled at the rather pompous speech which the chief had evidently prepared beforehand, but he answered gravely that he would indeed be indebted if Nennapuss could provide him with sleeping quarters. The chief assured him that the best in the town would be provided, and, turning, led Tumithak off in the direction from which he and his party had come.

They traversed several miles of deserted passages before they finally came to the inhabited halls of Nonone, but once here, the hospitality of Nennapuss knew no bounds. The people of Nonone were assembled in the "Great Square," as the juncture of the two main corridors was called, and in a florid, flowing speech that was characteristic of him, Nennapuss told them of Tumithak and his quest; and presented him, as it were, with the keys of the city.

After an answering speech by Tumithak, in which the Loorian worked himself up into a fine fury of eloquence on his favorite subject—his journey—a banquet was prepared; and even though the food was only the tasteless biscuits that constituted the sole diet of these people they gorged themselves to repletion. When Tumithak at last fell asleep, it was with the feeling that here, at least, a tentative slayer of shelks might find appreciation. Had not the proverb been buried in centuries of ignorance and forgetfulness, he might have mused that a prophet is, verily, not without honor save in his own country.

Tumithak arose about ten hours later and prepared to bid good-by to the people of Nonone. Nennapuss insisted that the Loorian have breakfast with his family and Tumithak willingly complied. The sons of Nennapuss, two lads in their early teens, were enthusiastic during the meal, with the wonderful idea that Tumithak had conceived. Though the idea of any other man facing a shelk was incredible to them, they seemed to think that Tumithak was something more than the average mortal, and plied him with a hundred questions as to his plans. But, beyond having studied the long route to the Surface, Tumithak's plans were decidedly vague, and he was unable to tell them how he would slay his shelk.

After the meal, he again shouldered his pack and started up the corridor. The chief and his retinue followed him for several miles and as they went Tumithak questioned Nennapuss closely as to the condition of the passages to Yakra and beyond.

"The road on this level is quite safe," said Nennapuss, in answer to his questions. "It is patrolled by men of my city and no Yakran ever enters it without our being aware of it. But the pit that leads to the level of Yakra is always guarded at the top by the Yakrans, and I do not doubt but that you will have trouble when you try to get out of that pit."

Tumithak promised to use an extra amount of caution when he reached this spot, and a short time later, Nennapuss and his companions said good-by to him and he trudged on alone.

He moved more warily, now, for though the Nononese patrolled these corridors, he knew quite well that it was possible for enemies to evade the guards and raid the corridors as had often been done in the past. He kept well in the middle of the corridor, away from the many doorways, any one of which may have concealed a secret road to Yakra, and he seldom passed one of the branching ways without peering carefully up and down it, before venturing to cross it.

But Tumithak was fortunate in meeting no one in the corridors, and after half a day he came at last to another apartment in which was located a shaft almost exactly similar to the one that had brought him to Nonone.

He mounted this ladder much more stealthily than he had the first one, for he was quite confident that a Yakran guard was at the top and he had no desire to be toppled backward into the pit when he reached there. As he drew near the end of the ladder, he drew his sword, but again luck favored him, for the guard had apparently left the room at the top of the well, and Tumithak drew himself up into the room and prepared to enter the corridor.

But he had moved only a scant half dozen feet when his luck deserted him. He bumped violently into a table that he had failed to notice in the gloom, and the resulting noise brought a bull-like bellow from the corridor without. The next moment, sword in hand, a veritable giant of a man dashed through the door and made for Tumithak.

CHAPTER III

The Passing of Yakra

That man was a Yakran, Tumithak would have known, had he met him in the depths of Loor. Though the Loorian knew of the Yakrans only through the stories of the older men, who remembered the wars with that city, he saw at once that this was just the kind of barbarian that had figured in the stories. He was fully four inches taller than Tumithak, and far broader and heavier, and his chin was covered with a tremendous, bristly growth of beard—sufficient evidence that the owner was of Yakra. His tunic was covered with bits of bone and metal sewn into the cloth, the former stained in various colors and sewn in a crude pattern. Around his neck was a necklace made of dozens of fingerbones threaded on a thin strip of skin.

Tumithak saw in an instant that he would have little chance with this huge Yakran if he were to stand fairly up to him, and so, even as he drew his sword and prepared to defend himself, he was casting about in his mind for some method to overcome him by strategy. The most probable plan, he decided at once, would be to drive him somehow into the pit; but to drive this colossus was almost as impossible as to defeat him by face to face fighting methods. And before Tumithak could devise any more subtle method of overcoming his adversary, he found his entire mind taken up with methods of defending himself.

The Yakran rushed at him, still shouting his rumbling war-cry, and it was but the merest lurch that enabled Tumithak to avoid the first terrific blow aimed at him. Tumithak dropped to one knee, but in a moment was up again and only just in time to avoid another sweep of that lightning sword. On his feet again, however, his defense was perfect, and the Yakran found it necessary to retire a step or two, in order to prepare another of his lunging rushes.

Again and again the Yakran rushed at Tumithak, and it was only the Loorian's uncanny skill at fencing, learned through many years in the hope of facing a shelk, that saved him. Around and around the table, now close to the pit and now farther away, they fought; until even Tumithak's steel-like muscles began to tire.

But as his body tired, his brain quickened, and at last a plan came to him to defeat the Yakran. He allowed himself to be gradually forced to the edge of the pit and then, as he parried a particularly powerful lunge, he suddenly threw one hand high in the air and screamed. The Yakran, believing that he had struck him, smiled a vicious smile and stepped back for a final rush. Sword pointing at Tumithak's breast, he dashed forward, and as he did so, Tumithak threw himself at his opponent's feet.

There was a wild howl from the giant as he stumbled over the recumbent form, but before he could recover himself, he dropped heavily at the very edge of the pit. Tumithak kicked wildly, and the great Yakran, grasping frantically at the air, dropped into the well! There was a hoarse cry from the darkness below, a heavy thud and then silence.

For several minutes, Tumithak lay panting at the edge of the pit. This was the first battle he had ever had with a man, and though he was the victor, it was only by a miracle, it seemed, that he had not been defeated. What would the people of Loor and Nonone say, he wondered if they knew that their self-appointed slayer of shelks had been so nearly defeated by the first enemy that had attacked him—and that enemy not a shelk, but a man, and a man of despised Yakra, at that? For several minutes, the Loorian lay, filled with self-reproach, and then, reflecting that if all his enemies were conquered with a margin even so small as this, his victory was certain, he arose, pulled himself together and left the room.

He was in Yakra now, and it was necessary for him to find some means of passing safely through the city in order to reach the dark corridors beyond. For only through these dark corridors might he win his way to the upper Surface. He continued cautiously on his way, turning over in his brain plan after plan that would enable him to deceive the Yakrans; but he was almost within sight of the inhabited walls of Yakra before he conceived an idea that seemed to him to be feasible. There was but one thing that all men in these pits feared, with a fear that was quite unreasoning. And it was upon this unreasoning fear that Tumithak decided to play.

He began to run. He ran slowly at first, a mere trot, but as he drew nearer the corridors where men lived, he increased his pace, running faster and faster until he was fleeing along like one who had all the demons of hell at his back. Which was precisely the effect that he wished to produce.

In the distance he saw a group of Yakrans approaching. They beheld him at the same time that he spied them, and in a moment more were charging down on him; quite aware, as he knew, that he was not a Yakran. Instead of trying to avoid them, he charged straight into their midst, screaming at the top of his lungs.

"Shelks!" he shouted as though in the last stages of terror, "Shelks!"

The bellicose attitude of the men changed at once to one of extreme fright. Without a word to Tumithak or even so much as a backward glance, they turned, and as he dashed past them, they sped panic-stricken after him. Had they been men of Loor, they might have paused long enough to investigate, or at least, have held Tumithak and questioned him. But not these Yakrans. This town was many miles nearer the Surface than Loor, and many of the older men could still remember the last time that the shelks had raided these halls on one of their rare hunting expeditions, leaving a trail of death and destruction that would never be forgotten while those that witnessed it lived. So the terror was far more of a living thing to Yakra than it was to Loor, to whom it was little more than a terrible legend of the past.

And so, without a word of question, the Yakrans fled down the long corridor after Tumithak, through branching hallways and through doorways that seemed mere entrances to apartments, but were actually roads to the main corridor. Several times they passed other men or groups of men, but at the fearful cry of "Shelks" these always dropped whatever they were doing and followed the frightened throng. A good many dashed down branching corridors, in which, they imagined, lay greater safety; but the majority continued on their way to the heart of the city, the direction in which Tumithak was going.

The Loorian was no longer in the lead now, several of the fleeter Yakrans had passed him, terror lending wings to their feet. And so the size of the mob grew and was augmented by greater and greater numbers as they came closer to the town center, until at last the corridor was filled with a screaming, terrified multitude in which Tumithak was completely lost.

They neared the wide main corridor, and here they found a great mass of people that had surged in from every one of the branching corridors. How the news had traveled so quickly, Tumithak was unable to guess, but apparently the entire city was already aware of the supposed danger. And like sheep, or rather, like the humans they were, all had been seized with the same idea—the desire to reach the center of the city, where they supposed, the greatest safety lay in the presence of the greatest numbers.

But now this frenzied confusion bade fair to defeat the plan that Tumithak had devised to cross the city safely under cover of the excitement he caused. To be sure, he had almost won to the center of the city without discovery, and the inhabitants were so wrought up that there would be little chance of any-one noticing that he was a stranger, but so thickly packed was the crowd that it became more and more certain that the Loorian was not going to be able to work his way through, in order to reach the corridors beyond. Yet in spite of the apparent hopelessness, Tumithak struggled along with the frantic mob, hoping against hope that he might gain a comparatively clear corridor beyond the city's center before the fright of the people died down to the point where they would begin the in-evitable search for the one who had started the panic.

The crowd, its fright enhanced by that strange sense of te-lepathy that is evident in any large assembly of people, was becoming dangerous. Men were using their fists freely to bet-ter their way, they passed their weaker brothers, and here and there voices could be heard, high pitched with anger. Tumi-thak saw a man stumble and fall, and a moment later, heard a scream as the unfortunate one was trampled on by the ones behind him. Hardly had the scream died away when there was another cry from the opposite side of the passage, where another man had fallen and found himself unable to regain his feet.

The Loorian seemed little more than a leaf borne along on the stream of shouting, gesticulating, Yakrans by the time he reached the center of the city. Time after time, he had almost been swept from his feet, only to regain his balance by what seemed a miracle. He had nearly gained the huge square that marked the crossing of the two main corridors when he stumbled over a fallen Yakran and almost went down. He attempted to pass on, and then stopped. The form beneath his feet was that of a woman with a baby in her arms!

Her face was tear-stained and bleeding, her clothes were torn in a dozen places, yet she was attempting bravely to prevent the injury of her child beneath the feet of the multitude. Tumithak instantly stooped over to raise her to her feet, but even before he could do so, the crowd had pushed him almost beyond the reach of her. Sudden anger swept over him, and plunging out wrathfully, he dealt blow after blow into the faces of the onrushing multitude of creatures, who would have crushed one of their own people in their anxiety for personal safety. The Yakrans yielded before his blows, poured on either side of him for a moment, and in that moment, Tumithak stopped and raised the woman to her feet.

She was still conscious, as the wan smile that she bestowed upon him showed, and though he knew she was an enemy of his people, Tumithak felt a momentary pity that his ruse to frighten the Yakrans had been so successful. She was trying to tell him something, but so great were the confused shouts that it was impossible for him to understand her. He bent down his head to hers to hear what she had to say.

"The doorway across the hall," she screamed in his ear, "Try to get through the crowd to the third doorway across the hall! There is safety there!"

Tumithak placed her in front of him and drove savagely into the crowd, his fists flashing out around her and protecting her as they moved. It was hard to keep from being hustled, against his will, into the central square, but at last he gained the doorway and thrust the woman through it. He followed her inside, and gave a great gasp of relief as he found himself free from the struggles of the crowd. He stood for a moment in the doorway, to assure himself that nobody intended to follow them, and then turned back to the woman with the child.

She had torn a small piece of cloth from the sleeve of her tattered garment and as he faced her, she paused from wiping the blood and tears from her face long enough to flash him a frightened, little smile. Tumithak could not but wonder at the apparent gentleness and refinement of this woman of savage Yakra. He had been taught to believe, since childhood, that the Yakrans were a strange race, not unlike our concept of goblins and witches, and yet, this woman might have been a daughter of one of the best families of Loor. Tumithak had to learn that in no matter what nation or age one finds oneself, he will find gentleness, if he looks, as well as savagery.

All this while the child, who had evidently been too frightened to cry, had been as silent as though dead, but now it set up a lusty screaming. The mother, after attempting for several moments to silence it with croonings and whispers, at last applied nature's first silencer, and as the child quieted down and began nursing, she arose and motioning Tumithak to follow, led the way to the doorway across the room and entered the rear of the apartment. She was gone a moment, and then she called to the Loorian, and with a realization of what she meant dawning in his mind, he followed her. In the next room, sure enough, the woman pointed to the ceiling and showed him the circular hole of a shaft leading straight upward.

"Here is the entrance to an old corridor that is not known to more than twenty people in all Yakra," she said, "It leads across the square to the upper end of the city. We can hide up there for days and the shelks will probably never know that we exist. Here is safety."

Tumithak nodded and began the ascent of the ladder, pausing only long enough to assure himself that the woman was following him. The ladder extended not more than thirty feet upward and then they found themselves in the dark in a corridor that must have been unused for many centuries. So dark was it that as soon as they moved away from the pit shaft, it was impossible to distinguish the faintest glow of light. Certainly the woman was right in calling this an unknown corridor. Even Tumithak's maps had never told him of this passage.

The woman seemed to be quite at home in the passage, however, for with a whispered word to Tumithak, she began to feel her way along the wall, only stopping now and then to whisper softly to her baby. Tumithak followed her, keeping one hand on her shoulder and so they felt their way along until they came at last to a spot where a single light glowed dimly, and here the woman sat down to rest. Tumithak did likewise, and the woman, reaching into her pocket, drew out a crude needle and thread and began to stitch the tears in her garment. Presently she spoke.

"Isn't it terrible," she whispered, her voice hushed as though she feared that even here the shelks might be listening. "What has started them to hunting again, I wonder?"

Tumithak made no reply and in a moment, she continued:

"My grandfather was killed in a shelk raid. That must have been nearly forty years ago. And now they have come upon us again! My poor husband! I separated from him almost as soon as we left our apartment. Oh! I do hope he reaches safety. He doesn't know about this corridor." She looked to him for comfort. "Do you think he will be safe?"

Tumithak smiled.

"Will you believe me if I tell you that he is surely safe from the shelks?" he asked. "Truly I can assure you that he will not be slain by the shelks in this raid."

"I only hope you are right," the woman began, and then, as if she had noticed him for the first time, she continued, suddenly. "You are not of Yakra!"

And then quite positively and harshly, "You are a man of Loor!"

Tumithak realized that the woman had at last noticed the Loorian clothes that he wore, and so made no attempt to lie.

"Yes," he answered, "I am of Loor."

The woman arose in consternation, clasping her baby tighter to her breast, as though to protect it from this ogre from the lower corridors.

"What are you doing in these halls?" she asked, fearfully, "Is it you that have brought this raid down upon us? I could well believe that the men of Loor would ally themselves with the shelks, if such a thing were possible. And surely, this is the first time in history that the shelks ever came upon us from the lower end of the city."

Tumithak considered for a moment. He saw no reason why he should not tell this woman the truth. It could do her no harm, and might at least put her mind at rest, regarding the safety of her husband.

"It will probably be the last time that the shelks ever come upon you from the lower end of the city, too," he said, and in a few brief words, he explained to her his ruse and its rather appalling success.

"But why should you desire to pass through Yakra?" she asked, incredulously. "Are you going into the dark corridors? What man in his senses would desire to explore them?"

"I am not seeking to explore the dark corridors," the Loorian answered, "My goal lies even beyond them!"

"Beyond the dark corridors?"

"Yes," said Tumithak, and rose to his feet. As always when he spoke of his "mission," he was, for the moment a dreamer, a fanatic.

"I am Tumithak," he said. "I am the slayer of the shelk. You wish to know why I seek to go beyond the dark corridors? It is because I am on my way to the Surface. For on the Surface is a shelk that, all unknowing, awaits his doom! I am going to slay a shelk!"

The woman gazed at him in consternation. She was quite certain, now, that she was alone with a madman. No other could even conceive such an incredible thought. She clasped her child tighter to her and drew away from him.

Tumithak was quick to notice her attitude. He had, many times before, seen people draw away from him in just the same manner, when he spoke of his mission. And so, quite unoffended by her unflattering opinion of him, he began to explain to her why he believed it possible for men to once more engage in battle with the masters of the Surface.

The woman listened for a while, and as he waxed more and more eloquent on his subject, Tumithak saw that she was beginning to believe. He told her of the book he had found, and how it had decided for him what his mission in life should be. He told her of the three strange gifts of his father, and how he hoped they would help him to be successful in his quest. And at last, he saw the look come into her eyes that he had often seen in Thupra's and knew that she believed.

The woman's thoughts, however, had been quite different from what Tumithak believed. She had listened to be sure, but as she listened, she was thinking of the fury with which Tumithak had attacked the terror stricken mob that had nearly crushed her. She was studying the erect, handsome form of him, the smooth-shaven face and keen eyes; and comparing him with the men of Yakra. And at last she believed, not because of Tumithak's eloquence, but because of the age-old appeal of sex.

"It is well that you saved me," she said at last, when the Loorian paused in his story. "It would have hardly been possible for you to force your way through the lower corridors. Up here, you may cross Yakra at your leisure, and leave it whenever you will. I will show you the way to the upper end of the city, now, if you wish."

She arose.

"Come, I will guide you. You are a Loorian and an enemy, but you saved my life, and one who would slay a shelk is surely the true friend of all mankind."

She took him by the hand (though that was hardly necessary), and led him on into the darkness. Minute after minute passed in silence and then, at last, she paused and whispered, "The corridor ends here."

She stepped into the doorway, and following her, Tumithak discerned a faint light coming up through a shaft from the corridor below.

He dropped down the ladder that he could see dimly in the gloom, and in a moment was in the lower corridor. The woman followed him, and when she reached the ground she pointed up the corridor.

"If you are really going to the Surface, your road lies that way," she said, "and we must part here. My road lies back into the town. I wish I might know you better, O Loorian," she paused and then, as she strode off, she turned to exclaim, "Go on to the Surface, strange one, and if you succeed in your quest, do not fear to pass through Yakra on your return. All the city would worship you then, and do you reverence."

As if afraid to say more, she hurried down the passage. Tumithak watched her for a moment and then, with a shrug, turned and walked away in the opposite direction.

He had expected to reach the dark corridors soon after leaving Yakra; but although his maps told him much concerning the route he must take, they were silent concerning the conditions of the various corridors; and it soon became evident to Tumithak that he was not to reach the dark corridors that day. Fatigue overcame him at last, and entering one of the many deserted apartments that lined the passage, he threw himself upon the floor and in a moment was sound asleep.

CHAPTER IV

The Dark Corridors

Hours after, the Loorian awakened with a start. He looked about him vaguely for a moment, and then started into full wakefulness. In the corridor without he had heard a soft rustling. Scarcely breathing, he arose and, tiptoeing to the doorway, peered cautiously out. The corridor was empty, yet Tumithak was certain that he had heard soft footsteps.

He stepped back into the room, picked up his pack, which he had removed before falling asleep, and adjusted it on his back. Then, once more carefully scanning the empty corridor, he stepped out and prepared to resume his journey.

Before going on, though, he drew his sword and looked thoroughly through all the neighboring apartments. It puzzled him to find them all deserted. He was quite sure that he had heard a noise, was quite sure, he felt, that someone, from somewhere, was watching him. But at last, he was forced to admit that unless he was mistaken in their existence, the watchers were more clever than he; and so, keeping well to the center of the corridor, he took up his journey again.

For hours, he kept up a continuous, monotonous pace. The route was steadily upward, the corridor was broad, and to Tumithak's surprise the lights continued undimmed. He had almost forgotten the cause of his sudden awakening, when, after traveling some eight or nine miles, he was suddenly aware of another soft, rustling sound, quite similar to the former one. It came from one of the apartments on his left, and he had scarcely heard it, when he sprang like lightning to the door from which it came, his sword flashing from its sheath. He dashed into the apartment, through the front room and into the rear one, and then stood foolishly, looking around him at the bare brown walls. Like the apartment which he had examined in the morning, this one was quite empty. There were no ladders up which the mysterious one might have escaped, indeed, there seemed to be no way in which anyone might have escaped discovery and, at last, Tumithak was forced to continue on his way.

But he moved more warily, now. He was as cautious as he had been before entering Yakra; in fact, even more so, for then he had known what to expect, and was facing the unknown.

As the hours passed, Tumithak became increasingly certain of the fact that he was being followed—was being watched. Time after time, he would hear the slight rustling noise, sometimes from the dark recesses of an apartment, sometimes from down the path of some dimly lighted branching corridor. Once he was certain that he heard the sound far ahead of him, in the hall that he was traversing. But never was he able to catch so much as a glimpse of the beings that caused the sound.

At last he came to a section of the corridors where the lights began to dim. At first only a few were affected, their light coming from the plates with a peculiar bluish glow, but before long the bluish tint was the rule rather than the exception, and many of the lights were out entirely. Tumithak traveled on in an increasing gloom, and realized that he was, at last, really approaching the legendary dark corridors.

Now, Tumithak was the product of a hundred generations of men who had fled from the slightest suspicious sound. For hundreds of years after the Invasion, an unusual sound had meant a man-hunting shelk, and a shelk had meant death, sudden, sure and unmistakable. So man had become a skulking, fleeing race of creatures that fled panic-stricken from the least suspicion of danger.

In deep-cut Loor, however, men had made a warren so intricate and lengthy that years had passed since a shelk had been seen. And so it came about that the men grew more courageous in Loor, until there arose, at last, a visionary who dared to dream of slaying a shelk.

But although Tumithak was bolder by far than any other man of his generation, it must not be supposed that he had overcome, entirely, the heritage that was man's. Even now as he trudged so firmly up the apparently endless hallway, his heart was beating wildly, and it would have taken little to send him back on the way he had come, his heart almost smothering him in his fright.

But apparently those who followed him knew well not to agitate his fears too greatly. As the corridors grew darker, the noises lessened, and at last, Tumithak decided that he was quite alone. Whatever had been following him, he felt, had turned back or continued down one of the branching halls. For over an hour, he strained his ears in an attempt to hear again the soft noises, but only silence was his reward; so his vigilance gradually lessened and he trod more and more carelessly up the hall.

He passed from a corridor of eternal gloom to one of eternal darkness. Here the lights, if there had ever been any, had long since ceased to glow, and for some time Tumithak felt his way along the passage, depending only on his sense of touch.

And in the corridor below, a number of dark, gaunt figures moved from the gloom to the darkness and hurried silently toward him.

As they went, they would have presented a strange appearance, could anyone have seen them. Gaunt almost to the point of emaciation, with strange, slate-colored skins, perhaps the most surprising thing about their appearance was their heads, which were wrapped with layer after layer of strips of cloth which completely covered their eyes, making it impossible for the slightest ray of light to reach them.

For these were the savages of the dark corridors—men born and raised in the halls of eternal night—and so sensitive were their eyes that the least light was an intolerable pain. All day long they had been shadowing Tumithak, and all day long their eyes had been veiled with the bandages, leaving the savages to move by their astounding senses of hearing and feeling alone. But now that they were again in the halls that were their home, they hastened to remove the cumbering cloths. And when this was accomplished they gradually closed in upon their intended victim.

The first intimation of their presence that Tumithak had after entering the darkness was when he heard a sudden rush behind him. He turned quickly, drew his sword and lashed out savagely. His sword cut through the air, he heard a sardonic laugh and then silence. Furiously he lunged again, and again his sword met only empty air, and then he heard new rustling in the hall behind him.

He turned, realizing that they had surrounded him. Sword flashing furiously, he backed to the wall prepared to sell his life as dearly as possible. He felt his blade strike something that yielded, heard a cry of pain and then suddenly quiet descended on the corridor. The Loorian was not to be deceived, however, he kept up the vicious beating about him with his sword, and presently had the satisfaction of hearing another groan of pain as he struck one of the savages who had attempted to creep under his guard.

But, though Tumithak continued to defend himself to the best of his ability, and lashed about with the courage born of desperation, he had little doubt as to the outcome of the struggle. He was alone, with his back to the wall; while his enemies, already numbering he knew not how many, were constantly having their numbers added to, by the arrival of others. Tumithak prepared to die fighting; his only regret was that he must die in this stygian darkness, unable even to see the opponents who conquered him—and then suddenly he remembered the torch, the first of his father's strange gifts.

With his left hand, he fumbled in his belt and drew out the cylinder. At least he would have the satisfaction of knowing what sort of creatures these were that had attacked him. In a moment he had found the switch and filled the hall with light.

He was totally unprepared for the effect that the brilliant beam of light had upon his enemies. Cries of pain and dismay burst from them, and Tumithak's first sight of the savages was that of a dozen or more scrawny, dark-colored figures that buried their heads in their arms and turned to flee in terror down the passage. Panic-stricken, bawling strange, harsh words to their companions, they fled from the light, as if Tumithak had suddenly been reinforced by all the men of Loor.

For a moment Tumithak stood dazed. He was, of course unable to account for the sudden flight of his attackers. The idea occurred to him that they fled from some danger that he was unable to see and he flashed his light about the corridor fearfully, but at last, as their cries diminished in the distance, the truth gradually dawned on him. These creatures were so much at home in the dark that it must really be, thought Tumithak, that they feared the light; and though he could not understand why this should be, he determined to keep the torch burning as long as his route remained in the dark.

So flashing its rays this way and that, up branching corridors and into open doorways, the Loorian continued on his way. He knew that any thought of sleeping in these dark halls was out of the question, but this bothered him little. Shut up in the pits and corridors for centuries, man had forgotten the regular hours that he had once kept, and although he usually slept eight or ten hours out of thirty, it was entirely possible for a man to go forty or fifty hours before he felt the necessity of sleep. Tumithak had often worked steadily, under his father, for as many hours as this, and so now he felt confident that he would be out of the dark corridors long before he gave way to fatigue.

He munched, now and then, on the biscuits of synthetic food that he had brought with him; but for the most part, his entire time was spent in carefully scanning the corridors before and behind him. And so the hours passed. He had almost reached the point where his fears were allayed sufficiently to allow him to enter one of the apartments and seek slumber, when he heard, far behind him in the corridor, a strange inhuman snarl. Fear seized him instantly. He felt a sudden crawling sensation at the back of his neck, and, darting instantly into the nearest doorway, he extinguished his torch and lay trembling in an excess of fear.

It must not be supposed that Tumithak had suddenly become a coward. Remember the courage with which he had faced the Yakran and the dark savages. But it was the inhumanity of the sound that terrified him. In the lower passages, with the exception of rats, bats and a few other small creatures, no animals had even been known. Except the shelks. They alone had followed man into his pits, and so it was natural that to them alone could Tumithak attribute the sound that had certainly come from some large creature other than man. He was yet to learn that there were other animals from the Surface that had been driven into these upper corridors.

So now he cowered in the apartment, vainly attempting to lash his courage to the point where he could go out and face his enemy. Suppose it were a shelk, he argued. Had he not come all these dangerous miles for the sole purpose of facing a shelk? Was he not Tumithak, the hero whom the high one had called to deliver Man from the heritage of fear that was his? And so, with arguments such as this, his indomitable spirit lashed his body into a semblance of courage, until at last he arose and again entered the corridor.

As he might have known, it appeared empty. His flashlight lit up the passage fully five hundred feet away, but the corridor was apparently quite deserted. He continued on his way; but as he went, he now paid more attention to the lower corridor than he did to the corridor above. And so, presently, he noticed, at the very limit of the light, a number of strange, slinking figures that followed him at a safe distance. His sharp eyes told him that these creatures were neither shelks nor men; but what they were, he was at a loss to guess. It was many generations since the men of the lower corridors had even heard of man's one-time friend the dog.

He paused uncertainly and watched these strange creatures. They slunk out of reach of the torch's rays at once, and after a moment Tumithak turned and continued his journey, half convinced that, in spite of their size, they were merely some large species of rat, as cowardly as their smaller brethren.

In this he was soon to find himself mistaken. He had continued for but a short distance, when he heard a snarl in the corridor ahead of him; and as though this were a signal, the beasts behind him began to draw steadily closer. Tumithak increased his pace, broke into a trot, and finally into a run; but fast as he went, the beasts behind him were faster, and gradually closed in on him.

It was when they were but a little less than a hundred feet behind him that he noticed their masters. The savages that he had vanquished a few hours before had returned, their faces buried in the swathings that they had worn when they stalked him in the corridors beyond Yakra. And with whispered urgings, they drove the dogs on until Tumithak again found it necessary to draw forth his sword and prepare to defend himself.

The beasts from the upper end of the corridor had appeared by this time and the Loorian soon found himself surrounded by a snarling, snapping pack of creatures against whose numbers it was utterly useless to attempt to defend himself. He slew one, another fell snapping at a great gash across its mangy back; but before he could do more, his light was knocked out of his hand and he felt a half dozen hairy forms leap upon him. He fell heavily to the ground with the dogs on top of him, his sword flying from his hand and disappearing in the darkness.

Tumithak expected to die then and there. He felt the hot breath of the monsters on various parts of his body, and that strange feeling of resignation came over him that almost every one feels in the presence of almost certain death, and then—the dogs were pulled away, and he felt hands on him and heard soft, muttering words as the savages felt over his body. He was pinioned to the ground by a half dozen wiry hands, and a moment later a band was tightened around him, fastening his arms firmly to his sides. He was picked up and carried away.

They carried him on up the corridor for some distance,

turned after a while into one of the branching halls and continued for a long time before they at last halted and threw
him upon the ground. Around him he heard many soft
sounds, whispered conversation and the rustling of moving
bodies, and he decided that he had been taken to the central
halls of these creatures. After lying for some time, he was
rolled over and a pair of thin hands felt him all over, and then
a voice spoke firmly and with authority. Again he was picked
up, and carried for a short distance and then he was unceremoniously dumped down upon the floor of what he suspected
was the floor of an apartment. Something metallic clanged on
the floor beside him and he heard the departing footsteps of
his captors in the corridor beyond the door.

For a while Tumithak lay still, gathering his thoughts. He
wondered vaguely why he had not been killed, little dreaming
that the savages knew well enough not to kill their meat until
they were ready for the feast. For these savages had no
knowledge of the preparation of the machine-made food, and
lived by preying on Yakra and other smaller towns that existed far down the branching corridors. Reduced to such desperate straits, anything that would provide sustenance became
their food and for many generations they had been cannibals.

After a while, Tumithak arose. He had little trouble in
working loose the bonds of cloth that he was tied with; the
knowledge of knots that the savages possessed was elementary, and so it took less than an hour for the Loorian to free
himself. He began feeling carefully over the walls of the
apartment, in an attempt to acquaint himself with the features
of his prison. The room was little more than ten feet square,
and the walls were broken by but a single door, the entrance.
Tumithak attempted to pass through this door, but was halted
immediately by a growl and a snarl, and a rough hairy body
pushed against his legs, driving him back into the apartment.
The savages had left the dogs to guard the entrance to his
prison.

Tumithak stepped back into the room and as he did so, his
foot struck an object that rolled across the floor. He remembered the metallic object that had been thrown into the apartment with him and wondered curiously what it was. Groping
around, he finally located it, and to his joy realized that it was
his flashlight. He was quite unable to understand why the savages had brought it here, but he decided that to their supersti-

tious minds, it was something to fear, and that they thought it best to keep these two dangerous enemies imprisoned together. At any rate, here it was, and for that Tumithak was grateful.

He turned it on and looked around as its rays filled the apartment with light. Yes, he had been right about its size and simplicity. There was little chance, none at all, in fact, of his escaping unless he passed through the beast-guarded doorway. And in the light, Tumithak saw that the savages had left him but little chance to escape that way. The entire pack of over twenty stood just without the doorway, their eyes dazzled and blinking in the sudden light.

From within the doorway, Tumithak could look far up the corridor, and he could see no one at all in that stretch of hallway, as far as his light reached. He flashed it down the hallway; it, too, was empty. He decided that it was probably the time of sleep for these savages, and realized that if he was to escape, no better time would offer itself than the present. He sat down on the floor of the apartment and gave himself up to thought. Somewhere in the back of his mind an idea was glimmering, a faint conviction that he possessed the means to escape those animals. He arose and looked at the pack, huddled together in the corridor as if to protect themselves from the unwelcome rays of the torch. He turned to study the room, but apparently found little there to favor his half-formed plan. Suddenly, though, he reached a decision, and feeling in the pocket of his belt, and pulling a pin from it, hurled it out among the pack and threw himself flat on his face!

It was the bomb, the second of his father's strange gifts. It struck the floor of the corridor without, and burst with a roar that was nothing short of deafening. In the confined space of the passage, the expanding gases acted with terrific force. Flat on the floor though he was, Tumithak was lifted and hurled violently against the opposite wall of the apartment. As for the beasts in the corridor without, they were practically annihilated. Torn bodies were flung in every direction, and when Tumithak, bruised and shaken, entered the corridor a few minutes later, he found it deserted of every living thing. But the scene resembled a shambles, with blood and torn bodies strewn all over the corridor.

Sick with the unaccustomed sight of blood and death, Tumithak hastened to put as much distance as possible between himself and the gruesome scene. He hurried on up the corridor, through the still smoke-laden air, until at last the air cleared and the horrors of the scene could be forgotten. He saw no signs of the savages, although twice he heard a whimpering from the doorway of some apartment and knew that a dark form probably cowered, terror-stricken, in the darkness. It would be many, many sleeps before the savages of the dark corridors forgot the enemy who had caused such destruction among them.

Tumithak emerged again into the corridor that led to the Surface. For the first time since he set out on that route, he retraced his steps, but it was with a definite object in view. He arrived at the place where he had battled with the dogs, and retrieved his sword, finding it without difficulty and noting with satisfaction that it was entirely unharmed. Then he once again took up his journey to the Surface, continuing for long without meeting with anything that could give him cause for alarm. At last he decided that he was past the dangerous parts of these halls, and entering one of the apartments he prepared himself for a long-needed rest . . .

He slept long and dreamlessly, awaking at last after more than fourteen hours of sleep. He immediately took up his journey again, partaking of his food as he went and wondering what this new march would mean for him.

But he was not to wonder for long. He was quite aware, from his maps, that he was now more than half through with his journey, and so he was not surprised when the walls of the corridors, which, ever since leaving Loor had continued as smooth and glossy as those of his own home, now began to assume a rough, irregular appearance, almost like that of a natural cavern. He was, he knew, approaching that section of the corridors which man had carved out in the days of his first panic-stricken flight into the earth. There had been little time, in those first days, to smooth down the walls of the corridors or to give them the regular rectangular appearance that they were to have in the lower corridors.

But though he was not surprised at this appearance of the passages, he was totally unprepared for their next change. He had travelled perhaps three or four miles through the winding, narrow caverns, when he came upon a well-concealed pitmouth that led far up into the darkness. He could see that there was a light at the top and gave a sigh of gratitude, for his light had began to show the first signs of failing. He climbed the ladder slowly, with his usual caution, and at last, emerging warily from the mouth of the shaft, he stepped into the strangest corridor he had ever beheld.

CHAPTER V

The Hall of the Esthetts

The hall in which Tumithak found himself was more brilliantly lighted than any he had ever seen. The lights were not all of the usual clear white, here and there blues and greens vied with reds and golden yellows to add beauty to a scene that was already beautiful beyond anything that Tumithak had ever imagined. For a moment, he was at a loss to understand just where the luminescence was coming from, for there were no shining plates in the center of the ceiling, such as he had always been familiar with. But after a while, an explanation of the system of lighting dawned on him, and he saw that all the plates were cleverly concealed in the walls, so that the light reflected from them produced an effect of soft, creamy mellowness.

And the walls—the walls were no longer of the familiar glossy brown stone; they were of stone of the purest milky white! And though this in itself was a wonder that must have excited the Loorian's astonishment, it was not the color of the walls that held his attention rivited to them. It was the fact that the walls were covered with designs and pictures, intaglios and bas-reliefs, to such an extent that not a clear space was visible on walls or ceiling, at any place along the corridor. And even the floor bore an intricate design of varicolored inlaid stone.

Now, Tumithak had never dreamed of the possibility of such a thing as this. There was no art in the lower corridors, there never had been. That had been lost to man long before the first passage had been blasted down to Loor. And so Tumithak stood lost in wonder at the marvel that confronted him.

Although most of the wall was covered with design, there were many pictures, too. They showed in detail many wonderful things, things that Tumithak could scarcely believe existed. Yet here they were before him, and to his simple mind the

fact that they were here in pictures were proof that somewhere they existed in reality.

Here, for instance, was a group of men and women dancing. They were in a circle and they danced around something
in the center, something that could only partly be seen. But as
he looked at it, Tumithak again felt the hair on the back of
his neck begin to rise—the creature had long and spidery legs,
and from somewhere in his subconscious mind a voice whispered, "Shelk."

Turning with a puzzled feeling of disgust from that picture,
he came upon another one—it depicted a long corridor, and
in it a cylindrical object that must have been eighteen or
twenty feet long. It was mounted on wheels and around it
were gathered a group of eager, waiting humans, with happy,
excited looks on their faces. Tumithak puzzled over the pictures for many moments, unable to understand them. They
didn't make sense. These people did not seem to fear the
shelks! He came upon a picture that proved it. It showed
again the long cylindrical object, and at its side were three beings that could be nothing but shelks. And grouped around
them, talking and gesticulating, were another group of humans.

There was one thing that particularly impressed Tumithak
in these pictures. The people were all fat. Not a one of them
but was florid and grossly overweight. But it was probably
natural, thought the Loorian, of people who lived near the
Surface and were apparently without any fear of the terrible
shelk. Such a people would naturally have little to do but live
and grow fat.

And so, musing and looking at the pictures, he continued
along his way, until he saw in the distance, up the corridor a
ponderous human form and realized that he was reaching the
inhabited part of these corridors. The form disappeared down
a branching corridor, almost as soon as he glimpsed it, but it
was enough to make Tumithak realize that he must go much
more carefully. So, for a long while, he slipped cautiously
along the side of the passage, using every opportunity that
was offered for concealment. He found a thousand things to
excite his wonder; indeed, ere long he found himself in a constant state of astonishment. Great tapestries were hung along
the wall at one spot; at another, his heart leapt into his mouth
as he came suddenly upon a group of statues. It was hard for
him to realize that these carven stones were not really men.

There had been no doorways on the sides of the corridors at first; but now the corridor widened until it must have been full forty feet broad, and apartment entrances began to appear. High and wide, these doorways were, and the "curtains" that covered them were of metal! It was Tumithak's first contact with true doors, for in Loor the cloth curtains were all that ever separated apartments from the corridor without.

Minute after minute passed, as Tumithak continued on his way. The pictures on the walls grew more elaborate, the corridor grew higher and even wider; and then, in the distance, Tumithak saw a number of human forms approaching him. He knew that he must not be seen, debated for a moment the advisability of turning about and retreating, and then he noticed an open door close to him. Before him was discovery and danger, behind him lay an unthinkable retreat. Tumithak had little choice in the matter; in a moment he had made his decision, had pushed the door wide open and stepped inside.

For a moment he stood, his eyes, used to the brilliant light without, failing him in the gloom of the apartment. Then he realized that he was not alone, for the room was occupied by a man who, to all appearances, was so frightened at Tumithak's sudden appearance as to be quite speechless. Tumithak took advantage of the other's evident fright to observe him carefully and to look about the room for some means of escape or concealment.

The room was lighted much more dimly than the hall, the light coming from two plates concealed in the wall near the ceiling. The walls were of a uniform dull blue and in the rear a tapestried door led to the back room. A table, a huge, padded chair, a bed, and a shelf that was filled with books, made up the furniture of the room. And in the midst of this bed lay this huge man.

The man was a veritable mountain of flesh. Tumithak estimated that he certainly must have weighed four hundred pounds. He was well over six feet tall and the bed on which he lay, and which would easily have held three of Tumithak's fellow citizens, was completely filled with his bulk. He was a florid, full-blooded type of man; and his pale blond hair and beard only served to accentuate the redness of his face and neck.

But the coarseness of the man's features was offset by the refinement of his surroundings. Never had such luxuries been dreamed of by the man of Loor. The clothes that the man wore were of the finest texture imaginable, sheer gauzes that were dyed in the most delicate shades of nacreous pinks, and greens, and blues. They flowed down over his form, softening and dignifying the immense obesity of him. The bed-clothes were as fine and sheer as the man's garments, but of a deep shade of green and brown. The bed itself was a revelation, a glorious triumph in inlaid metals that might have been wrought by some wonderful artisan of the Golden Age. And flung across the floor was a rug—And the pictures on the wall!—

The man suddenly regained control of himself. He set up a scream, a high-pitched womanly scream that seemed strangely absurd coming from one of his bulk. Tumithak was at his side in an instant, with his sword at the fat one's throat.

"Stop that!" he ordered peremptorily. "Stop it at once, or I'll kill you!"

The other subsided, his screams at once becoming a series of involuntary agonized groans. Tumithak stood listening, fearful that the first scream might have been effective, but the silence from without was unbroken. After fully a minute, the man spoke.

"You are a wild man," he said, and his voice was full of terror. "You are a wild man of the lower corridors! What are you doing here among the Chosen Ones?"

Tumithak ignored the question.

"Make another sound, fat one," he whispered, fiercely, "and there will be one less mouth to feed in these halls." He looked toward the door anxiously. "Is any one likely to enter here?" he asked.

The other attempted to answer, but apparently his fear had by now rendered him speechless. Tumithak laughed scornfully, a strange elation possessing him. It was indeed pleasant to the Loorian to find some one that feared him so terribly. Man had not felt this strange sense of power often in the preceding centuries and Tumithak was half tempted to increase the other's fears, but in the end this emotion was overcome by his curiosity. Seeing that the fat man's terror of the sword was a very real one, he lowered it and returned it to its sheath.

The fat man breathed easier then, but it was some moments before speech returned. Then when he did speak, it was only to repeat the question he had asked before.

"What are you doing here in the halls of the Esthetts?" he gulped fearfully.

Tumithak considered his answer carefully. These people, he knew, did not fear the shelk; clearly, then, they were friendly with them. The Loorian doubted the advisability of confiding in the obese craven, but at the same time it seemed absurd to fear him or any others like him. And the natural conceit that is a part of every great genius made Tumithak long to boast of his mission so that at last he decided to answer the question.

"I am on my way to the Surface," he said. "I come from the lowest pit of all, so far down that we have never even heard of the halls of the Esthetts, as you call them. Are you one of the Esthetts?"

"On your way to the Surface," said the other, who was now fast losing his fear. "But you have not been called! You will be killed at once. Think you that the Holy Shelks will permit any one to attain the Surface uncalled for?" His nose twitched scornfully. "And a wild man of the lower corridors at that!"

Tumithak was stung by the scorn in the other's voice.

"Listen, fat one," he said, "I do not ask the permission of any one to visit the Surface. As for the shelks, my whole object in reaching the Surface is that I might kill one of them."

The other looked at him with a look that Tumithak was at a loss to interpret.

"You will soon die," said the Esthett, calmly. "There is no need of my fearing you any longer. Surely any one who speaks such unthinkable blasphemy is doomed even as he says it." He settled himself more comfortably in his bed as he spoke, and looked at Tumithak curiously.

"From where, oh, Wild One, did such an impossible idea come to you?" he asked.

The Loorian might have had a feeling of anger at the other's attitude, had not this question shown him a loophole for expounding his favorite subject. He began to tell the Esthett, in elaborate detail, all the story of his mission. The latter listened attentively, so interested, apparently, that Tumithak grew more and more interested in the telling.

He spoke of his early life, of the finding of the book, and the inspiration it had given him; he told of the many years of preparation for his journey, and of the many adventures he had had since he left Loor.

The fat one was strangely interested, but to Tumithak, wrapped up in the story of his mission, it never once occurred that the Esthett was sparring for time. And so, when he was finished with his story at last, he was quite willing to listen to the Chosen One's story of his own life in the marble halls.

"We who live in these halls," began the Esthett, "are those chosen ones of the race of mankind who possess the one thing that the Holy Shelks lack—the power of creating beauty. Mighty as the Masters are, they have no artistic ability, but in spite of this they are quite capable of appreciating our art, and so they have come to rely upon us for the beauties of life, and they have given it to us to produce all the great works of art that decorate their wonderful palaces on the Surface! All the great art works that you see on the walls of these corridors have been executed by me and my fellow-citizens. All the rich paintings and statuary that you will see later, in our great square, all these are the rejected specimens that the Holy Shelks have no need of. Can you imagine the beauties of the accepted pieces that have found their way up to the Surface?

"And in return for our beauty, the shelks feed us and give us every luxury imaginable. Of all mankind, we alone have been chosen as worthy of being the friends and companions of the world's masters."

He paused for a moment, breathless with what was apparently an exceptionally long speech, for him. After resting a while, he went on:

"Here in these marble corridors, we of the Esthetts are born and educated. We work only at our art: we work only when it suits us, and our work is carefully examined by the shelks, and the choicest is preserved. The artists who produce this work—listen carefully wild man—the artists who produce this work are called from their homes to join the great guild of Chosen Ones who live on the Surface and spend the rest of their lives decorating the glorious palaces and gardens of the Holy Shelks! They are the happiest of men, for they know that their work is praised by the very Lords of Creation themselves."

He was panting with the effort caused by his story, but he struggled bravely on:

"Can you wonder that we feel ourselves superior to the men who have allowed themselves to become little better than animals, little more than rabbits skulking in their warrens, miles below the ground? Can you wonder that—"

His speech was suddenly cut off by a sound from the corridor without. It was the sound of a siren, whose tones grew shriller and shriller, higher and higher until it seemed to pass entirely beyond the range of sound heard by human ears. The Esthett was suddenly beside himself with eagerness. He began to struggle out of his bed, managed after several failures to get to his feet, waddled to the door and then turned.

"The Masters!" he cried. "The Holy Shelks! They have come to take another group of artists to the Surface. I knew they would be here soon, wild man, and it was not for nothing that I listened to your long, tiresome story. Try to escape if you can, but you know as well as I that none can escape from the Masters. And now I go to tell them of your presence!"

He slammed the door suddenly in Tumithak's face and was gone.

For several minutes, Tumithak remained motionless in the apartment. That shelks were so near to him seemed incredible. Yet he expected every minute to see the door open and to have the horrible spider-like creatures rush in and slay him. At last, it seemed, he was in a trap from which there was no escape. He shivered with fear, and then, as always, the very intensity of his fear shamed him and caused him to take a new grip upon himself; and though he trembled violently at what he was about to do, he moved to the door and examined it carefully. He had decided that the chances of escape would be greater in the corridor than if he waited here for the shelks to capture him. It was several minutes before he discovered the secret of the latch, but then he swung the door open and stepped into the corridor.

The corridor in Tumithak's vicinity was fortunately empty, but far up the hallway, the obese Esthett could still be seen, bustling ponderously on his way. He had been joined by others, many as fat as he; and all were hastening, as fast as their weight would let them up the corridor, in the direction in which the square of the city evidently lay. Tumithak followed them at a discreet distance, and after a while, saw them turn into another corridor. He approached the corridor cautiously, the determination forming in his mind to slay the fat one that intended to betray him at the first opportunity. It was well that he used care in his approach, for when he peered around the corner he saw that he was not a hundred feet from the town's great square.

He had never seen such a great square. It was a huge hall over a hundred yards in diameter, its tesselated marble floor and carved walls presenting an appearance that made Tumithak gasp in wonder. Here and there statues stood on varicolored pedestals, and all the doorways were hung with beautiful tapestries. The entire square was almost filled with Esthetts, over five hundred being present.

Not the hall, its furnishings nor its inhabitants had much effect on Tumithak. His eyes were occupied in observing the great cylinder of metal that lay in the center of the hall. It was just such a cylinder as the one he had seen on the carving when he first entered the city—eighteen or twenty feet long, mounted on four thickly tired wheels and having, he now perceived a round opening in the top.

While he looked, a number of objects shot out of the opening and dropped lightly before the crowd. One after another, just as jacks from a box, they leapt from the opening, and as they nimbly struck the ground the Esthetts raised a cheer. Tumithak drew hastily back, and then, his curiosity overcoming his caution, dared to peep again into the hall. For the first time in over a hundred years, a man of Loor gazed upon a shelk!

Standing about four feet high, they were indeed spider-like, just as tradition said. But close look showed that this was only a superficial resemblance. For these creatures were hairless, and possessed ten legs, rather than the eight that belong to a true spider. The legs were long and triple jointed and on the tip of each was a short rudimentary claw much like a finger nail. There were two bunches of these legs, five on each side, and they joined the creature at a point midway between the head and the body. The body was shaped much like the abdomen of a wasp, and was about the same size as the head, which was certainly the strangest part of the entire creature.

For the head was the head of a man: The same eyes, the same broad brow, a mouth with tight, thin lips, and a chin— all these gave the head of the creature a startling resemblance to that of a man. The nose and hair alone were missing, to make the face perfectly human.

As Tumithak looked, they entered at once upon the business that had brought them down into the corridor. One of them took a paper from a pouch strapped to his body, grasping it nimbly between two of his limbs, and began to speak. His voice had a queer, metallic clack about it, but it was not a bit hard for Tumithak to distinguish every word he said.

"Brothers of the Pits," he cried, "the time has come for another group of you to make your homes on the Surface! The friends who left you last week are eagerly awaiting your arrival there, and it only remains for us to call the names of the ones to whom the great honor has fallen. Listen carefully, and let each one enter the cylinder as his name is called."

He paused, allowing his words to sink in, and then in a silence that was impressive, he began to call the names.

"Korystalis! Vintiamia! Lathrumidor!" he called, and one after another, great, bull-bodied men strutted forward and climbed up a small ladder that was lowered from the cylinder. The third man called, Tumithak noticed, was the one who had conversed with him in the apartment. The look on his face, as well as on the faces of the others, was one of surprise and joy, as if some incredible piece of good luck had befallen him.

Now, Tumithak had been so absorbed in observing the shelks and their vehicle that he had forgotten momentarily the threat that the Esthett had made, but when he saw him approaching the shelks, the Loorian's terror returned. He stood, rooted in his tracks with fear. But his fear was unnecessary, for apparently this unexpected piece of good fortune had driven everything else from the simple mind of the Chosen One, for he climbed into the cylinder without so much as a word to the shelks standing about. And Tumithak gave a great sigh of relief as he disappeared into the hole.

There were six shelks, and six Esthetts' names were called; and as fast as they were called, their owners stepped forward and clambered, puffing and grunting, into the car. At last, the sixth had struggled down into the round opening and the shelks turned and followed. A lid covered the hole from below, and silence reigned in the hall. After a moment, the Esthetts began to drift away, and as several moved toward the corridor in which Tumithak was concealed, he was forced to dart back through the passage some distance and slip into an apartment to avoid discovery.

He half expected some Esthett to enter the apartment and

discover him, but this time luck was with him and after a few moments, he peered cautiously through the door to find the corridor empty. He emerged and quickly made his way to the main hall. It was deserted of Esthetts, now, but for some reason the cylinder still remained in the same spot; and Tumithak was suddenly seized with an idea that made him tremble with its magnitude.

These shelks had obviously come from the Surface in this car! And now they were going back to the Surface in it. Had not the Esthett, whom the shelks named Lathrumidor, told him that occasionally artists were called to live upon the Surface among the shelks? Yes, this car was certainly going to return to the Surface. And, with a sudden rush of inspired determination, Tumithak knew that he was going with it.

He hastened forward and in a moment was clinging to the rear of the machine, clambering for a foothold on the few projections he could find. He was not a moment too soon, for hardly had he gotten a firm grip on the machine than it leaped silently forward and sped at a vertiginous speed up the corridor!

CHAPTER VI

The Slaying of the Shelk

Tumithak's memory of that ride was a wild kaleidoscopic jumble of incidents. So fast did the car speed, that it was only occasionally, as they slowed to turn a corner or passed through an exceptionally narrow hall, that he could lift his eyes and look about him.

They passed through halls more brilliantly lighted than any he had yet seen. He saw halls of metal, polished and gleaming, and corridors of unpolished rock where the vibration of passing over rough rock threatened to hurl him at any moment from his precarious position.

Once they passed slowly through a marble passageway where Esthetts were lined on either side, chanting a solemn and sonorous hymn as the car of the shelks passed through. Tumithak was certain that he would be discovered, but if any of the singers saw him they paid little heed, evidently believing him to be a captive of the shelks. There were no longer any pits or branching hallways now, the entire road to the surface was one broad main corridor and along this corridor the car sped, carrying Tumithak ever nearer to his goal.

Although the car's speed was not great as measured by the speed of the cars we use today, it must be remembered that the fastest speed the Loorian had ever conceived was a fast run. So it seemed to him now that he rode upon the very wings of the wind, and his thankfulness knew no bounds when the car at last slowed to a speed that enabled him to drop to the ground in a section of the corridor that had apparently been uninhabited for many years. All thought of continuing the ride was abandoned now, his only desire was to end the devil's ride that he had so foolhardily undertaken.

For a moment, Tumithak was inclined to lie where he had fallen, at least long enough to regain control of his dazed faculties, but the sudden realization that the car of the shelks had stopped, not a hundred yards away, brought him instantly to his feet, and he flung hurriedly through the nearest open door. The apartment in which he found himself was dustladen and bare of furniture; it was obvious that it had been long unused, and so, convinced that no danger awaited him there, Tumithak returned to the door and looked out at the car.

He saw at once that the queer door or hatchway in the top of the car was open, but it was several moments before the occupants began to emerge. Then the fat head of one of the Esthetts appeared and its owner laboriously dragged himself up and over the side of the car. He was followed by a shelk, who leaped nimbly to the ground, after which the car slowly emptied until all twelve of its occupants were in the corridor. They all turned, then, and entered an apartment, the only one visible that bore a curtain over the door.

For a while, Tumithak remained in his hiding place debating his next move. His instinctive timidity urged him to remain in hiding, to wait—for days, if necessary—until the shelks had re-entered the car and departed. His curiosity demanded that he attempt to discover what the strangely allied party was doing beyond that great tapestry-covered door. And his wisdom told him that if he intended to continue on his quest, the best course was to keep on at once up the corridor, while the shelks were still within the apartment—for he knew that he was but a few short miles from the surface, toward which he had been traveling for so long.

His better judgment conquered at last and he chose the latter course, determined to forget the party, and so emerged from the room and began to run lightly and silently on his way; but as he passed the great doorway and saw how easily one might conceal himself in them, he determined to have one last look at the shelks and their strange friends before continuing. So, suiting the action to the thought, he stepped to the opening and, drawing the curtains around him, parted them slightly and looked into the room.

The first thing to strike his attention was the immense size of the room. It must have been eighty feet long and half as many wide, truly an enormous room to the Loorian; and its ceiling was lost in gloom. So high was it that the lights, which were arranged around the room at the level of the shoulder, were not bright enough to show any of its detail. Tumithak had a queer idea that there was no ceiling, that perhaps the walls rose higher and higher until at last they reached the Surface. He had little time to speculate on this possibility, however, for he had hardly noticed it when his eyes fell upon the table. A great low table, it was, a long table covered with a cloth of snowy whiteness and piled high with strange articles that Tumithak saw were intended to be foods. But the Loorian looked at them in wonder, for they were foods such as he had never before heard of, such as his ancestors had not known for many a generation, the thousand and one succulent viands of the Surface. And around the table were a dozen low divans, and on some of these divans the Esthetts were even now reclining, greedily partaking of the varied foods.

The shelks, strangely enough were not joining them in the feast. Behind each of the ponderous artists, a shelk had taken his place, and to Tumithak's notion, there was something ominous in the way they stood, silently watching every move the Esthetts made. But the self-styled Chosen Ones were quite at ease, gobbling their food and grunting appreciative interjections to each other, until Tumithak turned from looking at them in disgust.

And then, suddenly, there came a sharp command from the shelk at the head of the table. The Esthetts looked up in consternation, dismay and a pitiable incredulity in their faces. Ere they could move, however, ere they could even cry out, on each a shelk had leaped, his thin-lipped mouth seeking, finding unerringly, the jugular vein beneath the folds of flesh in the fat one's heavy throat.

Vainly the artists struggled, their slow, helpless movements were unavailing, the nimble shelks easily avoiding their groping arms while all the time their teeth sank deeper into the flesh. Tumithak gasped in horror. As one in a trance, he watched the movements of the Esthetts become feebler until at last all motion ceased. The Loorian's brain was in a daze. What—what on Venus could be the meaning of this? What connection could this grisly scene have with the lengthy explanation of the lives of these people that Lathrumidor had given him in the marble halls below? He gazed at the scene in horror, unable to move his eyes.

The Esthetts were quiet now, and the shelks had raised themselves from them and were busy with some new occupation. From beneath the table they had drawn several large, transparent jars and half a dozen small machines with long hoses attached. These hoses were fastened to the wounds in the necks of the Esthetts and as Tumithak looked on he saw the blood swiftly pumped from the bodies and ejected into the jars.

As the jars filled with the liquid, the bodies of the Esthetts collapsed like punctured balloons, and in a few moments they lay, pallid and wrinkled, on the floor about the table. The shelks showed no excitement in their work; apparently it was merely a routine duty with them, and their calm business-like methods served only to add to Tumithak's terror, but at last he overcame the paralytic fear that held him, and he turned and sped frantically away. Up the corridor he ran faster and faster, farther and farther, and at last, spent and breathless, unable to run another step, he darted into an open door and flung himself gasping and panting on the floor of the apartment it led into.

Slowly he regained control of himself, his breath returned, and with it some small measure of confidence. He berated himself harshly for his cowardice in so losing control of himself, yet, even as he did so, he trembled at the thought of the terrible sight that he had witnessed. As he grew calmer, he began to wonder at the meaning of the events that he had seen. Lathrumidor, the Esthett, had led him to believe that the

shelks were the kindly masters of the immense artists. He had
spoken of the journey to the Surface as being the culminating
honor of an Esthett's life. The shelk who had spoken in the
great hall, too, had intimated as much. Yet for some strange
reason, at the first opportunity after leaving the city, the
shelks had slain their worshiping servants, and slain them in a
way that seemed quite usual and commonplace to them.
Strive as he might, Tumithak could not account for this apparent anomaly. And so, cowering in the rear room of the
apartment, puzzling over the unnaturalness of the day's adventures, the Loorian fell into a troubled sleep.

It is not to be wondered that Tumithak was puzzled at the
strange events of the day. He knew of no relationship between
animals, such as existed between the Esthetts and the shelks.
There were no domestic animals in the pits and man had not
known of them for centuries. Other centuries were to go by
before they were to know of them again, so there was nothing
in Tumithak's life analogous to the status in which the shelks
held the Esthetts.

Today we know that they were—cattle! Lulled into a sense
of false security by hypocritical lies, bred for centuries for the
full-blooded, bovine stupidity that was characteristic of them,
allowed no means of intellectual expression except the artistic
impulse which the shelks scorned, they had become, after
many generations, the willing creatures of the Beasts of
Venus.

And by a strange combination of the lies of the shelks and
their own immense conceit, they had come to look forward,
from earliest childhood, to that happy day when they would
be taken to the Surface—to become, unknowing, the food of
their masters. Such were the Esthetts, strangest, perhaps, of
all the various races of men evolved by the breeding of the
shelks.

All this, however, was far beyond the comprehension of
Tumithak—or of any man of his generation. And so it was
that even after he awoke and resumed his journey, he was still
unable to account for the strange relationship. But the puzzles
which a semi-savage mind cannot solve, it soon forgets, and
so it was that before long Tumithak was strolling along on his
way, his mind entirely at ease

Since passing the hall of the singing Esthetts, during his
wild ride, Tumithak had seen no signs of habitation. Ap-

parently the corridors were entirely too near the surface to be inhabited by man. So Tumithak saw no one in the corridors and traveled for several miles undisturbed. At last he came to an abrupt end of the passage, and here found a ladder of metal set into the wall that rose higher and higher in the gloom. Filled with a suppressed excitement, his heart beating noticeably again, Tumithak began the ascent of what he knew to be the last pit before he reached the Surface. He emerged from it in a hall of strange black stone, and removing from his pouch the last of his father's gifts, he started along the upward slope, the weapon held gingerly in his hand. The corridor was narrower than any Tumithak had ever seen, and as he walked along, the walls drew still closer together, until it was not more than two feet wide. The grade became steeper and steeper and at last became a flight of stairs. Up these Tumithak strode, every moment his heart beating wilder, and at last he saw what he knew to be his goal. Far ahead, a light shone down in the corridor from above, a light far brighter and harsher than any of the lights of the corridors, and of a strange reddish tint. Tumithak knew, as he looked on it in awe, that the light was the light of the Surface.

He hurried forward; the ceiling became lower and lower and for the last few yards he was forced to stoop, and then, finally, he reached the top of the steps and found himself standing in a shallow pit, not more than five feet deep. He raised his head and a low gasp of absolute unbelief escaped from him.

For Tumithak had looked upon the Surface ...

The vastness of the scene was enough to unnerve the Loorian. It seemed that he had emerged into a mighty room or hall, so tremendous that he could not even comprehend its immensity. The ceiling and walls of this room merged into each other to form a stupendous vault like an inverted bowl, which touched the floor of the vault at a distance so far away that it seemed utterly incredible. And this ceiling and these walls in places were of a beautiful blue, the color of a woman's eyes. This blue glowed like a jewel, and was mottled with great billowy areas of white and rose, and as Tumithak looked he had a vague feeling that those enormous billowy spots were slowly moving and changing in shape.

Unable to take his eyes from the sky above him, Tumithak's wonder and awe began to turn into a great fear. The more he looked, the further away the great dome seemed to be, and yet, curiously and terribly, it seemed to be closing in on him, too. He was sure, after a moment, that the great billowy spots were moving, and he had a dreadful feeling that they were about to fall and crush him. Sick and terrified at the enormity of the scene before him, he darted back into the passageway and cowered against the wall, trembling with a strange, unreasoning fear. For, raised as he had been in the close confines of the corridor walls, living his whole life under the ground, Tumithak, when he first looked upon the Surface, became a victim of agoraphobia, that strange fear of open spaces, that in some people, even today, amounts to a disease.

It was nearly an hour before his reason was able to gain control over this strange fear. Had he come thus far, he argued with himself, only to return because of the appearance of the Surface? Surely, if that mighty blue and cloudy vault was to fall, it would not have waited all these years just to fall on him. He took a deep breath, and reason prevailing at last, he again looked out upon the Surface

But this time his eyes avoided the sky, and he directed his attention to the floor of the "room." In the vicinity of the pit this floor consisted of a thick brown dust, but not far away this dust was covered with a strange carpet consisting of thousands of long green hairs thickly matted together, completely hiding the dusty floor beneath. In the middle distance were a number of tall, irregular pillars whose tops were covered with a great huge bunch of green stuff, of the same color and appearance as the hairs of the carpet.

And then, as Tumithak looked beyond the grass and the trees, he beheld a wonder that surpassed the other wonders that he had seen, for hanging low in the dome above the trees was the light of the Surface, a brilliant, blinding orb that lit up, redly, all that vast space of the Surface.

Speechless with awe, Tumithak looked upon the sunset. Again came the dizzy, sickening rush of agoraphobia, but with it came a sense of beauty that made him forget his fear, and gradually calmed him. After a while he turned his eyes and looked in the opposite direction; and there, towering high above him, were the homes of the shelks!

Fully a dozen of the high towers were visible; obelisk-like they stood there, their metal walls gleaming redly in the light of the sinking sun. Very few of them stood perfectly erect, the strange unearthly artistic sense of the shelks causing them to be built at various angles from the perpendicular, some as much as thirty degrees. They were of varying heights, some fifty, some as much as two hundred feet high, and from their tops long cables hung, linking all the towers together. Windowless they were, and the only mode of ingress was a small round door at the bottom. Not one of all these towers was more than fifteen feet in circumference, so that they gave an appearance not unlike a bundle of huge needles.

For how long the Loorian gazed at these amazing scenes, he could not tell. Of all the wondrous sights, the strangest, to him, was the sunset, the gradual sinking of the great red light into what seemed to be the floor of the vast chamber. Even after the sun had disappeared, he remained gazing absorbedly at the walls, which still glowed redly where it had been . . . And then—

Tumithak had not heard a sound. Lost in wonder though he was, his ears had remained instinctively on the alert, and yet he had heard nothing. Until suddenly there was a scratching, rustling noise behind him and a clattering, metallic voice barked staccato words of command.

"Get—back—in—that—hole!" it spat, and Tumithak's blood turned to water as he realized that a shelk had stolen up behind him!

The next second seemed a year to the Loorian. He turned to face the beast, and in that turning a thousand thoughts raced through his mind. He thought of Nikadur and Thupra, and of the many years that he had known them; he thought of his father and even of his little remembered mother, he thought, strangely enough of the huge Yakran that he had tumbled into the pit and of how he had bellowed as he fell. All these thoughts rushed through his mind as he turned and then his arm flew up to protect himself. Utterly instinctive, the action was; it seemed that he was not in control of his body at all. Something outside of him—greater than himself —caused him to flex his fingers, and as he did, the revolver, the last of his father's three strange gifts spat flame and thunder? As in a dream, he heard its spitting bark, once, twice, thrice—seven times; and into the shallow pit tumbled the dead body of the shelk!

For a moment, the hero stared at it dumbly. Then, as the

realization that he had accomplished his mission came over him, a great feeling of exultation seized him. Quickly drawing his sword, he began to slash at the ten long finger-like legs of the shelk, humming, as he did so, the song that the Loorians sang when they marched against the Yakrans; and though there were strange, questioning clacks and clatters from the direction of the homes of the shelks, he methodically continued hacking until the head was free from the body.

Then, realizing that the voices of the shelks were much nearer, he stuffed the bleeding head into the bosom of his tunic, and sped like the wind down the steps of the corridor.

CHAPTER VII

The Power and the Glory

Tumlook of Loor, the father of Tumithak, sat in the doorway of his apartment, gazing out into the corridor. It was a lonely life that he had led for the past few weeks, for although his friends had tried to cheer him with the customary optimistic chatter, he could see that they all believed that his son would never return. And indeed, it would have been a bold man that would argue that Tumithak had even so much as passed the city of Yakra.

Tumlook knew the opinions of his friends and he was beginning to believe as they did, in spite of the fact that they did their best to make him think that they expected wondrous things of his son. Why, he wondered, had he ever let the youth depart on such a hopeless quest? Why had he not been more stern with him, and driven the idea out of his head while he was still young? So he sat and berated himself, in this hour just before the time of sleep, as the life of Loor passed by him in an irregular, intermittent stream.

After a while his face brightened a little. Coming down the hall toward him were the two lovers whose long friendship with Tumithak had made a bond that Tumlook felt that he had somehow inherited. Nikadur hailed him, and they drew near, Thupra ran up and kissed him impulsively on the cheek.

"Have you heard aught of Tumithak?" she cried, the question that had been almost a form of greeting between them.

Tumlook shook his head.

"Is it likely?" he asked. "Surely after all these weeks, we must look upon him as dead."

But Thupra was not to be discouraged. Indeed, of all Loor, it is probable that she alone still maintained the confidence that amounted to a certainty that Tumithak was safe and would return in triumph.

"I think he will return," she said now. "You know, we are sure that he reached Yakra. And has not Nennapuss told us of the huge giant that was found dead at the foot of the Yakran shaft? If Tumithak could conquer such a man as that, who could overcome him?"

"Thupra may be right," said Nikadur, gravely. "There are rumors in Nonone of a great panic in Yakra, during which a man of these corridors is supposed to have passed through the town. The rumors are vague and may be only gossip, but perhaps Tumithak did reach the dark corridors."

"Tumithak will return, I know," Thupra repeated. "He is mighty, and—" she paused. Far up the corridor, her ears caught a sound and she listened questioningly. Then Nikadur heard it, too, and last of all it reached the ears of Tumlook.

A shouting, a distant shouting that grew louder even as they listened. Several passing pedestrians heard it, too, and paused; and then two men turned and hastened off in its direction. The trio strained their ears in an endeavor to distinguish the meaning of the cries. Several more men came speeding up the corridor, running in the direction of the noise.

"Come," cried Nikadur suddenly, consternation written on his face. "If this be a raid of the Yakrans—" In spite of the cries of Thupra, he sped off, and Tumlook hesitated only long enough to dart back into his apartment and arm himself before he followed.

Thupra, however, was not to be left behind. She caught up with Nikadur in a moment, and in spite of his protestations, persisted in going with him. And so the three, joined soon by many others, rushed on in the direction of the excitement.

A man passed them, running the other way. "What is it?" came a chorus of a dozen voices, but the man's only answer was an unintelligible gabble of words as he ran on. The crowd's ignorance was not to continue for long, though, for at the very next turn of the corridor, they beheld the cause of the tumult.

Down the corridor came marching an incredible procession. A group of Loorians led the parade, dancing and cheering like mad, while behind them came marching a well-known figure—Nennapuss, chief of the Nononese, with his retinue of officers. Nennapuss was followed by what must have been almost the entire population of Nonone, all gabbling and shouting madly to the Loorians whom they passed. It was not at the Nononese that the Loorians stared, however, but at the ones who followed them. Behind Nennapuss' men came a crowd of Yakrans, each carrying aloft a white cloth on a stick that still, after so many hundreds of years, denoted a truce. Datta was there, the burly chief of the Yakrans, and his huge nephew, Thorpf, and many others of whom the Loorians had heard from the Nononese, and there, high on the shoulders of two of the mightiest Yakrans, was riding—Tumithak!

But when the eyes of the Loorians looked upon Tumithak, they looked no further. For the sight they beheld was so incredible that it seemed impossible to believe that they where not dreaming.

He was dressed in garments that, to their eyes, were beautiful beyond telling. They were of the finest texture imaginable, sheer gauzes that were dyed in the most delicate shades of nacreous pinks and greens and blues. They flowed down over his form, clinging to his body and giving him all the appearance of a god. Around his head was a metal band not unlike a crown, such a band as legend said the king shelks were wont to wear.

And, most unbelievable of all, he held his arm aloft, and in his hand was the wrinkled head of a shelk!

Tumlook, Nikadur and Thupra never knew when they joined the crowd. One moment they were rushing down the corridor toward the incredible procession, the next, it had absorbed them and they, too, were a part of the howling, enthusiastic mob that fought and laughed its way toward the great square of Loor.

They reached the crossing of the two main corridors and formed an immense crowd with Tumithak and the Yakrans in its center. The crowd continued its chattering and cheering for some moments and then Tumithak, mounting the stone pedestal that had long been used for speakers, held up his hand for silence. Quiet reigned almost instantly, and in the lull, the voice of Nennapuss, that instinctive master of ceremonies, could be heard.

"Friends of Loor," he cried. "Today is the day that will live forever in the archives of the three cities of the lower corridors. It has been unnumbered years since the three cities have all met on a friendly footing, and to bring that about it has taken an event so incredible that it is well-nigh impossible to believe. For at last a man has slain a shelk—"

He was interrupted by the booming voice of Datto, the much-decorated chief of the Yakrans.

"Enough of this talk," he shouted. "We are here to do honor to Tumithak, the Loorian, who has slain a shelk. Let us shout and sing songs in his praise. Let us bow to him, Nennapuss, we who are chiefs, let us call upon the chiefs of Loor to bow to him also, for who could slay a shelk if he were not far greater than he."

Nennapuss looked a little nettled at having been interrupted at his favorite pastime, but before he could answer, Tumithak began to speak. And at his word, Yakran and Nononese alike listened with respect.

"Fellow Loorians," he began. "Brothers of Nonone and Yakra, it was not for honor that I journeyed to the Surface and slew the beast whose head I hold in my hand. Since I was a boy I have felt that men could fight with shelks. It has been the ambition of my life to prove that fact to everyone. Surely no citizen of Loor was less of a fighter than I. Many, indeed, have scorned me for a mere dreamer of dreams. And I assure you that I was little more. Can you not see that man is not the weak, insignificant creature that you seem to think? You Yakrans have never cowered in fear when the men of Loor came against you! Loorians, have you ever trembled in your apartments when the Yakrans raided your halls?

"Yet the cry of the 'Shelk!' will send you all fleeing panic-stricken to your homes! Can you not see that these shelks, although mighty, are only mortal creatures like yourselves? Listen to the story of my deeds, now, and see if I have done aught that you could not have done."

He took up the recital of his adventures. He told of the passing of Yakra, and though the Loorians cheered a bit there was silence among the people of Yakra, and then he told of the dark corridors, and the Yakrans, too, cheered as he recited his story of the slaying of the dogs. He told of the halls of the Esthetts, and in glowing colors described to them the beauties there, hoping that he might arouse in them the desire to possess these beauties.

And then he tried to tell them of the Surface, but here words failed him; it was hardly possible, in the limited vocabulary of the corridors, to tell of the slaying of the shelk, and at last the story of his return.

"For some reason the shelks did not follow me," he said, "and I reached the first halls of the Esthetts in safety. And here I was discovered, and had to fight a battle with a half dozen of the fat ones before I could go farther. I slew them all," Tumithak, in that sublime unconscious conceit of his, failed to say how easy it had been to slaughter his huge opponents, "and taking from them these garments, continued on my way.

"I came again to the dark corridors, but even here no one opposed me. Perhaps the terrible smell of shelk was so great that the savages feared to come near me. So at last I came to Yakra, and found that the woman whom I had met on my upward journey had told her story to Datto, the chief, who was ready and eager to do me honor on my return home. And so I came to Nonone, and after a time to Loor."

He ceased his story, and again the crowd broke into cheers. The cheers increased, echoed back against the walls until the great hall rang like a bell. "Great is Tumithak of the Loorians!" They cried, "Great is Tumithak, slayer of shelks!" And Tumithak folded his arms and drank in the praise, forgetful for the moment that his entire mission had been to prove that it did not take a great man to kill a shelk.

After a while, the tumult began to die and the voice of Datto was heard again.

"Loorians," he shouted. "For many, many years, the men of Yakra have fought unending war with the men of Loor. Today that war ceases. Today we have found a Loorian who is greater than all Yakrans, and so we fight with Loor no more. And to prove that I speak truth, Datto bows in allegiance to Tumithak!"

Again the cheers, and at last Nennapuss arose.

"It is a good thing that you have done, O Datto," he said, "and truly Tumithak is a chief of chiefs if there ever was one. Now there has been little enmity between Loor and Nonone in the past, and so our cases are different. For it is said that in the olden days, the people of Loor and Nonone were one. Thus, we hear of the days of the great chief, Ampithat, who ruled—" here Datto whispered something fiercely into his ear, and the Nononese flushed and went on, "But enough of that. Suffice it that Nennapuss, too, bows to Tumithak, chief of chiefs and chief of Nonone."

Again there was a great demonstration and after a while, Datto began to speak again. Would it not be a seemly thing, he asked frowning fiercely, for the Loorians to recognize Tumithak as their chief also, thus making him king of all the lower corridors? The Loorians raised a cheer, and then Tagivos, the eldest of the doctors, arose to speak.

"The people of Loor have a government somewhat different from that of Nonone and Yakra," he said. "We have not had a chief for many years. However, it might be a good thing for the three towns to be united and so I will call a meeting of the council to decide on it."

The council was soon grouped together, Tagivos, Tumlook and old Sidango leading them, and after a while they announced that they were agreed to recognize Tumithak as their chief also. And so, amid wild cheering, that made it utterly impossible to distinguish a word that was said, Tumithak became chief of all the lower corridors.

Datto and his huge nephew, Thorpf, the foremost of the Yakrans, were the first to swear allegiance to him; then he accepted the fealty of Sidango, Tagivos and the other Loorians. It gave Tumithak a queer feeling to touch the sword of his father and to hear his oath, but he maintained his dignified bearing, and treated Tumlook in just the same fashion as the others, until the ceremony was over. Then he called for attention.

"Friends of the lower corridors," he said. "A new day dawns for man today. It has been over thirty years since war has visited these corridors and in all those years men have almost forgotten the arts of war. We have lived in a spirit of slothful peace, while above us the enemies of all mankind have grown stronger and stronger. But in making me your chief, you have ended that era of peace and brought upon yourselves new lives of action. I will not be a peaceful ruler, for I, who have seen so much of the world, will not be content to skulk idly in the deepest corridor. Already I plan to lead you against the savages of the dark corridors, to claim those halls as our own, and to fill them with the lights that still gleam in the deserted corridors that we no longer use.

"And if we conquer those savages, I shall take you against

the huge Esthetts to show you what beauty can do for the life of man. And the time will surely come, if the High One be willing, when I shall lead you against the shelks themselves, for what I have done, everyone of you can do, and shall do.

"And if anyone feels that the task I call upon you to do is too great, let him speak now for I will not rule over man against his will."

Again the cheers broke out, and gathered volume, and rang from wall to wall of the great square. In the excitement and enthusiasm of the moment, there was not a man in all the crowd that did not feel that he, too, might become a slayer of shelks.

And while they cheered and sang, and worked themselves into a frenzy. Tumithak stepped down from the stone and strode off in the direction of his home.

"Tumithak of the Corridors" was far and away the best and most exciting story I had ever read up to that time.

I must admit that when I reread these ancient stories, I don't, in my early fifties, get nearly the same charge I got when in my preteens. I am far more aware now than I was then of the structural and stylistic flaws. And what was new and astonishing then is not new and astonishing now.

Yet let it be said that the gap proved surprisingly small when I read "Tumithak of the Corridors." Even now, though my hair is graying, I found myself stirred very much as I had been once in junior high school.

I found the characters human and the hero all the more admirable because he could feel fear. I found the plot exciting and found a deep humanity in the sentence "Tumithak had to learn that in no matter what nation or age one finds oneself, he will find gentleness, if he looks, as well as savagery." This was an amazing viewpoint at a time when popular literature accepted racial stereotypes as a matter of course.

Most of all, though, there was (and is) something fascinating to me in the thought of endless corridors burrowing underground.

I'm a claustrophile. I enjoy the feeling of being closed in. I like tunnels and corridors and never mind the absence of windows. The office I work in I chose because it faces a court. I keep the shades pulled down and I work under perpetual artificial light.

I've always been that way. I remember that, in my younger days, when I took the subway to school I was always fascinated by the small newsstands there used to be on the stations. Late at night I would see them closed, and inside, I knew, were all those lovely pulps I never got a chance to read. And I would fantasize being shut into one of those things, with the lights on, of course, and, safely enclosed and with the sound of subway trains rushing past periodically, reading and reading and reading.

But don't get me wrong. I am not psychotic about it. The apartment I live in is on the twenty-third floor with wide windows overlooking Central Park, and the sunlight comes in steadily.

Well, I'm off the point. The corridors pleased me, and I never forgot them. When I wrote *The Caves of Steel*, in 1953, and lovingly described the underground city of the future, I did not forget "Tumithak of the Corridors."

One thing I noted, in rereading the story, that I had forgotten. It is told in the form of history. The narrator is in the far future looking back on events that took place in what was, to him, the legendary past. Apparently, that didn't impress me, for I did not remember.

Yet does one ever really forget? Eventually, when I wrote my Foundation Trilogy in the form of historical novels of the future, was there a dim unconscious memory of the manner of telling of "Tumithak of the Corridors?"

In my last months at junior high school, I decided to apply for entrance into Boys High School of Brooklyn. In the ordinary course of events I should have gone to Thomas Jefferson High School, which was closest to where I lived. The graduating body of J.H.S. 149 usually transferred to Jefferson *en masse* and did so this time too. I think I was one of only three boys who opted for Boys High.

You see, by this time I had ambitions of vague higher things, and Boys High School had a reputation for scholastic excellence. My parents, who wanted me to go to medical school eventually, thought this was a good move.

I have often pondered the consequences of that decision.

Jefferson High was coeducational. Had I spent my early teens there, I would undoubtedly have discovered girls. Automatically, I would have had a strong motivation to broaden my interests, learn to dance, for instance, learn to handle myself easily and well with the opposite sex. On the other hand, my schoolwork might have suffered disastrously.

At Boys High, with its purely masculine student body, I was plunged into a monastic existence in which there was little to distract me from schoolwork or to encourage me to broaden out.

In consequence, throughout my teens and very early twenties I remained ill at ease in the presence of girls. I got over it, to be sure, married at the age of twenty-two, and have, for many years, been noted for my suavity with the ladies. (I have even written a book called *The Sensuous Dirty Old Man*, and no one has ever cast doubt on my qualifications for undertaking that task.)

Nevertheless, what would have happened if I had gone to Jefferson High instead of Boys High?

But what's the use of dwelling upon it? Things might have turned out much worse. After all, the girls in my class would have been, for the most part, two and a half years older than I. Not only would I have seemed ludicrously young in their eyes, but I would also have been found to be lacking in the social graces and in worldly knowledge. I would undoubtedly have suffered rejection of all sorts, and who can tell how badly that might have affected me.

Nor was the monasticism of my early teens disturbed (or relieved, if you prefer) by the science fiction I was reading. In the 1930s, science fiction was almost entirely masculine. The readership was almost entirely masculine, after all, and so were the writers.

Of course, there were women in the stories, but they were there only to be caught and then rescued, only to be fought over by hero and villain (as in "Awlo of Ulm"). They had no life of their own and left no impression.

Once, in those early years, however, I recall being really moved by the relationship between a man and a woman as pictured in a science fiction story. It is perhaps inevitable that the woman involved wasn't really a woman.

The story in question was Jack Williamson's "The Moon

Era," published in the February 1932 *Wonder Stories*, and I
fell in love with the Moon woman whom Williamson called
the "Mother."

THE MOON ERA

by Jack Williamson

CHAPTER I

WE WERE seated at dinner in the long dining room of my uncle's Long Island mansion. There was glistening silver plate, and the meal had been served with a formality to which I was unaccustomed. I was ill at ease, though my uncle and I sat alone at the table. The business of eating, without committing an egregious blunder before the several servants, took all my attention.

It was the first time I had ever seen my uncle, Enfield Conway. A tall man, stiffly erect, dressed severely in black. His face, though lean, was not emaciated as is usual at his age of seventy years. His hair, though almost perfectly white, was abundant, parted on the side. His eyes were blue, and strong; he wore no glasses.

A uniformed chauffeur had met me at the station, in the afternoon. The butler had sent an entirely unnecessary valet to my luxurious room. I had not met my uncle until he came down to the dining room.

"I suppose, Stephen, you are wondering why I sent for you," he said in his precise manner, when the servants had carried away the last course, leaving cigars, and a bottle of mineral water for him.

I nodded. I had been instructor of history in a small high school in Texas, where his telegram had reached me. There had been no explanation; merely a summons to Long Island.

"You are aware that some of my patents have been quite profitable."

Again I nodded. "The evidence surrounds me."

"Stephen, my fortune amounts to upwards of three and a half million. How should you like to be my heir?"

"Why, sir—I should not refuse. I'd like very much to be."

"You can, if you wish, earn that fortune. And fifty thousand a year while I live."

I pushed back the chair and rose to my feet in excitement. Such riches were beyond my dreams! I felt myself trembling.

"Anything—" I stammered. "I'll do anything you say, to earn that! It means—"

"Wait," he said, looking at me calmly. "You don't know yet what I require. Don't commit yourself too soon."

"What is it?" I asked, in a quivering voice.

"Stephen, I have been working in my private laboratory here for eleven years. I have been building a machine. The best of my brains have gone into that machine. Hundreds of thousands of dollars. The efforts of able engineers and skilled mechanics.

"Now the machine is finished. It is to be tested. The engineers who worked with me refused to try the machine. They insist that it is very dangerous.

"And I am too old to make the trial. It will take a young man, with strength, endurance, and courage.

"You are young, Stephen. You look vigorous enough. I suppose your health is good? A sound heart? That's the main thing."

"I think so," I told him. "I've been coaching the Midland football team. And it isn't many years since I was playing college football, myself."

"And you have no dependents?"

"None.—But what is this machine?"

"I will show you. Come."

He rose, agilely enough for one of his seventy years, and led the way from the long room. Through several magnificent rooms of the big house. Out into the wide, landscaped grounds, beautiful and still in the moonlight.

I followed silently. My brain was confusion. A whirl of mad thought. All this wealth whose evidence surrounded me might be my own! I cared nothing for luxury, for money itself. But the fortune would mean freedom from the thankless toil of pedagogy. Books. Travel. Why I could see with my own eyes the scenes of history's dramatic moments! Finance research expeditions of my own! Delve with my own hands for the secrets of Egypt's sands, uncover the age-old enigmas of ruined mounds that once were proud cities of the East!

We approached a rough building,—resembling an airplane hangar,—of galvanized iron, which glistened like silver in the rays of the full moon.

Without speaking, Uncle Enfield produced a key from his pocket, unlocked the heavy padlock on the door. He entered the building, switching on electric lights inside it.

"Come in," he said. "Here it is. I'll explain it as well as I can."

I walked through the narrow doorway and uttered an involuntary exclamation of surprise at sight of the huge machine that rested upon the clean concrete floor.

Two huge disks of copper, with a cylinder of bright, chromium-plated metal between them. Its shape vaguely suggested that of an ordinary spool of adhesive plaster, from which a little has been used—the polished cylinder, which was of smaller diameter than the disks, took the place of the roll of plaster.

The lower of the massive disks rested on the concrete floor. Its diameter was about twenty feet. The cylinder above it was about sixteen feet in diameter, and eight feet high. The copper disk above was the same size as the lower one.

Small round windows stared from the riveted metal plates forming the cylinder. The whole was like a building, it burst on me. A circular room with bright metal walls. Copper floor and copper roof projecting beyond those walls.

My uncle walked to the other side of this astounding mechanism. He turned a projecting knob. An oval door, four feet high, swung inward in the curving wall. Four inches thick. Of plated steel. Fitting very tightly against cushions of rubber.

My uncle climbed through the door, into the dark interior. I followed with a growing sense of wonder and excitement. I groped toward him through the darkness. Then I heard the click of a switch, and lights flashed on within the round chamber.

I gazed about me in astonishment.

Walls, floor, and ceiling were covered with soft, white fiber. The little room was crowded with apparatus. Clamped against one white wall was a row of the tall steel flasks in which commercial oxygen is compressed. Across the room was a bank of storage batteries. The walls were hung with numerous instruments, all clamped neatly in place. Sextants. Compasses. Pressure gauges. Numerous dials whose functions were not apparent. Cooking utensils. An automatic pistol. Cameras. Telescopes. Binoculars.

In the center of the room stood a table or cabinet, with switches, dials, and levers upon its top. A heavy cable, apparently of aluminum, ran from it to the ceiling.

I was gazing about in bewilderment. "I don't understand all this—" I began.

"Naturally," said my uncle. "It is quite a novel invention. Even the engineers who built it did not understand it. I confess that the theory of it is yet beyond me. But what happens is quite simple.

"Eleven years ago, Stephen, I discovered a new phenomenon. I had happened to charge two parallel copper plates, whose distances apart had a certain very definite relation to their combined masses, with a high tension current at a certain frequency.

"The plates, Stephen, were in some way—how, I do not pretend to understand—cut out of the earth's gravitational field. Insulated from gravity. The effect extended to any object placed between them. By a slight variation of the current's strength. I was able to increase the repulsion, until the plates pulled upward with a force approximately equal to their own weight.

"My efforts to discover the reason for this phenomenon—it is referred to in my notes as the Conway Effect—have not been successful. But I have built this machine to make a practical application of it. Now that it is finished, the four engineers who helped design it have deserted. They refused to assist with any trials."

"Why?" I asked.

"Muller, who had the construction in charge, somehow came to the conclusion that the suspension or reversal of gravity was due to motion in a fourth dimension. He claimed that he had experimental proof of his theory, by building models of the device, setting the dials, and causing them to vanish. I would have none of it. But the other men seemed to accept his ideas. At any rate, they refused with him to have any part in the tests. They thought they would vanish, like Muller says his models did, and not come back."

"The thing is supposed to rise above the ground?" I asked.

"Quite so." My uncle smiled. "When the force of gravitation is merely suspended, it should fly off the earth at a tangent, due to the diurnal rotation. This initial velocity, which in these latitudes, amounts to considerably less than one thousand miles per hour, can be built up at will, by reversing gravitation, and falling away from the earth."

"Falling away from the earth!" I was staggered. "And where is one to fall."

"This machine was designed for a trip to the moon. At the beginning of the voyage, gravitation will be merely cut out, allowing the machine to fly off on a tangent, toward the point of intersection with the moon's orbit. Safely beyond the atmosphere, repulsion can be used to build up the acceleration. Within the gravitational sphere of the moon, positive gravitation can be utilized further to increase the speed. And reversed gravitation to retard the velocity, to make possible a safe landing. The return will be made in the same manner."

I was staring at him blankly. A trip to the moon seemed insane, beyond reason. Especially for a professor of history, with only a modicum of scientific knowledge. And it must be dangerous, if those engineers—. But three million—what dangers would I not face for such a fortune?

"Everything has been done," he went on, "to insure the comfort and safety of the passenger. The walls are insulated with a fiber composition especially worked out to afford protection from the cold of space, and from the unshielded radiation of the sun. The steel armor is strong enough not only to hold the necessary air pressure, but to stop any ordinary meteoric particles.

"You notice the oxygen cylinders, for maintaining that essential element in the air. There is automatic apparatus for purifying it. It is pumped through caustic soda to absorb the carbon dioxide, and through refrigerator tubes to condense the excess moisture.

"The batteries, besides energizing the plates, are amply powerful to supply lights and heat for cooking.

"That, I believe, fairly outlines the machine and the projected voyage. Now it is up to you. Take time to consider it fully. Ask me any questions you wish."

He sat down deliberately in the large, cushioned chair, beside the central table, which was evidently intended for the operator. He stared at me alertly, with calm blue eyes.

I was extremely agitated. My knees had a weak feeling, so that I desired to sit down also; though I was so nervous that I kept striding back and forth across the resilient white fiber of the floor.

Three millions! It would mean so much! Books, magazines, maps—I should have to economize no longer. Years—all my life, if I wished—abroad. The tombs of Egypt. The sand-covered cities of the Gobi. My theory that mankind originated in South Africa. All those puzzles that I had longed to be able to study. Stonehenge! Angkor! Easter Island!

But the adventure seemed madness. A voyage to the moon! In a craft condemned by the very engineers that had built it. To be hurled away from the earth at speeds no man had attained before. To face unknown perils of space. Dangers beyond guessing. Hurtling meteors. The all-penetrating cosmic ray. The burning heat of the sun. The absolute zero. What, beyond speculation and theory, did men know of space? I was no astronomer; how was I to cope with the emergencies that might rise?

"How long will it take?" I demanded suddenly.

My uncle smiled a little. "Glad you are taking it seriously," he said. "The duration of the voyage depends on the speed you make, of course. A week each way is a conservative estimate. And perhaps two or three days on the moon. To take notes. Photograph it. Move around a little, if possible; land in several different places. There is oxygen and concentrated food to last six months. But a fortnight should see you nearly back. I'll go over the charts and calculations with you."

"Can I leave the machine on the moon?"

"No. No atmosphere. And it would be too hot in the day, too cold at night. Of course an insulated suit and oxygen mask might be devised. Something like diving armor. But I haven't worked at that. You will be expected just to take a few pictures, be prepared to describe what you have seen."

I continued to pace the floor, pausing sometimes to examine some piece of apparatus. How would it feel, I wondered, to be shut up in here? Drifting in space. Far from the world of my birth. Alone. In silence. Entombed. Would it not drive me mad?

My uncle rose suddenly from the chair.

"Sleep on it, Stephen," he advised. "See how you feel in the morning. Or take longer if you wish."

He switched off the light in the machine. Led the way out into the shed. And from it into the brilliant moonlight that flooded the wide, magnificent grounds about the great house that would be one of the prizes of this mad adventure.

As he was locking the shed, I gazed up at the moon.

Broad, bright disk. Silvery, mottled. Extinguishing the stars with argent splendor. And all at once it came over me—the desire to penetrate the enigmatic mystery of this companion world, that men have watched since the race began.

What an adventure! To be the first human to tread this silver planet. To be the first to solve its age-old riddles. Why think of Angkor, or Stonehenge, of Luxon and Karnak, when I might win the secrets of the moon?

Even if death came, what did it matter against the call of this adventure? Many men would trade their lives eagerly for such a chance.

Suddenly I was strong. All weakness had left me. All fear and doubt. A few moments before I had been tired, wishing to sit down. Now vast energy filled me. I was conscious of an extraordinary elation. Swiftly I turned to my uncle.

"Let's go back," I said. "Show me as much about it as you can tonight. I am going."

He gripped my hand tightly, without a word, before he turned back to the lock.

CHAPTER II

Toward the Moon

It was in the second week, after that sudden decision came to me, that I started. At the end my uncle became a little alarmed, and tried to persuade me to stay longer, to make more elaborate preparations. I believe that he was secretly becoming fond of me, despite his brisk precise manner. I think he took the opinion of his engineers seriously enough to consider my return very uncertain.

But I could see no reason for longer delay. The operation of the machine was simple; he had explained it quite fully.

There was a switch to close, to send current from the bat-

teries through the coils that raised it to the potential necessary
to energize the copper disks. And a large rheostat that con-
rolled the force, from a slight decrease in gravity, to a complete reversal.

The auxiliary apparatus, for control of temperature and atmosphere, was largely automatic. And not beyond my limited
mechanical comprehension. I was certain that I should be
able to make any necessary repairs or adjustments.

Now I was filled with the greatest haste to undertake the
adventure. No doubt or hesitation had troubled me since the
moment of the decision. I felt only a longing to be sweeping
away from the earth. To view scenes that the ages had kept
hidden from human eyes; to tread the world that has always
been the symbol of the unattainable.

My uncle recalled one of the engineers, a sallow young fellow named Gorton. On the second morning, to supplement
my uncle's instruction he went over the machine again, showing me the function of every part. Before he left, he warned
me.

"If you are idiot enough to get in that darned contraption,
and turn on the power," he told me, "you'll never come back.
Muller said so. And he proved it. So long as the batteries and
coil are outside the field of force between the plates, the plates
act according to schedule, and rise up in the air.

"But Muller made self-contained models. With the battery
and all inside. And they didn't rise up. They went out! Vanished. Just like that!" He snapped his fingers. "Muller said the
things moved along another dimension, right out of our
world. And he ought to know. String of degrees a mile long.
Into another dimension. No telling what sort of hell you'll
blunder into."

I thanked the man. But his warnings only increased my eagerness. I was about to tear aside the veil of the unknown.
What if I did blunder into new worlds? Might they not yield
rewards of knowledge richer than those of the barren moon? I
might be a new Columbus, a greater Balboa.

I slept a few hours in the afternoon, after Gorton had gone.
I felt no conscious need of slumber, but my uncle insisted
upon it. And to my surprise, I fell soundly asleep, almost as
soon as I lay down.

At sunset, we went down again to the shed in which the
machine was housed. My uncle started a motor, which opened

the roof like a pair of enormous doors, by means of pulleys and cables. The red light of the evening sky streamed down upon the machine.

We made a final inspection of all the apparatus. My uncle explained again the charts and instruments that I was to use in navigating space. Finally he questioned me for an hour, making me explain the various parts of the machine, correcting any error.

I was not to start until nearly midnight.

We returned to the house, where an elaborate dinner was waiting. I ate almost absently, hardly noticing the servants of whom I had been so conscious upon my arrival. My uncle was full of conversation. Talking of his own life, and asking me many questions about my own, and about my father, whom he had seen last when they were boys. My mind was upon the adventure before me; I could answer him only disjointedly. But I was aware that he had taken a real liking for me; I was not surprised at his request that I postpone the departure.

At last we went back down to the machine. The white moon was high; its soft radiance bathed the gleaming machine, through the opened roof. I stared up at its bright disk. Was it possible that in a short week I should be there, looking back upon the earth? It seemed madness! But the madness of glorious adventure!

Without hesitation, I clambered through the oval door. A last time my uncle wrung my hand. He had tears in his eyes. And his voice was a little husky.

"I want you to come back, Stephen."

I swung the door into its cushioned seat, upon massive hinges, tightened the screws that were to hold it. A final glance about the white-walled interior of the machine. All was in order. The chronometer by the wall, ticking steadily, told me that the moment had come.

My uncle's anxious face was pressed against one of the ports. I smiled at him. Waved. His hand moved across the port. He left the shed.

I dropped into the big chair beside the table, reached for the switch. With my fingers upon the button, I hesitated the merest second. Was there anything else? Anything neglected? Anything I had yet to do on earth? Was I ready to die, if so I must?

The deep, vibrant hum of the coils, beneath the table, answered the pressure of my finger. I took the handle of the rheostat, swung it to the zero mark, where gravitation was to be cut off completely.

My sensation was exactly as if the chair, the floor, had fallen from under me. The same sensation that one feels when an elevator drops very abruptly. Almost I floated out of the chair. I had to grasp at the arm of it to stay within it.

For a few moments I experienced nauseating vertigo. The white crowded room seemed to spin about me. To drop away endlessly beneath me. Sick, helpless, miserable, I clung weakly to the great chair. Falling . . . falling . . . falling. Would I never strike bottom?

Then I realized, with relief, that the sensation was due merely to the absence of gravity's familiar pull. The machine had worked! My last, lingering doubt was killed. Strange elation filled me.

I was flying away from the earth. Flying.

The thought seemed to work a miracle of change in my feelings. The dreadful, dizzy nausea gave way to a feeling of exhilaration. Of lightness. I was filled with a sense of power and well-being, such as I had never before experienced.

I left the great chair, floated rather than walked to one of the windows.

Already I was high in the air. So high that the moonlit earth was a dim and misty plain before me. I could see many lights; the westward sky was aglow, above New York. But already I was unable to pick out the lights at my uncle's mansion.

The machine had risen through the open roof of the shed. It was driving out into space, as it had been planned to do! The adventure was succeeding.

As I watched, the earth sank visibly. Became a great concave bowl of misty silver. Expanded slowly, as the minutes went by. And became suddenly convex. A huge dark sphere, washed with pale gray light.

Presently, after an hour, when the dials showed that I was beyond the faintest trace of atmosphere, I returned to the table and increased the power, moving the rheostat to the last contact. I looked at charts and chronometer. According to my uncle's calculations, four hours at this acceleration were required, before the controls were set again.

I returned to the window and stared in amazement at the earth, that I had left vast and silver gray and motionless.

It was spinning madly, backward!

The continents seemed to race beneath me—I was now high enough to see a vast section of the globe. Asia. North America. Europe. Asia again. In seconds.

It was madness! The earth spinning in a few moments, instead of the usual twenty-four hours. And turning backward! But I could not doubt my eyes. Even as I watched, the planet seemed to spin faster. Ever faster! The continental outlines merged into dim indistinctness.

I looked away from the mad earth, in bewilderment. The firmament was very black. And the very stars were creeping about it, with visible motions!

Then the sun came into view, plunging across the sky like a flaming comet. It swung supernally across my field of vison, vanished. Appeared again. And again. Its motion became ever swifter.

What was the meaning of such an apparent revolution of the sun about the sky? It meant, I knew, that earth and moon had swung about the star. That a year had passed! But were years going by as fast as my chronometer ticked off the seconds?

Another strange thing. I could recognize the constellations of the Zodiac, through which the sun was plunging. And it was going backward! As the earth was spinning backward!

I moved to another window, searched for the moon, my goal. It hung still among spinning stars. But in its light there was a flicker, far more rapid than the flashing of the sun across the wild heavens. I wondered, then knew that I saw the waxing and waning of the moon. Months, passing so swiftly that soon the flicker became a gray blur.

The flashing past of the sun became more frequent. Until it was a strange belt of flame about the strange heavens, in which the stars crept and moved like living things.

A universe gone mad! Suns and planets spinning helpless in the might of a cosmic storm! The machine from which I watched the only sane thing in a runaway cosmos!

Then reason came to my rescue.

Earth, moon, sun, and stars could not all be mad. The trouble was with *myself!* My perceptions had changed. The machine—

Slowly it came to me, until I knew I had grasped the truth.

Time, true time, is measured by the movements of the heavenly bodies. Our day is the time of earth's rotation on its axis. Our year the period of its revolution about the sun.

Those intervals had become crowded so thick in my perception that they were indistinguishable. Then countless years were spinning past, while I hung still in space!

Incredible! But the conclusion was inevitable.

And the apparent motion of earth and sun had been backward.

That meant—and the thought was staggering—that the ages were reeling backward. That I was plunging at an incalculable rate into the past.

Vaguely I recalled magazine articles that I had read, upon the nature of space and time. A lecture. The subject had fascinated me, though I had only a layman's knowledge of it.

The lecturer had defined our universe in terms of space-time. A four-dimensional "continuum." Time was a fourth dimension, he had said. An extension as real as the three of what we call space, and not completely distinguishable from them. A direction in which motion would carry one into the past, or into the future.

All memory, he had said, is a groping back along this dimension, at right angles to teach of the three of space. Dreams, vivid memories, he insisted, carry one's consciousness in reality back along this dimension, until the body, swept relentlessly along the stream of time, drags it forward again.

Then I recalled what my uncle had told me of the refusal of his engineers to try the machine. Recalled Gorton's warning. Muller, they both had told me, had declared that the machine would move along a fourth dimension, out of our world. He had made models of the machine, and they had vanished when the power was turned on.

Now I knew that Muller was right. His models had vanished because they had been carried into the past. Had not continued to exist in the present time.

And now I was moving along that fourth dimension. The dimension of time. And very swiftly, for the years went past too fast for counting.

The reversal of gravitation, it came to me, must be some effect of this change of direction in time. But I am not a scientist; I can explain the "Conway Effect" no better than my uncle, for all the wonders that it has brought into my life.

At first it was horribly strange and terrifying.

After I had thought out my explanation of the mad antics of the earth and sun and moon, and of the hurrying stars, I was, however, no longer frightened. I gazed out through my small round ports at the melting firmament with some degree of equanimity.

I continued to watch the charts my uncle had prepared, and to make adjustments of the rheostat when they were indicated by the chronometer.

And presently, feeling hungry, I toasted biscuits on the electric stove, cut off a generous slice of a cheese that I found in the supplies, opened a vacuum bottle of steaming chocolate, and made a hearty and very satisfactory meal.

When I had finished, the aspect of the space about me was unchanged. Crawling stars, already forming themselves into constellations the most of which were unfamiliar. The sun a broad belt of burning gold, counting off the years too swiftly for the eye to follow. A living flame that girdled the firmament. The earth was a huge gray sphere, spinning so swiftly behind me that no detail was visible.

And even the moon, hanging in space ahead, was turning slowly. No longer was the same familiar face toward me, and toward the earth. Already I had reached a point in past time at which the moon was turning on its axis more rapidly than it revolved about the earth. The tidal drag had not yet completely stopped the moon's apparent rotation.

And if already the moon was turning, what would it be when I reached it? Hurtling into the past as I was, would I see oceans cover its dry sea-floors? Would I see an atmosphere soften the harsh outlines of its rugged mountains? Would I see life, vegetation, spread over its plains? Was I to witness the rejuvenation of an aged world?

It seemed fantastic. But it was taking place. The speed of rotation slowly increased as I watched.

The hours slipped past.

I became heavy with sleep. The two days before the departure had not been easy. I had worked day and night to familiarize myself with the machine's operation. The nervous strain had been exhausting. The amazing incidents of the voyage had kept me tense, sapped my strength.

The chart told me that no change was to be made in the controls for many hours. I inspected the gauges which showed the condition of the atmosphere in the chamber. Oxygen content, humidity, temperature, were correct. The air smelled sweet and clean. I completed the rounds, found everything in order.

I adjusted the big chair to a reclining position, and threw myself upon it. For hours I slept, waking at intervals to make a tour of inspection.

Sometimes, in the following days, I wondered if I should be able to go back. Muller's models had carried no operator, of course to start them on the flight back through time to the starting point. Would I be able to reverse the time-flight? If I followed the directions on the operating chart, on the flight back, would I be flung forward through the ages, back to my own era?

I wondered. But the speculation brought forth no conclusion. A strange, unique experience was mine. Glorious adventure. Death was not too high a price to pay.

It did not even occur to me to attempt to turn back earthward, when I found that I was slipping through time. And I did not have sufficient control of the machine to have done so, had I wished. Dependent upon the chart for navigating instructions, I could not have plotted a return path from the midway point. And I knew no way to stop my flight, except by using the repulsion of the moon's reversed gravitation.

My flight lasted six days, by the chronometer.

Long before the end, the moon was spinning very swiftly. And the edges of its outline had become hazy, so that I knew it had an atmosphere.

I followed the charted directions, until I was in the upper layers of that atmosphere. The moon's surface was sliding very rapidly beneath me, and the atmosphere with it, due to the swift rotation of the satellite. Consequently, fierce winds screamed about the machine.

I hung in the atmosphere, merely using enough power to balance the moon's comparatively feeble gravitational pull, until the pressure of that rushing wind swept me with it. The mistily indistinct surface slowed, became motionless beneath me.

With power decreased still further, I settled slowly, watching alertly through the ports.

A towering, crimson mountain loomed above the mists

below. I dropped toward it, increasing the power a little. At last I hovered motionless above a narrow, irregular plateau, near the peak, that seemed covered with soft scarlet moss.

Slowly I cut down the power. With hardly a shock, the machine settled in the moss.

I was on the moon! The first of my race to set foot upon an alien planet! What adventures might await me?

CHAPTER III

When the Moon Was Young

With the power cut off entirely, I ran to the ports. There had been no time to scan my surroundings during the uncertainties of the landing. Now I peered out eagerly.

The moonscape was as strange a sight as man had ever seen.

The machine had come down in thick green moss, that looked soft as a Persian rug. A foot deep it was. Dark green fibers closely intertwined. In an unbroken carpet it covered the sloping plateau upon which I had landed, and extended almost to the top of the rugged peak to northward.

To the south and west lay a great valley, almost level, miles across. Beyond it rose a dim range of green hills, rugged summits bare and black. A broad river, glinting white in the distance, flowed down the valley, from northwest, into the south. Then there must be an ocean in that direction.

Strange jungle covered that valley, below the green moss of the mountains. Masses of green. Walls of yellow lining the wide smooth river. Dense forests of gigantic plants, weirdly and grotesquely strange. They grew more luxuriant, taller than similar plants could upon the earth, because a much feebler gravitation opposed their growth.

Equally strange was the sky.

Darker than on earth, perhaps because the atmosphere was thinner. A deep, pure, living blue. A blue that was almost violet. No cloud marred its liquid azure splendor.

The sun hung in the glorious eastward sky. Larger than I had known it. Whiter. A supernal sphere of pure white flame.

Low in the west was an amazing disk. A huge ball of white, a globe of milky light. Many times the diameter of the sun. I wondered at it. And realized that it was—the earth! The earth young as Venus had been in my time. And like Venus, shrouded in white clouds never broken. Were the rocks still glowing beneath those clouds, I wondered? Or had the life begun——the life of my farthest progenitors?

Would I ever see my native land again, upon that resplendent, cloud hidden planet? Would the machine carry me back into the future, when I attempted return? Or would it hurl me farther into the past, to plunge flaming into the new-born and incandescent world?

That question I put resolutely from my mind. A new world was before me. A globe strange and unexplored. Why worry about return to the old?

My eyes went back to the broad valley below me, along the banks of the broad river, beneath the majestic range of green mountains. Clumps of gold, resembling distant groves of yellow trees. Patches of green that looked like meadows of grass. Queer, puzzling uprights of black.

I saw things moving. Little bright objects, that rose and fell slightly as they flew. Birds? Gigantic insects? Or creatures stranger than either?

Then I saw the balloons. Captive balloons, floating above the jungles of the valley. At first I saw only two, hanging side by side, swaying a little. Then three more, beyond. Then I distinguished dozens, scores of them, scattered all over the valley.

I strained my eyes at them. Were there intelligent beings here, who had invented the balloons? But what would be the object of hanging them about above the jungles, by the hundred?

I remembered the powerful prism binoculars hanging on the wall beside me. I seized them, focused them hurriedly. The weird jungle leaped toward me in the lenses.

The things were doubtless balloons. Huge spheres of purple, very bright in the sunlight. Anchored with long red cables. Some of them, I estimated, were thirty feet in diameter. Some, much smaller. I could make out no baskets. But there seemed to be small dark masses upon their lower sides, to which the red ropes were attached.

I left them and surveyed the jungle again.

A mass of the yellow vegetation filled the lenses. A dense tangle of slender yellow stems, armed with terrible rows of long, bayonet-like thorns. A thick tangle of sharp yellow thorns, it seemed, with no more stalk than was necessary to support them against the moon's feeble pull. A wall of cruel spikes, impenetrable.

I found a patch of green. A mass of soft, feathery foliage. A sort of creeper, it seemed, covering rocks, and other vegetation—though it did not mingle with the yellow scrub. Enormous, brilliantly white, bell-shaped blooms were open upon it here and there.

A flying thing darted across my vision. It looked like a gigantic moth, frail wings dusted with silver.

Then I made out a little cluster of curious plants. Black, smooth, upright stalks, devoid of leaf or branch. The tallest looked a foot in diameter, a score in height. It was crowned with a gorgeous red bloom. I noticed that no other vegetation grew near any of them. About each was a little cleared circle. Had they been cultivated?

Hours went by as I stared out through the ports, at this fascinating and bewildering moonscape.

Finally I recalled the pictures that my uncle had requested me to make. For two or three hours I was busy with the cameras. I made exposures in all directions, with ordinary and telescopic lenses. I photographed the scene with color filters. And finally I made motion pictures, swinging the camera to take a panoramic view.

It was almost sunset when I had done. It seemed strange that the day was passing so swiftly, until I looked at the chronometer, found that it was not keeping pace with the sun, and decided that the period of rotation must be rather less than twenty-four hours. I later found it to be about eighteen hours, divided into days and nights of very nearly equal length.

Darkness came very swiftly after sunset, due to the comparatively small size and quick rotation of the moon. The stars burst out splendidly through the clean air, burning in constellations utterly strange.

A heavy dew was soon obscuring the ports. As I later discovered, clouds almost never formed in this light atmosphere. Nearly the entire precipitation was in the form of dew, which, however, was amazingly abundant. The tiny droplets on the glass were soon running in streams.

After a few hours, a huge and glorious snow-white sphere rose in the east. The earth. Wondrous in size and brilliance.

The weird jungle was visible in its silvery radiance almost as in daylight.

Suddenly I realized that I was tired, and very sleepy. The anxiety and prolonged nervous strain of the landing had been exhausting. I threw myself down upon the reclining chair, and fell into immediate oblivion.

The white sun was high when I woke. I found myself refreshed. Keenly hungry. And conscious of a great need for physical exercise. Accustomed to an active life, I had been shut up in that little round room for seven days. I felt that I must move, breathe fresh air.

Could I leave the machine?

My uncle had told me that it would be impossible, because of lack of atmosphere. But there was plainly air about me, on this young moon. Would it be breathable?

I pondered the question. The moon, I knew, was formed of materials thrown off the cooling earth. Then should its atmosphere not contain the same elements as that of earth?

I decided to try it. Open the door slightly, and sniff experimentally. Close it immediately if there seemed anything wrong.

I loosened the screws that held the heavy door, tried to pull it open. It seemed fastened immovably. In vain I tugged at it, looked to see if I had left a screw, or if something was amiss with the hinges. It refused to budge.

For minutes I was baffled. The explanation came to me suddenly. The pressure of the atmosphere outside was much less than that within the machine. Since the door opened inward, it was the unbalanced pressure upon it that held it.

I found the valve which was to be opened to free the chamber of any dangerous excess of oxygen that might escape, and spun it open. The air hissed out noisily.

I sat down in the chair to wait. At first I felt no symptoms of the lessening pressure. Then I was conscious of a sensation of lightness, of exhilaration. I noticed that I was breathing faster. My temples throbbed. For a few minutes I felt a dull ache in my lungs.

But the sensations did not become unduly alarming, and I left the valve open. The hissing sound gradually decreased, and finally died away completely.

I rose and went to the door, feeling a painful shortness of the breath as I moved. The heavy door came open quite easily now. I sniffed the air outside. It bore a strange, heavy, unfamiliar fragrance which must have been carried from the jungle in the valley. And I found it oddly stimulating—it must have been richer in oxygen than the air in the machine.

With the door flung wide, I breathed deeply of it.

At first I had thought merely of strolling up and down for a while, in the moss outside the machine. But now I decided, quite suddenly, to hike to the lower edge of the green-carpeted plateau, perhaps a mile away, and look at the edge of the jungle.

I looked about for equipment that I should take, got together a few items. A light camera, in case I should see something worth taking. The binoculars. A vacuum bottle full of water, and a little food, so that I should not have to hasten back to eat.

And finally I took down the automatic pistol on the wall, a .45 Colt. It must have been included with the machine's equipment merely as a way of merciful escape, in case some failure made life in the little round compartment unendurable. There was only one box of ammunition. Fifty cartridges. I loaded the weapon, and slipped the remainder into my pocket.

Gathering up the other articles, I scrambled through the oval door, and stood upon the rim of the lower copper disk, drawing the door to behind me, and fastening it.

And stepped off, upon the moon.

The thick, fibrous moss yielded under my foot, surprisingly. I stumbled, fell into its soft green pile. And in scrambling to my feet, I forgot the lesser gravity of the moon, threw myself into the air, tumbling once more into the yielding moss.

In a few minutes I had mastered the art of walking under the new conditions, so that I could stride along with some confidence, going clear of the ground at every step, as if I had worn seven league boots. Once I essayed a leap. It carried me twenty feet into the air, and twice as far forward. It seemed that I hung in the air an unconscionable time, and floated down very slowly. But I was helpless, aloft, sprawling about, unable to get my feet beneath me. I came down on my shoulder, and must have been painfully bruised had it not been for the thick moss.

I realized that my strength upon the moon was quite out of proportion to my weight. I had muscles developed to handle a mass of 180 pounds. Here my weight was only 30 pounds. It would be some time, I supposed, before I could learn the exact force required to produce the result desired. Actually, I found myself adapted to these new conditions in a surprisingly short space of time.

For a time I was conscious of shortness of the breath, especially after violent exertion. But soon I was accustomed to the lighter air as well as the lesser gravitation.

In half an hour I had arrived at the edge of the red plateau. A steep slope fell before me to the edge of the jungle, perhaps two-thirds of a mile farther below. A slope carpeted with the thick fiber of the green moss.

A weird scene. Clear cerulean sky, darkly, richly blue. Huge white globe of the hot earth setting beyond the farther range of green mountains. The wide valley, with the broad silvery stream, winding among golden forests, and patches of green. The purple balloons floating here and yon, huge spheres swaying on the red cables that anchored them above the jungle.

I seated myself on the moss, where I could overlook that valley of eldritch wonder. I remained there for some time, staring out across it, while I ate most of the food that I had brought, and half-emptied the bottle of water.

Then I decided to descend to the edge of the jungle.

The sun was just at the meridian—the whole of the short afternoon, four hours and a half, was yet before me. I had ample time, I thought, to go down the slope to the edge of the jungle and return before the sudden nightfall.

I had no fear of getting lost. The glittering armor of the machine was visible over the whole plateau. And the jagged, triple peak to the northward of it was a landmark which should be visible over the whole region. There should be no difficulty about return.

Nor, while I realized that the jungle might hide hostile life, did I fear attack. I intended to be cautious, and not to penetrate beyond the edge of the jungle. I had the automatic, which, I was sure, gave me greater power of destruction than any other animal on the planet. Finally in case of difficulty, I could rely upon the superior strength of my muscles, which must be far stronger, in proportion to my weight, than those of native creatures.

I found progress easy on the long, mossy incline. My skill

at traveling under lunar conditions of gravity was increasing with practice: I found a way of moving by deliberate, measured leaps, each carrying me twenty feet or more.

In a few minutes I found myself approaching the edge of the jungle. But that was not so sharp a line as it had appeared from above. The first vegetation other than the moss was scattered clumps of a plant resembling the cactus of my native Southwest.

Thick, fleshy disks growing one upon another, edge to edge. They were not green, however, but of a curious pink, fleshlike color. They bore no thorns, but were studded with little black protuberances or knobs, of doubtful function. The plants I first approached were small and appeared stunted. The lower clumps seemed larger, and more thickly spaced.

I paused to examine one. Walked around it curiously. Photographed it from several angles. Then I ventured to touch it with my foot. Several of the little black knobs broke—they proved to be thin-walled vesicles, containing a black liquid. An overpowering and extremely unpleasant odor assailed me, and I retreated hastily.

A hundred yards farther on, I came upon the green creepers. Thick stems coiled like endless serpents over the ground, with innumerable fronds rising from them, terminating in feathery sprays of green. Here and there were huge white blooms, nearly six feet across, resembling great bells of burnished silver. From them, evidently, came the heavy perfume that I had noticed upon opening the door of the machine.

The creepers formed an unbroken mass of green, several feet deep. It would have been impossible to penetrate it without crushing the delicate foliage. I decided to go no farther in that direction. The creeper might have such means of protection as the malodorous sacs of the fleshy plants above. Or dangerous creatures, counterparts of terrene snakes, might lie concealed beneath the dense foliage.

For some distance I followed along the edge of the mass of creepers, pausing at intervals to make photographs. I was approaching a thicket or forest of the yellow scrub. A wall of inch-thick stems, each armed at intervals of a few inches with dagger-like thorns, all interwoven. A hundred feet high, I estimated. Interlaced so closely that a rat would have had difficulty in moving through it, without impaling himself upon a needlesharp spike.

Then I paused to watch one of the purple balloons, which seemed swaying toward me, increasing the length of the red anchor-cable which held it to the jungle behind. A strange thing, that huge purple sphere, tugging at the thin scarlet cable that held it. Tugging almost like a thing alive, I thought.

Several times I photographed it, but its distance was so great that I feared none of the images would be satisfactory. It seemed to be moving toward me, perhaps carried by some breeze that did not reach the ground. Perhaps, I thought, it would soon be near enough for a good picture.

CHAPTER IV

The Balloon Menace

I studied it closely, trying to see if it had an intelligent pilot or occupant. But I was unable to settle the point. There was certainly no basket. But black arms or levers seemed to project in a cluster, from its lowest part, to manipulate the cables.

Nearly an hour, I waited, watching it. It moved much closer during that time; until, in fact, it was almost directly overhead, and only a few hundred feet high. The red cable slanted from it back into the jungle. It seemed to be loose, dragging.

At last I got a picture that satisfied me. I decided to go on and examine the tangle of yellow thorn-brush or scrub at closer range.

I had taken my eyes from the purple balloon, and turned to walk away, when it struck.

A red rope whipped about me.

The first I knew, it was already about my shoulders. Its end seemed to be weighted, for it whirled about my body several times, wrapping me in sticky coils.

The cable was about half an inch in diameter and made of many smaller crimson strands, fastened together with the adhesive stuff that covered it. I recall its appearance very vividly, even the odd, pungent, disagreeable odor of it.

Half a dozen coils of the red cable had whipped about me before I realized that anything was amiss. Then it tightened suddenly, dragging me across the red moss upon which I had been standing. Toward the edge of the jungle.

Looking up in horror, I saw that the rope had been thrown

from the purple balloon I had been watching. Now the black
arms that I had seen were working swiftly, coiling it up again
—with me caught neatly on the end.

The great sphere was drawn down a little, as my weight
came upon it. It seemed to swell. Then, having been dragged
along until I was directly beneath it, I was lifted clear of the
ground.

I was filled with unutterable terror. I was panting, my heart
was beating swiftly. And I felt endowed with terrific strength.
Furiously I writhed in my gluey bonds, struggled with the
strength of desperation to break the red strands.

But the web had been spun to hold just such frightened,
struggling animals as myself. It did not break.

Back and forth I swung over the jungle, like a pendulum.
With a constantly quickening arc! For the cable was being
drawn up. Once more I looked upward, and saw a sight to
freeze me in dreadful stupefaction of horror.

The whole balloon was a living thing!

I saw its two black and terrible eyes, aflame with hot evil,
staring at me from many bright facets. The black limbs I had
seen were its legs, growing in a cluster at the bottom of its
body—now furiously busy coiling up the cable that it had
spun, spider-like, to catch me. I saw long jaws waiting, black
and hideously fanged, drooling foul saliva. And a rapier-thin
pointed snout, that must be meant for piercing, sucking body
juices.

The huge purple sphere was a thin-walled, muscular sac,
which must have been filled with some light gas, probably hydrogen, generated in the body of the creature. The amazing
being floated above the jungle, out of harm's way, riding free
on the wind, or anchored with its red web, lassoing its prey
and hauling it up to feast hideously in the air.

For a moment I was petrified, dazed and helpless with the
new horror of that thin snout, with black-fanged jaws behind
it.

Then fear bred superhuman strength in me. I got my arms
free, dragging them from beneath the sticky coils. I reached
above my head, seized the red cable in both hands, tried to
break it between them.

It refused to part, despite my fiercest efforts.

Only then did I recall the pistol in my pocket. If I could
reach it in time, I might be able to kill the monster. And the
gas should escape through the riddled sac, letting me back to

the surface. I was already so high that the fall would have been dangerous, had I succeeded in my desperate effort to break the web.

The viscid stuff on the cable clung to my hands. It took all my strength to tear them loose. But at last they were free, and I fumbled desperately for the gun.

A red strand was across the pocket in which I had the weapon. I tore at it. It required every ounce of my strength to slip it upward. And it adhered to my fingers again. I wrenched them loose, snatched out the automatic. It touched the gluey rope, stuck fast. I dragged it free, moved the safety catch with sticky fingers, raised it above my head.

Though it had been seconds only since I was snatched up, already I had been lifted midway to the dreadful living balloon. I glanced downward. The distance was appalling. I noticed that the balloon was still drifting, so that I hung over a thicket of the yellow scrub.

Then I began shooting at the monster. It was difficult to aim, because of the regular jerks as the ugly black limbs hauled on the cable. I held the gun with both hands and fired deliberately, very carefully.

The first shot seemed to have no effect.

At the second, I heard a shrill, deafening scream. And I saw that one of the black limbs was hanging limp.

I shot at the black, many-faceted eyes. Though I had no knowledge of the creature's anatomy, I supposed that its highest nervous centers should be near them.

The third shot hit one of them. A great blob of transparent jelly burst through the faceted surface, hung pendulous. The thing screamed horribly again. The black arms worked furiously, hauling me up.

I felt a violent upward jerk, stronger than the regular pulls that had been raising me. In a moment I saw the reason. The creature had released the long anchor cable, which had held it to the jungle. We were plunging upward. The moon was spinning away below.

The next shot seemed to take no effect. But at the fifth, the black limbs twitched convulsively. I am sure that the creature died almost at once. The limbs ceased to haul upon the cable, hung still. But I fired the two cartridges remaining in the gun.

That was the beginning of a mad aerial voyage.

The balloon shot upward, when the anchor cable was

dropped. And after it was dead, the muscular sac seemed to relax, expand, so that it rose still faster.

Within a few minutes I must have been two miles above the surface. A vast area was visible beneath me; the convexity of the moon's surface, which, of course, is much greater than that of the earth's, was quite apparent.

The great valley lay below, between the green mountain ranges. Splotched with blue and yellow. The white river twisting along it, wide and silvery. I could see into other misty valleys beyond the green ranges, and on the curving horizon were more hills, dim and black in the distance.

The plateau upon which I had landed was like a green-covered table, many thousands of feet below. I could distinguish upon it a tiny bright disk, which I knew was the machine that I had left so unwisely.

Though there had been little wind at the surface, it seemed that I rose into a stratum of air, which was moving quite rapidly into the northwest. I was carried swiftly along; the floor of the great valley glided back beneath me. In a few minutes the machine was lost to view.

I was, of course, rendered desperate at being swept away from the machine. I kept myself oriented, and tried to watch the landmarks that passed beneath me. It was fortunate, I thought, that the wind was driving me up the valley, instead of across the red ranges. I might be able to return to the machine by following down the great river, until the triple peak, near which I had left the machine, came into view. Despair came over me, however, at the realization that I was not likely to be able to traverse so vast a stretch of the unknown jungles of this world, without my ignorance of its perils leading me into some fatal blunder.

I thought of climbing the web to that monstrous body, and trying to make a great rent in the purple sac, so that I should fall more swiftly. But I could only have succeeded in entangling myself more thoroughly in the adhesive coils. And I dismissed the scheme when I realized that if I fell too rapidly, I might be killed upon striking the surface.

After the first few minutes of the flight, I could see that the balloon was sinking slowly, as the gas escaped through the bullet-holes in the muscular sac. I could only wait, and fix in my mind the route that I must follow back to the machine.

The wind bore me so swiftly along that within an hour the

triple peak that I watched had dropped below the curved horizon. But still I was above the great valley, so that I should be able to find my way back following the river. I wondered if I could build a raft, and float down it, with the current.

The balloon was carried along less rapidly as it approached still drifted at considerable speed.

Hanging helpless in the end of the red web, I anxiously scanned the jungle into which I was descending. Like that which I had first seen, it was of dense tangles of the thorny yellow scrub, broken with areas covered largely with the luxuriant green creeper.

Never would I be able to extricate myself alive, I knew, if I had the misfortune to fall in the thorn-brush. And another danger occurred to me. Even if I first touched ground in an open space, the balloon, if the wind continued to blow, would drag me into the spiky scrub before I could tear myself free of the web.

Could I cut myself free, within a safe distance of the ground, and let the balloon go on without me? It seemed that only thus could I escape being dragged to death. I knew that I could survive a fall from a considerable height, since the moon's acceleration of gravity is only about two feet per second,—if only I could land on open ground.

But how could I cut the web? I was without a knife. I thought madly of attempting to bite it in two, realized th that would be as hopeless as attempting to bite through a manila rope.

But I still had the pistol. If I should place the muzzle against the cable and fire, the bullet should cut it.

I reached into my pocket again, past the adhesive coil, and found two cartridges. Though they clung to my sticky fingers, I got them at last into the magazine, and worked the action to throw one into the chamber.

By the time I had finished loading, I was low over an apparently endless jungle of the yellow thorns. Swaying on the end of the web, I was swept along over the spiky scrub, dropping swiftly. At last I could see the edge, and a green patch of the great creepers. For a time I hoped that I would be carried clear of the thorns.

Then they seemed suddenly to leap at me. I threw up my arms, to shelter my face, still clinging fiercely to the pistol.

In an instant, I was being dragged through the cruel yellow

spikes. There was a sharp, dry, crackling sound, as they broke beneath my weight. A thousand sharp, poisoned bayonets scratched at me, stabbed, cut.

Intolerable agony racked me. I screamed. The razor-sharp spikes were tipped with poison, so that the slightest scratch burned like liquid flame. And many of the stabbing points went deep.

It seems that I struck near the edge of the thicket. For a moment I hung there in the thorns. Then, as a harder puff of wind struck it, the balloon leaped into the air, dragging me free. I swung up like a pendulum. And down again, beyond the thorny scrub—over a strip of bare sand beside the thicket.

Bleeding rapidly from my cuts, and suffering unendurable pain from the poison in my wounds, I realized that I could not long remain conscious.

Moving in a haze of agony, I seized the red cable with one hand, put the muzzle of the automatic against it, pulled the trigger. The report was crashing, stunning. My right hand, holding the gun, was flung back by the recoil—I should have lost the weapon had it not been glued to my fingers. The cable was jerked with terrific force, almost breaking my left hand, with which I held it.

And it parted! I plunged downward, sprawled on the sand.

For a few minutes I remained conscious as I lay there on the hard, cold sand—the first soil, I recall thinking vaguely in my agony, that I had seen not covered with vegetation.

The clothing had been half stripped from my tortured body by the thorns. I was bleeding freely from several deeper cuts—I remember how dark the blood was, sinking into the white sand.

All my body throbbed with insufferable pain, from the poison in my wounds. As if I had been plunged into a sea of flame. Only my face had been spared.

Weakly, dizzy with pain, I tried to stagger to my feet. But a coil of the red web still clung about my legs. It tripped me, and I fell forward again, upon the white sand.

Fell into bitter despair. Into blind, hopeless rage at my inane lack of caution in leaving the machine. At my foolhardiness in venturing into the edge of the jungle. Fell into gentle oblivion. . . .

A curious sound drew me back into wakefulness. A thin,

high-pitched piping, pleasantly melodious. The musical notes beat insistently upon my brain, evidently originating quite near me.

On first awakening, I was aware of no bodily sensation. My mind was peculiarly dull and slow. I was unable to recall where I was. My first impression was that I was lying in bed in my old rooming place at Midland and that my alarm clock was ringing. But soon I realized that the liquid piping notes that had disturbed me came from no alarm.

I forced open heavy eyes. What startling nightmare was this? A tangle of green creepers, incredibly profuse. A wall of yellow thorns. A scarlet mountain beyond. And purple balloons floating in a rich blue sky.

I tried to sit up. My body burst into screaming agony when I moved. And I sank back. My skin was stiff with dry blood. The deeper wounds were aching. And the poison from the thorns seemed to have stiffened my muscles, so that the slightest motion brought exquisite pain.

The melodious pipings had been abruptly silenced at my movement. But now they rose again. Behind me. I tried to turn my head.

Recollection was returning swiftly. My uncle's telegram. The flight through space and time. My expedition to the jungle's edge, and its horrible sequel. I still lay where I had fallen, on the bare sand below the spiky scrub.

I groaned despite myself, with the pain of my stiff body. The thin musical notes stopped again. And the thing that had voiced them glided around before me, so that I could see it.

A strange and wonderful being.

Its body was slender, flexible as an eel. Perhaps five feet long, it was little thicker than my upper arm. Soft, short golden down or fur covered it. Part of it was coiled on the sand; its head was lifted two or three feet.

A small head, not much larger than my fist. A tiny mouth, with curved lips full and red as a woman's. And large eyes, dark and intelligent. They were deeply violet, almost luminous. Somehow they looked human, perhaps only because they mirrored the human qualities of curiosity and pity.

Aside from red mouth and dark eyes, the head had no human features. Golden down covered it. On the crown was a plume or crest of brilliant blue. But strange as it was, it possessed a certain beauty. A beauty of exquisite proportion, of smooth curves.

Curious wing-like appendages or mantles grew from the sides of the sleek, golden body, just below the head. Now they were stiffened, extended as if for flight. They were very white, of thin soft membrane. Their snowy surfaces were finely veined with scarlet.

Other than these white, membranous mantles, the creature had no limbs. Slim, long, pliant body, covered with golden fur. Small, delicate head, with red mouth and warm dark eyes, crested with blue. And delicate wings thrust out from its sides.

I stared at it.

Even at first sight, I did not fear it, though I was helpless. It seemed to have a magnetic power that filled me with quiet confidence, assured me that it meant only good.

The lips pursed themselves. And the thin, musical piping sound came from them again. Was the thing speaking to me? I uttered the first phrases that entered my mind, "Hello. Who are we, anyhow?"

CHAPTER V

The Mother

The thing glided toward me swiftly, its smooth round golden body leaving a little twisting track in the white sand. It lowered its head a little. And it laid one of the white mantles across my forehead.

The strange red-veined membrane was soft, yet there was an odd firmness in its pressure against my skin. A vital warmth seemed to come from it—it was vibrant with energy, with life.

The pipings came again. And they seemed to stir vague response in my mind, to call dim thoughts into being. As the same sounds were repeated again and again, definite questions formed in my mind.

"What are you? How did you come here?"

Through some strange telepathy induced by the pressure of the mantle upon my head, I was grasping the thought in the piping words.

It was a little time before I was sufficiently recovered from my astonishment to speak. Then I replied slowly, phrasing my expressions carefully, and uttering them as distinctly as I could.

"I am a native of Earth. Of the great white globe you can see in the sky. I came here in a machine which moves through space and time. I left it, and was caught and jerked up into the air by one of those purple, floating things. I broke the web, and fell here. My body was so torn by the thorns that I cannot move."

The thing piped again. A single quavering note. It was repeated until its meaning formed in my mind.

"I understand."

"Who are you?" I ventured.

I got the meaning of the reply, as it was being piped for the third time. "I am the Mother. The Eternal Ones, who destroyed my people, pursue me. To escape them, I am going to the sea."

And the thin, musical tones came again. This time I understood them more easily.

"Your body seems slow to heal its hurts. Your mental force is feeble. May I aid you?"

"Of course," I said. "Anything you can do—"

"Lie still. Trust me. Do not resist. You must sleep." When the meaning of the notes came to me, I relaxed upon the sand, closed my eyes.

I could feel the warm, vibrant pressure of the mantle on my forehead. Vital, throbbing force seemed pulsing into me through it. I felt no fear, despite the strangeness of my situation. A living wave of confidence came over me. Serene trust in the power of this being. I felt a command to sleep. I did not resist it; a strong tide of vital energy swept me into oblivion.

It seemed but an instant later, though it must have been many hours, when an insistent voice called me back from sleep.

Vitality filled me. Even before I opened my eyes, I was conscious of a new and abounding physical vigor, of perfect health; I was bubbling with energy and high spirits. And I knew, by the complete absence of bodily pain, that my wounds were completely healed.

I opened my lids, saw the amazing creature that had called itself the Mother. Its smooth golden body coiled beside me on the sand. Its large, clear eyes watching me intently, with kind sympathy.

Abruptly I sat up. My limbs were stiff no longer. My body

was still dried with blood, clothed in my tattered garments;
the sticky scarlet coils of the web were still around me. But
my ragged wounds were closed. Only white scars showed
where they had been.

"Why, I'm well!" I told the Mother, thankfully. "How'd
you do it?"

The strange being piped melodiously, and I grasped the
meaning almost at once. "My vital force is stronger than your
own. I merely lent you energy."

I began tearing at the coils of the crimson web about me.
Their viscid covering seemed to have dried a little; otherwise I
might never have got them off. After a moment the Mother
glided forward and helped.

It used the white, membranous appendages like hands.
Though they appeared quite frail, they seemed able to grasp
the red cable powerfully when they were folded about it.

In a few minutes I was on my feet.

Again the Mother piped at me. I failed to understand,
though vague images were summoned to my mind. I knelt
down again on the sand, and the being glided toward me,
pressed the white, red-veined mantle once more against my
forehead. An amazing organ, that mantle, so delicately beautiful. So strong of grasp when used as a hand. And useful, as I
was to learn, as an organ of some strange sense.

The meaning of the pipings came to me clearly now, with
the warm, vibrant mantle touching my head.

"Adventurer, tell me more of your world, and how you
came here. My people are old, and I have vital powers beyond
your own. But we have never been able to go beyond the atmosphere of our planet. Even the Eternal Ones, with all their
machines, have never been able to bridge the gulf of space.
And it has been thought that the primary planet from which
you say you came is yet too hot for the development of life."

For many hours we talked, I in my natural voice, the
Mother in those weirdly melodious pipings. At first the transference of thought by the telepathy which the wonderful mantle made possible was slow and awkward. I, especially, had
trouble in receiving, and had many times to ask the Mother to
repeat a complex thought. But facility increased with practice,
and I at last was able to understand, quite readily, even when
the white membrane did not touch me.

The sun had been low when I woke. It set, and the dew fell

upon us. We talked on in the darkness. And the earth rose, illuminating the jungle with argent glory. Still we talked, until it was day again. For a time the air was quite cold. Wet with the abundant dew, I felt chilled, and shivered.

But the Mother touched me again with the white membrane. Quick, throbbing warmth seemed to flow from it into my body, and I felt cold no longer.

I told much of the world that I had left, and of my own insignificant life upon it. Told of the machine. Of the voyage across space, and back through aeons of time, to this young moon.

And the Mother told me of her life, and of her lost people.

She had been the leader of a community of beings that had lived on the highlands, near the source of the great river that I had seen. A community in some respects resembling those of ants or bees upon the earth. It had contained thousands of neuter beings, imperfectly developed females, workers. And herself, the only member capable of reproduction. She was now the sole survivor of that community.

It seemed that her race was very old, and had developed a high civilization. The Mother admitted that her people had had no machines or buildings of any kind. She declared that such things were marks of barbarism, and that her own culture was superior to mine.

"Once we had machines," she told me. "My ancient mothers lived in shells of metal and wood, such as you describe. And constructed machines to aid and protect their weak and inefficient bodies.

"But the machines tended to weaken their poor bodies still further. Their limbs atrophied, perished from lack of use. Even their brains were injured, for they lived an easy life, depending upon machines for existence, facing no new problems.

"Some of my people awoke to the danger. They left the cities, and returned to the forest and the sea, to live sternly, to depend upon their own minds and their own bodies, to remain living things, and not grow into cold machines.

"The mothers divided. And my people were those that returned to the forest."

"And what," I asked, "of those that remained in the city, that kept the machines?"

"They became the Eternal Ones—my enemies.

"Generation upon generation their bodies wasted away.

Until they were no longer natural animals. They became mere brains, with eyes and feeble tentacles. In place of bodies, they use machines. Living brains, with bodies of metal.

"Too weak, they became, to reproduce their kind. So they sought immortality, with their mechanical science. And still some of them live on, in their ugly city of metal—though for ages no young have been born among them. The Eternal Ones.

"But at last they die, because that is the way of life. Even with all their knowledge they cannot live forever. One by one, they fall. Their strange machines are still, with rotting brains in their cases.

"And the few thousands that live attacked my people. They planned to take the Mothers. To change their offspring with their hideous arts, and make of them new brains for the machines.

"The Mothers were many, when the war began. And my people a thousand times more. Now only I remain. But it was no easy victory for the Eternal Ones. My people fought bravely. Many an ancient brain they killed. But the Eternal Ones had great engines of war, that we could not escape, nor destroy with our vital energy.

"All the Mothers save myself were taken. And all destroyed themselves, rather than have their children made into living machines.

"I alone escaped. Because my people sacrificed their lives for me. In my body are the seed of a new race. I seek a home for my children. I have left our old land on the shores of the lake, and I am going down to the sea. There we shall be far from the Eternal Land. And perhaps our enemies will never find us.

"But the Eternal Ones know I have escaped. They are hunting me. Hunting me with their strange machines."

When day came, I felt very hungry. What was I to do for food in this weird jungle? Even if I could find fruits or nuts, how could I tell whether they were poisonous? I mentioned my hunger.

"Come," the Mother piped.

She glided away across the white sand, with easy, sinuous grace. Very beautiful, she was. Slim body, smooth, rounded. Compactly trim. The golden down was bright in the sunlight; sapphire rays played over the blue plume upon her head. The wondrous, red-veined mantles at her sides shone brilliantly.

Regarding her strange beauty, I stood still for a moment, and then moved after her slowly, absently.

She turned back suddenly, with something like humor flashing in her great dark violet eyes.

"Is your great body so slow you cannot keep up with me?" she piped, almost derisively. "Shall I carry you?" Her eyes were mocking.

For answer I crouched, leaped into the air. My wild spring carried me a score of feet above her, and beyond. I had the misfortune to come down head first upon the sand, though I received no injury.

I saw laughter in her eyes, as she glided swiftly to me, and grasped my arm with one of the white mantles to assist me to my feet.

"You could travel splendidly if there were two of you, one to help the other out of the thorns," she said quaintly.

A little embarrassed by her mockery, I followed meekly.

We reached a mass of the green creeper. Without hesitation, she pushed on through the feathery foliage. I broke through behind her. She led the way to one of the huge white flowers, bent it toward her, and crept into it like a golden bee.

In a moment she emerged with mantles cupped up to hold a good quantity of white, crystalline powder which she had scraped from the inside of the huge calyx.

She made me hold my hands, and dropped part of the powder into them. She lifted what she had left, upon the other mantle, and began delicately licking at it with her lips.

I tasted it. It was sweet, with a peculiar, though not at all unpleasant, acid flavor. It formed a sort of gum as it was wetted in my mouth, and this softened and dissolved as I continued to chew. I took a larger bite, and soon finished all the Mother had given me. We visited another bloom. This time I reached in, and scraped out the powder with my own hand. (The crystals must have been formed for the same purpose as the nectar in terrene flowers—to attract raiders, which carry the pollen.)

I divided my booty with the Mother. She accepted but little, and I found enough of the sweetish powder in the calyx to satisfy my own hunger.

"Now I must go on down to the sea," she piped. "Too long already have I delayed with you. For I carry the seed of my race; I must not neglect the great work that has fallen upon me.

"But I was glad to know of your strange planet. And it is good to be with an intelligent being again, when I had been so long alone. I wish I could stay longer with you. But my wishes are not my master."

Thoughts of parting from her were oddly disturbing. My feeling for her was partly gratitude for saving my life and partly something else. A sense of comradeship. We were companion adventurers in this weird and lonely jungle. Solitude and my human desire for society of any sort drew me toward her.

Then came an idea. She was going down the valley to the sea. And my way led in the same direction, until I could see the triple peak that marked the location of the machine.

"May I travel with you," I asked her, "until we reach the mountain where I left the machine in which I came to your world?"

The Mother looked at me with fine dark eyes. And glided suddenly nearer. A white membranous mantle folded about my hand, with warm pressure.

"I am glad you wish to go with me," she piped. "But you must think of the danger. Remember that I am hunted by the Eternal Ones. They will doubtless destroy you if they find us together."

"I have a weapon," I said. "I'll put up a scrap for you, if we get in a tight place. And besides, I'd very likely be killed, in one way or another, if I tried to travel alone."

"Let us go, Adventurer."

Thus it was decided.

I had dropped the camera, the binoculars, and the vacuum bottle when the balloon-creature jerked me into the air. They were lost in the jungle. But I still had the automatic. It had remained in my hand—stuck to it, in fact—when I fell upon the sand. I carried it with me.

The Mother objected to the weapon. Because it was a machine, and machines weakened all that used them. But I insisted that we should have to fight machines, if the Eternal Ones caught us, and that fire could be best fought with fire. She yielded gracefully.

"But my vital force will prove stronger than your rude slaying machine, Adventurer," she maintained.

We set out almost immediately. She glided off along the strip of bare sand beside the wall of thorny yellow scrub. And began my instruction in the ways of life upon the moon, by informing me that there was always such a clear zone about a thicket of the thorn-brush, because its roots generated a poison in the soil which prevented the growth of other vegetation near them.

When we had traveled two or three miles, we came to a crystal pool, where the abundant dew had collected at the bottom of a bare, rocky slope. We drank there. Then the Mother plunged into it joyously. With white mantles folded tight against her sides, she flashed through the water like a golden eel. I was glad to remove my own garments, and wash the grime and dried blood from my body.

I was donning my tattered clothing again, and the Mother was lying beside me, at the edge of the pool, with eyes closed, drying her golden fur in the sunshine, when I saw the ghostly bars.

Seven thin upright pillars of light, ringed about us. Straight bars of pale white radiance. They stood like phantom columns about us, enclosing a space ten yards across. They were not above two inches in diameter. And they were quite transparent, so I could see the green jungle and the yellow wall of thorn-brush quite plainly through them.

I was not particularly alarmed. In fact, I thought the ghostly pillars only some trick of my vision. I rubbed my eyes, and said rather carelessly to the Mother:

"Are the spirits building a fence around us? Or is it just my eyes?"

She lifted her golden, blue-crested head quickly. Her violet eyes went wide. I saw alarm in them. Terror. And she moved with astonishing speed. Drew her slender length into a coil. Leaped. And seized my shoulder as she leaped, with one of her mantles.

She jerked me between two of those strange columns of motionless light, out of the area they enclosed.

I fell on the sand, got quickly to my feet.

"What——" I began.

"The Eternal Ones," her sweet, whistling tones came swiftly. "They have found me. Even here, they reach me with their evil power. We must go on, quickly."

She glided swiftly away. Still buttoning my clothing, I followed, keeping pace with her easily, with my regular leaps of half a dozen yards. Followed, wondering vainly what danger there might have been in the pillars of ghostly light.

CHAPTER VI

Pursuit!

We skirted a continuous wall of the spiky yellow scrub.

The strip of clear ground we followed was usually fifty to one hundred yards wide. The mass of yellow thorn-brush, the poison from whose roots had killed the vegetation here, rose dense and impenetrable to our right. To the left of our open way limitless stretches covered with the green creeper. Undulating seas of feathery emerald foilage. Scattered with huge white blooms. Broken, here and there, with strange plants of various kinds. Beyond were other clumps of the yellow scrub. A red mountain wall rose in the distance. Huge purple balloons swayed here and there upon this weird, sunlit moonscape, anchored with their red cables.

I suppose we followed that open strip for ten miles. I was beginning to breathe heavily, as violent exercise always made me do in the moon's light atmosphere. The Mother showed no fatigue.

Abruptly she paused ahead of me, and glided into a sort of tunnel through the forest of thorns. A passage five feet wide and six feet high, with the yellow spokes arching over it. The floor was worn smooth, hard-packed as if by constant use. It seemed almost perfectly straight, for I could see down it for a considerable distance. Twilight filled it, filtering down through the unbroken mass of cruel bayonets above.

"I am not eager to use this path," the Mother told me. "For they who made it are hostile things. And though not very intelligent, they are able to resist my vital force, so that I cannot control them. We shall be helpless if they discover us.

"But there is no other way. We must cross this forest of thorns. And I am glad to be out of sight in this tunnel. Perhaps the Eternal Ones will lose us again. We must hasten, and hope that we encounter no rightful user of the path. If one appears, we must hide."

I was placed immediately at a disadvantage upon entering the tunnel, for I could no longer take the long leaps by which

I had been traveling. My pace became a sort of trot. I had to hold my head down, to save it from the poisoned thorns above.

The Mother glided easily before me, to my relief not in such haste us before. Slender and strong and trimly beautiful —for all her strangeness. I was glad she had let me come with her. Even if peril threatened.

I found breath for speech.

"Those ghostly bars," I panted. "What were they?"

"The Eternal Ones possess strange powers of science," came the thin, whistling notes of her reply. "Something like the television you told me of. But more highly developed. They were able to see us, back by the pool.

"And the shining bars were projected through space by their rays of force. They meant some harm to us. Just what, I do not know. It is apparently a new weapon, which they did not use in the war."

We must have gone many miles through the tunnel. It had been almost perfectly straight. There had been no branches or cross-passages. We had come through no open space. Roof and walls of yellow thorns had been unbroken. I was wondering what sort of creature it might be, that had made a path through the thorns so long and straight.

The Mother stopped suddenly, turned back to face me.

"One of the makers of the trail is approaching," she piped. "I feel it coming. Wait for me a bit."

She sank in golden coils upon the trail. Her head was raised a little. The mantles were extended stiffly. Always before they had been white, except for their fine veining of red. But now soft, rosy colors flushed them. Her full red lips were parted a little, and her eyes had become strange, wide, staring. They seemed to look past me, to gaze upon scenes far-off, invisible to ordinary sight.

For long seconds she remained motionless, violet eyes distant, staring.

Then she stirred abruptly. Rose upon tawny, golden coils. Alarm was in her great eyes, in her thin, melodious tones.

"The creature comes behind us. Upon this trail. We have scant time to reach the open. We must go swiftly."

She waited for me to begin my stumbling run, glided easily beside me. I moved awkwardly. With only the moon's slight gravitational pull to hold me to the trail, I was in constant danger from the thorns.

For tortured hours, it seemed to me, we raced down the straight passage, through the unbroken forest of yellow thorns. My heart was laboring painfully; my breath came in short gasps of agony. My body was not equipped for such prolonged exertions in the light air.

The Mother, just ahead of me, glided along with effortless ease. I knew that she could easily have left me, had she wished.

At last I stumbled, fell headlong, and did not have energy to get at once to my feet. My lungs burned, my heart was a great ache. Sweat was pouring from me; my temples throbbed; and a red mist obscured my sight.

"Go—on," I gasped, between panting breaths. "I'll try—to stop—it."

I fumbled weakly for my gun.

The Mother stopped, came back to me. Her piping notes were quick, insistent. "Come. We are near the open now. And the thing is close. You must come!"

With a soft, flexible mantle she seized my arm. It seemed to me that a wave of new strength and energy came into me from it. At any rate, I staggered to my feet, lurched forward again. As I rose, I cast a glance backward.

A dark, indistinguishable shape was in view. So large that it filled almost the whole width of the tunnel. A dim circle of the pale light of the thorn forest showed around it.

I ran on . . . on . . . on.

My legs rose and fell, rose and fell, like the insensate levers of an automaton I felt no sensation from them. Even my lungs had ceased to burn, since the Mother touched me. And my heart ached no longer. It seemed that I floated beside my body, and watched it run, run, run with the monotonously repeated movements of a machine.

My eyes were upon the Mother before me.

Gliding so swiftly through the twilight of the tunnel. Trim, round golden body. White mantles extended stiffly, wing-like, as if to help carry her. Delicate head raised, the blue plume upon it flashing.

I watched that blue plume as I ran. It danced mockingly before me, always retreating. Always just beyond my grasp. I followed it through the blinding mists of fatigue, when all the rest of the world melted into a gray blue, streaked with bloody crimson.

I was astonished when we came out into the sunlight. A strip of sand below the yellow wall of thorns. Cool green foliage beyond, a sea of green. Sinister purple balloons above it, straining on crimson cables. Far-off, a scarlet line of mountains, steep and rugged.

The Mother turned to the left.

I followed, automatically, mechanically. I was beyond feeling. I could see the bright moonscape, but it was strange no longer. Even the threat of the purple balloons was remote, without consequence.

I do not know how far we ran, beside the forest of thorns, before the Mother turned again and led the way into a mass of creepers.

"Lie still," she piped. "The creature may not find us."

Gratefully, I flung myself down in the delicate fronds. I lay flat, with my eyes closed, my breath coming in great, painful, sobbing gasps. The Mother folded my hand in her soft mantle again, and immediately, it seemed, I felt relief, though I still breathed heavily.

"Your reserve of vital energy is very low," she commented.

I took the automatic from my pocket, examined it to see that it was ready for action. I had cleaned and loaded it before we started. I saw the other raising her blue-crested head cautiously. I got to my knees, peered back along the bare strip of sand, down which we had come.

I saw the thing advancing swiftly along the sand.

A sphere of bright crimson. Nearly five feet in diameter. It rolled along, following the way we had come.

"It has found us!" the Mother piped, very softly. "And my vital power cannot reach through its armor. It will suck the fluids from our bodies."

I looked down at her. She had drawn her slender body into a golden coil. Her head rose in the center, and the mantles were outspread, pure white, veined with fine lines of scarlet, and frail as the petals of a lily. Her great dark eyes were grave and calm; there was no trace of panic in them.

I raised the automatic, determined to show no more fear than she, and to give my best to save her.

Now the scarlet globe was no more than fifty yards away. I could distinguish the individual scales of its armor, looking like plates of horn covered with ruby lacquer. No limbs or external appendages were visible then. But I saw dark ovals upon the shell, appearing at the top and seeming to drop down, as the thing rolled.

I began shooting.

At such a distance there was no possibility of missing. I knelt in the leaves of the green creeper, and emptied the magazine into the globe.

It continued to roll on toward us, without change of speed. But a deep, angry drumming sound came from within it. A reverberating roar of astonishing volume. After a few moments, I heard it repeated from several points about us. Low and distant rumblings, almost like thunder.

In desperate haste, I was filling the clip with fresh cartridges. Before I could snap it back into the gun, the creature was upon us.

Until it stopped, it had presented a sphere of unbroken surface. But suddenly six long, glistening black tentacles reached out of it, one from each of the black ovals I had seen evenly spaced about the red shell. They were a dozen feet long, slender, covered with thin black skin corrugated with innumerable wrinkles, and glistening with tiny drops of moisture. At the base of each was a single, staring, black-lidded eye.

One of those black tentacles was thrust toward me. It reeked with an overpowering, fetid odor. At its extremity was a sharp, hooked claw, beside a black opening. I think the creature sucked its food through those hideous, retractable tentacles.

I got the loaded clip into the gun, hastily snapped a cartridge into the chamber. Shrinking back from the writhing tentacular arm, I fired seven shots, as rapidly as I could press the trigger, into the black-lidded eye.

The deep drumming notes came from within the red shell again. The black tentacles writhed, thrashed about, and became suddenly stiff and rigid. The sound of it died to a curious rattle, and then ceased.

"You have killed it," the Mother whistled musically. "You use your machine well, and it is more powerful than I thought. Perhaps, after all, we may yet live."

As if in ominous answer, a reverberating roll of distant drumming came from the tangle of yellow thorns. She listened, and the white mantles were stiffened in her alarm.

"But it has called to its kind. Soon many will be here. We must hasten away."

Though I was still so tired that movement was torture, I rose and followed the Mother, as she glided on along the sand.

Only a moment did I pause to examine the very interesting creature I had killed. It seemed unique, both in shape and in means of locomotion. It must have developed the spherical shell of red armor through ages of life in the spiky scrub. By drawing its limbs inside, it was able to crash through the thorns without suffering any hurt. I supposed it contrived to roll along by some rhythmic muscular contraction, inside the shell—such movement being much easier on the moon that it would be on earth, because of the lesser gravity. Where it could not roll, it dragged or lifted itself with the long, muscular appendages that I have called tentacles.

Since we were in the open air again, I was able to resume my progression by deliberate, measured leaps, which carried me forward as fast as the Mother could move, and with much less effort than I had spent in running. I had a few moments of rest as I glided through the air between leaps, which compensated for the fiercer effort of each spring.

From time to time I looked back, nervously. At first I could see only the scarlet shell of the dead creature, there by the green vines where we had killed it. Always smaller, until it was hardly visible.

Then I saw other spheres. Emerging from the tangle of yellow thornbrush. Rolling along the strip of bare soil, to congregate about the dead being. Finally I saw that they had started in our direction, rolling along rather faster than we could move.

"They are coming," I told the Mother. "And more of them than I can kill."

"They are implacable," came her piping reply. "When one of them sets out upon the trail of some luckless creature, it never stops until it has sucked the body fluids from it—or until it is dead."

"Anything we can do?" I questioned.

"There is a rock ahead of us, beyond that thicket. A small hill, whose sides are so steep they will not be able to climb it. If we can reach it in time, we may be able to scramble to the top.

"It will be only temporary escape, since the creatures will never leave so long as we are alive upon it. But we shall delay our fate, at least—if we can reach it in time."

Again I looked back. Our pursuers were rolling along like a group of red marbles, at the edge of the yellow forest. Gaining upon us—swiftly.

The Mother glided along more rapidly. The white mantles were stiffly extended from her golden sides, and aglow with rosy colors. The muscles beneath her furry skin rippled evenly, gracefully.

I increased the force of my own leaps.

We rounded an arm of the tangle of scrub, came in sight of the rock. A jutting mass of black granite. Its sides leaped up steep and bare from a mass of green creepers. Green moss crowned it. Thirty feet high it was. Perhaps a hundred in length.

Our pursuers were no longer merely marbles when we saw the rock. They had grown to the size of baseballs. Rolling swiftly after us.

The Mother glided on, a tireless strength in her graceful tawny body. And I leaped desperately, straining to drive myself as fast as possible.

We turned. Broke through the thick masses of verdure to the rock. Stood beneath its sheer wall, grim and black.

The red spheres were no more than a hundred yards behind. A sudden rumble of drums came from them, when we halted by the rock. I could see the dark ovals on their glistening red armor, that marked their eyes and the ends of their concealed tentacles.

"I can never climb that," the Mother was piping.

"I can leap up!" I cried. "Earth muscles. I'll carry you up."

"Better that one should live than both of us die," she said. "I can delay them, until you reach the top."

She started gliding back, toward the swiftly rolling spheres.

I bent, snatched her up.

It was the first time that I had felt her body. The golden fur was short, and very soft. The rounded body beneath it was firm, muscular, warm and vibrant. It throbbed with life. I felt that a strange sudden surge of energy was coming into me from contact with it.

I threw her quickly over my shoulder, ran forward a few steps, leaped desperately up at that sheer wall of black granite.

My own weight, on the moon, was only thirty pounds. The Mother, compact and strong though she was, weighed no more than a third as much. Combined, our weight was then some forty pounds. But, as she had realized, it was an apparently hopeless undertaking to attempt to hurl that mass to the top of the cliff before us.

At first I thought I should make it, as we soared swiftly up and up, toward the crown of red moss. Then I realized that we should strike the face of the cliff before we reached the top.

The face of the black rock was sheer. But my searching eyes caught a little projecting ledge. As we fell against the vertical cliff, my fingers caught that ledge. A moment of dreadful uncertainty, for the ledge was mossy, slippery.

CHAPTER VII

The Eternal Ones Follow!

My left hand slipped suddenly off. But the right held. I drew myself upward. The Mother slipped from my shoulder to the top of the rock. Grasped my left hand with one of the white mantles, drew me to safety.

Trembling from the strain of it, I got to my feet upon the soft scarlet moss, and surveyed our fortress. The moss-covered surface was almost level, a score of feet wide at the middle, where we stood, and a hundred in length. On all sides the walls were steep, though not everywhere so steep as where I had leaped up.

"Thank you, Adventurer," the Mother whistled musically. "You have saved my life, and the lives of all my people to come."

"I was merely repaying a debt," I told her.

We watched the red globes. Very soon they reached the foot of the cliff. The rumble of drums floated up from the group of them. And they scattered, surrounding the butte.

Presently we discovered that they were attempting to climb up. They were not strong enough to make the leap as I had done. But they were finding fissures and ledges upon which their long tentacles could find a grasp, drawing themselves up.

We patrolled the sides of the rock regularly, and I shot those which seemed to be making the best progress. I was able to aim carefully at an eye or the base of a tentacle. And usually a single shot was enough to send the climber rolling back down to the green jungle.

The view from our stronghold was magnificent. On one side was an endless wall of yellow scrub, with crimson mountains towering above it in the distance. On the other, the green tangle of the luxuriant creepers swept down to the wide silver river. Yellow and green mottled the slope that stretched up to scarlet hills beyond.

We held out for an entire day.

The sun sank beyond the red mountains when we had been upon the butte only an hour or two. A dark night would have terminated our adventures on the spot. But fortunately the huge white disk of the earth rose almost immediately after sunset, and gave sufficient light throughout the night to enable us to see the spheres that persisted in attempting to climb the walls of our fort.

It was late on the following afternoon that I used my last shot. I turned to the Mother with the news that I could no longer keep the red spheres from the walls, that they would soon be overwhelming us.

"It does not matter," she piped. "The Eternal Ones have found us again."

Looking nervously about, I saw the bars of ghostly light once more. Seven thin upright pillars of silvery radiance, standing in a ring about us. They had exactly the same appearance as those from which we had fled at the pool.

"I have felt them watching for some time," she said. "Before, we escaped by running away. Now that is impossible."

Calmly she coiled her tawny length. The white mantles were folded against her golden fur. Her small head sank upon her coils, blue crest erect above it. Her violet eyes were grave, calm, alert. They reflected neither fear nor despair.

The seven pillars of light about us became continually brighter.

One of the red spheres, with black tentacles extended, dragged itself upon the top of the butte, with us. The Mother saw it, but paid it no heed. It was outside the ring formed by the seven pillars. I stood still, within that ring, besides the Mother, watching—waiting.

The seven columns of light grew brighter.

Then it seemed that they were no longer merely light, but solid metal.

At the same instant, I was blinded with a flash of light, intolerably bright. A splintering crash of sound smote my ears, sharp as the crack of a rifle, infinitely louder. A wave of pain flashed over my body, as if I had received a severe electric shock. I had a sense of abrupt movement, as if the rock beneath my feet had been jarred by a moonquake.

Then we were no longer upon the rock.

I was standing upon a broad, smooth metal plate. About its edge rose seven metal rods, shining with a white light, their positions corresponding exactly to the seven ghostly pillars. The Mother was coiled on the metal plate beside me, her violet eyes still cool and quiet, revealing no surprise.

But I was dazed with astonishment.

For we were no longer in the jungle. The metal plate upon which I stood was part of a complex mechanism, of bars and coils of shining wire, and huge tubes of transparent crystal, which stood in the center of a broad open court, paved with bright, worn metal.

About the court towered buildings. Lofty, rectangular edifices of metal and transparent crystal. They were not beautiful structures. Nor were they in good repair. The metal was covered with ugly red oxide. Many of the crystal panels were shattered.

Along the metal-paved streets, and on the wide courtyard about us, things were moving. Not human beings. Not evidently, living things at all. But grotesque things of metal. Machines. They had no common standard of form; few seemed to resemble any others. They had apparently been designed with a variety of shapes, to fill a variety of purposes. But many had a semblance to living things that was horrible mockery.

"This is the land of the Eternal Ones," the Mother piped to me softly. "These are the beings that destroyed my people, seeking new brains for their worn-out machines."

"But how did we get here?" I demanded.

"Evidently they have developed means of transmitting matter through space. A mere technical question. Resolving matter into energy, transmitting the energy without loss on a light beam, condensing it again into the original atoms.

"It is not remarkable that the Eternal Ones can do such things. When they gave up all that is life, for such power. When they sacrificed their bodies for machines. Should they not have some reward?"

"It seems impossible—"

"It must, to you. The science of your world is young. If you have television after a few hundred years, what will you not have developed after a hundred thousand?

"Even to the Eternal Ones, it is new. It is only in the time of my own life that they have been able to transmit objects between two stations, without destroying their identity. And they have never before used this apparatus, with carrier rays that could reach out to disintegrate our bodies upon the rock, and create a reflecting zone of interference that would focus the beam here—"

Her piping notes broke off sharply. Three grotesque machines were advancing upon us, about the platform. Queer bright cases, with levels and wheels projecting from them. Jointed metal limbs. Upon the top of each was a transparent crystal dome, containing a strange, shapeless gray mass. A soft helpless gray thing, with huge black staring eyes. The brain in the machine! The Eternal One.

Horrible travesties of life, were those metal things. At first they appeared almost alive, with their quick, sure movements. But mechanical sounds came from them, little clatterings and hummings. They were stark and ugly.

And their eyes roughened my skin with dread. Huge, black, and cold. There was nothing warm in them, nothing human, nothing kind. They were as emotionless as polished lenses. And filled with menace.

"They shall not take me alive!" the Mother piped, lifting herself beside me on tawny coils.

Then, as if something had snapped like a taut wire in my mind, I ran at the nearest of the Eternal Ones, my eyes searching swiftly for a weapon.

It was one of the upright metal rods that I seized. Its lower end was set in an oddly shaped mass of white crystal, which I took to be an insulator of some kind. It shattered when I threw my weight on the rod. And the rod came free in my hands, the white glow vanishing from it, so I saw it was copper.

Thus I was provided with a massive metal club, as heavy as I could readily swing. On earth, it would have weighed far more than I could lift.

Raising it over my head, I sprang in front of the foremost of the advancing machines—a case of bright metal, moving stiffly upon metal limbs, with a dome-shaped shell of crystal upon it, which housed the helpless gray brain, with its black, unpleasant eyes. I saw little tentacles—feeble translucent fingers—reaching from the brain to touch controlling levers.

The machine paused before me. An angry, insistent buzzing came from it. A great, hooked, many-jointed metal lever reached out from it suddenly, as if to seize me.

And I struck, bringing the copper bar down upon the transparent dome with all my strength. The crystal was tough. But the inertia of the copper bar was as great as it would have been upon the earth; its hundreds of pounds came down with a force indeed terrific.

The dome was shattered. And the gray brain smashed into red pulp.

The Eternal Ones would certainly have been able to seize the Mother, without suffering any harm. And probably any other creature of the moon that might have been brought with her on the matter-transmitting beam. But they were not equipped for dealing with a being whose muscles were the stronger ones of earth.

The two fellows of the Eternal One I had destroyed fell upon me. Though the copper bar was not very heavy, it was oddly hard to swing, because of its great inertia. The metal limbs of the third machine closed about my body, even as I crushed the brain in the second with another smashing blow.

I squirmed desperately, but I was unable to twist about to get in a position to strike.

Then the Mother was gliding toward me. Blue crest erect upon her golden head, eager light of battle flashing in her violet eyes. From her smooth, tawny sides the mantles were stiffly outstretched. And they were almost scarlet with the flashing lights that played through them. My momentary despair vanished; I felt that she was invincible.

She almost reached me. And then rose upon her glossy coils, and gazed at the brain in the transparent dome of the machine that held me, her membranes still alight.

Abruptly the machine released me; its metal limbs were relaxed, motionless.

My encrimsoned copper mace rose and descended once more, and the machine fell with a clatter upon its side.

"My mental energy is greater than that of the Eternal One," the Mother piped in calm explanation. "I was able to interfere with its neural processes to cause paralysis." She looked about us suddenly.

"But smash the delicate parts of this machine that brought us here. So that if we have the good fortune to escape, they cannot soon bring us back. I know it is the only one they have, and it does not look as if it could be quickly repaired."

My club was busy again. Delicate coils were battered beneath it. Complex prisms and mirrors and lenses shattered. Delicate wires and grids in crystal shells, which must have been electron tubes, destroyed.

The three machines we had wrecked had been the only ones near. But a score or more of others were soon approaching across the metal-paved court, producing buzzing sounds as if of anger and excitement. Some of them were near before my work was done.

Too many of them to battle. We must attempt an escape.

I stooped, picked up the Mother's warm, downy body, and ran across the platform, toward the ring of approaching machine-beings. Near them, I leaped, as high and as far as I could.

The spring carried me over them, and a good many yards beyond. In a moment I was in the middle of a worn pavement of metal. The street, almost empty of the machines, ran between ancient and ugly buildings, toward a lofty wall of some material black and brilliant as obsidian.

I hastened desperately toward the wall, moving with great leaps. The Eternal Ones followed in humming, clattering confusion, falling swiftly behind.

They had been taken quite by surprise, of course. And, as the Mother had said, dependence upon the machine had not developed in them the ability to respond quickly to emergencies.

As we later discovered, some of the machines could travel much faster than could we. But, as I have remarked, the things were not of a standard design, all differing. And none of those behind us happened to be of the fastest type.

I do not doubt that they could easily have destroyed us, as we fled. But their object would have been defeated. They wanted the Mother alive.

We reached the shining black wall well ahead of our pursuers. Its surface was smooth and perpendicular; it was fully as high as the cliff up which I had leaped with the Mother. And there was no projecting ledge to save us if I fell short.

I paused, dropping the heavy mace.

"You could toss me up," the Mother suggested. "Then leap."

There was no time for delay. She coiled quickly up into a golden sphere. I hurled her upward, like a football. She vanished over the top of the wall. I lifted the mace, threw it up, and to one side, so it would not strike her.

The Eternal Ones were close behind. A mob-like group of grotesque machines. Buzzing angrily. One of them flung some missile. There was a crashing explosion against the black wall, a flare of green light. I realized the danger of being separated from the Mother, even as I leaped.

My spring carried me completely over the wall, which was only some five or six feet thick.

I descended into a luxuriant tangle of the green creepers. Foot-thick stems covered the ground in an unbroken network, feathery leaves rising from them higher than my head. I fell on my side in the delicate foliage, struggled quickly to my feet. The green fronds cut off my view in all directions, though I could see the top of the black wall above.

Before I struck the ground I had glimpsed a vast green plain lying away eastward to the horizon. In the north was a distant line of red mountains. The city of the Eternal Ones lay westward.

I saw nothing of the Mother; I could not, in truth, see a dozen feet through the exotic jungle.

"This way," her cautious whistling tones reached me in a moment. "Here is your weapon."

I broke through the masses of delicate fronds in the direction of the sound, found the Mother unharmed, coiled in a golden circle beside the copper bar. She glided silently away; I picked up the bar and followed as rapidly and quietly as I could.

Once I looked back, when we passed a narrow open space, and saw a little group of the Eternal Ones standing upon the black wall. They must have been looking after us, but I do not suppose they saw us.

For the rest of the day—it was early afternoon when we escaped—and all night when the jungle was weird and silvery in the earth light, and until late on the following day, we hastened on. We did not stop except to drink and bathe at a little stream, and to scrape the sweet white powder from a few of the great argent flowers we passed. We ate as we moved. The jungle of creepers was unbroken; we were always hidden in the luxuriant, delicate foliage.

At first I had been sure we would be followed. But as the hours passed and there was no sign of pursuit, my spirits rose. I doubted now that the Eternal Ones could follow the trail swiftly enough to overtake us. But I still carried the copper mace.

The Mother was less optimistic than I.

"I know they are following," she told me. "I feel them. But we may lose them. If they cannot repair the machine which you wrecked—and I am sure they cannot do it soon."

We had approached a rocky slope, and the Mother found a little cave, beneath an overhanging ledge, in which we rested. Totally exhausted, I threw myself down, and slept like a dead man.

It was early on the next morning when the Mother woke me. She lay coiled at the entrance of the cave, the frail mantles stiffened and flushed a little with rosy light, violet eyes grave and watchful.

"The Eternal Ones follow," she piped. "They are yet far-off. But we must go on."

CHAPTER VIII

An Earth Man Fights

Climbing to the top of the rocky slope, we came out upon a vast plateau, covered with green moss. The level surface was broken here and there by low hills; but no other vegetation was in view before us. At a distance, the plain resembled a weird desert covered with green snow.

It took six days to cross the moss-grown table-land. We finished the white powder we had carried with us on the fourth day; and we found no water on the fifth or sixth. Though, of course, those days were of only eighteen hours each, we were in a sorry plight when we descended into a valley green with the creepers, watered with a crystal stream whose water seemed the sweetest I had ever tasted.

We ate and rested for two nights and a day, before we went on—though the Mother insisted that the Eternal Ones still followed.

Then, for seventeen days, we followed down the stream, which was joined by countless tributaries until it became a majestic river. On the seventeenth day, the river flowed into a still greater one, which came down a valley many miles wide, covered with yellow thorn-brush and green creepers, and infested with thousands of the purple balloon-creatures, which I had learned to avoid by keeping to the green jungle, where they could not throw their webs with accuracy.

We swam the river, and continued down the eastern bank —it was flowing generally south. Five days later we came in view of a triple peak I well remembered.

Next morning we left the jungle, and climbed up to the little moss-carpeted plateau where I had left the machine. I had feared that it somehow would be gone, or wrecked. But it lay just as I had left it on the day after I landed on the moon. Bright, polished, window-studded wall of armor, between two projecting plates of gleaming copper.

We reached the door, the Mother gliding beside me.

Trembling with a great eagerness, I turned the knob and opened it. Everything was in order, just as I had left it. The oxygen cylinders, the batteries, the food refrigerator, the central control table, with the chart lying upon it.

In a week—if the mechanism worked as I hoped it would— I should be back upon the earth. Back on Long Island. Ready to report to my uncle, and collect the first payment of my fifty thousand a year.

Still standing on the narrow deck outside the door, I looked down at the Mother.

She was coiled at my feet. The blue plume upon her golden head seemed to droop. The white mantles were limp, dragging. Her violet eyes, staring up at me, somehow seemed wistful and sad.

Abruptly an ache sprang into my heart, and my eyes dimmed, so that the bright golden image of her swam before me. I had hardly realized what her companionship had come to mean to me, in our long days together. Strange as her body was, the Mother had come to be almost human in my thoughts. Loyal, courageous, kind—a comrade.

"You must go with me," I stammered, in a voice gone oddly husky. "Don't know whether the machine will ever get back to earth or not. But at least it will carry us out of reach of the Eternal Ones."

For the first time, the musical pipings of the Mother seemed broken and uneven, as if with emotion.

"No. We have been together long, Adventurer. And parting is not easy. But I have a great work. The seed of my kind is in me, and it must not die. The Eternal Ones are near. But I will not give up the battle until I am dead."

Abruptly she lifted her tawny length beside me. The limp, pallid mantles were suddenly bright and strong again. They seized my hands in a grasp convulsively tight. The Mother gazed up at my face, for a little time, with deep violet eyes—earnest and lonely and wistful, with the tragedy of her race in them.

Then she dropped, and glided swiftly away.

I looked after her with misty eyes, until she was half across the plateau. On her way to the sea, to find a home for the new race she was to rear. With a leaden heart, and an aching constriction in my throat, I climbed through the oval door, into the machine, and fastened it.

But I did not approach the control table. I stood at the little round windows, watching the Mother gliding away, across the carpet of moss. Going ahead alone . . . the last of her race. . . .

Then I looked in the other direction, and saw the Eternal Ones. She had said the machines were near. I saw five of them. They were moving swiftly across the plateau, the way we had come.

Five grotesque machines. Their bright metal cases were larger than those of the ones we had encountered in the city. And their limbs were longer. They stalked like moving towers of metal, each upon four jointed stilts. And long, flail-like limbs dangled from the case of each. Crystal domes crowned them, sparkling in the sunlight—covering, I knew, the feeble gray brains that controlled them. The Eternal Ones.

Almost at the edge of the plateau they were when I first saw them. I had time easily to finish sealing the door, to close the valve through which I had let out the excess air upon landing, and to drive up through the moon's atmosphere, toward the white planet.

But I did not move to do those things. I stood at the window watching, hands clenched so that nails cut into my palms, set teeth biting through my lip.

Then, as they came on, I moved suddenly, governed not by

reason but by an impulse that I could not resist. I opened the door and clambered hastily out, picking up the great copper mace that I had left lying outside.

And I crouched beside the machine, waiting.

Looking across the way the Mother had gone, I saw her at the edge of the plateau. A tiny, distant form, upon the green moss. I think she had already seen the machines, and realizing the futility of flight had turned back to face them.

As the machine-things came by, I was appalled at their size. The metal stilts were fully six feet long, the vulnerable crystal domes eight feet above the ground.

I leaped up, and struck at the brain of the nearest, as it passed. My blow crushed the transparent shell and the soft brain within it. But the machine toppled toward me, and I fell with it to the ground, cruelly bruised beneath its angular levers.

One leg was fast beneath it, pinned against the ground, and its weight was so great that I could not immediately extricate myself. But I had clung to the copper bar, and when another machine bent down, as if to examine the fallen one, I seized the weapon with both hands, and placed another fatal blow.

The second machine fell stiffly beside me, an odd humming sound continuing within it, in such a position that it almost concealed me from the others. I struggled furiously to free my leg, while the other Eternal Ones gathered about, producing curious buzzing sounds.

At last I was free, and on my knees. Always slow in such an unexpected emergency, the machine-beings had taken no action, though they continued the buzzing.

One of them sprang toward me as I moved, striking a flailing blow at me with a metal arm. I leaped up at it, avoiding the sweeping blow, and struck its crystal case with the end of the copper bar.

The bar smashed through the crystal dome, and crushed the frail brain-thing within it. But the machine still moved. It went leaping away across the plateau, its metal limbs still going through the same motions as before I had killed the ruling brain.

I fell back to the ground, rolling over quickly to avoid its stalking limbs, and struggling to my feet, still holding grimly to the copper bar.

The remaining machine-beings rushed upon me, flailing out with metal limbs. Desperately, I leaped into the air, rising ten feet above their glistening cases. I came down upon the case of one, beside the crystal dome that housed its brain. I braced my feet and struck, before it could snatch at me with its hooked levers.

As it fell to the moss, humming, buzzing, and threshing about with bright metal limbs, I leaped from it toward the other, holding the bar before me. But I struck only the metal case, without harming it, and fell from it into the moss.

Before I could stir, the thing drove its metal limb down upon my body. It struck my chest with a force that was agonizing . . . For a moment, I think I was unconscious. Then I was coughing up bloody foam.

I lay on the red moss, unable to move, the grim realization that I would die breaking over me in a black wave, that swept away even my pain. The metal limb had been lifted from me.

Then the Mother was beside me. She had come back.

Her warm smooth furry body was pressed against my side. I saw her violet eyes, misty, appealing. She laid the rose-flushed mantles over my side. The pain went suddenly from it. And I felt new strength, so I could get to my feet, though red mist still came from my nostrils, and I felt a hot stream of blood down my side.

The remaining machine-monster was bending, reaching for the Mother. I seized the copper mace again, struck a furious blow at the crystal shell that housed its brain. As it crashed down, beating about blindly and madly with its great metal limbs, my new strength went suddenly from me and I fell again, coughing once more.

A flailing limb struck the Mother a terrific blow, flinging her against the moss many yards away. She crept back to me, brokenly, slowly. Her golden fur was stained with crimson. Her mantles were limp and pale. There was agony in her eyes.

She came to where I lay, collapsed against my side. Very low, her musical tones reached my ears and died abruptly with a choking sound. She had tried to tell me something, and could not.

The last of the Eternal Ones that had followed was dead, and presently the machines ceased their humming and buzzing and threshing about upon the moss.

Through the rest of the day we lay there, side by side, both unable to move. And through the strange night, when the huge white disk of the earth bathed us in silver splendor, and in my delirium I dreamed alternately of my life upon it, and of my adventures upon this weird moonworld, with the Mother.

When the argent earth was low, and we were cold and drenched with dew, lying very close together to benefit from each other's warmth, the wild dreams passed. For a few minutes I was coldly sane. I looked back upon a life that had never had any great purpose, that had been lived carelessly, and impulsively. And I was not sorry that I had come to the moon.

I remained with the Mother until she stirred no more, and no effort on my part could rouse her to life. With tears in my eyes, I buried her beneath the green moss. Then stumbling to the ship I climbed in. Sealing the door and starting the machinery, I felt the ship lift quickly toward the distant beckoning earth.

When I began writing science fiction myself, I still had had no dates with girls and I made very little effort to deal with women in my stories (see *The Early Asimov*). I had, however, learned the power of the understated romance from "The Moon Era" and other, less remarkable stories.

There came a time when I used the device of an implicit love developed across an impossible gap, either social or biological, and underplayed it every time. "The Moon Era," even if unconsciously, influenced me in my short stories "Sally," "Lennie," and "The Ugly Little Boy," to say nothing of my novel *The Naked Sun*.

In September 1932, I entered Boys High School, but spent the first half of the tenth grade (or as we called it, "the third term," since my last year at junior high had embraced the first and second terms of high school) at Waverley Annex. This was a small, ramshackle school that served as a reservoir, intended to keep the student body at Boys High itself from overflowing its bounds.

The Annex contributed a column to the high school newspaper (a "news from Waverley" thing), and I volunteered to write it. I don't remember how many columns I did, but I do remember that on one occasion there was a mini-stir occasioned by the fact that I had naïvely reported that we had been let out early one day, when that had been done against the rules. (The head of the Annex found he had to do some explaining, and from then on he read my column before I was allowed to pass it on to the newspaper office.)

This column was the first occasion on which I had written anything for publication. It was the first time I had ever seen any words of my own in actual print with my own name on them. (In *The Early Asimov*, I said that an essay I had written in 1934 was my first published piece. That was wrong. I had forgotten about this earlier material, and it is only now, when I am rummaging about in the ancient lumber of my mental attic, that I have come across it.)

I had assumed when I was in the Annex that once I went to Boys High School itself, I would join the staff of the school paper. It seemed natural to me to do so, since I had no doubt of my writing ability at all. That, however, was never to come to pass.

For one thing, I found that working on the paper meant all kinds of after-school activity, and I *couldn't* work after school. I had to get back to the candy store. For another thing, the students on the staff of the paper were all considerably older than myself and seemed to my frightened self to be very cynical and wordly-wise. I was overawed and backed away.

The result is that I *never* worked on a school paper, either in high school or in college. My brother, Stanley, however, when it was his turn to be in his teens, was a much more self-possessed youngster. He worked on the papers, was eventually editor of a school paper, made newspapers his lifework, and is now Assistant Publisher of the Long Island *Newsday*. He is very highly thought of in the field.

I'm not sorry. I'd have made a rotten reporter and a rottener editor.

I CAN only hope, by the way, that now that you have come to the end of this book, you find yourself reluctant to leave the stories of the 1930s and perhaps also to leave me at the age of twelve.

If that's how you feel, cheer up. This is not the end of the book. The book is three times as long but the kind people at Fawcett did not think they could make a soft-cover three times this thick and have it do anything but fall apart, filling you with chagrin and themselves with embarrassment.

So they end it here with the assurance that you will find it (and me) continued in Book 2 and, finally, in Book 3. I'll see you then.

ISAAC ASIMOV's
Startling Tales of the Far-Distant Future

THE STARS, LIKE DUST   P2373 $1.25

Half a century before, the Nebular Kingdoms had been conquered by the cruel war lords of Tyrann. Now Biron Farrill's father had disappeared and Biron himself was marked for murder. But why had he and his father been singled out for destruction? The answer takes Biron to the "Rebellion World"—the hidden planet that shelters a conspiracy against the Tyranni and holds the only hope of peace for man's future.

I, ROBOT   P2355 $1.25

What do you do with a drunken robot? You may not believe it, but robots have problems too. Just like humans. In these nine mind-spinning stories, Isaac Asimov brings us an astonishing and delightful vision of a tomorrow filled with marvels and miracles—of computers in human form so incredibly real you cannot tell the man from the machine without a scoreboard.

THE NAKED SUN   P2261 $1.25

The planet Solaria could destroy Earth in two seconds flat and probably would—eventually. Solaria was power-hungry and had developed the ultimate weapon—a massive army of robots that could obliterate Earth. But now that would have to wait. One of Solaria's eminent scientists had been murdered. Only Earth's famous detective, Elijah Baley, could solve the baffling mystery. Baley didn't want to go. But how could he refuse? Earth's very existence was at stake.

FAWCETT

Wherever Paperbacks Are Sold

BY ISAAC ASIMOV

"FASCINATING."
—*The New York Times*

THE EARLY ASIMOV, BOOK ONE   Q2425 $1.50

These thirteen classic tales from the fantastic imagination of Isaac Asimov range from interplanetary collisions to Galactic Congresses, from Rigellian psychologists to Martian professors. "The stories are chronologically arranged so that the development of this towering young mind becomes as engrossing as the stories themselves."

—*The New York Times*

THE EARLY ASIMOV, BOOK TWO   P2323 $1.25

Fourteen fantastic stories by the master of science fiction. Along with the stories, Asimov has included a fascinating commentary on the stories, the times, and himself as a writer. "Asimov was writing when science fiction was really the literature of ideas, and it is wonderful, intricate, informative ideas that he crams into these stories."

—*Amazing Science Fiction*

"Vintage Asimov!"
—*Washington Post*

FAWCETT CREST
BESTSELLERS